THE
MIND'S
ECHO

DOUGLAS VAUGHN

ISBN: 978-1-954814-86-8 (Paperback)
ISBN: 978-1-954814-12-7 (E-Book)
ISBN: 978-1-954814-99-8 (Audiobook)

Library of Congress Control Number:

First Edition 2022

Credits:
Book Cover and Formatting by Miblart – www.miblart.com
Editing by – Stardust Book Services and Elite Authors

Obsidian Wolf Publishing
www.obsidianwolfpub.com
PO Box 1086
Salem, UT 84653

CHAPTER 1

Dr. Theo Raden stepped into the exam room to see his first patient of the day and was assaulted by the odors of vomit, trash, and body odor. This would not have been surprising if he were still volunteering at the homeless shelter on Imperial, but this was an entirely different atmosphere. The neighborhoods surrounding Scripps Mercy were student apartments, higher-end condos, and middle to upper class houses. Hunched on the table was a girl his age sitting with her head between her legs, shaking wildly. The moment he strode in her direction, her head snapped up, and she stared at him unblinking, as if he were going to attack her. The look she held was fierce, primitive, and untamed.

Momentarily glancing down at the chart, he read, "'Jane Doe.'" Theo said tentatively to the girl, "Hello, Miss. This is Scripps Mercy Hospital, and I'm Dr. Raden. Do you know why you're here?"

She did not answer but tilted her head back and forth as she stared at the wall behind him. Her eyes were unfocused.

Theo added, "How long have you been pregnant?"

Her face remained emotionless, and he wondered if she'd even heard him. He continued, "I just want to see how you are doing. Would that be all right?" He took a tentative step forward.

Her hands became fists at the sound of his shuffling feet, and Theo halted.

There was a knock on the door. Without saying anything, Theo moved back to the door and opened it. Jane Hardy, his most experienced nurse, stood with a knowing smile. She whispered, "I knew this was going to be interesting. I brought popcorn."

Theo leaned closer. "She hasn't said anything."

Nodding, Jane added, "Nor did she during my screening."

"I did find it amusing that you named her Jane Doe."

"We look like sisters. You never know," Jane said, winking playfully.

Pointing over his shoulder, he asked, "How old do you think she is?"

"Could be anywhere from late teens to early thirties. It's hard to say."

A sound from behind them caused Theo to turn back to the patient. Jane Doe was now standing, her feet on the small built-in step of the exam table, staring at them, a small smile playing on her face.

"Hello," Theo said.

The girl squeaked, "Hello." Her head weaved side to side as if impervious to the moment.

The transition of her facial features could not have been more obvious. Jane Doe now appeared calm and relaxed.

Theo repeated, "I'm Dr. Raden. You're at the hospital. How long have you been pregnant?"

The girl answered, "Hello, Dr. Rodeo. You funny. I not pregnant."

Theo was shocked by how childlike her voice sounded. If he'd not been staring at her mouth when she spoke, he would've never imagined that voice coming out of this girl.

"Okay." The word came out slowly. "Why are you here?"

"That is easy, silly. Dr. Happypants sent me."

A giggle escaped from his nurse, Jane, and Theo tried to contain his own laugh.

As if she were on stage, the girl's face contorted once again, and a third personality emerged. Theo did not like where this was going. Just by the expression on her face, this one was angry and demented. Jane Doe glanced down at her hands, lifted both arms into the air, and brought them down again and again as she punched her own stomach.

Theo was caught off guard, as if he'd been sucker-punched himself; then he reacted and launched forward. His right hand gripped one wrist, and he pulled it backward. The nurse must've reacted at the same time, and she clasped the other wrist. Together, they forced Jane Doe back onto the exam table. Spittle and froth, like from a rabid dog, splattered the air. Jane Doe wrestled, moved, kicked, and screamed.

Despite her size and having no use of her hands, the girl did not give up. She planted her feet and pushed upward. Theo felt his grip loosening. The door opened, and Ralph, the security guard, leaped into the fray.

Jane Hardy, Theo's nurse, breathed loudly. "Over here. Help me. I can't hold on any longer."

Ralph moved expertly and with one hand seemed to gain control over Jane Doe's movements. Theo was not as lucky as he lost his grip, and Jane Doe smacked him in the nose. His eyes watered for several seconds as they secured her wrist again.

Jane asked, "Dr. Raden, what do we do?"

Speaking mostly to himself, he said, "We could restrain her." Glancing at Ralph, he asked, "Are there any handcuffs around?"

Ralph answered, "On the other side of the hospital, maybe, but cuffing her could be an administrative problem if she isn't arrested."

Theo said, "So could the miscarriage if she keeps hitting herself." He thought for a moment. "We could medically restrain her, then get her to the emergency room."

"So...a shot?" Jane asked.

It didn't take long for him to decide. "Give her Ativan. Two milligrams."

Nurse Jane sprinted from the room as Jane Doe continued flailing. Theo's arms began to feel the burn. Sweat glistened on his hands, arms, and back and slid down his face, but he and Ralph held on.

Nurse Jane returned a few minutes later with a syringe in her hand. She asked, "Where?"

"Pick an arm," Theo wheezed.

As Nurse Jane approached, Jane Doe shot out both of her legs as if anticipating what was coming. The nurse quickly jumped out of the way, approaching the patient from the side.

"I've got this," Ralph said, and he somehow pinned both of her legs with one of his and extended her right arm to allow for the shot in one full, smooth motion. By then, Theo could barely control her other arm.

"It's in," Jane said.

Thirty seconds after the injection, Theo watched as the fight left Jane Doe's eyes. She no longer flailed or attacked or even appeared angry in the slightest. He nodded at Ralph, and they both let go, stepping backward. Jane Doe folded both of her arms protectively over her chest and tried pulling up her baggy clothing. Her clothes were several sizes too big. She was either having difficulty finding the right size clothes or trying hard to hide her pregnancy.

The girl maneuvered to sit back on the table. She shook her head as if clearing it. When she looked up, her eyes found his, and she appeared focused. "Hello," she said in a healthy, rational, and calm voice. As she glanced around, she added, "What am I doing here?"

Theo said, "You're at Scripps Mercy Hospital. I am Dr. Raden."

Confusion crossed her face, but she wasn't agitated. He thought the medication was starting to take effect, which might mean she would need a nap. Nurse Jane hurried forward and adjusted the back of the exam table.

Jane Doe mumbled, "Thanks." Peering up, she asked, "Do you know Dr. Had...Dr. Happy?"

"No," Theo said, his eyes meeting Jane's. "Who is Dr. Happy?"

Ignoring this, she asked, "Have I done something wrong?" The pleading look on her face caused Theo's world to tilt ever so slightly.

This girl might be the most pathetic patient he'd seen this month. She was clearly homeless, sickly, and pregnant, but there was something more within those blue-green eyes. He had never felt such compassion for a patient.

Theo asked, "Where do you live?"

"In a house, a beautiful house, but there are...like a hundred other people who live there. I've seen Dr. Happy there." She shook her head as if trying to adjust the memory.

"Is it a motel?"

She shrugged, and her interest shifted to a string hanging from her pants. She began pulling at it and soon became mesmerized.

"Do they clean your room every day?"

"Nope."

"Have you ever slept outside?"

"Lots."

Theo considered his options. At least she was answering his questions and had stopped the self-harm. This was a vast improvement from just minutes ago. She would still likely be admitted to the hospital. "Can you remember the name of the place you were living?"

"Saint Marks?"

Theo asked, "Are you sure?"

"Saint something," she mumbled, her eyes appearing heavy.

Theo knew of a few homeless shelters in San Diego, but none were called St. Marks. Could it be St. Jude's in the East Village? Maybe the rescue mission, or even Father Joe's? He asked again, "Who is Dr. Happy?"

Jane Doe said, "Not Dr. Happy but Dr. Had…" She shook her head. "I can't remember his name. Why am I here?"

Theo checked the chart. "It looks like you were found wandering the streets. An officer picked you up and brought you to our hospital. You couldn't tell him anything about yourself, and he was worried. I'm Dr. Raden. This is Jane, my nurse, and Ralph, the security guard. You're in this hospital because you're pregnant and you need to be checked."

"Not possible," said Jane Doe dismissively. "You can't trick me."

"It's no trick," Theo replied.

"There's no freaking way," the girl snapped.

"Look down," Nurse Jane said, and Theo could hear the doubt in her voice.

Instead of taking in her own appearance, Jane Doe's eyes searched the room as if a hidden camera was lurking. Finally, she focused on her stomach. Her eyes widened in surprise, and her hands touched her belly. She exhaled and muttered, "It's not possible."

Tears began running down her face, and she tore at her pathetic clothes until she pulled up her shirt and exposed her belly. She slumped back into the chair, and it took a few minutes for Jane Doe to regain control of her emotions.

Theo glanced at Nurse Jane, who rolled her eyes and mouthed, "Is she for real?"

Finally, Jane Doe asked, "What is really going on here? How far along am I? Is something wrong with the pregnancy?"

Theo said, "By the looks of it, six or seven months along."

"You don't know exactly?"

Theo stepped closer. "This is the first time we've ever seen you. We don't even know your name."

"It's Sophia." Her name spilled from her mouth with such ease.

Theo shared another glance with Jane. To Ralph he said, "I think we've got this from here."

"Is there something wrong with me?" She pushed a few more times at her belly as if confirming her horror as Ralph stepped from the room.

"Well, actually," Theo said, "you've been acting strange since you arrived. At first, you refused to talk to us. We couldn't get you to concentrate. In fact, I'm rather worried about your mental health."

Jane, his nurse, added skeptically, "And let's not forget that whole episode of beating your own stomach."

"What?" Sophia screamed. "I did what? There's no way."

Theo said calmly, "You did. That's why Ralph was here." Theo reached over and pulled out two latex gloves. Stepping closer to Sophia, he pointed to his arm. "You see these red marks? You caused these."

"I scratched you?"

"You did more than that. You hit yourself hard."

She rubbed at her draining nose. "I can't remember doing that. How's that possible?"

"I promise you, it happened," Jane said as she handed her a tissue. "Take a look at your clothes. By the looks of it, you've worn the same items for the last several days. Your hair has something sticky in it, and there are clumps. We're just trying to understand if there's a mental illness and if your baby is okay. I hope you aren't playing a game with us, Miss."

"What? Games?"

Theo rested his hand on her shoulder. "What was your name again?"

"Why do you keep asking me that?" she hissed.

Theo pulled his stool closer and sat down. "I appreciate your confusion. But from our standpoint, this is all somewhat concerning. You are pregnant. You are homeless and started attacking yourself. Now you say you can't remember doing it. We don't know your name or anything about you. Anything is on the table right now."

"I'm Sophia LaCross, and I moved from San Francisco two years ago. I moved here after some college and after my parents died. I have no siblings. I have a roommate, and we live in the Lemon Grove apartments." Sophia touched her sweatshirt. A sob unhitched from her chest, and she began shaking. "Shit. How can I be pregnant?"

"What was the last thing you remember?"

"Let me see…" She glanced up as if concentrating.

"I remember working at Bank of America, and my roommate is Mary. We hung out after work, I think, but I certainly wasn't pregnant. I remember talking with

Mary about trying to find a way to make some extra money. I haven't had a boyfriend since I moved here, and I've never had sex before. How can I really be pregnant?"

Again, Theo glanced at Jane. He added, "Well, that's a start."

"How can we find out if the baby is all right?" Sophia asked, almost frantic.

Standing, Theo said, "Sit tight. We'll need to do some blood tests and an ultrasound today and watch you for a while. We may need to admit you, but we'll make sure everything is okay."

"Admit me for what?" Sophia retorted.

"Just to make sure you and your baby are safe."

Sophia's voice calmed quickly. "You're right. Whatever it takes, Doctor. I would never hurt my own child. Never." In a small voice, she added, "I just can't believe I'm pregnant."

"Okay. We'll get started in a few minutes. You're going to be here for a few hours at least." Her head bobbed up and down as Theo and Jane stepped from the room.

As they walked down the hallway, Jane asked, "What the hell just happened in there? I mean, is she for real? Does she have multiple personalities? I've always wanted to see that."

"That's the million-dollar question."

"What's our next step?"

"Let's check to make sure the baby is all healthy. I'm still leaning toward admitting her. I'll never be able to get her hitting her stomach out of my mind."

Jane huffed loudly in response.

Theo responded, "We can try to convince her to self-admit for mental health testing or call Dr. Jeffery and get a 5150 signed for a seventy-two-hour hold."

Jane smiled. "Well, you've still got three more patients, and with Miss Unpredictable, I think your day is far from done. I need to get her ultrasound done as soon as possible. I don't know if I trust that girl, but there is something weird going on."

"I agree."

CHAPTER 2

An hour and a half later, Theo exited the room of his third patient for the day. It was nearing 11:00 a.m., and he was starving. He had not come to a final decision about Sophia but also couldn't keep her off his mind. For some reason, every time he thought about admitting her, it felt like the wrong thing to do. But professionally, it might be his only option.

The updates throughout the morning had been better than expected. The ultrasound was normal, and she was having a girl. Sophia had burst into tears of joy upon hearing the news. Her blood work had shown some typical problems, such as anemia, and there was a possibility of a urinary infection, but Sophia and the baby were doing well. Additional tests, including for sexually transmitted diseases, were still pending.

Sophia had eaten three meals and still seemed hungry, which was another good sign. Her behavior and outlook were far better than when she arrived. But this information didn't tell him what he needed to do. He had no idea how she had gotten into this situation or if she would sink back into it the moment she was discharged from the hospital. He had an obligation to his patient and the unborn child. Sophia was doing better now, but what long-term risk did she pose to herself?

Lost in thought, Theo strolled to the nursing station. Jane was huddled with Nurse Susan as if planning a sinister scheme.

"How hard would it be to get her admitted?" Susan asked in a low tone. "You know that is his only option."

"Maybe. I just don't think we can trust her at all." Jane stopped suddenly, her face turning bright red, as Theo approached.

"What is my only option?" Theo asked, aware that his day had become a no-win situation.

Nurse Susan, fiftyish, with brown hair, was half his size but had twice his energy. She swiveled, sized him up, and said, "You can't help this girl. She has problems bigger than you can see."

"I know that," he said confidently. "But you also haven't seen the remarkable changes."

"She could be playing you for a fool," Jane said.

"To what end?" Theo said, and some of his inner monologues were coming out in coherent thoughts. "Maybe she is hoping to have a roof and some food over her head for a few days. Maybe she wants some healthcare for her child. I don't know. But these aren't bad things. We have housing and other programs we can offer her."

Susan interrupted him. "She needs a psych eval."

Theo knew this was an option. "You might be right, but that could take several days. Let's monitor her for the next few hours and see what happens."

Jane added, "You know where she lives. And she has a roommate."

"Do you think I should talk to her roommate first before making a decision?"

"It's up to you."

"Honestly," Susan huffed, "are you going to personally help every single pregnant woman that walks through our doors? That isn't was residency is."

"No. But for some reason, this one feels different."

"I knew it," Jane said. "I knew from the look you had on your face when she started remembering things."

"What look?"

"I knew it," Jane repeated.

Susan stepped away from her computer. "I'm a spiritual woman, and this girl has some bad omens. Whatever you do, be careful. I don't imagine this is going to go well for you."

"I'll take your recommendation under advisement."

Susan said, "I've got your eleven-thirty appointment in the waiting room. I'll get her vitals."

As Susan walked away, Jane said, "You have nothing on your schedule for tomorrow."

"What can I really do?" Theo asked. "What will Dr. Jeffery think?"

"It's fine." Jane smiled knowingly. "You could spend the rest of today and tomorrow helping our new friend."

"I swear that a few hours ago, you weren't buying her story."

"I'm sitting on the highest fence, like back home, and watching all the passersby. I see Susan's point, but I also know that things have changed with Sophia. She slept for an hour, and the blood work is back, and the ultrasound showed a girl. Everything points to healthy. The due date is less than sixty days away." Jane twirled her hair with her finger. "Since we gave that injection, this girl is back to normal. I mean, it's incredible to think about. But she has no one to help her. At least drive her home and see what you can learn."

"Are you kidding?" Theo said, laughing. "I'm not a detective. I've no idea where to start or what I would be looking for."

"Didn't you tell me that you went through the police academy?"

"I went through the academy when I got a job at the prison as an EMT. It certainly wasn't more than that."

"See, you're already a pro."

"That was nearly five years ago, back before I started med school." He leaned closer. "Maybe if I admit her, we can get a psych eval this weekend, and we can get her placed somewhere in a few days."

Jane's face revealed nothing. "The choice is yours, Dr. Raden."

"Fine. I'll let you know what I've come up with by the end of lunch."

Jane nodded, but she didn't walk away.

Theo asked, "What do you think happened to her?"

"I can't pretend to know. But you'll figure it all out with your police training and all your officer experience at the prison."

Theo's mind recalled some of the memories of him working at the prison. It had been an incredible first experience in medicine. He saw and did things that prepared him to understand both the successes of medicine and some of its failures. Inmates were often extremely complicated patients. He had worked with some of the best and most dedicated staff. Some of the officers he met had gone on to work for the police department and even the Federal Bureau of Investigation.

"I'm going to look in on Sophia," Theo said, and he walked down the hall just as Susan brought back his last patient for the day.

He opened the door but did not fully step in, as if his mind hadn't been made up. Sophia sat there, rubbing her belly and crying at the same time.

"Is everything okay?"

Sophia wiped her eyes. "It's a lot to process."

"We'll have more answers for you in the next few minutes."

"Thank you."

Sophia glanced up, and her look was fleeting. She seemed to be staring at him without really seeing anything; then she was back to caressing her stomach. A pang of empathy as if he was slapped in the face sent Theo's world spinning. He barely managed to step out of the room. Theo closed the door and leaned back against the wall, hardly able to remain standing.

"Oh. My. Word," he muttered.

His heart raced, and his mind whirled back to the last time he had seen such an aching countenance. That same expression haunted his dreams because he had missed its meaning from a girl that had nearly stolen his heart. At work, Hannah Evans had been strong and patient, direct and sympathetic. Theo had asked her out three times before she agreed to a group date. She was shy and elusive, and he never knew where he stood with her. The last night he'd seen Hannah, he had thought everything was becoming clearer between them. She had made some promises, and it had been the best night of his life. The look that he missed came at the end of the night. He had been too preoccupied with his insecurities. The moment passed. Hannah had smiled kindly, kissed him, and got into her car, never to be seen alive again.

The next day, his life was shattered when he arrived at work only to learn that his best friend and coworker had been murdered just hours after he had last seen her. It was discovered that she had a violent ex-boyfriend, another coworker, who had been stalking her for months. There were hundreds of threatening texts on her phone. The worst one had been sent while Theo and she had been walking to her car. That missed moment would haunt him forever, and it would be the last thing he remembered of her.

Theo sucked in breath after breath, trying to slow his heart rate. Shaking his head, he absorbed the truth. Sophia had given him the same look, and he was determined to do whatever it took to get her the answers she needed.

"Theo. Are you okay?" asked Jane, who hurried down the hall.

"I want to help Sophia. I just don't know how," he managed to say, his voice rising in his throat.

"You can. I have faith."

"Why do you say that?"

"It's in your personality."

"I'm not sure that's a good thing."

"It might not be, but it doesn't change the facts." She leaned in. "We didn't officially put her into our system. She's still a Jane Doe."

"What do I do next?"

"I'll let Dr. Jeffery know what's going on. Well, sort of. Start by bringing Miss LaCross home. Call me if you have any problems."

Theo took a deep breath and walked back into Sophia's room. Sophia sat in a chair next to the exam table, reading a magazine. Her hair was still matted, and her clothes were filthy.

"Sophia, it's me, Dr. Raden."

"Who died?"

"What are you talking about?"

"You sound as if your dog got kicked. Did you really think that I forgot who you were?"

"Well…sort of."

"So, what's the plan? Are you going to admit me to the psych ward? I overheard you talking with your nurses earlier. Is it really that bad?" Theo saw the hurt and anger on her face.

"No. I'm not exactly sure what to do. I'll help you get home, then we'll take it from there."

"How did I get here?"

"Like I said before, it looks like an officer found you on the streets. He was worried, and he brought you here. We have programs that can help the homeless."

"Am I going crazy?" she asked honestly as she turned to face him.

"Aren't we all?" Changing the topic, he said, "My car is old, and I'm not sure you have another choice unless you want to call your roommate."

Sophia's face faltered. "Nurse Jane let me use the phone. Mary's cell phone went directly to voicemail several times. That's weird because she always picks up."

"Maybe you have the wrong number," said Theo.

"Maybe."

"Are you okay if I take you home?"

"You would do that for me?"

"I have one patient left to see, and then we can go."

"I guess." Sophia smiled. "Thank you."

He found Susan monitoring things closely at the nurse's station. She glared at him as he approached. "Don't say that I didn't warn you."

"It'll be fine. I won't really be doing much, just helping her get settled. I'm sure she has friends and a roommate."

"Why don't they come and get her, then?" she asked.

"No one answered."

Susan bristled for only a moment longer. Soon she added, "Mrs. Parker is in room number two. And Dr. Jeffery wants to talk to you before you leave."

"Thank you, Susan."

Theo cringed at both prospects awaiting him. It wasn't that he hated his attending physician. It was exactly the opposite. He was a talented doctor and a great guy. It was just that Dr. Steven Jeffery quizzed him on everything. After his shift yesterday, Dr. Jeffery interrogated him for over an hour about several patients, particularly one with preeclampsia. This condition, a potentially serious problem, can occur during pregnancy. It happens when the patient experiences elevated blood pressure as a direct result of the pregnancy.

In many cases, it can be managed throughout the pregnancy. Things become problematic if seizures or other complications are added on top. Dr. Jeffery blasted Theo with question after question and even asked him to write a paper about it. He'd been up until two this morning finishing it. Theo pulled the paper out of his backpack and hurried down the hall, turning the corner and running directly into his attending physician.

"Dr. Raden, are you already finished with your clinic?" Dr. Jeffery asked.

"No, sir. Just coming to turn in the assignment from yesterday. Nurse Susan said you needed to see me."

"Not for anything important. Your clinic will close for the weekend. You're going out of town, correct?"

"Yes, sir."

"We'll have another intern cover the call schedule. I'm also out of town this weekend.

"Where to?"

"Seattle. Off to see some family and get away from this horrible weather."

"Really?" Theo asked.

"Even perfect weather gets boring."

"If you say so."

Dr. Jeffery smiled. "Have a good few days off. Do something fun."

"Yes, sir." Theo handed him his preeclampsia paper and strolled back to the nurse station feeling guilty.

Before stepping into the next exam room, Jane caught up with him, a broad smile on her face. "Today has been as enjoyable as a night on Bourbon Street. Can we do this again tomorrow? Oh, wait—you and I will be miles away from this place."

"You're not picking up any overtime this weekend?" he asked.

"Not on your precious life," the tall blond nurse from New Orleans said with a Southern drawl that mesmerized even the most logical. "I've got plans."

Jane had been assigned to him a few months back. She was knowledgeable, trustworthy, punctual, good with the patients, and the most attractive person in the hospital. She was a good five years older than Theo. Rumor had it that she'd been deemed "too pretty" for her last two residents. She privately claimed harassment, and some of the other nurses had urged her to become more vocal to the administration. Theo knew that she just wanted to keep her head down and work. He'd also been told by management that, "this was her last stop if things didn't work out." Despite everything he had heard, he got along perfectly well with Jane.

Theo said, "Thanks for your help today. Any idea what's going on with Mrs. Parker?"

"Of course. She wants to discuss her scary things—the Braxton hicks…again." Her voice was serene, but she rolled her eyes.

Theo knew that Mrs. Parker had been at the clinic all five days last week and two days this week with one concern after another. He mused aloud, "I wonder if something else is really the problem."

"Not the foggiest idea. That would make as much sense as my mother's Sunday dinner. She always has a second agenda, like whom I was dating that week." Her drawl was incredibly thick, and it was Theo's turn to roll his eyes.

Jane Hardy had grown up on the north side of New Orleans, and she had no desire to return anywhere close to that state. The craziness that she'd experienced in her upbringing blended into her everyday perspectives and was the reason she became a nurse. Just last week, she had described Mrs. Norton by saying, "That woman's so scary that even a blind man looking for a call girl on Bourbon Street would've run off in terror." And in some bizarre way, this described Mrs. Norton perfectly.

The problem surfaced when he and Jane realized that her verdict had been given within earshot of Mrs. Norton. Theo had apologized for a full ten minutes. He'd promised her repeatedly that Jane was talking about her sister, who'd run off with an old college professor, gained weight, and was now on the hunt for a new man. Theo was certain they would never see Mrs. Norton again.

"Wish me luck," said Theo as he opened the door. Inside, he found Mrs. Parker sitting on the exam table and reading a copy of *Vogue*. Theo never understood why *Vogue*, *Seventeen*, or any other glamorous magazine was at the disposal of his pregnant patients. These magazines tended to make most nonpregnant women anxious about their own looks. Add an extra twenty to fifty pounds, and Theo often was forced to give them oxygen and anxiety medication just to get them out the door. Mrs. Parker was no exception.

Mrs. Parker had a look of wishful thinking as she asked, "Dr. Raden, do you think I'll ever look like her again?"

Theo walked forward and glanced at the picture. "Mrs. Parker, that girl doesn't even look like that. You do know that her picture has been photoshopped." In a soothing voice, he added, "Pregnancy is a rare blessing, and one with an amazing gift. Sometimes physical changes are seen during and after pregnancy. I know this is your first pregnancy, but you're doing great."

Mrs. Parker shifted slightly. "You can call me Pam. My sister had five children. I bet she would never call them a blessing or heavenly. She calls them 'her little monsters.' My body is taking on forms that I'd never imagined. Breastfeeding better make this all go away!" Pam gazed down and shuddered.

Theo opened the chart. "It looks like you're approaching the thirty-ninth week of your pregnancy. Your baby's heart rate is fantastic and consistent. Nurse Hardy said that things are going pretty good for you. Her notes say that everything went well on your vitals and urine sample this morning." Theo gave her a scrutinizing look. "This is when you are supposed to be taking it easy. Are you still working?"

"You know that I am. You asked me that last week. Sunday is my last day. I promise," Pam said.

"Good. Tell me about the labor pains you're feeling."

Twenty minutes later, after several attempts to calm Mrs. Parker, he found out that Mr. Parker, her husband, was really the one to blame. He'd lost any desire for sexual contact with Pam and had let slip comments about her weight, and ever since, they'd been fighting. He'd promised that he hadn't meant what he had said, but the comments had been hurtful. Theo gave doctor's orders for a special night together, even going as far as writing it on a prescription pad.

CHAPTER 3

Not long after Theo's shift ended, he and Sophia headed northeast on Martin Luther King Jr. Freeway toward Lemon Grove. He felt slightly embarrassed, leaving the hospital with his patient, but the encouraging smiles from his nurses convinced him that this was the right thing.

Theo knew relatively little about Lemon Grove or the surrounding neighborhoods of San Diego, but Sophia was quite talkative. She was a completely different person than the one he had met this morning. He caught himself staring at her when she spoke. It was as if she had been in prison and was getting out for the first time in months.

"Lemon Grove is in San Diego County, with over twenty thousand residents. The single most important item in town is the large lemon on display when you first arrive. It's the largest in the world." She pointed to the large lemon decoration as they drove into town.

"That's a large, yellow piece of junk," Theo joked.

"And we're proud of it." Her eyes sparkled, and despite her attire, dirtiness, and smell, she could easily be described as beautiful.

They turned onto Broadway and drove several blocks to Washington Street. A quarter of a mile on the left, they turned into a set of apartments: the Golden Grove Apartments.

"Fabulous name. A town called Lemon Grove and apartments called Golden Grove. Totally original."

"You should see Dead Grove cemetery and Detained Grove police department—they're pretty incredible as well."

Theo laughed loudly. "I get your point." He was surprised by his ease and comfort with Sophia. She was intelligent, thoughtful, and fiercely independent. A far cry from the homeless, downtrodden, and psychotic girl he had met earlier this morning.

As they parked, he asked, "When's the last time you remember coming here?"

"Before I was pregnant, so it's been a while."

"Do you have a key?"

"If I do, I've no clue where it is."

"Didn't you say something about a roommate?"

"Yes, Mary."

Theo pulled out his cell phone. "What was her number again?"

She said, "I tried. Directly to voicemail."

Theo closed his phone. "It's possible Mary has a new roommate, so this could be a little weird."

"I never thought of that," Sophia muttered. "But Mary was the only true friend I had the entire time I was living here. Even if she has a new roommate, I bet she'll help me."

Theo said, "Stay here. I'll go knock on the door and see if anyone is there."

Sophia nodded. "It's that one on the left. The first one across the parking lot."

As Theo stepped from his car, he glanced back, wondering if this had all been a ruse and if his car would be gone by the time he came back. He noticed a pool behind him and several buildings surrounding the main parking lot. He thought he saw some trash bins behind some of the buildings. This wasn't the newest complex he had ever seen, but it wasn't bad. He crossed the asphalt and stepped onto the sidewalk.

After a dozen steps, he turned left and headed straight for the door. The curtain in the window, to the left of the doorway and behind some shrubs, was closed. He couldn't see any lights on. He knocked loudly on the door and waited. Five minutes later, there was still no answer, and he headed back to the car. He exhaled when it came into view.

"No one's inside," Theo said as he sat down. "This makes it more challenging."

She shifted in her seat. "What should we do?"

"We could either break into your apartment or go ask the manager for a key. Your choice."

"Let's break in!" Sophia said with a surprising amount of humor. She pulled down the visor and stared into the mirror. "Look at me. If I go walking into the office, the police will be called."

"I'll talk to the manager." Theo pushed open the door and turned off the car. "Wish me luck." This time, he took his car keys, because as funny and calm as she had been, he still didn't trust her.

The manager's building was not far from the parking lot. It was just in front of the large pool that seemed to divide the apartment complex. As he stepped into the main room, a plan formed in his mind. Sparkling glass doors met him, and several large, beautiful fake plants welcomed him. There was an overwhelming smell of cleaners, likely bleach.

"Hello! Welcome to Golden Grove Apartments." A bubbly woman in her early twenties with bright orange hair stood behind the counter. "Sorry about the smell. We were forced to make some changes to our pool outside. Don't worry, it's almost finished and should be up and running in the next few weeks."

Theo nodded as he approached the desk, but the air irritated his eyes.

"Have you been here before?" she asked quickly.

"No, I haven't."

"We have quite a deal going on. Three months free, and we'll waive the sign-up fee."

Theo smiled politely. "I'm not here to consider renting, though this does look like a great spot." He gauged her reaction, but there was none. He leaned closer and whispered, "You see, I'm here for a friend. She lives here and is in the car, and she's still hungover from last night. I'm her ride home, and she has misplaced her keys."

"Oh, I see," the girl behind the counter said in a normal voice, as if this happened every other day.

Theo continued, "We need to get her back into her apartment."

"Are you sure she lives here?"

"I can bring her in here if you want, but she might throw up on your carpet. I thought it would be easier for me to come inside."

"What's her name?"

"Sophia LaC—" Theo didn't get the second half of the name out before she gasped, though it was more like a choke of astonishment.

"Are..." she whispered. "Are you sure?"

"Positive." Theo smiled politely but took a step back. It was impossible to miss the perplexed look on the girl's face. He mumbled, "She's really not feeling so good."

"I can imagine."

Theo asked, "So, you know Sophia?"

"Oh, sure. Everybody here knows Sophia. She is so, well, uh—cute and all. But it has been months since anyone has seen her. We weren't sure if she vanished or what."

"She is very cute," Theo agreed. "She has been going through a lot. She's fine, but she can't remember where she lost her keys. I was hoping you could help."

"Oh, yes—her keys."

Theo added, "Maybe someone else found them and turned them in."

The girl began frantically searching the drawers next to the desk. Squinting up at him, her face betrayed a look of confusion and alarm.

Theo asked, "Should I speak with the manager?"

"Oh, no!" she screamed. "That would be a bad thing!"

"What? Why?"

The girl examined Theo closely. She was about to say something but stopped.

"What's going on?" he asked.

The girl shook her head back and forth as if convincing herself that she shouldn't talk.

Theo said, "Sophia is truly sick. She needs to get inside and lie down."

The girl responded hesitantly. "We haven't seen Sophia in several months. The manager thought she'd moved out without paying only a few months into her year lease. Mary tried covering for her. That was until last week."

"Mary is her roommate. I know. Are they behind in rent? Could you call her?"

"They're not behind," the girl said, and she peeked over her shoulder.

Reading her name tag, he asked, "Is your name Rachael?"

The girl nodded slowly.

"Look, Sophia is in the car. I think it would be better if I brought her in here."

"I don't know," Rachael said slowly. "I don't want anyone to get in trouble."

"Trouble," he said. "That seems unlikely. Rachael, can you tell me what's going on? It would really help."

Rachael motioned for him to step into an adjacent room with fewer windows and a single desk, like an office. The smell only slightly improved. They stopped, and she whispered, "Sophia started acting differently a few weeks before she vanished. She couldn't remember anyone, she got lost, and Mary came in and spoke to the manager about it. At first, they thought it was nothing serious. But soon, my boss thought she was on drugs, and he wanted to kick Sophia and Mary out. After that, it was only Mary that we saw. She kept making excuses for Sophia and why she was never around."

"How long ago was this?"

"Eight or nine months ago?"

"No one has seen Sophia since that time."

"Mary would say that she was working late and leaving early. Then she was out of town. There was always something."

"Who was paying for her rent?"

"At first, no one was."

"For how long?"

"Two months at the most. Then, one day, someone called and paid the balance of what was owed and an advance for the next year."

"Then why's the manager so upset?"

Rachael released her breath as if she'd been holding it for a lifetime. "There was a party three nights ago, and a lot of people from the apartment were there. I heard that someone thought they saw Sophia but that she looked homeless and had gained a lot of weight. At the end of the night, I was helping to clean up, and there was something near the bottom of the deep end of the pool. Derek, one of the residents, dove in and pulled up a body. It was that of Mary Sneider, Sophia's roommate, and she was dead."

CHAPTER 4

As Theo escorted Sophia to her apartment, his mind was in overdrive. He had just walked into a hornet's nest of problems. He saw no one watching them as they rushed up the walkway toward the front door. Theo placed a jacket and an arm around Sophia to hide her belly.

He learned that there had been plenty of alcohol at the party, but Rachael insisted she hadn't seen Sophia at all. The police had arrived and questioned several partygoers and some of the neighbors. Rachael reported that the manager had been in a whirlwind of a mood ever since.

Rachael had escorted the police over to Mary's apartment two days ago and had waited outside as they searched around. They even called her in to make sure that everything was in its place. They asked about Sophia, but Rachael insisted that Sophia hadn't been around in months. She had overheard a police officer saying that Mary, presumably, had fallen in and drowned during the party.

If anyone saw Sophia today, in this state, the police would be called again. Movers were scheduled to come and remove all the items in the apartment in two days, but if Sophia planned to stay around, Rachael promised that she would cancel that appointment.

Rachael handed over the key without any complaints. She didn't ask him where Sophia had been the last several months, which was good, because he didn't yet have an answer.

Unlocking the door, Theo helped Sophia inside and onto the couch. A large flat-screen TV was against the far wall to his left. The entire apartment looked like it had been trashed, with slashes in the cushions and foam everywhere. There were broken dishes, glass on the floor, and a spider web crack was smashed into the television.

Sophia put her head in her hands and began to cry. Theo quickly closed the door.

He promised, "We'll figure this out. Try not to worry."

"Aren't you a damn saint? Trying to keep a positive spin on everything. It can't possibly get any worse than this."

He whispered, "Stay here while I look around."

He found a small wooden table overturned in the kitchen, and two of the four chairs were shattered. The back glass door was locked, but a liquid had been splashed on the back and had dried, so he couldn't see outside clearly. Most of the kitchen drawers were open. He darted down a hall just off the kitchen and reached the bathroom on his right. The mirror was cracked, but otherwise, it was untouched. The last two rooms were bedrooms on the left. The first looked relatively unharmed, with only a few figurines broken and the bedding tossed onto the floor. Clothes and towels were strewn across the carpet.

The last room was not as fortunate. The mattress had been slashed, just like the couches, and everything that could be broken was. A desk, a mirror, a plastic lamp, and a chair had been demolished. The entire contents of the closet had been thoroughly searched. Theo returned to Sophia, who was sobbing uncontrollably.

Theo placed a cushion on an exposed area of the couch and sat down. He wrapped his arms around Sophia and held her for a long time. He felt guilty that he didn't tell her right away. He just didn't want to cause her any more pain.

After more than twenty minutes, Sophia lifted her head and gently pushed him away. She said, "I'm fine."

Theo swallowed. "Actually, I have some more bad news."

"I can't handle more news. I just can't."

"I think you need to understand what's going on."

"What do you mean?"

"No one has seen you around the apartment in months. Mary has been paying your bills, and she has been covering for you. Some unknown person called and paid everything for a year."

"That sounds like Mary."

"Everything changed a few days ago."

"What's that supposed to mean?" Sophia asked, and her face turned white.

"A girl named Rachael works in the office, and she told me that there was a party poolside three days ago. Mary fell in and drowned. I guess she'd been drinking a lot."

Sophia wrapped both arms around her stomach and sat forward. Theo was certain that she was going to lose control again. How in the world had he thought it was a good idea to help her? This was a horror show. But he couldn't imagine her doing this on her own. Despite everything, he was going to see this through. That's when the tears came. At first, they were silent and controlled, but soon the barrier fell again. Theo wrapped Sophia as tightly as he could and let her sob.

In a hoarse voice, she said, "Mary hated to swim, though she loved the water. She wouldn't have gone swimming."

"Maybe she just stumbled into the water. No one found her until after the party."

"How's that even possible?"

Theo shook his head. "How deep is the pool?"

"Ten feet, maybe."

"It might've been nearly impossible to see the bottom of the pool, especially if it was dark."

"She would have struggled."

"According to Rachael at the front desk, she was quite intoxicated. If she'd fallen and hit her head, or if she just fell unconscious, she might not have struggled at all."

"That just sounds horrible. How could I not have been here? Where in the hell was I?"

Sophia's head fell onto his shoulder, and she was silent for the next few minutes. Suddenly, her head rose, and she looked around the apartment as if for the first time. "So, did someone break in here to steal everything they could?"

Theo stepped away, giving her some room. "The police have already searched the place. Rachael said she escorted them. That was two days ago. I've seen enough cop shows to know that a flat-screen TV would've been the first thing taken during a robbery. Whoever came in here did so in the last few days, and they were searching for something else."

"We didn't have anything of value." She frowned, stood, and began walking around. "It just doesn't make sense. What the hell am I going to do now?"

Theo calmly pointed out, "The bathroom isn't too bad—you can take a shower. I'll start cleaning up the kitchen."

"You're my doctor, not my housekeeper."

"I have a little component of OCD; it'll make me feel better."

"How bad is my room?"

"Which one is yours?"

"The last one."

"The worst." Theo thought for a moment. Most of her clothes were trash. "Do you have a large sweatshirt or some ex-boyfriend's clothes?"

"Maybe a large sweatshirt or something. I'll take a look." Sophia stepped from view.

Theo turned his attention back to the kitchen and the living room. He found a broom in the hallway closet and swept the linoleum floor. Broken glass and dishes were everywhere, fragmented as if in an artist's abstract portrait. Theo had watched a guy—a friend really—who called himself an artist, spray several colors of paint onto a canvas and call it art. He was told later that someone spent $5,000 on that same canvas. He doubted he could get five dollars for what he was staring at.

Soon, he heard a door close, and the water turned on. Sobs resonated through the small apartment, and he could do nothing but clean.

An hour later, four trash bags had been collected, and the kitchen and front area were remarkably better. After stuffing the fluff back inside the cushions, he surgically placed duct tape, and things appeared liveable. Under the last cushion was a cluster of papers. Sitting down, he rifled through them. There were receipts from the gym, the grocery store, and a few bars in downtown San Diego. Two of the bars were the Fleetwood and the Gaslamp. He'd been to Fleetwood and its "all you can eat" Tuesday dinner. He suddenly found himself starving just thinking about food.

He'd never been to Gaslamp but hadn't heard anything bad about it. For him, word of mouth was the key to the bar scene in San Diego. If he heard about a few bad experiences from his friends, then Theo would never step foot inside. That had been the case with a bar off

Dewey Street. A bunch of underage kids had slipped in and added things to people's drinks. It turned out to be a disaster for the club. Theo didn't drink, at least not for the last few years, but he still liked to go occasionally. The dates of the receipts in his hands were from about a month ago. He guessed that Mary really enjoyed partying and drinking. Theo added the papers to the rest of the trash.

Soft steps echoed from down the hallway, and Sophia came into view. The transformation was startling. Gone was the girl who was homeless, dirty, and pathetic. Now she was clean, scared, and alone. A flash of the look resurfaced on her face; she was nervous. She stood in the hall, unsure if she should come in. A jolt of anger caused an irrational desire to punch whoever had done this to her.

Theo said, "The kitchen has had a makeover, and so have you. You look refreshed."

She smiled tentatively; a few strands of hair fell and covered her blue-green eyes. She said, "Thanks for everything."

"How was the shower?"

"A dream come true. But I can't seem to get everything out of my hair. It's so thick; I washed it three times. Looks like I'll be getting a haircut tomorrow."

"Oh," he said, half transfixed at her transformation. She could pass as any college girl he'd seen during his time at the University of California, Irvine, for med school. Her sweatshirt read "San Francisco Giants," the baseball team. He mumbled, "So, you like the Giants?"

"Giants and the 49ers."

"Cool."

She stared at him, giving him the impression that she was still unsure if she should come into the kitchen.

Theo tried to think of something to say. He asked, "Do you want to get some sleep or some food?" Before she answered, he blurted, "Or, if you don't want me here, I'll leave and see you in clinic next week."

"Don't go." Sophia's voice came in a whisper, startling him. "I know that this was not what you signed up for. But I don't know what I would've done without you."

"What do you mean?"

"You've been so nice and helpful." Her voice shook. "I've some friends, but none of them would've helped—as you did."

Theo said quickly, "It seems like you've been through so much. Food or sleep?"

"I'm so hungry and tired, I can't even think straight." Her teeth chattered, and tears slid down her face. She took a few tentative steps forward. "I can't be here alone. Truthfully, I thought you were going to be long gone when I came out."

"Why?" Theo stood.

"Because this isn't your problem."

"It is now."

"Thank you." She leaned in and let him hold her. She cried again.

After a pause, he said, "Okay. What do you want to eat?"

"I don't know, but I need to get out of here, just for a few minutes. It makes me sad to look at this place and know that Mary is never coming back."

"So we'll eat out."

"Please." Sophia moved to the closet and opened the door. Two coats hung in the closet, and both had been sliced apart. Slamming the door closed, she said, "Let's go."

Theo slid an arm under hers. "You choose where you want to eat, and we'll plan out what we're going to do tomorrow."

Using the sleeve of her sweatshirt, she wiped her eyes. "So, you're willing to stay and help me."

"I've got tomorrow off and no other plans." Theo instantly thought about Danielle Shaw, his on-and-off girlfriend for the last six months. He knew that she was probably working late. He hadn't seen her in over two weeks. As a new associate lawyer at a full-service firm downtown, she didn't get much time off. But when she did, it was like a tornado of emotions between them. He decided he would text her when he could.

Theo kept a few lights on and locked the door behind them. It was nearly seven o'clock, but this April evening was cooler than usual. He would have to grab a jacket from the trunk of his beat-up 1988 Honda Accord. As they neared the parking lot, a loud whistle burst from behind another building. Theo glanced around as two guys stepped into view.

Sophia groaned, and her arm slipped from Theo's.

"Hey, Soph...it's been a while. How are you?"

"Good, Derek, I'm good." Derek was the skinnier of the two, as if he were a long-distance runner. Theo knew a thing or two about running, but even with his three miles a day, he was far from the running shape that Derek was in.

Sophia seemed to avoid eye contact with the second guy. She finally asked, "How are you, Clayton?"

Clayton said nothing, but he glared at Theo as if he'd just eaten the last piece of cake on the planet and hadn't bothered with sharing.

"Who's this douchebag?" Clayton finally asked. "Is he your boyfriend or something else?"

"Why do you have to be like this?" Sophia protested. "It doesn't matter. He's a friend."

Clayton took a step closer, his face as angry as anybody's that Theo had ever seen. "Where've you been, Soph?"

"Around." Sophia took a step back.

"You've changed," Clayton added. "What's wrong?"

Sophia looked up. "Were you here when Mary died?"

"Yeah," Derek said, his voice calm and reassuring. "We were at the party and going back and forth between my place and the pool. Damn shame that she died. Did you know that I dove in to get her? I can never unsee that."

"You found her?" Sophia exclaimed. "Why was she at that party in the first place?"

Clayton added, "I talked with a lot of people that night. I never saw her once."

"I can't believe she is gone."

"Is that why you're back?" Derek asked.

As much as Derek resonated calm, Theo sensed that Clayton was about to explode.

Sophia said, "Mary was my best friend. I'm just having a hard time dealing with everything."

Derek smiled, but not fully. "We all are, Soph."

"Where have you been?" Clayton demanded.

"I've been sick. I'm hoping to be better now."

Clayton shook his head and raised a hand, pointing at Theo. "Who's this guy, really?"

Sophia stepped between them, but Theo answered, "You can call me T. Everyone does."

"Dude, that's a stupid name."

Theo answered, his voice unwavering, "It is what it is, Clayton."

Sophia pushed Theo back several steps. She said, "We've got to be going."

Clayton protested loudly, "Hey girl, stay and hang with us. Don't go with this guy. We haven't seen you in months."

"See you guys around." Sophia raised her hand and waved. "I'll catch up with you in a few days."

Theo watched as Derek put his hand out and pulled at Clayton's forearm, trying to restrain him. Theo and Sophia walked away, and soon he was opening the door for Sophia. As Theo drove away, he glanced in the rearview mirror and saw the boys at the edge of the parking lot, watching them.

A moment later, Theo said, "Clayton's an interesting guy."

"He would kick a dead dog if he thought it would convince me to go out with him. He borders on the side of a stalker."

Theo shivered. "What about Derek?"

"He's totally nice on his own, but he's best friends with Clayton. They live in the apartment complex, on the far side of the pool. They were here before I moved in. Derek may have even been with Mary a few times." She slumped back in the seat. "Can we head out of town?"

"I don't think they noticed that you were pregnant."

"Maybe. I'm not sure how I'm going to explain this to any of my friends."

"Do you think you'll stay in Lemon Grove Apartments without Mary?"

"I have no idea. I'm so overwhelmed right now. Leaving seems like the right idea, but that's way too much for me to process. Learning I'm pregnant is one thing, but not having Mary around is totally different."

They drove north toward La Mesa and found a sandwich shop just off the freeway. The shop was almost deserted, as it was approaching 8:00 p.m. Theo chose peppered turkey and Havarti cheese, while Sophia ordered the chicken club. They both got chips and a drink, found a seat in the back, and engulfed their food in silence.

After finishing his last bite, Theo asked, "Tell me about yourself?"

Sophia said, "I'm twenty-four and from San Francisco. I graduated three years ago from the state college up there. I moved down here after my dad died."

"Sorry to hear that."

"It was a car accident," she said as if reading his thoughts. "My mom left when I was younger. She's not in the picture. I came down here to look for a new job and to escape."

"Is it working?"

"I thought it was."

Theo asked, "Where do you work?"

"Bank of America back in Lemon Grove, but I can't imagine that I still have a job after all of this." She smacked both sides of her bag of chips playfully, and the pop echoed around the room. "What about you?"

"Born and raised in Dallas." Theo's drawl became pronounced and overdone. He reverted to his normal tone as he added, "Parents split while I was in high school, and I moved to San Diego for my senior year. I stayed here for the first three years of college and then transferred back to Dallas and finished up at the University of Texas in Austin. During the summer after high school, I got a job at Pleasant Valley Correctional Facility as an EMT and worked there for three years until moving back home. After I graduated from college, I was lucky enough to be accepted to medical school here."

"And your parents?"

"They eventually got back together, and that's why we moved back home. They both went to counseling and are doing great. It was weird for a while."

She stared at him more closely. "How old are you?"

"Twenty-five, turning twenty-six next month."

"Any siblings?"

"Two brothers. Both are doctors on the East Coast. I rarely see them."

"So it's a family affair."

"It is."

A silence fell between them, and Theo wasn't sure if it was awkward or uncomfortable. He asked, "Tell me the last thing you remember before today?"

"I've been thinking about it. I don't remember getting or being pregnant." She peered out of the window, concentrating. "That's a tough one. I vaguely remember leaving work, and I was probably heading out to a club. But of course, I can't be certain. That's what Mary and I did almost every night."

Theo's eyebrows rose. He remembered that the last time he had asked this question, she had said something about making some extra money.

Shaking her head, she offered, "I don't meet guys at clubs. I love dancing. It's purely for fun. No take-home boyfriends."

"Well..." Theo's head tilted, unconvinced.

"I know. Pregnancy only happens one way, but I wasn't interested in that. If you must know, I've never been with a guy, or a girl, like that, as far as I can remember."

"We can't rule anything out, since you can't remember the last several months."

"I guess. But it's not like my personality changed."

"Actually, it did. When you first came into the hospital today, you were talking about a Dr. Happypants, and you were talking in gibberish. We gave you some medications and you calmed down. I think that helped."

"It seems so surreal," she muttered. After a moment she asked, "What are other options that could explain my pregnancy?"

"In vitro, surrogate, or something worse." He cringed at the thought.

She asked, "What's in vitro?"

"Where you go to a clinic, and someone else puts a fertilized egg into you?"

"Why would anyone do that?"

"People do it if they can't get pregnant on their own. It's an option, but it's expensive. But if you're a surrogate, you can get paid a lot of money. I remember you said that you were looking for additional ways to make money. Could this be it?"

"No way. Not on your life. I'm too selfish for that."

"To be honest, this is really the starting point of figuring this all out. If we learned who the father was, that would go a long way."

"So you believe me?"

"Clayton, maybe?"

"Get out," she protested. "That's the worst possibility."

"With the way he looks at you…"

"I know." She rolled her eyes. "That would never happen."

"Try thinking back to what you've been doing for the past several months. You must've been living somewhere, even if it was on the streets. Your hair was a mess, but you weren't sickly underweight."

"Was I that bad?"

Theo nodded. "You hit your stomach several times. I was worried."

"Then why are you helping me? Maybe I am just crazy? What if I'm just tricking you?"

"It's crossed my mind a few times. But something weird is going on here. Your apartment was trashed after the police were there. Your roommate died recently. Although that may be a coincidence, she was obviously covering for you until someone called and paid your rent. There are too many questions."

"I realize that. But why did you agree to help me in the first place?"

After a long pause, Theo wondered how much he should say. He opened his mouth but quickly closed it again. He tried once more, but nothing came out. He inhaled deeply and stared at the table. He finally whispered, "I had a close friend a few years ago. We liked each other, and we were hanging out. One night we had a great time. There were times during the night when she became slightly distracted and glanced at her phone. I thought she was nervous. Just before I said good night, she had this look on her face of...helplessness. I was so worried about if I should kiss her or not that I missed understanding the look. Something bad happened to her, and I regret not grasping the look for what it was. You had a similar look today...of helplessness. I promised myself that I would never make the same mistake twice."

CHAPTER 5

As they got back into the car after dinner, Theo asked, "What do you want to do next?"

"I need sleep, a haircut, and some new clothes. I know it sounds dumb, but this girl needs some pampering after everything that's happened today. I can't go for the next several weeks in men's sweatshirts and pajamas."

"And after that?"

"Not sure. It depends on how far we want to push this."

"What do you mean?"

"I could just accept my lot in life and move on, or I can try to figure out where the last seven months have gone."

"Could you really live with not knowing how you got pregnant, and by whom?"

Sophia shot him daggers. "I know you're a doctor and all, but you need a little work on comforting a girl."

"What? I've been such a gentleman. I haven't made you pay for a single thing."

"I should also call my work and apologize for skipping out on them. They've always treated me well."

Theo said, "Sounds like you have a plan."

"Uh…Theo."

"Yes," he said as he started the car.

"I doubt I still have a car. Would you stay over tonight and drive me around tomorrow? I really don't want to be alone."

"Sure." Theo considered their options. They could go to his condo, but his roommate, Barrett, wouldn't be thrilled that he brought over a girl. Staying at her apartment would be uncomfortable, but Sophia could have a room of her own. "Do you want to stay at your apartment?"

"It hasn't completely sunk in that Mary's gone, but yeah, that's the best place for me."

Theo drove for a while, contemplating what he had agreed to do. He wanted to help Sophia as much as he could. He felt sorry for her. He had tried to remain impartial but had come to believe that something awful had happened to Sophia LaCross. There was no way he could abandon her now.

"Any other ideas of what we should do tomorrow?" Sophia asked, interrupting Theo's thoughts.

"Your bank is a great option. If we can see where you've been spending your money, that could give you some information. Also, when you first arrived at the clinic, you were talking crazy, but you did mention a homeless shelter. We could check a few of them out. They might have a record of you."

"A shelter," she said to herself. "That doesn't sound like me, but it's worth a try."

"Okay," Theo replied.

Suddenly Sophia screamed, "Stop!"

"What?" Theo yelled as he slammed on the brakes causing the car to swerve.

When he had finally pulled over, Theo noticed that Sophia had a half smile and a guilty look. "Vision's Hair Solutions is still open. It's over in the strip mall. Do you mind?"

Gasping, Theo said, "My pleasure." He safely crossed traffic and turned into the parking lot, his heart thudding.

As she stepped out, he said, "I'll just stay here for a moment." It took several minutes for his breathing to return to normal.

Sophia walked out of the hair salon an hour later, her transformation complete. It was difficult to picture that scared, smelly, homeless, dirty girl he had met and treated just eight hours ago as this completely stunning, confident girl who climbed into his car.

"What do you think?"

Her hair was still blond but six inches shorter. Blue mascara surrounded her blue-green eyes. She was still wearing the sweatshirt and pajama bottoms, but she stood out as neither psychotic nor homeless.

"Well, you're still hiding a basketball under your shirt, but no one would ever confuse you for a homeless girl."

*　*　*　*

When he awoke the next morning, his joints felt like they were thick with peanut butter and honey. Sophia was fast asleep, and he snuck out to get a change of clothing, including underwear, from the trunk of his car. It never hurt to have a few extra sets of clothes when working at the hospital. He was convinced that he'd run into Derek or Clayton, but he didn't see a soul this early on a Saturday morning. His joint tightness improved considerably with a long and hot shower.

His thoughts turned to Sophia's roommate, Mary, and he deemed it heartbreaking that she had died while Sophia was missing. He wondered if he should suggest that they talk with Derek and Clayton again to see what they had heard about Mary's death. Then he wondered why Sophia's apartment had been trashed. What were they searching for? That question didn't gel with his other thoughts. Finally, he felt sympathy for Sophia, who had been thrust into a completely different life. Her roommate and friend were gone, she was pregnant and alone, and he was almost certain she didn't have anywhere else to turn.

Last night, they had checked all the locks to ensure they were safe. Sophia had slept in her room, and Theo had slept in Mary's room without any reservation. Mary was dead, but this didn't give him any reason not to sleep in her room. It was far more comfortable than the torn-up couch. He thought he heard Sophia crying a few times during the night, but whenever he got up, she was still in her room.

Stepping out of the bathroom, he was surprised to find that Sophia was dressed and ready to leave. She again wore the pajama bottoms and sweatshirt. "I couldn't find anything else to wear." Her eyes were red from crying.

"How are you feeling?"

"Antsy. I called the bank. I talked to my boss and told him what happened. Well, everything except for not remembering the last several months."

"How did that go?"

"He offered me my old job back."

"No way."

"Yeah." She seemed as dazed as he felt. "Let's get food on the way. There's nothing edible here. Give me five minutes to put some makeup on, and we can go."

Theo watched for Derek and Clayton when they left the apartment. He had a nagging feeling that they weren't too far away. Sophia carried a purse that she had found in the back of her closet the night before.

As he slid behind the wheel, he asked, "So, your boss was cool with everything?"

"My boss is the best. When I didn't show up one day, he was shocked. He even called the cops. He is relieved to hear that I'm okay."

"How long ago did you stop working?"

"That's the scariest part. Nine or ten months ago."

"What did the cops say?"

"That I wasn't missing just because I'd quit my job. They thought that I ran away or moved."

"How much did you tell him?"

"I told him that I got amnesia, became homeless, and had just recently recovered. He wants a doctor's note." She winked and relaxed in the passenger seat, staring out of the window.

"Are you kidding?"

"It's a luxury to have my own personal doctor."

"And how, exactly, are you going to describe this little bun in the oven?"

"A great question. Maybe I'll have you come in and explain how babies are made."

Theo mumbled, "Oh, boy, you're in a mood."

She directed him to a local bakery, where they picked out several doughnuts and two coffees.

A few blocks later, Theo asked, "Can I ask a question about Mary?"

"Depends." She shifted uncomfortably in the car.

"How well did you know her?"

"As well as possible, I guess. We were roommates for twelve months, maybe more."

"I can't stop thinking about her," Theo said honestly.

"I'm listening."

"Could she be involved in drugs or stolen property or anything else you can think of?"

Sophia laughed. "Mary! Absolutely not. She's the last person who would do anything illicit. She's about as harmless as a rash. Why do you ask?"

"Well, to the first point, some rashes can be deadly. There's your medical tip for the day."

"Wow. I'm impressed."

Theo continued, "Your television is expensive. It's like four thousand dollars or more. It was cracked but not stolen. Whoever broke into your apartment was looking for something specific, and maybe a little angry."

"Not sure what that could be," Sophia assured him. "Maybe they were looking for small things to sell for drugs. Stealing a television is sort of obvious. Someone might've seen them."

Theo considered this for a moment, "Maybe...but I think there's something more."

"Your guess is as good as mine."

He said, "It would help to get my hands on Mary's autopsy report."

"How?"

"Her cause of death would enable us to better understand what happened to her. There may have been something in the autopsy that wouldn't have been seen at the time of death. Some things become more apparent a few days after death."

"Is that a public record?"

"Not really. And probably not until they decide on the cause of death."

"Is there a way you could look at it?"

"I have a few friends. Not sure that they can help, but I'll call them."

"Any other questions on Mary?"

"Not yet, maybe later."

The friends he was referring to were Patrick Mulder and Zorn Davies, both born and raised in San Diego. Theo met them during his time working at the Pleasant Valley Correctional Facility. They were correctional officers while he was an EMT. Both Patrick and Zorn were a good four or five years older than he was and had been at the jail for more than five years when he started. But somehow the three of them became inseparable best friends, at least for a few years. Now, several moons later, Patrick worked as a detective in San Diego, and Zorn had climbed the ladder all the way to the FBI. Theo doubted that Zorn could help in this case, but Patrick might be able to answer a few questions. Today being Saturday, there was a fifty-fifty shot of reaching him.

Theo parked the car across from the bank, and Sophia reached for the door handle. "So, we're good to go inside."

"You go in first. I'll watch for anything suspicious out here."

"Why?"

"I think it's prudent that we are careful. When you're inside, don't give away too much information. You can say that you're pregnant, but don't tell them you were missing. Say you were sick or something, and that you're seeing a doctor. Don't open up about your memory loss or anything else."

"If you say so."

Sophia stepped out and crossed the street as Theo scanned the area but saw no one suspicious. He opened his phone and dialed the number, speaking for a few minutes. He gave just the basics, and Patrick agreed to see what he could find out. As the words came from his mouth, he realized how crazy they sounded. Luckily,

Patrick loved this type of mystery and was willing to find some information.

After hanging up the phone, he slipped out of the car and walked down the street. He had no intention of going inside. He found a bench across from the bank and played a game on his phone for a few minutes. Several minutes later, his cell phone rang, and he listened to his friend.

When Sophia stepped out of the bank, she appeared flustered and scurried to the car. Theo tried catching up to her, but she rushed to her side of the car.

"Is everything all right?" Theo asked, concerned.

"I'm not sure." Her voice sounded bleak and distant.

"What is it?"

"Just open the door." She was pale and sweat poured down her face.

Theo quickly jumped in and started the car.

"Just drive," she hissed, clutching her purse.

He waited until Sophia could speak. Finally, she said, "My account must've been hacked."

"What do you mean?"

"Shit," she mumbled as she pulled open her purse, and Theo gasped.

"It's ten thousand dollars, and I've got another hundred and forty thousand sitting in my account. How's this even possible?"

Theo reached into the purse and pulled out a stack of twenty-dollar bills, then another and another.

"It was so easy to ask for a withdrawal. The manager obviously knows me, but even he was surprised that I had so much money—especially since I just walked out of there ten months ago and never came back. He knows how much I made. He explained that another account wired the money into mine six months ago, as far as he could tell. That account is now closed."

"Looks like you don't need a job there after all."

"He said the same thing." Her cheeks reddened. "How could I have been living homeless and have this much money in my account?"

"Can you think of anyone who could have put this into your account? Anyone?"

"No one I know has that kind of money."

"Unbelievable."

"I can't even give it back unless I throw it out the window. It's mine," Sophia added.

Theo said hesitantly, "I also have some news. I don't remember if I've told you, but I have a friend who works for the police. His name is Patrick. I didn't give him any real information. But he works as a detective for the San Diego Police Department."

"Is that a good thing?"

"I called, and he was willing to investigate a few things. I've known him forever. He's a good friend and we worked at the prison together."

"Did you tell him about me?"

"Sort of. My focus was more on Mary. He told me that her body was taken to the San Diego County medical examiner's office. Her autopsy is probably already done. He's trying to get me clearance to go in as a medical student. We should probably head that direction next if you're okay with it."

"Can your friend help us? Maybe I should just talk with him."

"He might be able to help, but he's going to keep his distance for now."

Meeting his eyes, she insisted, "I will find out what happened here. Memory loss, money in my account, I'm freaking pregnant, and Mary's dead. These all can't be coincidences. What the hell is going on?"

Thirty minutes later, he parked at the coroner's office. The idea of seeing Mary was too much for Sophia, and she was dropped off at a nearby coffee shop. Patrick called and confirmed his approval with the coroner's office. The building was big, new, and a few stories high. Several large windows with bright lights were at the front of the building. The north side held no windows and only a single door. A road cut along the north side, disappearing around the back. Stepping inside, he found the lobby was large and unwelcoming. Clean and sterile, it screamed *"icy and sterile death."* He found three expensive couches forming a triangle around a full oak table to his left. Artwork, statues, and even a small water fountain took up most of the remaining space, and these felt impassive and cold. The reception desk was nestled into the far back-right corner.

A young and attractive blond girl sat behind the desk. As Theo approached, she dazzled him with a confident smile and mesmerizing green eyes. She said, "Welcome to the medical examiner's office. Do you have an appointment?"

"I'm a medical student at UCSD, and I was told I would have access to an autopsy report." He reached into his wallet and pulled out his school ID. The receptionist wrote down his name and passed back the ID.

"Do you know which pathologist you will be meeting with?"

"I don't. I will be reviewing the autopsy of a young woman who died by drowning."

"I don't know the exact patient load or who you will be meeting with. Give me a moment to call back and verify."

Five minutes later, she waved him over. "You will need to go through the back doors, and someone will help you."

He arrived at a metal door at the far end of the hallway. Stepping closer, he heard a slight click, and it opened automatically. A surprisingly bright hall greeted him with white walls and dark gray tiles. There were a few tasteful paintings on the wall, which was decorated far differently than the one in the lobby. But the smell was more overwhelming than he had remembered. It was a combination of death and bleach. He'd spent a month helping with autopsies at the hospital last summer. He was suddenly shocked that he had forgotten this smell.

A skinny, tall man practically crashed into him as he scurried out of a door connecting to the corridor. Theo leaped to the side. The man didn't seem to see him. keeping his head down as he concentrated on a purse in his gloved hand. This worker wore black pants, a black shirt, and black shoes. His spiky black hair and black eyeliner were visible only for a second. He wore a white lab coat that looked out of place, and he wore something around his neck, an ID holder. The man took several steps down the hall, swiped the ID tag at another door at the end of the hall, and disappeared. Theo pictured him entering a room of dead bodies, autopsy rooms, and instruments.

After another few steps, he reached an open, circular room, that felt like an office space. Four corridors, including the one he was coming from bisected this area. The tile from each corridor met in the middle. This created four separate office-like zones with different colored carpets and desks. The individuality of each section was on full display.

The desk immediately to his right was near the wall, and a large palm tree to the right of the desk went to the ceiling. Several clear bottles of sand sat on a shelf, as did six bobbleheads of half-naked men and women who nodded repeatedly. A beach towel covered a wooden beach chair pushed into the desk. There was a gigantic picture of a white sandy beach with turquoise water and a beautiful sunset. An opened set of shark jaws was mounted on the far wall.

The next desk, against the back wall, farther to the right and past the first hallway, was expensive dark oak. There were five shadow boxes of dead insects arranged neatly, as if in picture frames. Theo could see beetles, butterflies, moths, spiders, and things he didn't even want to recognize. Another set of insects was on the desk in small, clear containers. A balding man sat at this desk, and the nameplate said "Dr. Phillip Bowthorpe." He thought the man could be in his sixties. He looked skillful with his hands as he worked at the table with a bright light, a magnifying glass, and several instruments. He was not dissecting the insects but expertly pinning them to a board.

The third desk, immediately to Theo's left, was covered with charts and files but equally strange. It was dark black but expensive. The chair was a black gamer's chair that looked comfortable. The lamp on the desk was red oak and had a black shade that gave off a weird vibe. A checkered, black-and-white board was attached to the wall. Surrounding this, eight masks adorned the wall, but these were different than the masks hanging up at his condo. These were evil rather than artful, depicting death, an afterlife, hatred, envy, guilt, sadness, rage, and contempt. He quickly searched for the name on this desk. Dr. Lucas Daniels.

The last desk in the room, across and to his left, was designed with an appreciation for books. The desk was old, sturdy, and painted a deep blue. A Victorian desk lamp illuminated the covers of several old books on a shelf. He was enchanted by this desk. It was arranged neatly, with a picture of a house overlooking the ocean, an expensive pen set, stacks of papers, and several files.

On the wall next to the older desk, hung a marble slab that was divided by black tape into eight equally sized squares. Eight pictures, autopsy headshots, were the central point in each square with some writing below and to the left of the pictures. From this distance, Theo thought they probably were the heights, weights, and eye and hair colors of those who had been autopsied. Glancing around to ensure no one was staring at him, Theo strode toward this display. He stared closely at the first picture and saw an old man with vacant eyes and a crushing injury to his frontal lobe, his head had been smashed in by a significant force. The date of his death, where he was found, and several other pertinent facts were outlined to the left of the picture.

The second box held a picture of a woman who seemed to be in her fifties. She looked peaceful but still dead. Next to her photo was the cause of death—pulmonary embolism, a blood clot in her lungs. It was not always fatal, but it was a hard way to go when it was. Her date of birth confirmed that she was fifty-six.

Eyeing the others, he found that the next three pictures were of drug overdose, old age, and child abuse. A beautiful black girl was the sixth picture. His eyes flickered to her cause of death: drowning. Theo's heart raced, and his eyes shifted to her name. He read the name—Mary Sneider.

CHAPTER 6

"Excuse me. Can I help you?" a high-pitched voice asked with authority from down the hall. As he turned, a woman was marching toward him, having come out of one of the three autopsy rooms behind her. Two of the glass rooms had frosted windows, and Theo guessed that the occupant could control the change. Inside the middle room, a man lay supine, clearly undergoing a procedure, his chest cavity having already been opened.

The woman wore a blue body covering, white boots, a mask, an eye shield, and something over her head. She had just disposed of her gloves.

Theo, caught off guard, said nothing.

The woman demanded, "Can you hear me? Do I need to call security?"

"No," he finally managed. "I am a medical student and was approved to come in this morning and talk with someone."

Theo glanced at the picture of Mary, and it suddenly made things real in his mind. He felt sorry for Sophia and Mary and everything that had happened.

The woman removed her mask and eye shield, and Theo noted that she was maybe ten years older than he was. Her skin was soft, and her lipstick was pink. However, she looked far from happy to see him.

He added hastily, "I'm Theo Raden. I mean, Dr. Raden, from UCSD, and I'm here to go over a drowning victim.

I just wasn't told who I'd be shadowing." He pulled out his student ID and held it up as if he were getting carded at the liquor store.

"Oh," she said, clearly annoyed. "That would be with Dr. Daniels, but I haven't seen him in an hour or so." She glanced in the direction of the black desk first, then to the back of the head of the balding man farther away, and rolled her eyes. "You can follow me for a few minutes until he gets back."

She stalked back to the outside of the autopsy room and discarded her blue top and pants. She set aside her shield but tossed her mask. She wore black slacks and a white blouse top. As Theo got a full picture of her, she was attractive and professional. She removed her boots and slid into black flats with pointy ends. She had black hair and was around five foot ten.

"I'm sorry to receive you like this. I'm sure it seems like I don't have time for students, and the truth is, I don't. But I can also appreciate the importance of mentoring students; I just wish you had given me more time than a few hours before you dropped by. It has been a busy day."

"I'm sorry," he managed to say.

She picked up a white coat on a hook and said, "Grab yourself a white coat and put some booties on your feet. It doesn't appear that you're ready to help with a single autopsy. Didn't one of your instructors tell you how things would be?"

"I'm actually a first-year resident. Someone called today and cleared me to review the drowning case."

The lady stopped, turned, and stared at Theo. Her head tilted as if reevaluating him, or worse. She asked, "You mean Miss. Sneider?" Her tone left very little confusion.

"Yes, ma'am."

The annoyance she'd shown a few seconds ago had evaporated and was now replaced with simmering anger and suspicion. He unconsciously stepped backward from her glare. She was no longer trying too hard to be hospitable. Theo finally asked, "Is there something wrong?"

"Why in the world would you need to come all the way down here and examine *her* body? And why would a detective that I've never worked with call and tell me that I need to let you, a student, into my building?"

"Uh," Theo stuttered. "He's doing me a favor to get more experience."

She stared at him knowingly. "Who are you really with?"

"I work at Scripps Mercy—"

She reached out, grabbed his shirt, and pulled him down a hallway leading away from the autopsy rooms. "Is someone on my staff being investigated? Are you with internal affairs or with the mayor's office?" She took a menacing step forward.

Theo retreated until his back hit a wall. "Doctor. I've no idea what you're talking about. I really am a fifth-year student."

"Just because I haven't confirmed the death as a drowning doesn't mean that we need to be investigated."

Theo stirred over this statement. "So she didn't die from the swimming pool?"

"It actually seems like she did. Dr. Daniels hasn't given me the final report yet. Why are you so interested in this case?"

"I'm looking for more experience, and this case would really help me."

She stopped suddenly and shook her head. She asked quizzically, "Do you know who I am?"

He felt his face redden. "I'm sorry. I don't."

Her facial features relaxed considerably. She pointed to a small closet. "Put on the coat and booties and join me in autopsy three. I think we need to start over. You have a lot of explaining to do."

Theo hesitantly found a white coat in a closet nearby, and he placed thin, blue tissue socks over his shoes. He scrubbed his hands in the same manner as he did when assisting with surgery. The smell of death was stronger as he passed through the glass doors into the autopsy room. The male body was positioned on the metal slab. He was covered with a white sheet.

"I'm Dr. Lazar, Celeste Lazar. I don't think I told you my name. And you are... Theo...?"

"Raden," he muttered.

"I see." She still wore her white coat and had changed back into her boots and face mask. She didn't change back into the blue protective covering, and Theo assumed the body had already been fully cut open.

She lifted open the chest cavity, which had already been opened, removed the heart, took a few steps to her left, and placed the heart onto a scale. "How did you hear about Mary Sneider's death?"

"From a friend." Theo's eyes feverishly watched at her work.

Unperturbed, Dr. Lazar continued, "When did you hear about it?"

Theo hesitated. "Yesterday."

"You're taking a large interest in someone you just heard about yesterday."

"It's a friend of a friend and hard to explain." He doubted that this would placate her, but he wasn't sure what else to say. He muttered, "I haven't had a lot of experiences with death and its causes. My attending thinks I should get experience with the living and the dead."

"Interesting."

Theo hoped he hadn't said the wrong thing.

She returned to the body, reaching in and pulling out the liver. Blood did not ooze out of the chest cavity. This almost seemed unnatural since all wounds *should* have a release of blood. Dr. Lazar nodded at a countertop at the back of the room. "Miss Sneider's preliminary file is at the back. I remind you that it is not finished. Open it and tell me what you think."

Theo had read several autopsies before, but he wasn't an expert by any means. The first few lines spelled out what he was looking at. He read phrases like "death from asphyxia due to suffocation caused by a liquid entering the lungs" and "resulting in the prevention of the absorption of oxygen, which leads to cerebral hypoxia." He realized that in essence, drowning was the suffocation of the patient. The cause was a liquid spilling into the lungs. Without the ability to breathe, hypoxia soon followed. Moderate pulmonary edema was noted as well. Hypoxia, the lack of oxygen, led to brain damage and was often the ultimate cause of death. He knew that in some cases, a cardiac event like a heart attack could result from the lack of oxygen or a change in chemicals inside the body. But a severe cardiac event was not seen in Mary's case. To Theo, this spelled out that she was indeed a drowning victim.

There was a large amount of water found in her stomach. This was likely a result of the involuntary swallowing of water during the drowning. Mainly, part of the water went into the lungs and part into the stomach. Rigor mortis had set in by the time the autopsy was performed. No strangulation marks or postmortem bruises were seen. Alcohol was found in the blood at elevated levels, and this was confirmed using urine and vitreous humor, a liquid from the eye. The last thing that Theo checked was for any tissue samples under her fingernails. This was often a sign of a struggle if there had been one. Dunking someone's head underwater could result in quite a skirmish.

But nothing was found under her nails. It was surprising, though, as noted by Dr. Lazar, that her nails had recently been cleaned and trimmed. It probably meant nothing. It was concluded that Mary Sneider had likely cleaned her own nails prior to the party at the pool. This made perfect sense to Theo.

He finished and found Dr. Lazar staring at him. "What do you make of the report?"

"It appears to be a simple death by drowning. No defensive wounds, no signs of a struggle. No cardiac or other preceding event. She had alcohol in her system. A pretty open-and-shut case."

"I agree," said Dr. Lazar. "Do you see anything suspicious that would make me think otherwise?"

Theo reread the file. "I don't."

She nodded as if this was what she had expected. "Two things appear peculiar and not what I call conclusive. The first was the alveolar tissue itself. Look here—fresh water is less salty than the fluid inside the human body, and this can cause the water to be rapidly absorbed. At least at first. But what I found contained more sodium chloride than expected. By contrast, when there is salt water, water from the pulmonary circulation comes into the alveolar spaces because the water is saltier than the human body."

"Are you saying that she drowned in saltwater?"

"It's inconclusive, at this point, and impossible to prove or disprove. The second issue is that there was a layer of silt lining the alveolar tissue and in her stomach."

"Where would she get that from?"

"From the pool, probably, but it's an oddity nonetheless."

Theo asked, frustrated, "Dr. Lazar, is this death suspicious or not?"

"I don't think so, but my colleague Dr. Daniels will present the findings soon. There was pool water in her stomach and chest. These are just small findings. I imagine he will finish the report by Monday as a non-suspicious drowning."

Theo replaced the file on the counter. "Thank you for the chance to see this file."

Dr. Lazar returned to the patient. The chest cavity was now empty. She asked, "Are you sure you don't want to stick around for this case? This could be interesting."

"How would an eighty-year-old man be interesting?"

"Because all signs point to a possible poisoning that resulted in the man's intestines turning mush. Can't you tell by the smell?"

Theo laughed uncomfortably. "I think I'll pass." He felt a slight lurch in his stomach. "Maybe next time." He hustled quickly to the door, shouting, "Thanks again, Dr. Lazar."

Upon exiting the autopsy room, he pulled off his booties, tossed them into the trash, and placed the white coat into a laundry bin. Retracing his steps, he passed by the desks, and soon he was turning the key to his car as he took deep, calming breaths.

Sophia sat in the back of the coffee shop, sipping her coffee with a partially eaten pastry in front of her. She was pale and lost in her own thoughts as he approached. Theo ordered a coffee and pulled up a chair beside her.

She didn't ask him anything immediately and waited for Theo to start.

After his coffee arrived, Theo whispered, "Looks like a drowning, plain and simple."

"You sound disappointed."

"I'm not," he assured her. He described the first part of the encounter with Dr. Lazar. They both found it bizarre that she thought he was there for an investigation into the lab. He moved on to the basic findings and the two anomalies that were given.

"So, it's not suspicious?"

"No two deaths are alike. Autopsy findings can be consistent with each other, but not everything matches up all the time. There is fluidity to everything. There are some questions, but more importantly, she found no foul play involved."

"Where does that put us?" Sophia asked, but she was visibly shaking.

He tried assuring her. "I know that this is hard. I'm just glad you stayed here. We've lost nothing, and we have a clearer picture. Are you all right?"

Sophia wiped her eyes and her nose. When she spoke again, she asked, "Does that mean we will look at some homeless shelters?"

"I think so."

"That's as good of a place as any for our next step," Sophia said. "I had to be living somewhere, but as you said, I was well-fed. I don't have any track marks, and there were no signs of drugs in my system, so a shelter is likely the best bet."

"I agree." Theo took a drink of his coffee.

"But after that, we need to go shopping for some new maternity clothes."

"Sounds like a plan. But I'm not going to help you pick out anything. You know that, right? I'm staying far away."

"We'll see. I might need your expert opinion."

"No way. Why would you need me for that?"

"I'll give you a thousand dollars."

"Are you bribing me to go shopping with you?"

"Call it whatever you want. Are you in?"

"Well…"

"Don't make me ask Clayton or Derek for help. I won't come out and model it for you."

"Fine." He smiled. "Not sure how I got talked into any of this in the first place."

CHAPTER 7

The St. Jude's Village homeless shelter was the third location on their schedule and the last one for the day. They had found nothing helpful at their two previous stops. It was nearing 4:00 p.m., and Theo and Sophia were tired of walking and asking questions. At the other shelters, they were escorted to a waiting room until someone was willing to answer their questions. It had been a long, drawn-out process. Neither place had any records for Sophia LaCross, even for her first name, or anyone that recognized her.

The outer concrete of St. Jude's was cracked, and the walls were crumbling. The structure was gigantic, and there were dozens of people milling around in open parking lots, along the streets, and around the nearby buildings and homes. A few groups huddled together on the far street corners, while others were half hidden on steps or in alleys. At this point, he wished they were at the mall with Sophia trying on maternity clothes rather than standing near the front door.

They had parked in a large lot facing the front of the building, but really, it seemed like St. Jude's took up the entire block. A large stucco fence went in both directions, turned the corner, and continued onward.

"Let's walk inside as friends," Theo suggested. "Not with you as my patient."

"Why?"

"I'm not sure what we're going to find here. This place is bigger than I expected. There are a lot of people, and we didn't have luck at the last two locations. Having a doctor look into the facility might not open the right doors."

"Maybe they didn't know my real name, like when I first met you."

"Maybe," he said as they strolled toward a large, wooden front door. His mind recalled some information he had learned about St. Jude's Village. It was more than a shelter; it was a small community with housing, several open areas during the day, a church, mental health advocates, food resources, and safety for those accepted to its program. The doors closed at 10:00 p.m., and you couldn't walk around the community at night. Someone he remembered from when he worked at the prison told him there was a grass courtyard, and there were stone tables, chessboards, large trees, and several buildings. The inmate had nothing but good things to say about St. Jude's.

Just to the right of the door was a group of kids. Several vials of some clear liquid were being passed under their coats or clothes and between newspapers. The realization hit him immediately, and he knew he shouldn't be surprised that selling drugs was happening so close to a shelter. They were only a few blocks from several large parks and the ocean. This might be considered a prime location.

The outer wooden doors were covered with marks, carvings, and graffiti. A second set of doors, metal and thick, were located under an archway just inside a walkway. They were open, and he and Sophia entered a long hall. He shook his head at the impossibility of some people escaping addiction. From his experience working at the prison, he had learned that some people could never escape no matter how hard they tried. Society expected them to avoid the streets, find new homes, and get new jobs but provided them with very few resources or second chances.

For these people and thousands of others, overcoming or avoiding being homeless was more complicated than you could imagine. Drug and alcohol addictions, difficult family dynamics, mental health complications, posttraumatic stress disorder, and a slew of other problems prevented thousands of people from finding a normal life, whatever that was. Theo had seen his fair share of those types of patients and inmates. Some shelters and homes really wanted to help. He wasn't completely sold on St. Jude's because of the simple fact that kids were selling drugs right on their doorsteps. But what did he know?

Through the metal doors, the stone walkway sparkled with cleanliness. There were pictures of men and women lining the walls. On one side were photos of employees and on the other side were success stories from the shelter. The success stories had a "before" and an "after" photo, and Theo gasped at some of the differences. Each stood outside the shelter in front of the main wooden doors. Maybe he'd spoken too soon, and they would find something helpful about Sophia after all.

Two women neatly dressed in long skirts and white shirts sat behind a glass window at the far end of the hall, welcoming a line of people into the village. They professionally scrutinized each person; some they recognized and welcomed to pass through a third door, into a place Theo could only imagine was more protected than the White House.

"Is that where the magic happens?" Theo whispered. "Are we going to see the wizard?"

"Without a doubt," Sophia agreed. "I mean, how could it not be."

Ten minutes later, it was Sophia's turn. She politely smiled at the attendant behind the desk. "I was hoping that you could help me. I think I was here for the past few weeks. I seem to have some memory issues. Could I talk with someone who might be able to help me?"

The woman concentrating on her paperwork glanced up, and recognition crossed her face. Theo watched it melt away as she seemed to remember something else. "Are you sure that it was here?" she asked.

"Pretty positive. I just need to talk to someone. Do you have medical staff here or just those helping with housing issues?"

The attendant fumbled for the phone. "Let me call someone." Her body leaned away as she spoke into the phone. After hanging up, she glanced back at Sophia and said, "I can let you through. Take the first right."

Theo stood close but still out of the way.

The lady continued, "Hurry on through, into the big open building, and someone will come and meet you."

Sophia walked to the door, and they heard a click. "Guess that means we're home free."

Theo caught up as the door opened. As they turned to the right, he looked back and caught the same women cursing at him for slipping in. Not so professional after all. She quickly picked up the phone and dialed it again. Ahead, several men and women were busy helping or guiding groups of people around a large and spacious room. It felt like a church, with a high ceiling, candles, benches, and several small groups listening to someone reading a Bible. The doorways into different rooms or hallways were enormous, and the entire room was well decorated.

He and Sophia veered to the left near one of the side walls. They stopped near a window that stared out onto the courtyard. There were a dozen trees, benches, large stretches of grass, pathways, and two gardens. It was an impressive sight with more than a hundred people in it. The inner structure was magnificent and a far cry from the crumbling outer walls.

"Is that yoga over there?" Theo pointed to the center of the courtyard.

"Looks like it."

"I'm officially impressed."

"Not too shabby," she agreed.

Sophia pulled on his arm. Straight in front of them was a doorway leading to an area that appeared to be a cafeteria. They found several different aromas competing in their senses as they stepped through. Three spacious kitchen areas were situated in separate alcoves, and a dozen people were busy at work. The room felt inviting and comforting. It was decorated like he imagined a Christian convent would be. The walls were bright white, with several large crosses; a brown trim stretched around the alcoves, the doorways, and even the ceiling. Several wooden tables were centered in the room, giving an almost café sort of feeling. A good seventy clients could eat at one time in this room.

Counselors, who sat farther back at more private and smaller tables, were busy talking with clients and their families. Briefcases, papers, and books were at most of these tables. This area was bustling and animated. Three halls split from the room and traveled to different portions of the village. At the top of each hallway were signs that read "St. Josephs," "Good Shepherd," and "New Beginnings".

"Do any of those sound familiar?" Theo asked, pointing to the signs.

"I don't think so."

"Can I help you?" an older man in a brown sports coat asked from the closest of the four counselor tables.

"I think that I might have been staying here. I was wondering if I could've left any possessions."

"I see," the man grumbled, and he gave Theo the once-over. "Follow me. There's a receptionist back here that can help." The older man nodded at the couple he was talking with, two women holding hands, then grasped Sophia's arm and whisked her toward the doorway that read "New Beginnings". Theo remained a few steps behind.

The man glared back sharply at him twice. He leaned in and whispered something to Sophia. She laughed and turned back to Theo with a wicked grin. She rubbed her belly softly, and Theo realized that this man thought he was the dirtbag boyfriend who'd left his pregnant girlfriend at a homeless shelter.

This portion of the building was older and even more charismatic. The decorations were subtle, plain, and inviting. They were led to another wooden doorway, where the man knocked twice and entered. A wooden desk matching the door was positioned ten feet inside the room.

"Hello, Father James. What can I do for you?" asked an older woman who sat working.

Father James took another long stare at Theo. "This young lady says she was a client here. She's wondering if she left anything behind. She's here with one of her _friends_." He tilted his head in Theo's direction. No names were asked, and no introductions were given. Sophia was the important one here, not him.

"I see," said the woman. When she peered up at Sophia, Theo thought he saw recognition cross her face, just like at the front doors. The woman dropped something to the floor and bent low to pick up the item, her pen. "Are you sure you've been here before?" Her voice wasn't friendly or compassionate. The reaction bothered Theo, and an inner voice told him to leave immediately.

Sophia smiled kindly and said, "I think so."

The woman turned to Father James, "Father, I thought today was your day off."

"It is, Gretchen. I had an urgent meeting scheduled. When I finish, I will be leaving for my vacation."

Father James did not come across as much more than a social worker. Theo expected a priest's attire, whatever that might be.

"You deserve it. You do so much for our parish."

He gave one last disapproving look at Theo and stalked from the room.

Gretchen turned back to Sophia. "Perchance, do you remember what housing you were in?"

"I'm sorry, I don't."

"But you are sure that it was here?"

Theo stepped forward to put his arm under Sophia's. He wanted to whisper to her to leave, but she brushed him off.

"Quite sure."

"Was your friend here with you before?"

"No."

"How long have you been pregnant?"

"About seven months."

"I see." Gretchen asked, "Have you been seeing a doctor?"

"I think so." Sophia turned and glanced at Theo.

Taking a step forward, Theo muttered, "I'm a…"

Gretchen stood and snarled, "I was talking with the client about personal and confidential information. If you could wait in the next room, Sophia and I will be just a few more minutes."

Theo was shocked at her outburst.

Sophia said, "No. It's okay. I would prefer for him to stay. He is my friend."

Gretchen recovered quickly. "That's fine, dear. We just need to protect the innocent. I hope you can understand. Would you be willing to wait in the waiting room, and I'll have someone come to talk with you in a minute?"

"I guess," said Sophia, but Theo pulled her arm.

"We'll stay just for a few minutes."

"That's a good choice," replied Gretchen. "In here."

They were led to a room with four chairs, a table, and two doors. The glass was frosted, and no one could see in or out of the rooms. Once the door closed, he said, "We need to go."

Sophia sighed. "There's something here that we need to know. I can feel it."

Maybe," he said skeptically. "But there's something off about this place. A few people have recognized you, then pretended they didn't. Gretchen is no saint."

"It looks fantastic to me."

"Maybe on the outside. But I think it might be hiding something."

"Like what? You're overreacting. We're about to get some of the information we need…"

Theo took her hand in his. "I promise you that there's something wrong here. Let's get out of here. We can come back another day."

"I can't. I…"

The door swung open, and a tall man strolled casually into the office. He had dark brown hair and a deep tan. His features were taut against his face, almost chiseled—except for his smile, which reminded Theo of a car salesman. He could see the anger on his cheeks, in his clenched teeth, and especially in his eyes. He refused to acknowledge Theo as he swept toward Sophia. He wore expensive business-casual clothing. This man could pass for someone working on Wall Street or an incredible college professor who was entertaining and thought-provoking.

"I'm so glad that you're safe," the man said calmly.

"You know me?"

"Of course!" His voice dripped with contempt, and he stepped even closer. "Don't be silly. You've been in my care for the last few months. Our nurses have been so worried about you. You're a high-risk pregnancy, and we can help. We're so glad that you're safe."

High-risk, Theo thought to himself.

She smiled and tried glancing at Theo.

The man quickly touched her belly. "Looks like you're progressing right along, Tosh." The name slipped out. The man glanced at Theo, and his smile faltered for just an instant. Then the moment passed, and he was smiling again at her.

"Tosh?" she asked. "My name is Sophia. I can't remember Tosh."

"No worries. It's a nickname one of the other girls came up with for you. Sophia is what we normally call you."

Sophia turned to Theo again. "This is my friend..."

Theo held out his hands and answered, "Clayton." It was the first name that came to his mind. He wanted to keep himself and Sophia safe from this man.

In a dismissive voice the man said, "Hello Clayton, nice to meet you."

"Actually, we need to be going." Theo stood quickly and reached for Sophia.

"Who are you?" Sophia blurted at the man.

The man bristled but said, "Dr. Thomas Haderly. I'm your doctor and have been treating you for the last several months. You've been struggling, but we were making real strides. I hope you haven't forgotten everything we've been working on."

Theo tried to forward to put his arm around Sophia, but Dr. Haderly blocked his movement.

He asked, "How are you feeling? I hope you aren't having any complications or problems?"

Sophia said quickly, "I don't think so. I can't remember anything about being here."

"Really?" Dr. Haderly pondered. "That's quite concerning. I've seen you three times a week for the last few months. As your doctor, I've been planning with you for your delivery. We've done three ultrasounds to monitor your progress. I could show them to you. Have you been taking your medications?" His voice changed, and Theo could see exactly where this was going.

Theo interrupted, "Yes, Doctor, she's fine and has been taking her medications. She's just tired right now. We have an appointment to get to. We really must be going."

Glaring at Theo, Dr. Haderly asked, "Oh, Tosh…I mean, Sophia. Are you sure that everything's all right?"

"I'm just confused, that's all." Sophia tried catching Theo's eye.

"I see," Dr. Haderly said gravely, as if pronouncing a death sentence. He nodded quickly as if mentally checking a box.

Theo reached out intending to grab Sophia's hand and pull her from the room. Dr. Haderly stepped between them and yelled, "Security!"

Sophia gasped. "What's going on?"

Theo tried stepping closer. "Sophia and I need to go."

The doctor spread his arms as if protecting Sophia. "Sir, you need to leave at once."

"I'm not leaving without her," Theo said, pointing to Sophia.

"This girl is my patient. She's having a nervous breakdown. You need to leave the premises immediately."

Theo tried sidestepping Dr. Haderly. Before he'd taken a step, an arm reached around his neck from behind, and Theo was dragged backward. A second arm grasped him as two men roughly the size of Mount Rushmore pulled him in the direction of Gretchen's office. He watched as a door opened just behind Sophia, and two men in white coats entered the room and pulled her from his sight.

She screamed, "Theo! Theo! Where are they taking me?"

Within seconds, she was gone.

Dr. Haderly straightened, a slight smile on his face. His voice was calm as he said, "You must understand, Theo, she's quite sick if you haven't noticed. This pregnancy is causing what we call a psychotic episode. She thinks that she's someone that she's not. She's been under strict observation for the last few weeks. Somehow, she got out. I'm sorry that you had to see that. She'll be fine."

"I need to see her. I can calm her down."

The pressure on his neck tightened.

Dr. Haderly took a few steps closer. "We're trained professionals. Would you mind coming into the office and leaving your number with Gretchen? When she gets better, we'll call you, I promise. But let me guess. She can't remember how she got pregnant. She can't remember a lot of things. We've seen this before."

Theo felt his anger rise. "I'm not leaving her."

Dr. Haderly continued in a reassuringly and frighteningly well-trained voice. "She's in the right place. You did an excellent job. How did you find us by the way?"

Theo allowed them to walk him a few steps. Reaching up, he tried brushing the man's hand away from his neck. Dr. Haderly nodded, and the man let go just as the second man opened the door. The instant he was free, Theo broke away and sprinted into Gretchen's office. The lady let out a scream as Theo lowered his shoulder and crashed through the far door. Glancing back and forth, Theo hoped to spot Sophia, but the hallway was empty. He tore off in the direction of an exit with two men mere steps behind.

He dodged around two clients and heard their cries a moment later, as if they had been knocked aside. An exit sign illuminated the far wall. Theo had to swerve around another group of clients, knocking over a trash can and dashing forward. He sucked in gulps of air as he went, his head pounding, but he didn't dare look back.

He flew through two more doors before seeing the stone hallway where he and Sophia had entered the building. The same ladies were talking and answering the phone. The security guards behind him yelled to have the metal doors closed. One lady reacted a moment too late as Theo lunged through the first set of doors and past the closing metal ones. He exited the building, turned left, and sprinted away from St. Jude's.

As he ran, he flipped open his cell phone and dialed nine and one. Before hitting the third number, he slammed the end button. He knew what would happen. A licensed physician had done precisely what Theo himself was on the verge of doing. Invoking a 5150 was an acceptable action in this situation, and how well did he know Sophia? It would take weeks before a hearing would take place. He didn't know her that well and he would never win against Dr. Haderly.

CHAPTER 8

Three weeks later, he'd forgotten about Sophia LaCross as much as he'd forget a rip-roaring cavity that had festered and worsened over time. While back at work but could barely focus on anything but Sophia. He had no idea that bringing her to St. Jude's would go so badly. Thinking back, he wished he had done something more. But what could he have done? When he had finally reached his car, outside the shelter, he called his friend Patrick.

There was an answer on the third ring. "Detective Mulder."

"Patrick, it's Theo."

"Surprise, surprise. Twice in one week. This better not be about that dead girl. I've done everything I can. There has already been some blowback for allowing you into the ME's office. That was already a stretch. How many times do I need to tell you to steer clear of this?"

"Patrick. Will you listen to me?"

"I'm listening. Why does it sound like you are in a wind tunnel?"

"Someone was chasing me."

"What?"

"I've got a huge problem."

"Like what?"

Theo said, "That girl I was telling you about."

"The crazy one or the dead one?"

"Dude!" Theo screamed. "Sophia, the pregnant girl, was just kidnapped at a homeless shelter we visited."

"What are you talking about?"

"Someone recognized her, a doctor. And he led her down a hall, and now she's missing."

"Was this doctor treating her?" Patrick asked calmly.

"He said he was."

"And when you first saw Sophia, wasn't she acting paranoid and doing some self-harming?"

"She's different now."

"What did the doctor say?"

Theo stared at the front door as he talked with Patrick. Soon, men and women in scrubs were searching the area around the building, including the parking lot. He sunk lower in the driver's seat. "That she needed specialized treatment. But she didn't want to go. She wanted to stay with me."

"There's nothing anyone can do. The doctor's order is more concrete and protected by the law than anything you can do. You would have to have someone witness a malpractice incident or an unnecessary risk. Without that, you won't get a court order for Sophia to be released from this doctor's care."

"What can I do?"

"You could petition the court, but that might take weeks, and you better have damn good evidence."

"This is ridiculous."

"No," Patrick said. "What's ridiculous is that you allowed yourself to get sucked into a situation with a girl you didn't even know. What have you found out?"

"Her roommate died by drowning, but there were some unusual circumstances. Someone called and paid her rent and other utilities, and when we stopped by the bank, she had some unexpected money in her account."

"This doesn't add up to anything substantial."

"I feel it. There *is* something wrong going on here."

A nurse or a tech had begun searching all the cars in the parking lot. Theo realized that he needed to leave, or he would be spotted. Starting his car, he waited for the precise moment that the man's back was facing the front door of St. Jude's. Theo eased out and drove away slowly.

"I can't just do nothing," he hissed.

"Theo. You don't have a choice. Go home and get back to your normal life."

Nurse Jane sat down next to Theo in the break room of the hospital as he ate lunch. She asked knowingly, "Are you obsessing over Sophia again?"

"It's been three weeks, and there has been no sign of her."

Jane asked, "How late were you watching St. Jude's last night?"

"Midnight."

"Have you been careful of any cameras?"

Theo nodded. The transformation from homeless Jane Doe to stunning Sophia was impossible to ignore. She was vulnerable but strong. She needed him to help, but he also thought she could take care of herself. If she had been lying to him the entire time, she could be a superb actress, but what was her motive? There were several things he didn't understand but tricking a med student seemed like a reach. Above all, she'd left all the money with him. That didn't seem like the thing a woman con artist would do.

Jane said, "You told me about your conversation with Patrick. Why didn't he want to help?"

"I don't think it was a matter of want. He saw no evidence to suggest that he needed to get involved."

Theo's mind flashed to the last few words Patrick had said that night: "Just so you know. I called back the ME's office. I didn't get a chance to talk with Dr. Daniels, but Dr. Lazar seemed pleasant despite all the rumors."

Theo had asked, "What rumors?"

"Dr. Celeste Lazar is not getting along with the department, and most of her colleagues don't like her. She's going to be a short timer in San Diego." Patrick added, "Dr. Lazar said that the case was an open-and-shut case. The drowning was unremarkable."

Theo thought about those words. Dr. Lazar had seemed nice enough and let him read the preliminary autopsy. She had said that she would wait for the final report from Dr. Daniels. But she had also acted strangely at first, nearly accusing him of performing an investigation on her department. Theo wondered if any of this meant anything.

For the second time in a matter of minutes, Jane brought his thoughts back to the present. "Have you seen Dr. Haderly at all?"

"I've driven by the shelter nearly four times a week. I haven't seen any sign of him or Sophia."

"That one time I came with you, we noticed several expensive cars. You wrote down some license plates. Have you seen any of those cars again?"

"Not a single one."

"So frustrating," Jane said, and she patted his arm. "You did your best."

Theo said, "I'm thinking of going back to Sophia's apartment tonight."

"You've already done that a few times," Jane answered. "It's a dead end. Sure…you found something about

Dr. Cavanaugh the first time, but there isn't anything else to find."

"I don't know what else to do."

"Maybe you should just relax tonight. Give it a rest, and you'll think of something else."

"Maybe," Theo said.

Jane glanced back and forth across the break room. She leaned in and whispered, "Look. Others have started to notice that you've lost some weight and aren't as well-dressed as before. They're starting to think something is going on."

"Like what?"

"Don't be surprised if you get a random drug screening or something next week."

"Random?"

"You know what I mean."

Theo felt his face, and he hadn't shaved in two weeks. He was wearing the same scrubs as yesterday.

"You're not helping anyone by letting this consume you."

Theo nodded.

Jane said, "Now tell me again about Dr. Cavanaugh. Remind me about her."

Theo rolled his eyes. He had already told this story to Jane a few times, but he appreciated her willingness to listen.

"Well…inside a pair of Mary's jeans, I found a business card for Dr. Cavanaugh from the San Diego Health Department. The next day, I called and made an appointment."

"How many times did Dr. Cavanaugh meet with Mary?"

"A few times, but only once with Sophia."

"So, do you think that Mary knew that Sophia was pregnant?"

"When I met with Dr. Cavanaugh, I first thought it was only for Mary. After I explained why I was there and that Mary had died, she told me that Mary had come with someone who resembled Sophia. I guess the girl kept calling herself Tosh."

"Wasn't that the name Dr. Haderly used for her?"

"Yes."

"When was this?"

"It must've been a few weeks before Mary died."

"So…like a little more than two months ago." Jane rocked her chair back and forth.

"I guess," Theo answered.

"How did Sophia look at the time?"

"Pregnant and homeless. Don't forget the smell."

"Just like when she was here in our clinic."

"Yes."

"Go on."

"Mary was worried because Sophia couldn't remember basic things like where she lived or how well she knew Mary. The pregnant girl became erratic at the end of the visit and took off running out of the building. Mary sprinted after her. Mary returned two more times without Sophia, still trying to locate her. Mary had called the day before she died and scheduled an appointment to talk with Dr. Cavanaugh again, but she never showed."

"Anything else you can think of?"

"That's everything."

Jane said, "You'll figure this out."

"You have far more confidence in me than I do." He sat back in his chair.

The outer door opened, and Nurse Susan poked in her head. "Pam Parker is in room three."

"Thanks. I'm on my way."

Mrs. Parker was his last patient for the day, and she would be a fitting end to this extremely long week. She was in a frantic mood about the thirty pounds of weight she had gained over the last few months. Theo and Jane spent the next hour calming her down, which had become a daily ritual. Her self-worth had been shattered by her pregnancy, and anything he said only helped for a few days. Jane stood patiently with Theo as they listened to her complaints and offered kind words. In the end, she left satisfied and upbeat.

Nurse Susan stood outside waiting for Theo and Jane. She glared at him. "How long are you going to mope around? I told you that girl was a fake." Susan had repeated the same phrase a dozen times.

"Hello, Susan. I'm not moping. Things are fine. What can I do for you before we all head out for this much-deserved weekend?"

She said, "Dr. Jeffery had to leave early, so he wanted me to pass along to you that Dr. Simmons has coverage for the weekend and into midweek. He thinks you need a few days off to relax and come back refreshed. Be ready to present three patients next Wednesday when Dr. Jeffery comes back."

"Thank you," replied Theo. "Have a good weekend."

Nurse Susan headed to the staff locker rooms, and Theo walked slowly down the hall toward the nursing station. He charted his visit with Mrs. Parker and turned off his computer.

Jane and Susan walked out with Theo. Jane said, "Get some rest. Let your girlfriend spoil you over the next few days. If you find anything out about Sophia, let me know."

A hollow laugh escaped Theo. "Danielle and I broke up earlier this week. She said I was too preoccupied with work."

"Can't say that I'm overly surprised. She's stopped by here twice. You've barely said her name in weeks. She wasn't the right one for you."

"I'm not looking for the right one. I just want someone to hang out with and enjoy, with no serious expectations. Danielle and I were in a relationship of convenience."

Jane cleared her voice and asked, "Have you ever had a serious girlfriend?"

Theo stopped in the middle of the hallway. "Why does it matter?"

"Staff around here talk. You've never been the topic of anyone's gossip list."

"And that's a bad thing?"

"It means," Susan said deliberately, "that you're either playing for keeps or playing with the wrong people."

"No," Theo scoffed. "I'm just not playing."

"What happened?" Jane asked.

Theo wasn't sure what Jane was searching for. Finally, he said, "I've had one serious relationship, and it ruined my chances with all others. Now I'm just trying not to screw up everything in my life."

"You're doing a terrible job," Susan said. "But you are great to work with. Have a good weekend."

Theo and Jane watched Susan head to her car. After a moment, Jane asked, "Want to get dinner and talk about it?"

"Not tonight."

"Call me if you find any information."

"I will."

Jane rushed to her car. Theo realized that he had told Jane and Susan pretty much everything but one piece of information. It was the money. For some reason, he kept that to himself. But a thought struck him.

"Hey, Jane!" he yelled.

Stopping near her car, Theo motioned her back over.

As she walked up, she asked, "Change your mind?"

"No. But I've been holding something back from you. But I just had an idea, and I want your opinion."

"You purposely withheld information from me? Like what?"

"Her bank account."

"Why would that matter?" Jane asked.

"She had a cool hundred and fifty thousand dollars in her account. And she didn't know where a cent of it came from."

"Are you serious?" Jane asked, her voice dropping low.

"She pulled out ten thousand dollars. I still have most of it at my condo."

Jane mouthed slowly. "Ten thousand aces?"

"Yep."

"Why hold out on me?"

"I don't know. But something just clicked today. Maybe they're after the money."

Jane asked, "Does she have credit cards?"

"I don't know."

"I bet that one of your friends can check on that. If I were you, I'd have them peek at Mary's cards as well. You never know what they might find."

"Maybe." He wasn't sure this was a real option, but it was a good idea.

"Hop to it," Jane said. "And have a good weekend."

"You too."

Theo headed to his car and drove home. An hour later, as he finished showering at his condo his phone began to ring. It was Patrick, and he was excited to hear back so quickly.

However, Patrick's voice seemed to be laughing at him. "I knew it. So predictable."

Theo growled, "I'm not in the mood. Did you get my message?"

"I knew that you couldn't keep this off your mind."

"Hell, I tried. I really did. Guess you were right once again."

"You are a glutton for punishment. Why are you pushing this?"

"I met her; you didn't. So keep all of your hypercritical comments to yourself."

"Fine. Do you want to hear what I've found or not?"

"Of course I do," Theo said slowly, quieting his anger.

"One of my colleagues did a credit card search for the past few months. Mary Sneider went to a few bars and clubs up to the day before she drowned. She frequented these types of places in the three months before her death. She never bought drinks on the card, just used it to get inside and sometimes order food. She was probably hoping that someone would buy her a drink. You know how it works. It paints a picture of a shit-ton of drinking and an unfortunate drowning incident."

"Can I get a copy of the those?"

"That I can't do. My boss will kill me if I give you a list of the names. Trust me, she was a heavy drinker."

"Maybe." Theo thought for a moment. "But something else is going on. What about March fifteenth to the twentieth?"

"Hold on." A minute later, Patrick returned. "Lunch, a movie, some clothes, and a night of partying on March eighteenth."

"Can you tell me the name of the location where she went on March eighteenth?"

"I can't."

Theo refused to let his disappointment show in his voice. "This helps a ton."

"Why this specific date?"

"Mary and Sophia visited a doctor at the health department on March nineteenth. Sophia was acting strange."

"What are you thinking?"

"I don't know. What about Sophia's credit card?"

Patrick answered, "It doesn't look like she owned or used a credit card in the last six months. Her last one had a balance of four thousand and some change until it was paid off fully in September of last year. We couldn't find another one listed under her name."

"The first part is not totally unexpected. I wonder who paid off her card?"

"It doesn't say." Patrick asked, "Any new information that you want to share?"

"I'll keep it to myself until I figure out more."

"What's going on, Theo?"

"A lot, and I'm going to find a way to prove it to you."

"You don't need to do that. I'll try to see things your way."

Theo was tempted to explain his ideas and theories. The prospect of bouncing things off of Patrick was easy enough, but he also knew his friend well enough to know that it would get him nowhere. Suspicions, thoughts, and theories meant very little to him. Theo needed more evidence. Theo said, "You've helped a lot. Thank you. If I do find something, I'll let you know.

"Can't ask for more than that. Try to avoid letting your feelings cloud your judgment."

"What does that mean?"

"I think you know."

Theo hung up the phone, frustrated and disappointed in his friend. It was always like this with him. Patrick knew how to needle him and never hesitated. It was as if Patrick's life mission was to parent Theo. It was why they would go months without talking. Mary's credit card information was unsettling. He had hoped there was more. Patrick's excuse of purposely going to a bar to have someone else buy her drinks might make sense. He wished he had someone he could ask.

Theo's next thought was a stretch. Maybe he should visit some of the clubs Mary had been going to. He had found some receipts at the girl's apartment. Mary must have had a purse. Where was it? Could some of Mary's personal items still be at the ME's office? He was running out of ideas, but these new thoughts provided a sliver of hope.

Pulling out his phone, he dialed Dr. Lazar's work number intending to leave a message. It was late Friday, and she was probably long gone.

Instead, Dr. Celeste Lazar answered, "Hello."

"Ah, yes, Dr. Lazar, it's Dr. Raden. We met a few weeks ago. Sorry to bother you this late on a Friday."

In a professional tone, she asked, "How can I help you?"

"I wanted to ask you another thing or two about the case of Mary Sneider," Theo said quickly.

"Her cause of death was officially reported as an accidental drowning."

"I'm sure. But I was wondering if any personal items came in with her? What about her clothing?"

"There were a few items."

"Do you happen to still have any of those things?"

"Not all accidental drowning occurs because the individual intended to swim and was wearing a bathing suit."

"Was Mary wearing a bathing suit?"

After a long pause, he heard some papers shuffling. "No, she wore blue jeans and a light-blue and purple shirt. Inside her pockets, she had her keys—six total. She wore five bracelets and a watch. She had some receipts, but they couldn't be salvaged. There was a single piece of paper with a long list of bars or nightclubs on it. That piece survived the water."

"A list of bars?" Theo said, interested.

"This was one of the more convincing pieces of evidence. Half the places were scratched off. She'd been searching for bars, presumably got drunk, and made it back to the party. She was heavily intoxicated, with a blood-alcohol level of 0.23. It's not rocket science, Dr. Raden."

"Patrick said 'a few bars,' not a ton." He said this out loud, as if contemplating its meaning. "She used her credit card to get in but didn't buy a single drink."

"It happens, Dr. Raden."

"What does?"

"Girls, especially good-looking girls who want to drink, don't always need to pay money for their drinks." A deep and enchanting laugh echoed through the phone. "They flirt for a free drink."

Theo replied quickly, "And you know this from experience?"

She did not answer.

Theo added, "Nothing else found with the body? No purse?"

"There was a jacket, but there was nothing in the pockets."

"Thank you, Dr. Lazar."

"You sound disappointed."

"I was hoping for something more. I had a hunch, and now I'm not so sure. The list of bars piques my interest, but your explanation of how to get drinks makes sense."

"I still don't understand why you are going through all this trouble."

"I don't like unanswered questions."

"Interesting," she said, her voice thawing slightly. "I will have to remember that. Maybe you and I could sit down and have a drink. Have a good night."

Dr. Lazar hung up before Theo had time to reply. Leaning back in his chair next to his desk, he concentrated on a black mask staring back at him. It was the second of the six masks on his bedroom wall, like what he had seen in the medical examiner's building. Except these masks were far different from the ones he had seen. This one was from Africa, and the face was molded to be entirely blank, void of any expression, far from what he was feeling.

The masks were a collection he'd begun in Africa last summer as a medical student bringing medicine and help to those in need. He'd been there for eight weeks. He'd personally found three of the masks. The other three had been given to him by patients, often a day or two before they died. One small village had called him "the hidden doctor," regarding the masks.

The first two masks were carved out of wood, and he understood that their faces had been bleached and then painted. The first mask was almost entirely red, and the second was white. Their noses were similar, as were their pursed lips. The third mask had tribal decorations on its head, while the fourth held a sly smile. The last two, his favorites, were similar to each other in their message. They were made for two lovers who, because of their families, were forced to hate each other. But in truth, they were in love. Therefore, both faces were divided into two. Half the mask was hatred, while the other half was love. Theo was confident that almost everyone he knew wore a mask of some sort or another.

The masks on the wall of the ME building were those of a jester, intended to poke fun at fear and hatred, like Halloween masks. They weren't art but more like costumes. African art was closely connected—intimately, in fact—with African religious beliefs and traditions, especially with the seen and unseen of the spiritual worlds. Aboriginal tribes were often thought to be unique to Africa. Theo had learned this the hard way by embarrassing himself in front of an Elder of an indigenous tribe. Aborigines can be found from Australia to Canada and everywhere in between.

Opening his bedroom door, Theo hesitantly listened for his roommate, Barrett. Thankfully, he was nowhere to be found. If he were home, he would be in front of the television, spending hours playing video games. For the first time in weeks, the condo was quiet. An idea suddenly struck him, and he hurried to his room and changed his clothing. He pulled out a long sleeved, black shirt with a Texas Longhorn symbol on the chest and black pants. He grabbed Sophia's keys and left.

Thirty minutes later, he slowly put her key into the door once again. He had left the kitchen light on the last time he was here, and it didn't appear that anything had changed. He had tied a small string a few inches above the bottom of the door, across the sidewalk. It hadn't been moved. Only an animal or someone walking through the front door would do the trick. He stepped over the string and realized the fallacy of his plan immediately. The inside of the apartment was exactly as they had left it. He closed the door, locked it, and turned off the kitchen light.

He took two steps toward the hallway when a rustling sound could be heard from outside. A shadow crossed the sliding glass kitchen door, and Theo ducked down as three shapes materialized in the darkness. One of them blocked the light and caught his attention. The face of Rachael, the receptionist, pressed against the glass as if looking inside. Theo remained still as he guessed that the other two figures were Derek and Clayton. Rachael reached down and tried opening the sliding glass door, but it was locked.

She turned to say something to the other two figures, and Theo retreated down the hallway toward the two bedrooms. He came to a stop and considered escaping out the front door; instead, he snuck into Sophia's room and planned to wait them out. She had spent some time cleaning the room, but the mattress was still destroyed, and the desk was broken. He used the light from his cell phone to look around. He attacked her closet first, and after five minutes, he'd found nothing. He stopped and listened. He hoped that Derek and the others were just watching the apartment. He began checking under, around, and on her bed. But again he came up empty-handed.

There was a noise at the window. Keeping low, he progressed farther into the room, listening for several minutes. After a while, he felt they had gone, and he silently pulled open the drawer of the broken desk.

Rummaging inside, he found the usual papers, pens, and other expected items. As he pushed the drawer, it caught on something and wouldn't completely close.

He shifted the drawer silently and finally pulled it completely out. He bent down, reached inside, and felt something that was preventing the drawer from closing. He gave it a tug, and a few seconds later, he pulled out the object. A brown bracelet two inches thick and made of string, lay in his hand. He'd never seen anything like it. A yellow plastic jewel was centered and entwined in the bracelet. He tried picturing Sophia wearing this around her wrist like a family heirloom of sorts.

The thud at the bedroom window was louder as if someone was trying to pry open the glass. Leaving the drawer on the ground, Theo retreated to Mary's room with the bracelet in his hand. He pocketed it and watched as a flashlight beam shone on the floor. He hid in the closet just as insistent pounding erupted on the front door. This lasted for a full thirty seconds. When it was quiet, he began searching this room. He checked under the mattress, between clothing, and on a shelf in the back of the closet. He was fairly certain that Mary had a purse, and he was desperate to find it. A few minutes later, he had retrieved two hand-sized purses, but both were empty.

The front door opened, and Theo melted as far as possible into the closet. Voices rang from the front room, and one sounded like Derek. "Why didn't you bring the key with you in the first place?"

"Sorry," Rachael muttered.

"Look. The television has been smashed. I knew something was going on."

Derek added, "No one has been here for a few weeks. I've been watching."

"Then why is the kitchen light off?" asked Clayton. "Didn't you say it was on last night?"

"What should we do?" Rachael asked softly.

"Watch the front door while we search the apartment."

The last thing Theo wanted was to be caught, but he was trapped.

Clayton protested, "We should've come in here sooner. What's going on with Sophia? Where is she? That guy she was with before was sketchy. I'm worried about her."

"You think everyone near Sophia is sketchy. Even Mary."

"She was totally paranoid. I wouldn't have been surprised if she wore an aluminum hat."

Rachael said, "Speak nicely of the dead."

Derek said, "I'm going to Sophia's room. Clayton, look in Mary's."

The door to the bedroom crept open and inch or two, and Theo stopped breathing.

Rachael asked, "Did you guys see a flashing light?"

"Why are you even here?" Clayton snapped and Theo knew he was just outside the room. "You didn't want to come with us in the first place. Chill out."

"I'm outta here," said Rachael.

"What?" Derek asked. "Why?"

"First, I'm not taking Clayton's abuse. Second, the cops are coming. I can hear the sirens."

The footsteps in the hall pounded as all three of them fled the apartment. The door slammed closed, and Theo considered his options. He didn't want to get caught here either.

He heard Derek shout, "Make sure we lock the door."

Theo crept from the closet and checked the window. He waited until he couldn't hear Rachael, Clayton, or Derek anymore and escaped out the window. He tried closing the window as best he could. Whirling, he sprinted off toward his car, glad he chose not to park in the main parking lot. As he turned the corner of the next building, something connected with the side of his head so hard that everything went pitch black.

CHAPTER 9

As he opened his eyes, Theo's head pounded as if he had been run over by a semi, and everything in his vision was double. He blinked several times and rubbed at his eyes until most of his vision normalized. It was still nighttime, but an overhanging light a dozen feet away caused the searing pain in his head to explode as he tried to stand. Theo eased himself back to the ground.

While gathering his energy, splashes of light blinked on the building next to him, and memories of the last few hours rushed back at him. He touched his head, and it came away wet with blood. Shielding his eyes, he tried crawling to get a better view. This was the wrong move, and his stomach lurched, and he vomited onto the ground. After several deep breathes, he tried again. He faced a building and couldn't see any windows, and he doubted anyone had seen him except his attacker. He thought it was impossible for Derek or Clayton to get to this precise spot fast enough to attack him. It had to have been someone else, but who?

He still had his keys, his phone, and his wallet. He checked twice and found that nothing was missing. Then the realization hit him. The woven bracelet with the yellow bead was gone. It was the only thing he'd taken from the apartment.

When his stomach was calm, he tried standing again. This time it worked, and he found two police cars thirty feet away, their doors closed but their lights flashing. It appeared as if two people with flashlights were searching the building next to Sophia's. They scoured the bushes and knocked on a few doors. Theo used this moment to slip away.

The blood began dripping down his back as he drove home. There were several tears in his black shirt with some abrasions. Once there, he showered and, with the help of his roommate, shaved a small area around the head wound. The cut was almost three inches in length. He found a medical staple gun holding ten staples. He carefully unleashed the first staple into his scalp.

Barrett said, "I see how it works. Can I do the rest?"

"I guess. Just make sure it looks good."

"What happened?" A huge smile was plastered on his roommate's face, as if he were enjoying this. The big man's shoulders shook when he spoke, but his hands were steady. His eyes squinted as he stared at the wound.

Theo answered quickly, "I hit a window when I was trying to stand up."

"That sounds stupid."

"Tell me about it. It feels worse than it sounds."

Theo downed a couple of over-the-counter medications once Barrett had finished. He wasn't starving but needed to stay awake. He and his roommate sat on the couch and watched television for the next two hours. He knew that Sophia might be in danger, and he craved getting back out there, but that would be a mistake. He needed to rest. It wasn't until near the end of the movie that Theo started to feel better, and Barrett ordered a pizza. It turned out to be one of the most normal nights he'd had with his roommate.

The next morning, he downed another cocktail of medications, and after a thirty-minute shower his headache started to ease. It was already two in the afternoon, and half his day had vanished. He dressed and scarfed down four eggs and a large glass of chocolate milk. He could not run or lift weights this morning, so he decided to take a stroll around the park near his condo. There was a large pond in the center, open grass, two soccer fields on the far side, and a playground. An asphalt path encircled most of the space. Around four-thirty, he drove to Jane's place and picked her up.

They headed straight to St. Jude's Village and parked in his usual spot on Sixteenth Street, a block away from the front door. Their view consisted of half of the front door and part of the building across the street. It was the best view they had to work with.

Theo said, "There are a lot of people out tonight. This is more than I usually see."

Jane pointed to a group of women. Theo was shocked. There were at least a dozen pregnant women all huddled in a corner. Jane said, "Guess this is the new rave for the preggos. Wow, count me as jealous."

"Do you see Sophia?"

"Hard to tell," said Jane. "Want me to try to sneak up and pretend I'm pregnant?" Searching Theo's car, she added, "Got anything I could put under my shirt?"

"Are you for real?" Shaking his head, he said, "Not the brightest of ideas."

"Oh, Theo, how hard could it be to pretend to be homeless?"

She stuffed some clothes under her belly and left the car. Theo tried protesting, but Jane was determined, and one look told him that he wouldn't convince her otherwise.

He watched as she slowly crossed the street and headed in the direction of the girls. She spoke with a few of them. After fifteen minutes, she continued up and down the street, talking with several people. Finally, she crossed over and slowly made her way back to the car. She was a natural.

"How did it go?"

"Most everyone was talkative enough. I got offered drugs like five times."

"Lovely neighborhood," Theo said. "But no Sophia?" he asked flatly.

"No one recognized the name."

"Did you ask about Tosh or describe her to anyone?"

Jane nodded. "No one seemed to be unwilling to talk or hiding anything. I really don't think they know her."

Theo pointed to the group of girls near the door. "What are they doing?"

"Waiting for their next shot. It's supposed to really make them feel better. Helps with the withdrawals."

"Really?" Theo questioned. "Like Suboxone or something?"

"They didn't know."

They stopped talking and watched the front door for the next few hours. They were on high alert tonight. Something about all the foot traffic gave Theo hope. He pointed at several people, but Jane shook her head each time. A police car shot through the area and continued its pursuit elsewhere. The pregnant women were long gone. The new arrivals were few, and many were pushing carts or settling in for the night. Makeshift tents were created, and Theo's hope evaporated. Jane shifted uncomfortably, and not just because of the time spent in the car.

Theo said, "I think it's time to call it. Thanks, Jane, for joining me on this stakeout. I'm sure you had better things to do."

"No problem. It wasn't as boring as I thought it was going to be. I'm glad you—"

Theo was reaching to start the ignition when Jane touched his arm and pointed out of the front window. A tall man with a thin, brown trench coat stepped into the light. Theo recognized him immediately as Dr. Thomas Haderly. No beefy security guards shadowed him this time. The doctor crossed the street and headed in their direction. It was too late to pull out onto the street; if they moved at all, they would be seen. They sank low in their seats and peered over the console. Dr. Haderly was nearing their car, still a dozen feet away.

Peering around, it seemed to Theo that Dr. Haderly was nervous. His eyes landed on Theo's car, and Dr. Haderly stopped mid-stride, staring at the car expectantly. Theo felt his heart race, and Jane's breathing quickened. Dr. Haderly's face relaxed, and he took a tentative step and another and crossed Sixteenth Street. A black sedan drove in front of St. Jude's, turned left, and quickly caught up to Dr. Haderly. The dark-tinted window on the passenger side rolled down at the precise moment Dr. Haderly lifted his arm. The exchange was perfect. A large, almost square briefcase was passed through the window as the smaller leather one disappeared inside. In stride, Dr. Haderly turned down an adjacent side street and vanished.

The black sedan drove past, heading in the opposite direction, and Theo started the car. He needed to make a quick decision: follow Dr. Haderly or the black sedan. A car rumbled to life ahead of them and a silver Lexus peeled out and drove in the opposite direction.

"Which way?" he asked Jane.

"Depends on what you want to find."

"Choices, choices," he mumbled to himself.

Before Jane said another word, he accelerated after the black sedan.

"Good move," whispered Jane as she fastened her seatbelt.

It took some maneuvering for Theo to catch up with the sedan. Once he did, he stayed back at a reasonable distance. The sedan was two blocks ahead and heading toward Petco Park, the Major League Baseball stadium for the San Diego Padres. The season was a month old, and there was optimism about some new players, including a star rookie.

"Slow down," Jane hissed at the precise moment he ran a red light to keep up. "Was that necessary?"

"Can't lose them."

"If they see us, it won't matter."

"Relax. Two other cars ran the same light. It's the Californian way. You're only guilty if you're the last one through."

The black sedan made an abrupt turn onto G Street, and Theo crossed two lanes of traffic, barely missing the front end of an SUV. By the time he turned the corner, the sedan was almost out of sight.

Slamming the gas, he nearly rear-ended an old Chevy junkmobile that pulled out in front of them. Theo crossed the double yellow line to pass, and a very elderly lady flipped them off as they went by.

"Did you see the smile on her face?" Jane asked as she burst into laughter. "The time of her life."

Theo just shook his head in amazement.

Two minutes later, Jane said, "The car is slowing."

The black sedan turned left into a single lane of a large parking structure. A moment later, it was out of sight. Turning right before the parking garage, Theo drove down a side street until he found a place to turn around. He ended up parking so that they faced the building nestled behind the structure.

"BioPharm," she said, reading the glowing block letters. "Have you ever heard of them?"

"Doesn't ring a bell. You?"

"Nada." Jane clicked on her phone for a few seconds. "BioPharm is a pharmaceutical company that has been around for about ten years. They are a small-scale firm, but one that is rapidly making a name for itself. It looks like they have three different sectors or research ventures. They study emerging medications, virology, or the study of viruses, and community outreach."

"You found all of that on your phone?"

"Do you even have a cell phone?" Jane smirked.

"I have a pager."

"Lovely. Like I was saying…BioPharm is looking to get into military or government contracts, new patents, FDA approval of several drugs, and more. This company means business, and it is growing fast."

"What is a pharmaceutical company doing with military contracts?"

"The world of medicine is changing," Jane insisted. "Marijuana and other medications, especially controlled substances, could be going through a coming-of-age. Changes are essential. Being linked to the government is where you would want to be. Treatment for PTSD, mental health, poly-substance abuse, and any other mental health issue is at the forefront of treatment discussion. Substance abuse among the military is very high. There are any number of options."

"How do you know all this?" Theo asked.

Jane smiled. "I've got a friend. He wants marijuana to be legal in all states. He is trying to get special approval from the government to use his land to grow. If you were a pharmaceutical company and received approval for marijuana to help treat PTSD in the military, that would be huge."

"So that's what they're doing here, growing marijuana?"

"Not necessarily. Marijuana and CBD oil are big right now, but what if they were working on a contract to study veterans with marijuana or any number of other things?"

"What does Dr. Haderly have to do with this?"

"Maybe nothing. Maybe everything."

"Should I approach Dr. Haderly, tell him I am a doctor, and see how he responds?"

After a moment of thought, she said, "That's a tough one. I'd say no. You already tricked him once. I can't see how it would end well."

"He'd have to tell me where Sophia is!"

"Actually, my dear, he wouldn't have to tell you anything more than a prostitute from Metairie, Louisiana—my hometown, by the way—would have to tell you about her own clientele. And really, what we saw tonight likely has nothing to do with Sophia. She isn't mixed up with a pharmaceutical company. I bet this is one of Dr. Haderly's other adventures. Doctors will do anything to get rich."

"Hello!" he said.

Rolling her eyes, she amended, "Present company excluded."

"What if he is not working with the pharmaceutical company in the way we're thinking?"

"What do you mean?"

"What if he's getting marijuana and selling it to groups of kids around the shelter, or to the pregnant girls?"

Jane caught on quickly. Nodding, she added, "If he ever got caught, he could just say he was trying it out for a pharmaceutical study."

"That's pretty ingenious," said Theo.

"You said Mary was going around to some of the clubs. What if they're using the clubs to pass drugs through? Maybe Sophia was involved, and so was Mary."

"That's crazy enough to work."

"What clubs did Mary visit?"

"I wrote down a few in my phone."

"I thought you only had a pager."

Ignoring this, he said, "The Fleetwood and the Gaslamp. Credit cards say she visited a lot more and the ME said she has a list."

"Wow," said Jane. "You've discovered a lot of things. Who would've guessed? Who has the complete list?"

"Dr. Lazar."

"She's the medical examiner, right?"

"Yep."

"Is she cute?"

It was his turn to roll his eyes as he dialed her number.

It was nearing eleven, but Dr. Lazar answered on the first ring. "Theo, this is certainly a surprise. Have you given my request a second thought?"

Jane covered her mouth with her hand as Dr. Lazar's voice boomed in the car.

"Um. Sorry to call so late at night, Dr. Lazar." He felt his cheeks redden.

"I'm sure that you are." Her voice was soft, and livelier than usual. "Can you please just call me Celeste unless we're at my office?"

"I'll try," he said hesitantly.

Celeste whispered softly, "I need to know, is this phone call for work or pleasure?"

After a moment of hesitation, Theo answered, "For work."

"Somehow," she said, her tone hardening, "I should've known." She coughed, and when she spoke again, it was all business. "Why are you calling me so late, Dr. Raden?"

"I need to see that list of bars and clubs."

After a short pause, she said, "If you stop by Monday morning, I'll have my secretary give you a copy."

"Is it at all possible to see it sooner?"

"No," she said hastily. "Take it or leave it."

Resignedly he said, "I'll take it, Dr. Lazar." She hung up without another word, and Theo tossed his phone onto the console.

Jane avoided any questions as they drove back to her house. Before she closed the door, she said, "Good night, Theo. You're a good man for doing this."

"For failing?"

"For trying, and yes…for failing and then continuing to try again."

"Good night."

As he drove away, he turned up the radio, having nowhere he wanted to go and hating the idea of heading back to his condo empty-handed.

His phone rang, and he ignored it. When it rang for the second time, he searched the console blindly until his fingers wrapped around the phone, and he brought it to his ear.

"What?"

"Hey, Theo." The voice was soft and wistful.

"Danielle. I wasn't expecting to hear from you."

"I know, babe. I was just missing you," she said, soothing him playfully.

Theo instantly recognized what was happening. "Where are you?"

"At home."

"Are you alone?"

"Of course, babe."

"How much have you been drinking?"

"Not nearly enough. Come join me."

"I don't know, Danielle." He held his breath. He had no desire, yet…

"Oh, pleeeease, T."

"You know I love it when you call me T."

"I know. I'll leave the door unlocked."

He squeezed his eyes shut, just for an instant. "I can't."

"You with someone else already?" Danielle joked.

"No."

"It's always someone else."

Under his breath, he said, "Not again."

"I heard that."

He quickly said, "It's no one else. I've had a bad day and need some rest. That's all."

"Come over, T."

"No. I'm heading home."

Danielle's voice turned harsh and bitter. "Were you out to see her?"

"Uh, no."

'I don't believe you."

"Sorry, Danielle. It really is late."

"No way. I knew it. You went to see her."

"I'm hanging up now."

Her sobs resonated through the phone. "Don't hang up. Don't hang up."

"Danielle, you've got to let this go."

"I can't." More sobs escaped through the phone. "Was she really that much better than I am?"

"Good night, Danielle. I'll call you tomorrow."

She screamed, "If you can't stop seeing her, don't ever call me again!"

"You know I can't see her. Hannah, our dear friend, is dead. Whenever you drink, you seem to forget that fact." He hung up and tossed the phone onto the seat.

His phone began ringing almost instantly. He loathed the idea of answering it but was also worried about Danielle. He debated back and forth, but the call ended before he made up his mind.

Danielle, his on-and-off-again girlfriend, had been a friend before they started dating. She was connected to Hannah Evans and Cassandra Billings; those three had been besties since high school. Hannah went off to nursing school, but they all kept in touch. Theo had met Danielle and Cassandra a few times over the year and a half that he worked at the jail. After Hannah died, they had barely kept in touch until a few years later, during a happenstance meeting, he ran into Danielle. Four months later, he moved things to the next level. He stayed over only a few times a month, but lately he felt that he might be holding her back, or vice versa. When she broke up with him recently, he felt relieved.

Theo slowed his car, reached for his phone, and dialed Cassandra. They hadn't talked in over a year. She had graduated with an MBA and gone in a different direction. He should have fixed things between them. He'd even missed her wedding. He was the worst type of friend.

Cassandra answered, annoyed, "Theo. What do you want? I'm pretty sure I told you to never call me again."

"It's about Danielle. She's a mess."

"I just saw her the other day." Cassandra added, "Why did you have to date her?"

"It just happened."

"And now, it's just ended." Her voice was cold and unfriendly.

"Danielle just called me. She's been drinking. She wanted me to stop by."

"Tell me you aren't going over. That would only make things worse."

"Exactly what I was thinking. But she started going on about Hannah. You're the only one who can talk with her when she's like this."

At the time of their friendship, when Hannah had died, Cassandra was dating Jessie Simkins. They'd married a few years later. Her voice calmed, as she said, "I'll call and talk with her. I'll work it out."

"Thanks, Cassandra. And sorry about everything. I hope you're doing well."

She didn't hang up right away. There were a few beats of silence. "I'm pregnant."

"What?" he managed to say after a few coughs to clear his throat. "Congratulations. That's incredible."

"I'll talk to you later, Theo."

He pulled to the side of the road. Everything around him was getting stirred up like a river after a muddy misstep. Closing his eyes, he tapped his phone on his forehead. When he had settled his nerves, he glanced at the screen and found that he had a voicemail. Thinking it was from Danielle, he clicked and listened.

"Hey, Theo. It's Celeste. Sorry about before. Meet in an hour at the morgue, and I'll get you that copy."

CHAPTER 10

The medical examiner's office still had a few lights on inside when Theo pulled up. He felt conflicted and hoped that the list would provide answers, but he was also worried about Danielle. She needed help, just not from him. The rain began falling on his drive over, and along with the fog it cast a luminescent shadow on the building. He got out and walked to the front door. A car on the street adjacent to the building flashed its lights, catching his attention. Theo jogged in the BMW's direction and opened the passenger door, slipping inside. Dr. Celeste Lazar sat in the driver's seat, looking radiant. Her black hair was wet and pulled into a ponytail. She wore dark yoga pants and a cream shirt. He couldn't help thinking that she might be only a few years older than he was.

She smiled at Theo knowingly. "You're so strange. What's got your ass in a binder about this death?"

"A hunch."

"Look, you're cute and all, but it's past midnight. Why don't you let me in on your little problem?"

"What problem?"

"Did you know the victim?"

"You mean Mary?"

With ease, she pulled her right leg to her chest. "That's the one."

Realizing that she would not budge, he began explaining. "I've never met her. But her roommate came into my ob-gyn clinic at Scripps Mercy completely paranoid. I mean, she didn't even know that she was pregnant. She was psychotic, punching her own stomach, and had lost her memory. We gave her medication to calm her down, and her memory suddenly improved, as if she had settled down enough to think clearly. Don't ask me how."

"What's her name?"

Theo considered this for a moment, but in the end, he didn't see any harm. "Sophia."

"So what's the problem?"

"Sophia is now missing, and there's something inconsistent with how everything is playing inside my head."

"How's she missing?"

Theo kept things vague. He explained about taking Sophia to a clinic, where a doctor became concerned and took her into the back room. Then he was rushed out as if he were a criminal. He didn't know why he didn't tell her everything.

"Did you tell him you were a doctor?"

"No. Being a first-year residency student in my own clinic doesn't mean much. I doubt it would've helped with him either."

"Probably not." She sighed and leaned back in her seat. "But she's not really missing. The clinic should know where she's at."

"If they do, they aren't saying."

Celeste gazed at him for a long time. "Tell me more about Sophia."

"Well, not only did she not know about her pregnancy, but she was also dressed like she was homeless. But when her memory came back, she told me exactly where her apartment was and her job. She'd been gone for several months."

"What's the connection with this list of bars?"

"Not sure. Mary and Sophia were roommates. Mary was seen at the health department with Dr. Cavanaugh in the weeks before she died. Mary was worried about how Sophia was acting, as if she were someone different. Sophia went missing again, and Mary ended up dead. I'm not sure why Mary was going to a bunch of bars and searching for Sophia at the same time."

"Is that everything?"

"Mostly."

"Are you leaving something out?" She eyed him suspiciously.

"A few things. But you've got the main story."

"A copy of the list is at my house."

"Why didn't we meet there?" The answer hit him before she could answer. "Never mind. Stupid question."

"I needed to see if I could trust you."

"Trust me?" he asked, confused.

"There's someone out for my job. I'm trying to make sure it isn't you."

Theo remembered something Patrick had said: "Dr. Celeste Lazar is not getting along with the department, and most of her colleagues don't like her. She's going to be a short timer in San Diego."

Theo said, "Well, it isn't me."

Celeste laughed hesitantly. "Follow my car; I'll show you to my house."

"It's late. I don't want to bother you."

She smiled but wasn't angry. "You probably should've thought of that before calling me late at night for a piece of paper."

Theo pulled open the door handle. "Good point."

Twenty minutes later, a beautiful two-story home on a cliff next to the ocean came into view. She lived in one of the more expensive neighborhoods in San Diego. Her house was quaint, with white stucco and a red roof. The front of the house was partially blocked from the street by several trees, but once he drove into the driveway, a swimming pool and a majestic view of the ocean made it all worth it.

Celeste unlocked the front door as Theo asked, "How long have you had this place?"

"Ten years." She sighed, turned off the alarm, and strolled down the hall. "Why don't you take a seat in the kitchen? My notes on the case are upstairs."

Theo closed the door and felt like he'd stepped into a different world. He was in awe. He recognized an oil painting by Paul Cézanne on the wall. "Is that the original?" he asked himself. In another corner sat a full-height statue of a naked angel carved from white stone. This was the most impressive room he'd ever been in except for a museum. His own condo was postmodern dirt compared to this.

Inside the kitchen was a black square table with four chairs. The tabletop and countertop were marble. They were identical colors. A collection of saucepans were arranged above the counter, and Theo became convinced that this was an Italian retreat house.

When Celeste returned, she wore black silk sweatpants and a tight-fitting yellow shirt. "What do you think?" she asked as she walked through the oval doorframe.

"Did we teleport to Italy?"

"Have you ever been to Italy?"

"No. But I saw an incredible documentary on villas in Florence, and this looks exactly like them."

"Glad you approve." She placed a soft leather briefcase on the counter. It was locked, and she hit a few numbers on the dial. Once it was open, she pulled out several files, one with Mary's name emblazoned on it in red letters.

"The view is magnificent, but so is all this art."

"Some people dream about hiking a white-covered mountain or through a forest of trees or even of sky diving, but the ocean gives me a sense of breathlessness."

"Well, you've certainly got your dream." Theo eyed the room. "You live here alone?"

Celeste shifted ever so slightly and asked, "Are you asking professionally or personally?"

"Both."

She considered the question. "I live here alone." Celeste continued talking as she flipped through the chart. "I met the man of my dreams early on during medical school, and things were great. I mean, the whole fairy-tale thing, romantic and just incredible. We married, and six months later, it was a catastrophe. I mean a shit-fiasco. When we divorced, I was just finishing school in D.C. He was already a neurosurgeon and ten years older than I was. His practice blossomed, and I was a casualty in his professional and personal evolution. Maybe we were just too different. My grandmother passed away around the same time. She left me some money, and this was the first house I looked at. The rest is history. I came to San Diego to start my forensic fellowship but did so alone. The picture-perfect marriage had fallen apart. Somehow, I landed at the medical examiner's office; it was the surprise hiring of the century. I do a good job, but..." Her voice trailed off.

"Things are rocky?" Theo asked.

"That's an understatement."

"You have a pretty remarkable story."

Celeste switched gears. "I want to hear yours."

Theo laughed. "Mine? Not much to tell."

"Indulge me."

Theo sat at the kitchen table. "I went to medical school here in San Diego, and I, as you know, am at Scripps Mercy finishing my first year as a recruited hostage. I graduated from the University of Texas. My parents split up for a while but got back together and are better than ever. Two brothers—both doctors on the East Coast. The story of your ex reminds me of my brothers. They are both surgeons, one in North Carolina and the other in Florida."

"Why didn't you follow in their shoes?"

"I wanted a life. They're divorced, bitter, and angry. Then they remarried." He raised his eyes to meet hers.

"Go on," she insisted.

He added, "They each got divorced sometime during medical school. It was too stressful. They advised me strongly to avoid marriage until after I finished school."

Celeste asked, "Want a drink before we get to the good stuff?"

"I'd love one."

"Alcohol or no alcohol?"

Theo answered, "I'm on a strict non-alcohol diet. Water, please."

"There sounds like a story here?"

"Story and problems. The short of it is that I was a big drinker in college. Almost got kicked out twice. A few years ago, I was drinking too much and was out with a friend, and I missed a huge nonverbal gesture and some facial expressions and something bad happened. I've slipped up a few times, but I do my best."

"Wow, you're full of surprises."

Theo shifted uncomfortably. "How did you manage to become the medical director so quickly? You obviously know someone I don't."

She laughed, almost spilling his water. "Once you graduate, you're a doctor. But things were different for me, good and bad."

"What do you mean?"

"In school, we were all told that grades are just a formality. And that's sort of true. I came out here, but my grades got me into my forensic fellowship, and I met my mentor, Dr. Stranton. Essentially, he got me my job. But really, I'm the lead forensic pathologist because of my looks, and I know it. My predecessor lost his job and some high-profile cases because he lacked good hygiene and didn't know when to say the right thing. My current colleagues are irate because they don't think I've earned my way to where I am. Maybe they're right."

"I saw some of your colleagues. They seemed a little quirky."

"Did you get a chance to meet Dr. Daniels? The one who wears all black?

"I didn't meet him, but I think I saw him."

"He's decent at what he does. All my staff are. There are four pathologists total in the lab, but none of the others could be on camera for more than a minute. That's where I fit in. I have experience and come from the East Coast; it was a perfect way to get in the door. But my looks and my ability to say "no comment" or "we're doing all we can," on camera have come to serve me well. But I'm also damn good at my job."

"So you're the face of the medical examiner's office?"

"For now. I can't seem to escape the stereotype of the newbie. Except for two cases, all my requests get moved to the back of the line, even with the police."

He nodded at the file lying open on the counter. Celeste reached over and pulled out a sheet half the size of a notebook.

"Here's your copy."

The paper was passed to him, and he took it greedily. Was it trash or a clue? He hoped for the latter. Flipping it over, he scanned the list of clubs and bars. There were about twenty in total. More than half had been crossed out. He wondered what this could mean. He recognized several of them, but others were unknown.

"I haven't been completely honest with you."

"Uh…what do you mean?" He glanced around the room apprehensively.

"Dr. Daniels was the primary on this case. When you visited, it caused me to reexamine all the evidence again. You called me before and asked a bunch of questions."

"I remember," Theo said slowly.

"I told you that there was a jacket—"

"But nothing in the pockets," Theo finished.

"That was true. But I did find this list of clubs in a pocket that was sewn closed, and it was inside a plastic bag."

Theo shook his head at this new information.

"Officially," Celeste continued, "It doesn't change the outcome of the final report, but I wanted you to know the truth."

"Thank you." He stood, feeling slightly awkward. "I owe you big time, Celeste. Let me know how I can repay you."

She responded swiftly, "How about dinner next Friday, here?"

"Are you asking professionally or personally?"

Her laugh made him smile despite his bewilderment at this latest news.

"That will be hard to refuse," he finally answered.

She stood up and stepped close to him. Theo watched a wisp of her bangs fall into her face. She whispered, "So don't."

"I'll be here around six."

Her face leaned in, and she quickly kissed his left cheek and then his right. "It's customary to kiss cheeks in Europe, especially when saying goodbye."

Theo's heart raced, and he almost completely forgot why he was leaving. She must have seen something in his eyes, because she stopped and stared at him. Shaking his head, he regained his senses and moved to the door. "Thanks again. Have the most amazing week, and I'll see you next Friday."

CHAPTER 11

Theo stepped inside the outer door of his building at one-thirty in the morning and expected to find Danielle passed out on the floor next to his door. That had happened more times than he cared to admit. She was unpredictable and stubborn, and if she decided she would wait for Theo to get home, she would. The ground was empty, and he silently let himself into his condo only to find his roommate playing *Call of Duty* with a wide-eyed, over-caffeinated expression. He barely glanced up as Theo closed the door.

"Don't you ever get sick of this game?"

"Impossible." At that moment, he must've died, as he reached over and paused the game. "Guess you had a late night. Feeling better?"

Theo lied, "Just out with some friends, and I feel great. Thanks." He pointed to his head and added, "The doctor did an excellent job."

"No problem."

"How was your night?"

"Good...until Danielle showed up irate that you weren't here."

Theo closed his eyes.

Barrett continued, "She lay on your bed for two hours waiting for you, crying and asking me to get her another beer. Another friend of yours—I think her name is Cassandra—

showed up and pounded on the door like she was trying to break it down. I answered, and she rushed in and dragged Danielle from your room. It was super fun for me."

Theo sat on the couch. "Danielle and I broke up. She's impossible when she drinks. She called, but I never thought she would show up here."

"Right. 'Cause she's never done that before.'"

Theo said, "Cassandra promised that she was handling things."

"Your love life sucks."

"Thanks for pointing that out. What about you?"

"I get plenty of love from the girls online. To them, I'm a god."

"Here we go again," Theo mumbled, but he smiled weakly.

"I'm telling you, meeting people in the real world is overrated. I get plenty of pics and stories that I'm perfectly satisfied with."

Theo stood quickly. "I don't want to hear any of this."

"Fine. Your loss." Barrett asked, "Are you up for a *Call of Duty* marathon tomorrow?"

"Rain check. I'm working on something for the next few days, and then I'm on call for the rest of the week and this weekend. I'll have some free time next week."

"Dude, it seems like even when you are off, you're still too busy."

"Story of my life." Theo walked to his door. "Sorry about the drama with Danielle. It'll get better."

"Keep telling yourself that."

Theo stepped in and closed his door. When he turned on his light, he found the word "asshole" sprayed on the wall next to his bed in capital letters. It was bright red and impossible to miss.

"Yep," he muttered, stepping into the bathroom.

When he finished getting ready, he flipped off the lights and fell into a restless sleep. His mind took Sophia's face and put it on Hannah's body. Both of their voices spoke to him as if he had failed each of them. Danielle's hysterical laugh badgered him as he tossed and turned the entire night.

He fitfully slept until 10:00 a.m., and when he pulled himself out of bed, he searched the internet to learn about the eight clubs that hadn't been marked off of Mary's list. He believed the list might be more than just drinking destinations if she kept it hidden in a pocket. A plan materialized in his mind for which clubs he could visit that night. Turning his attention to his wardrobe, he realized he had nothing to wear. He had hidden Sophia's purse in his dirty clothes basket and was thankful that he did. If Danielle had seen a purse in his room, the condo would've been set on fire.

He retrieved the bag and dumped its contents onto the bed. He separated the bundles of cash and found her driver's license, some prepaid Visas, a debit card from Bank of America, and a picture of her at a party with Mary. He was again struck by how beautiful both girls were. They were happy and free. The pregnancy had added some weight to Sophia, but that was expected. So much had changed since that photo was taken. He pulled out some female items: tampons, hair clips, a small bag of make-up, nail clippers, and headache medicine. Two condoms tumbled out.

After returning the unnecessary items, he left to find some paint and some new clothing. At four-thirty that afternoon, he locked his condo and took the elevator down to the first floor. He felt different—better. He wore a crisp, button-down black shirt, tailor-made black slacks, and expensive shoes. This was the most lavish set of clothing he had ever owned. He didn't feel an ounce of remorse for using Sophia's money. It was actually a relief. He'd researched five bars or clubs to visit tonight from the list that Mary had written down. She had already scratched off ten. If things didn't work out tonight, there were still a few more for tomorrow.

The closest location was the SD Club, a hotspot back in the eighties that was far less impressive today. He had visited it twice before with Danielle and found it boring. The SD Club was called the STD Club back in its prime, and the name spoke volumes about what happened inside.

The smell of stale beer and smoke assaulted his senses as he stepped through the front door. It was filled with less than 20 percent capacity, and Theo walked to a side booth against the back wall. The service was slow, and it was several minutes before he received a bottle of beer. Another twenty minutes passed before he ordered some food. When his chicken tenders and onion rings arrived, he nibbled in relative silence. The food was horrible, and the atmosphere was worse. Nothing noteworthy had happened here in a decade. The darkness of his bottle prevented anyone from seeing that he wasn't drinking. A few minutes later, he paid the bill and left.

Clubs two, three, and four on the list were also complete failures. He'd been the best dressed and only non-drunk person inside. In two of them, there wasn't anyone younger than fifty besides himself. The best part of the night so far had been when he was hit on by a male and female duo at Six Degrees, but Theo smiled politely and declined.

Club Jazzed was the final club on his list. It was the most intriguing new club in San Diego. But its popularity still couldn't match the top two: Fluxx and Vanish. Both had already been crossed off of Mary's list. Getting through the front doors of either Fluxx or Vanish was nearly impossible. He heard that Club Jazzed got busy, but he was optimistic that since it was before eight on a Monday, a quick entrance wouldn't require his left kidney.

The difference between this club and the others was clear before he placed a foot inside. Two bouncers patrolled the front doors, and they could've passed for Greek titans. Theo gave a cool hundred dollars in a handshake to the closest giant, and he was ushered inside without delay. His first few steps inside were by the way of a small room. It was almost like a changing room, or a foyer.

A gray mist, almost refreshing, hung in the air and several colors splashed on the walls as he stepped into the main part of the club. The music was modern and upbeat. The mist cast an energetic buzz and excitement over the room as the smell of damp pleasure ran wild. Tables were positioned expertly around a dance floor. A staircase leading up and around the building was situated to his left. There appeared to be larger rooms for general seating on the higher levels. But on the third floor he thought he saw a VIP sign and a second bar. The focal point was the open space directly in front of him with a dozen smaller tables and dance floor. Many customers from above had a great view of this area. The ceiling was vaulted with an enormous chandelier hanging down.

The waitresses and bartenders were young and extremely attractive, both the boys and the girls. They all shared a similar appearance and presence, as if on stage. The clientele was young and old, rich and middle-class, though the rich seemed to get the better seats. Most of the tables were taken, and everyone was enjoying themselves.

"What suits your fancy?"

Theo stared at the beautiful girl, about his age, who awaited his response. "I'm from out of town and heard that I must check this place out. Wherever you want to put me, darling."

She winked. "There's a great table on the second floor. It gives you some privacy, but you can also have some fun."

"Perfect."

He was escorted up the stairs, and by the time he arrived, she had already told him that her name was Shelby and given him her number. "Don't hesitate to call before you head out of town."

"I'll do that," he replied.

From his table, he had a decent view of half of the main floor. Twenty barstools sat in front of a bar as long as two limos. A waitress passed by, handing him a menu so quickly that he didn't get a chance to look at her. The menu was one page that was black with gold lettering. When his waitress arrived five minutes later, Theo's jaw opened slightly. He managed to say "calamari," and "double IPA." She smiled, wrote nothing down, and vanished.

The hype for this club was spot-on. He recalled a group of baseball players for the Padres insisting that they were headed here after the first home series sweep of the year. A rookie phenom pitcher, Devon Burks, had even signed his rookie contract before the season started on the black marble countertop of the bar on the first floor. That was the same day the club opened.

"Here's your beer," said the long-legged blonde who wore a revealing black dress that had less material than his underwear. After she dropped off the beer, she remained at the table expectantly.

"Thanks," he muttered. "Have you been working here long?"

"Just over a year."

"Do you like it?"

She looked at him awkwardly. "I guess."

He lowered his eyes and asked, "Can I ask you something kind of unexpected?"

She smirked and added, "Be careful what you ask. The wrong question might get you more than kicked out."

His voice stuttered. "It's…it's just about the type of people that come here."

"Why don't you spit out your question and save yourself the embarrassment?"

"Do a lot of pregnant women come here?"

Her face didn't react at first; then her expression slowly changed to bemusement. "Are you looking for a wife or a girlfriend? Is she yours or someone else's?"

"No," he said quickly. "I'm here for a good time, but a pregnant friend suggested this place." He pointed to a group of dancers that had just come onto the dance floor. The five of them had on tight red dresses with even less material than his waitress's. "This doesn't seem like the place for my pregnant friend, and maybe I'm missing something."

"We get all types," she said as she moved to an empty table and collected her tip.

"Are you serious?"

"As a heart attack." She stopped and gave him the once-over. "I've never had anyone ask me about a pregnant woman at this club. Well…I take that back, but it was a guy whose wife was no longer pregnant. I guess that pregnancy thing really turned him on. But I don't think that counts."

"Yeah, that's not what I'm looking for." This time he pretended to take a deep chug of his draft. When his eyes searched around the room, he was surprised to see his waitress staring at him.

She asked, "Is this really your scene?"

"Honestly, I'm just looking for my pregnant friend. She's in some trouble. She owes someone some money. She's missing, and I just need to find her. I thought she said that she used to come here. Do you know anyone who worked here and became pregnant?"

"I don't think so." His waitress glanced around the room, appearing distressed for the first time."

Theo leaned closer. "I think you know something. Can you help me?"

"Are you for real?" she asked, but her tone contradicted her facial expression.

In a louder voice, she added, "I'll come back with your food in a few minutes." Without another word, she left.

Theo wasn't sure what had just happened. He thought she was responding pretty well to him. He hoped he hadn't pushed her too hard. Glancing down at his beer, he hated the idea of drinking, especially tonight, but he was worried that he might have grabbed the attention of one of the club's bosses. A man from the first floor was watching him closely. Theo understood why his waitress had acted as she had. Reluctantly, he took a long gulp of his beer, leaned forward, and gawked at the girls below.

The number of gorgeous women in the building was astonishing. The men working the bar or dancing could've been on the cover of magazines and were eye candy for many patrons. It must've been a prerequisite on the application form. Four girls, not dancers, came out of a hidden door on the first floor. The door was built into the wall, and Theo thought they had spontaneously appeared, as if for a purpose. The girls' clothing was more elegant than that of the dancers; they wore long, flowing, silky white dresses that were backless with spaghetti straps.

The same club boss that had been watching him nodded, and all four girls rushed to a central table with four older, rich men. The girls giggled, swooned, and played with their hair as they sat in the men's laps. Soon the girls pulled the men onto the dance floor and rubbed up against them seductively.

A plate of calamari was set on the table, and Theo jerked up. His waitress asked quietly, "Why are you asking about a pregnant girl here? Is she your girlfriend?"

"She is my friend. Do you know her?"

"And you think she might have worked here?"

"Maybe," Theo said. The reality of the situation was becoming murkier. These girls were in top form and as skinny as possible. Why would Mary think Sophia had come here? Why would Sophia be in a club like this in the first place? She had a job and money. The night's adventure suddenly seemed like a waste of his time.

Loudly, the girl said, "Enjoy your food. Let me know if you need anything else." Before leaving, she softly whispered, "I have a friend in the back. I'll see if she'll talk with you." The waitress vanished, but this time, Theo noticed her name tag. It read, "Tina."

Theo started eating, again confused about what was happening. He continued watching the room. Ten different things were happening at once. The four girls and their older men had vanished. A new set of men, this time three, were sitting at the same tables as the men before them had. Drinks were being passed out by another lovely waitress. Four male dancers were on the floor, shirtless, and their chests glistened. Women in the crowd began screaming and shouting. The louder someone was, the closer the male dancer got. When he found his girl, he lifted her off her feet and carried her to the dance floor.

Theo thought he saw something on the wrists of some of the dancers and he stood to get a better look. From the corner of his vision, he saw his waitress approaching with another girl. The new girl was dressed casually in tight jeans and a tight black shirt with a square neckline and short sleeves. As with everything in the club, it was incredibly revealing.

Tina dropped off another beer and whispered, "This is my friend. Call her Cindy. She was just leaving. I told her about your questions, and she thinks she may have an answer for you." The waitress walked off casually, and Theo took another drink of his beer. He was already feeling the effects of the first one.

Cindy glanced around and sat, her back facing the open room. She was neither comfortable nor uncomfortable, but she was wary. Theo sat forward in anticipation as Cindy stared at him as if sizing him up. Her next words brought him back to reality. "It'll take a hundred dollars for me to tell you anything."

"What if I don't like what you tell me?"

"That's the risk. Take it or leave it."

Pulling out sixty dollars, he passed them across the table and said, "You'll get the rest when you tell me something useful. I'm just searching for my friend."

Cindy scoffed, evidently amused. "We get thousands of people in here a day. There's no way I would know if it was your pregnant friend. But I'll tell you what I know."

He nodded for her to continue.

"Well, actually, I don't know anything about your pregnant friend." Cindy continued, "What I can say is that you're the second person in the last six weeks that came here asking the staff about their pregnant and missing friend. She was much more convincing than you are."

Theo asked, "What did she look like?"

She stared at the money on the table, and he pulled out the rest of the cash and slid it across the table.

"She was young, pretty, and black. She wasn't pregnant, in case you were wondering. She knew a bit more about this person than you did. She also reported the girl was missing. She insisted that she had seen her friend holding a worker ID card for this club. The girl didn't have the ID card with her and only showed a picture. I didn't see it, but none of the other girls recognized the girl in the picture."

"How do you know we're talking about the same girl?"

"I've been here for eight months, and no one else has ever asked about a pregnant girl, especially one working here. I'm going to tell you the same thing the other girl was told. You got the wrong spot. No pregnant girl has ever worked here."

"Why's that?"

"At Club Jazzed, if you're pregnant, you're fired."

Theo saw the logic in this immediately. Business wouldn't improve with a bigger belly from what he was seeing.

"Is it possible my friend could've been working here before she was showing?"

"Maybe. But again, no one recognized the girl in the photo."

"Did you ever talk with the girl who came asking questions?"

"No," she said emphatically. "But I did see her leave through the front door. I haven't seen her again, so maybe she was wrong, and her friend didn't work here after all."

"Maybe," Theo said. He considered his options. He thought about asking to talk with whomever Mary had talked to, but he didn't think he would get any more information than he had already received. He pulled out the picture of Mary and Sophia and placed it in front of Cindy. He said, "This is the girl I'm looking for."

Cindy blanched ever so slightly. She said, "I can't be sure. Doesn't look familiar."

Theo was slightly surprised by her reaction. Why would she describe Mary but not point her out in the picture?

The blond waitress was back with a third and fourth drink. This time she placed one in front of Cindy and the other next to Theo. She hissed, "Cindy! Mr. Jack and Trevin are on their way."

"Oh, shit," hissed Cindy. "I'm screwed."

To Theo, Tina said, "We're both screwed if you don't smooth this out. Tell them you came here to pay for something."

"Like what?" he hissed.

"Look around and guess." She appeared genuinely terrified.

Two figures approached from the stairs on his right. The club boss from earlier walked next to a freight train of a man, heading directly to his table.

Theo said loudly, "Have a drink. It's on me. I'm sure it'll be fine."

The expressions on the faces of Cindy and Tina were of pure terror, but they tried hard to relax.

Tina said, "Are you ready to order?"

"Yes. I want the ribeye steak, medium. Fries and mashed potatoes."

Tina remained standing, but Cindy had nowhere to go. Theo asked, "So. Can I have your number?"

Silkily, Cindy fell into character. These words seemed to have a profound effect on her. She said, "It takes some convincing to give it out. I'm not sure you've done enough." Her tongue slid over her lips as she pouted with noticeable charm.

Theo's mouth dropped open. He managed to say, "No harm in asking, but what will it take to convince you?"

The statement lingered in the air for a moment. Before Cindy could respond, the club boss swept up to the table. His voice boomed, "Ms. Fletcher, there better be a great reason to be bothering this gentleman." But the man's tone was anything but compassionate. The bouncer, likely Trevin, stood as a silent warning.

Theo took a long drink, holding up his hand as he finished his second glass.

Cindy responded quickly but with surprising control. "This boy caught me as I was leaving. He wanted to buy me a drink, Mr. Jack. I can't drink with him while on shift. He also asked for my number."

"Is that so?" Mr. Jack asked. His cold, calculating eyes focused on Theo. "And who do we have here?" Trevin leaned forward.

This was where he was to put up or shut up. The former would result in some pain, likely in an alley out back.

"Lincoln Reynolds from San Francisco." Theo stared directly at Mr. Jack and added, "This is quite a place. Meets and surpasses all expectations."

"We aim to please." His voice was tense.

Theo could tell that Tina and Cindy understood the underlying threat. They both cringed.

Mr. Jack said dismissively, "Cindy, if he offered you a drink, it looks like you're off shift, so enjoy. But Tina, you have a few customers waiting for you."

Tina blanched at her dismissal and scurried away.

"What are your plans tonight, Mr. Reynolds?" Mr. Jack as he and Trevin remained motionless.

Theo leaned back in his chair and reached into his pocket, pulling out a handful of bills. He dumped these on the table and smiled as broadly as possible. "You see, sir, I'm here for fun, and a hell of a lot of it. I'm going fishing tomorrow after my meeting and heading down to Tijuana the day after that. I'm not here to cause any problems. Just want to have a great night tonight." He passed a few hundred-dollar bills to Mr. Jack.

"I've never seen you here before," Mr. Jack said, but the tone of his voice had changed.

Theo said, "A colleague from my office insisted that this was a hell of a place to visit." Nodding to his table, he said, "I'm going to eat, drink, and maybe dance a little. But I hope I haven't caused any problems with Cindy here. I'm only a guy. She was walking by, and I couldn't help but ask her to sit down."

"No. I completely understand." Mr. Jack laughed, almost sincerely. "We heard there might be a problem up here. It certainly wasn't with you." Turning back to Cindy, he said encouragingly, "Cindy, you've worked hard, and as you said, you've finished your shift. Have a drink. Enjoy your time!"

"Perfect!" Theo said emphatically, and he pulled more cash from his pocket.

Mr. Jack reached out and shook Theo's hand. "If you need anything, don't hesitate to ask."

"Will do." He passed another $200 into Mr. Jack's hand.

Cindy smiled as if onscreen, her eyes dazzling, and the smile was convincing. As Mr. Jack walked down the stairs, her eyes betrayed her confusion.

Theo pushed $200 to Cindy. "Sorry about that. You'd better get out of here. I'll leave in a few minutes."

"If I leave now, they'll know something was up. Looks like I'll be leaving with you tonight."

"Is that against Mr. Jack's policy?" he asked mischievously. He felt the calmness of his drinks overpowering him. He'd felt this same feeling dozens of times. He wasn't a mean drunk, just a stupid one who thought himself invincible. It had been several months since his last drink. He wasn't sure anything was worth his sobriety.

"It was…until you pulled out that cash. When that happens, all bets are off. What's really going on here?"

"I'm just looking for my friend. Nothing more and nothing less."

Cindy said, "The girl in the photo is the one who came here. The other girl was the one she was looking for."

"I thought so," Theo said, unsure what it really meant.

They talked for the next half hour, and Theo learned a surprising number of personal details about Cindy Fletcher. He also shared more than he would have wanted. He kept Sophia's name out of the conversation. His steak arrived, and it was fabulous. Cindy allowed him to get her a club sandwich and fries. She drank two beers.

Their conversation wasn't labored but was surprisingly calm, as if they had been friends for years. Cindy talked about why she moved to San Diego from Vegas and how she loved the ocean and the weather here. Her questions and answers were thoughtful and expansive.

Theo asked, "Why are you telling me all of this?"

"Mr. Jack, of course. He'll ask me about you. You can bet on that. He will ask you something about me if he ever sees you again. If you don't know the answer, he'll become suspicious."

"He knows everything about you?"

Her face reddened. "Most things. But not everything."

After another thirty minutes, Theo bought drinks for the five closest tables, and soon a party was gathered near their tables. His money was speaking to their hearts. All the while, Mr. Jack appeared to be busy but found time to stop by every now and then.

Two girls were sent over by Mr. Jack, and they performed a very personal dance for Theo. Other customers blushed, cheered, or drooled. Two men in the back screamed loudly. The girls went back and forth between tables, but most of their attention was on Theo. Cindy stared blankly at them, as if she'd done it a hundred times. Theo was convinced that this was a test, despite the buzz in his head. He clapped enthusiastically, reached out and pinched one of the girls, and gave them each a hundred dollars as they left. They waved passionately as they returned to the main floor.

Cindy whispered, "That was good. You had me convinced. You're plenty drunk right now. It's probably time that we can go. Is your car here?"

"Yes," Theo said loudly. "I'm not sure I want to go yet." His words slurred.

"I'm sober. There has been no alcohol in any of my drinks. Tina made sure of it."

Theo leaned in, finding amusement in his words, "Damn. Why couldn't she do that for me? Aren't we good friends?"

"You needed to be convincing. You've done an outstanding job. By the way, did you know that you gave each of those girls five hundred dollars?"

"No, I didn't. Only a hundred."

"Yeah. You're definitely not driving."

"How did you let me get into this mess?"

Cindy smiled genuinely for the first time. She said, "I think you did that yourself."

"Stupid me." He leaned closer. "I should tell you, I was trying to avoid drinking. Do you want to hold my money?"

"No. You'll need to give another five hundred to Mr. Jack. After that, we're good to go."

Cindy called over Tina, and they whispered for a few seconds. Theo paid for his meal along with everyone else's drinks. The bill was nearly $5,000, and he left Tina a $500 tip. He was cheered by fifteen people when he stood unsteadily. They sang to him as he headed down the stairs.

Theo blew everyone kisses.

Mr. Jack arrived just as Theo reached the bottom floor. He said, "I hope you had a good time?"

"A great time," Theo slurred. "Never better, in fact."

Mr. Jack asked, "Where did you say you were from?"

Theo's head shouted at him to be careful. He said, "San Jose." Shaking his head, he tried again, "San Fernando. I mean, nope. San Francisco. Here for business and some fishing."

Mr. Jack pulled him aside and asked, "Are you looking for anything else while you are here?"

"Some flash, a good time, and some excitement. Anything you've got."

"I know exactly what you mean." Mr. Jack passed him a black business card from an inside pocket. "If you stop by later this week or next, after Tijuana and fishing, show this to the front staff. They'll know precisely what to do. See you soon." Mr. Jack waved over Cindy, who swooped in.

Mr. Jack whispered, "Good job tonight, Cindy. Make sure he gets home without too many problems."

"Yes, Mr. Jack."

CHAPTER 12

Theo woke as bright light snuck through the blinds, attacking his eyes, and a stabbing headache exploded. He rotated a few inches and the light disappeared, and the pain in his head receded. As he stared at the unfamiliar room, he wondered, *Where the hell am I and what happened?*

He was in a large, spacious room with a window to his back. If he had to guess, this apartment was on the ground floor and near some train tracks. The walls were concrete, and there was a kitchen, a dining area with a table, a living area with a huge television, and a bedroom all in the same space. He was lying on a long couch, and he sat up. The bed was positioned closer to the window, and Theo saw a girl lying there asleep, wearing only panties and no bra. She was face down and breathing deeply, a blanket only partly covering her shoulder and left leg. Her face was turned away from him.

He tried desperately to remember what happened last night and the girl's name. After a few minutes, the name Cindy came to his mind, and he had some snatches of memories of Club Jazzed. His recollections did not continue past leaving the club or the drive here. He groaned at the likelihood that something had transpired last night and the realization that she would be pissed to learn that it was only a one-night thing. He hoped she wouldn't be too upset.

Checking his watch, he found that it was six-thirty. There was a buzzing sound, and he stood, finding that he wore only his boxers. He reached over to a white table and grabbed his cell phone. The message read, "9-1-1 at the hospital! Mrs. Parker is going into labor. Come now." It was from Jane.

His stomach lurched as he searched for his clothes. He found them neatly folded on the table. Two minutes later, he was only partly dressed and making his way to the door when he heard a voice and froze.

"Can you tell me one thing?" Cindy's voice surprised him.

Theo felt caught and awkward trying to sneak away. He turned guiltily. "I'll try."

She was sitting up, having pulled up a sheet to cover herself. "Are you going to go back to the club?"

"I don't know." He shrugged. "Probably."

Her long legs reached out and touched the floor. "If you do, don't tell them anything about me except what we agreed. Don't tell them where I live or what we talked about last night. Not even Tina knows my real name. I'm not sure why I told you in the first place, but you can't tell a single person why I'm really here."

"Uh," Theo muttered. "I don't think that'll be a problem at all."

"So you'll keep quiet?"

"No problem there." He felt his cheeks redden.

A tiny smile curved at the side of her mouth. "You don't remember last night."

He laughed softly. "Much of what happened after the club is fuzzy. I have no idea how I got here or what happened when I did."

"We talked for a few hours," she said as she stood and walked toward the kitchen. "The rest was pretty good too."

"What?"

"Just kidding." She sized him up. "Go into the bathroom and throw some water on your hair, or better yet, take a quick shower. I'll have something to drink when you get out."

"I have to be going," Theo insisted.

"Something interesting is going on with you." She opened a cupboard and rummaged through the shelf. She continued talking, but her voice was firm. "But I'm also doing something interesting. You almost ruined that for me last night."

"I still need to be going." He took a few steps toward her, but she motioned to the bathroom door behind him. "Not with that stuff in your hair. You can take a shower in like two minutes."

He glanced in the bathroom mirror and was horrified at how pale he looked. His cheeks were sunken, and he did not recognize the substance in his matted hair. He turned on the water to take a quick shower. He had spare scrubs in his car that he could change into before getting to the hospital. That was if his car was close by.

A voice echoed through the door. "There's soap and shampoo under the sink."

Three minutes later, after turning off the shower, he felt a hundred times better. The grogginess of the night had mostly vanished. Dressing quickly, he combed his hair and opened the door. Cindy, now dressed in pajamas, sat at the table waiting for him with coffee and a pastry.

He said, "I'm sorry about risking your job last night. Thanks for talking with me."

She stared at him with a mixture of confusion and amusement. "Either you're the best liar in the world, or you don't really remember much about last night."

Reaching for the coffee, he said, "There are several reasons why I don't drink anymore. Now I need to go."

"If your memory does come back, keep your promises."

"Did I do or say anything that I shouldn't have?"

"Nothing that I would worry yourself over. I did most of the talking."

"What am I missing?"

"Nothing important. If you see me again, act as before and we'll be fine." She opened the door for him.

"Is my car here?"

"In the parking lot."

He stepped outside, turned, and stared at Cindy. She stared back at him with a mixture of vulnerability and fierceness. He asked, "Can I help you in any way?"

"Just don't get in my way." She smiled kindly and closed the door before he could say anything else.

Peering around, he was surprised to find that he was next to a parking lot, and the building he'd just stepped out of was an old train car that had been significantly renovated. There were another five or six train cars in far worse shape than the one he'd just left. His vehicle was in the parking lot along with a dozen others in different shapes and sizes. They were close to the harbor. As he looked back at the train car, he found Cindy watching him. She raised her cup of coffee and disappeared.

Twenty minutes later, he pulled up in front of Scripps Mercy. By the time he arrived on the delivery floor of the hospital, dressed in his scrubs, there was an ominous tension throughout this area of the hospital. Theo smiled as he walked down the hall until he saw Jane leaning against a closed door.

"How's Mrs. Parker?" As her head turned to see him, relief flooded her face.

"There's a problem."

"What is it?" A sense of calm extended into his body the instant he walked through the hospital's front doors. He'd always felt more in control at work, especially in emergency situations. Much of his fatigue and worry had evaporated. Even his concerns about Sophia had been temporarily placed on hold.

"Dr. Jeffery started noticing a change in the baby's heart rate. At first, they thought it was the expected heart rate change as they moved toward delivery. A few minutes later, though, it became obvious that something serious was going on. He and another attending tried to calm Mrs. Palmer. It didn't work and they gave her medications to settle down, but she kept screaming about her baby."

"Is the baby distressed?"

"It was." Silence punctuated the air. She finally added, "But now… they can't find the baby's heartbeat."

"So they are doing a caesarian section."

"They needed to move fast," said Jane. "I think they want you inside the delivery room."

"Let's go."

She shook her head. "They want me to stay out here. Dr. Collier, who is helping Dr. Jeffery, and I don't get along. I've said no to his advances…if you get my meaning."

"Come on," Theo said as he seethed.

"It's better for everyone that I stay here. You need to get in there."

Theo had been part of several planned C-sections; they were intense under the best of circumstances. Jane nodded at him, and he opened the door. Theo quickly washed his hands and dressed in a mask, surgical gloves, and a gown. The inner door opened, and he stepped into the room with Dr. Jeffery and Dr. Collier.

Dr. Jeffery started the first incision as Theo approached. A curtain was draped across Mrs. Parker's chest, and the abdomen was exposed. Theo walked to the left side of the table and the two doctors acknowledged him. They asked questions, always teaching, and he answered as well as possible.

Time passed in quick bursts over the next several minutes. It could only be described as a coordinated commotion. Nurses moved in and out of the surgical room. Theo was asked to hold things here and there. The buzzing sounds of the machines sitting just a few feet away from Mrs. Parker would not calm a hospital visitor, but it was music to Theo's ears. She'd been given an IV upon arrival, but a more sedating medication had been given.

Theo replayed the anatomy lesson in his mind and what he would do if he were leading the surgery. His mind calculated risks versus benefits and what could go wrong. He could see every movement and hear every command. The tension rose with every passing minute as the baby's monitor did not improve. The relief and anxiety culminated in everyone's worst nightmare becoming a reality. The limp body of the baby was pulled from Mrs. Parker's abdomen. Another team was standing by to work on the baby.

The infant was laid on the cart, and a group of medical workers attacked with an oxygen mask, a blanket, and other supplies. Theo knew from experience that there was an extremely low chance of survival at this point. Too many minutes had already passed without a heartbeat. The baby was whisked out of the delivery room to be worked on in a different room.

When Theo tottered out of the delivery room, he was exhausted. He removed his gloves, gown, and mask. His movements were slow, and he felt like he was in a dream state. He was personally connected to Mrs. Parker, and he felt horrible. He repeated in his mind the baby being removed from the abdomen. He had been allowed the opportunity to close the abdomen and did so in a semi-detached state, but with precision. The text that confirmed what he already knew came as he stepped into the hall. The baby had died. Jane and some of the other nurses were crying at the nurse's station.

Jane located him half an hour later, after he had showered and changed. She said, "I wasn't sure you would come."

"Why not?"

"Because it isn't your week to be on-call."

"What does that matter?"

"Quite a bit. I've had several other residents that were too wasted to come in on a similar case. It isn't that they don't care, but sometimes, on their day off, it's just too much to handle."

"I can see that. But I've been seeing Mrs. Parker for months. I needed to be here."

"I'm sure she'll be happy to see you." She gave his arm a tight squeeze. "Any news on Sophia?"

"No. I've only found more dead ends and more unanswered questions."

"Fill me in when you get a chance."

"I will."

They set off together to find Mrs. Parker's room. They waited outside the door until it was appropriate to enter. Jane said, "Maybe you could give me a few minutes to talk with Mrs. Parker alone. It's always easier to hear bad news from a nurse, no matter how good your intentions will be."

He began pacing the hall. Dr. Jeffery joined him but remained quiet. Finally Theo asked, "Dr. Jeffery, what happened?"

"I'm not sure exactly. The patient's contractions were progressing, and she had cervical dilation and effacement. I believe that the baby's position changed before I was called into the room. A cord entanglement resulted, and as hard as we tried, we couldn't fix it in time." He shook his head, clearly disappointed. "I've seen this a few times, but I've never had a patient so close to delivery have this happen." Theo could feel the despair in his voice.

Theo added, "Everyone did everything they could."

"I know. I reviewed your charting with her, and everything was on course. No problems to speak of. Though the fetus could've had the entanglement before active labor began, there were no signs of any distress. It progressed so quickly."

This was the first patient Theo had ever lost, or at least the first that he was actively treating. He'd been involved with patients recovering from car accidents, cancer, and other traumatic events. But this was the first patient who was healthy, and then something bad happened. Somehow this felt different.

Dr. Jeffery, as if sensing Theo's distress, said, "This is a very unfortunate thing to occur, but certainly no one is at fault. Nothing is perfect in medicine, especially childbirth."

"I thought Dr. Simmons was on call?"

"Not for this."

Theo nodded back in the direction of Mrs. Parker's room. "I'd better go in and talk with her."

"That's very decent of you. Send her my regards."

"I will."

Theo's legs felt weighed down as he approached the door. He found Jane holding hands with Mrs. Parker, and both women were crying. He tried to keep his emotions in check.

"Hello, Mrs. Parker. How are you feeling?" He knew how ridiculous this question must sound. He felt equally stupid asking it.

Her anguish was almost tangible. Her voice shook when she asked, "What went so horribly wrong?"

Theo glanced around the room. "Where's Mr. Parker?" He remembered hearing so much about her husband and some of the insecurities they had.

"He's at a conference in Seattle." Mrs. Parker continued to cry softly. "He's trying to get a flight back here as soon as possible. He didn't want to go … but I needed some time for myself."

Theo moved toward the edge of the bed and sat. "Is there anyone else that could come in and share this with you?"

"My mom is on her way, but she's still a few hours away. She's driving down from the north." Her eyes pleaded with him for something.

"Okay. I talked with Dr. Jeffery, who oversaw the delivery. Things started off well. But as your labor progressed, your baby started to become distressed. Her heart rate escalated. A caesarean section was the only option to release what was causing her distress."

Theo noticed the dryness of Mrs. Parker's lips when she asked, "What caused the distress?"

"It's likely that the umbilical cord became entangled with your baby. It could have been that way for a while, but it wasn't causing any problems. Or it could've just happened. As labor progressed, the cord became tighter. Do you understand what I am saying?"

She half tilted her head as tears swam down the side of her face. "Is this common?"

"Having the umbilical cord do its own thing can be somewhat common. But usually it isn't dangerous. In this case it was. They did everything they could, but..." his voice trailed off.

Jane squeezed Mrs. Parker's hand. "They did a really good job. They were so quick, and they took good care of you and your baby."

"I know, I just wish..."

Jane added quickly, "I'll stay with you honey...at least until your mom gets here."

"Where's my baby now?"

"She's being taken care of down the hall."

"Can I see her?"

Jane hesitated for a moment. "Sure. They can bring in your baby, and you can hold her for a little while."

"I'm exhausted."

"I'll go talk with the nurses and be back in a few minutes." Jane stood, and Theo began to follow her.

Mrs. Parker said quickly, "Thank you, Dr. Raden, for everything you did."

"Take care, Mrs. Parker."

They walked in silence back to the nursing station. Jane said, "She's better than I could've imagined."

"I doubt the shock of everything has really hit her. Wait until her mother gets here."

Jane laughed out a sob of her own. "I always cried harder when I saw my mom."

Jane half hugged Theo. "See you tomorrow?"

"Bright and early."

Theo left the hospital feeling dazed and tired, but he couldn't get Mrs. Parker out of his mind. This was the worst heartbreak he could imagine for her. His mind slowly transitioned to Sophia. She was somewhere, all alone. He hoped she wouldn't have to go through anything this traumatic. He doubted that Dr. Haderly would care about what happened to Sophia. He needed to find her, and soon.

CHAPTER 13

Theo was so burned out that he spent the rest of the afternoon and evening resting in his condo. He wasn't sure what his next step should be. He considered calling Dr. Lazar to see if there was any new information on the lab findings. He couldn't imagine what else there was to find. At this point, he needed to locate Sophia, determine what happened to her, and find out if Mary's death had been an accident or something else. But for tonight, he tried taking his mind off of everything by playing video games and gorging on take-out Chinese food.

Around midnight, he picked up his phone and called Danielle. He still hadn't heard back from her. To his surprise, it was Cassandra who answered. She didn't sound happy.

"Why are you calling Danielle?"

"Remember when I phoned you, worried about Danielle? I haven't heard from either of you. I was being a good friend and checking in."

"At midnight? Maybe you were looking for a little booty call?"

"No one calls it that. Whatever. How's Danielle?"

"In rehab."

"What?" Theo asked. "I didn't see that coming."

"By the time I got to her apartment, she was passed out. I stayed with her until the night she came to see you and wrote those kind words on your wall. She was in bad shape, and I immediately took her to the ER, and she was admitted. She just got placed in a thirty-day rehab."

"And you kept this from me." He couldn't hide the hurt in his voice.

"You're partly the reason why she is there. I thought you would run down and try to save the day, as you always do."

"That's not fair. You could've texted that she was fine."

"I knew that you would call sooner or later."

"I don't try to save everyone."

"You do—if they're pretty enough."

"What?" Theo shouted.

"Anything else?"

"Seriously, Cassandra. I don't get you. It's like you're pissed at me."

"Bravo, Sherlock. Have you noticed that everything you touch gets worse? Leave Danielle alone for a long time."

Theo was stung and confused by Cassandra's comments. She'd always been supportive of everything he had done. "Whatever you say, Cass. You're the smart one. I'll stay far away from both of you. Take care."

"Theo…"

He hung up the phone. Without another word, he pulled back his covers and slipped inside. He just wanted this day to be over.

The next morning, he dragged himself kicking and screaming back to the hospital, but on the drive over, he promised himself that despite everything, he was going to be there for each of his patients. He had laser focus as he stepped through the doors. His last patient of the day was a pregnant woman coming for her first appointment. As he opened the door, his sense of smell was overwhelmed by something slightly familiar. His heart raced as he glanced up, expecting to see Sophia after all these weeks. The disappointment of seeing another homeless pregnant girl staggered him.

A middle-aged woman with gaunt eyes stared back at him. Her look of despair, riddled with addiction, was almost too much to handle. She was far different from Sophia, but he couldn't stop the flood of memories. This woman wasn't as strong as Sophia, and her life had been cruel. He felt a sense of empathy for her, but mostly for the child in her belly. That fetus didn't have a choice of parents, and the chances of a good life were now that much harder.

Theo searched for her name. "Hello, Ms. Banks."

"Call me Tanya," she hissed angrily.

"All right, Tanya, I'm Doctor Raden." He let out a slow breath and rummaged through his mind for peace and comfort. He found both.

She held up both hands. "Look. I'm here 'cause the judge said. Else he was going to throw me into the cage."

"I hear you."

"Just sign my damn paper and let me go."

With a crooked smile, he added, "I'll feel more comfortable in signing the paper after I perform an exam."

Her lip quivered with anger. "Look, fool. I understand that you've got to do what you've got to do. But can't you just sign something that says I'm fine?"

"Not really. Let's get started. Is this your first pregnancy?" he asked.

Tanya angrily described her history, beginning with her first pregnancy at age sixteen. She aborted the first three pregnancies. Now, at age thirty-five, she had decided to keep this one. She was eight months pregnant and had gained a grand total of five pounds. She had a belly and had gained only baby weight. There was almost no chance that this baby was going to be healthy. Even worse, it had a greater risk of addiction and child-development problems.

"Tell me about your weight gain."

"You've got the chart, so why don't you tell me."

Theo took a deep breath, "Two pounds of weight loss from since last appointment with the jail doctor. You need to be gaining weight."

"What I need is for you to sign a paper so I can be released from jail. If you sign it, they will let me go, and I can have this baby and get on with life."

"We'll get to that."

"I'm done." Tanya stood. "I don't need to be treated like a criminal."

Theo's voice elevated. "You're not. I'm trying to help."

"Damn you, this ain't no help at all."

"I'm not signing anything until I get an exam."

"You can take your pen and shove it where even the missus can't find it." The officer in the room rushed forward, and although Tanya was half dressed, the officer efficiently cuffed her with wrist cuffs, before she could attack. The standard for cuffing pregnant women had changed since his time at Pleasant Valley Correctional Facility. The officer escorted Tanya from the room, and soon they were in a van heading back to prison. He didn't feel bad about not signing her papers. Sometimes jail or prison was the best thing for the mom and child.

Jane bustled in with a smile across her face. "How was the criminal?"

"Angry."

"What did she really want?"

"For me to give her clearance to leave the jail before giving birth so she could spend the next few weeks higher than a kite."

"I'm guessing she didn't get what she wanted."

"No, she didn't." And something clicked in his mind. He felt a plan coming together. He'd watched St. Jude's so many times, maybe he needed to do something different.

The next day, after clinic and a meeting with Dr. Jeffery that lasted over two hours as they discussed his patients from the week, Theo was free for the next few days. He went directly to St. Jude's. This time he brought a few extra things with him. He parked a few blocks from the shelter, farther north, and found a grocery store, and changed.

When he stepped out of the bathroom, the employee behind the register gave him a look. "You filthy trash. You'd better not have stolen anything, or I'll call the cops."

Theo lifted both arms in the air and retreated out the door.

As the door shut, he heard, "Don't you ever come back here."

Once outside, he located some dirt and rubbed it thoroughly into his hair and clothes and onto his skin. He rifled through some trash and poured something nasty onto his pants. Returning to his car, he carefully placed some plastic on the front seats and moved his car closer to St. Jude's, where it was concealed by several trees. Pulling a glass bottle of root beer from a paper bag, his hands could barely grip the bottle, as dirty as they were. Theo stumbled to the corner and brought out a sign asking for money. He walked back and forth in front of two shopping carts tipped on their sides. Blankets were strewn between the two carts, and two men, smelling worse than he, were unconscious under the makeshift tent. Today, no one even saw him. He felt invisible.

Two hours later, his mood was already starting to drop. He was drenched in sweat and perched on the ground. He had made thirty-seven dollars and watched half a dozen drug deals, but no pregnant women were wandering the streets. He gulped down the last of his warm drink and concluded that his only option was to get back inside the shelter. If he posed as someone homeless, he might learn a few things. For all he knew, Sophia was holed up in a locked room. He tried standing, but his legs had a tingling sensation. He stumbled up the street. The entrance to St. Jude's was on the far side of the building, to his left, and out of sight. His last attempt for the night would be to walk completely around the compound.

He reached the crosswalk that would bring him closer to the entrance. There were several people already waiting. Some had to be supported by their friends. Behind him, there was a slamming door, like someone was trying to knock the building down. Theo turned and recognized a large apartment complex. It was high-end, especially for this part of town. There was a high metal fence, and there were several security cameras. However, the cluster of three girls that exited the main doors were different from what he expected. All three wore oversize clothing, with matted hair and vacant looks. There was a good chance they were pregnant. Rushing to the green metal fence, Theo tried to get a better look. A man—tall, well-dressed, and athletic— kept back several steps, like a bodyguard, but watched the girls like a hawk. The first girl, plump, with brown skin, stepped to one side, and Sophia came into view.

Theo's heart pounded, and he silently thanked the heavens. He felt an avalanche of emotions, but it was more vital than ever that he remained focused. Sophia was close but still so far away. The green metal fence, like one around the old manor in the center of town, surrounded the apartment complex. Several high spires were at the corners. The goal was to keep everyone out. Back down the road, there was a sliding gate that gave vehicles access to an underground garage. Ahead was the same road that crossed in front of the shelter, where he had spent countless days watching. Sophia and the other girls were walking toward another gate. It was possible that she was heading over to the shelter. If she left the gated apartment, that would be his best option. If she didn't, he would be forced to come back tonight.

The well-dressed man hurried past the girls and removed a key, unlocking a door. Sophia and the other girls stepped onto the sidewalk, turned left, and headed in his direction. The crosswalk was now nearly empty of people, as most had just crossed the street. Theo sunk back into the shadows, pulling out his sign.

The group stopped at the crosswalk and waited to cross. Within thirty seconds, a dozen more people arrived. Theo stepped from the shadows and pushed past three or four people until he was directly behind Sophia. He whispered, "Sophia, can you hear me?"

There wasn't the slightest sign of a response.

The walk sign glowed. The man stepped out first, as if clearing the way across the street. Sophia was the last of the girls, and Theo reached out and tugged her arm, pulling her back onto the sidewalk. He didn't say anything but kept dragging her toward his car. She didn't struggle but stared up at him. She didn't seem to understand what was happening or who he was.

After five steps, she asked, "Do I know you?"

"I'm your doctor. You need a second opinion. Please come with me."

"Okay."

Sophia let him guide her, and Theo walked as briskly as he could.

Sophia asked, "Why do I need to see a doctor?"

"For an exam."

"Okay." After another few steps, she said, "I'm so thirsty."

He wrapped his arm around hers, almost shielding her, and said, "I've got something right over here."

Shouts erupted behind him, on the opposite corner. "Tosh! You come back here right now! Where did you go?"

Sophia stiffened. "I got to go back."

"No," Theo said forcefully. "We're almost to your drink and your appointment."

"Do I know you?"

"I'm a friend." Theo hoped that his body was shielding Sophia enough that they couldn't see her.

A man yelled, "Over there! Someone is trying to kidnap her."

Sophia froze.

Theo reacted, swooped down, and picked Sophia up off her feet. She slapped in the face a few times and wiggled her feet. Theo sprinted as fast as he could down the block.

"Stop right now," a voice yelled.

His car was still twenty feet away. As he carried Sophia, he tried unlocking his doors at the same time. It took a few attempts, but he finally disengaged the door.

Sophia started screaming, "Help!"

The two men sleeping under the makeshift tent awoke. They lumbered out and stood as Theo hurried past.

Theo roared, "They're trying to steal my money. Those assholes behind me."

The two men glared at Theo, then glanced behind him. They did not react.

Sophia wailed loudly.

Theo spoke to Sophia, trying to calm her. "A bad man is coming for you. We have to get out of here."

"You're bad."

"No! Someone scary is chasing us."

"I'm not going to go with you."

Theo reached the driver's door. He pinned Sophia against the car door and added, "Mary called me—she wants to see you."

Sophia's eyes narrowed. "Mary?"

He heard the footsteps approaching. He cried, "Yes! She wants to see you. The doctor said it would be okay."

"Really," she said quickly. "I want to go."

Theo shoved her inside the car and closed the door behind him. She landed better than expected except that her feet were in his lap. He slid his key into the ignition and started the car. He slammed down the accelerator and tried pushing Sophia's legs out of the way.

An elbow collided with the driver's side window, and glass shot inward, spraying Theo. A hand reached in and tried grasping Theo's arm. He released the steering wheel and punched the arm repeatedly, and the car swerved across the two lanes. The man's grip was strong. He grasped the wheel to avoid crashing. As soon as he could, he let go of the wheel again and reached up, grabbing the man's shirt, and instead of pushing him away, he jerked him toward the car. A sick sound resonated as the man's head collided with the top of the car. A moment later, he limply fell away. Several horns erupted as Theo regained control of his car. He drove for several blocks before finding a freeway entrance ramp.

Sophia began crying. "You stole me." Through her tears, she shouted, "Help! Help!" Her fingernails dug into his arms. He pushed her back into her seat and held her as best he could. This mollified her for only a few seconds. Soon she tired pulling the hair out of the back of his head.

Theo screamed, "Dr. Happypants is going to punish you."

Sophia's arms stopped mid slap, and she halted all attacks. A moment later, he leaned over and pulled down her seat belt and buckled her in. Theo drove swiftly up Route 163, heading north past the San Diego Zoo.

After five minutes of silence, he whispered, "Dr. Happypants and Mary are at the hospital. We'll be there in twenty minutes."

In a very childlike voice, she asked, "Will he be mad at me? Will he hurt me?"

Theo couldn't understand how this twenty-four-year-old college graduate was the same person he'd talked to just a few weeks ago. She didn't recognize him, and she was a completely different person.

"No. He wants to help."

Her next question held no serious emotions. "What happened to your window? The air is blowing too much in here."

He managed to say, "The bad people were trying to take my car."

"So they weren't after us?"

"No…no."

"You did a good thing. You drove super fast. Like a race car. I'm sorry that I hit you."

"It's all right. We're almost there, so you can see your friend and the doctor."

"That's good."

Ten minutes later, he pulled into the parking lot of the hospital, careful to ensure that no one could see his broken window. She allowed him to help her inside, and he placed her in an exam room and shut the door.

"Do I need to call security?" a voice demanded.

Theo turned to find Nurse Jane approaching with her coat and purse in hand.

"It's me," he muttered.

"What in the Louisiana hell are you doing here?" She stepped a few feet closer, her hand quickly covering her nose. "And why do you smell worse than the French Quarter after Mardi Gras?"

"Part of my disguise."

"To enamor zombies?"

Theo pointed over his shoulder. "Looks like I found the right one."

"Is Sophia in there?"

"She is. And I need to give her something to calm down, like we did before."

Ten minutes later, Jane, now dressed in her scrubs, walked in with a shot. She moved past Theo quickly, having learned her lesson last time. Theo told Sophia, "Doctor Happypants wants you to have this before he gets here. He wants you to take this medicine."

Sophia appeared apprehensive. "Is it going to hurt? Shots always hurt me."

"Maybe a little," he said encouragingly. Theo held both of her hands as Jane walked up behind Sophia. She said nothing as she pulled out the needle and gave her the shot in the hip.

Sophia jerked and screamed as if she had just had a toenail ripped off. Theo and Jane stepped back several steps and waited.

Jane whispered, "Where was she? She looks even worse than before."

Sophia's clothes were baggy like when he first saw her. This time, half her face was black and blue and swollen. She hobbled with a limp. Her shirt and pants were three times her size. He thought there was puke in her hair, and the smell was similar, but Theo had barely noticed it. He was relieved that she was safe.

Twenty minutes later she had calmed considerably but was still erratic and confused. Her memory had not improved as it had before. Theo had expected that she would snap out of her behavior once she calmed. He muttered, "She looks the same."

"Just a calmer version of crazy," replied Jane.

"Isn't this what we did before?"

"I can't remember. I think so."

He pondered the steps they had taken. Something clicked in his mind. "Did we give her Valium or Ativan today?"

"We gave her Valium."

"Let's try Ativan."

Jane's eyebrows rose, but she remained quiet. She quickly left the room. Five minutes later, she returned with a second injection. By this time, Sophia was so comatose that she didn't complain. Theo gave her the injection, and they both sat and watched in anticipation. The reaction was significant and impressive, occurring after only a few minutes. They observed Sophia shaking her head as if confused. She shook it again…once…then twice…then right before their eyes, the cobwebs fell free. She glanced from ground to ceiling, confused.

Sophia's eyes moved around the room until they fell onto Theo and Jane. She glared at both of them. When she spoke, it was in her strong voice. "Who are you?" Her head rolled back and came to rest on the cushioned portion of the exam table. The medications were starting to set in fully.

"Sophia? It's me...Theo."

She answered without the slightest hesitation, "Theo who?" She didn't move her head, but her eyes rolled in his direction.

Jane took a step forward. "Ms. LaCross, I'm a nurse at Scripps Mercy Hospital, and this is Dr. Raden. You're here because you're pregnant."

She smiled confidently. "There's no way. I haven't had a boyfriend in a long time. I can promise you that I'm not pregnant."

Patting Sophia's arm, Jane continued kindly, "I know that this is probably a hard thing to understand, but you are pregnant. Take a look at your belly." Nurse Jane helped move Sophia's head into a better position.

Sophia's confident smile did not falter until she stared at her swollen and pregnant stomach. She began to cry, and Jane helped her recline the exam table so she could relax. Sophia closed her eyes and cried. Jane comforted her as Theo watched. A few minutes later, she fell asleep and immediately started snoring.

CHAPTER 14

Two hours later, Theo and Jane walked back into Sophia's room. Her eyes were open, and she still looked tired but seemed more aware of her surroundings. Theo had showered and changed and he felt delight and surreal at seeing Sophia again. She was safe, for now.

Sophia muttered, "Is this as bad as things can get? How could I possibly be pregnant?"

Theo asked, "What is the last thing you remember?"

"I remember going inside a room with a friend of mine, but he was forced to leave."

"Do you remember who that friend was?"

Sophia continued staring at the wall. "I can't exactly remember the details."

"It was me," Theo said.

For the first time, she peered at him.

He said, "Let me explain."

Somehow talking with Sophia this time was far more difficult. He watched her closely as he tried explaining everything that had happened. It went from bad to worse as he described Mary's death, her apartment, and the visit to St. Jude's. If Jane hadn't stepped in to corroborate his story, he was almost certain that Sophia would've called the cops.

After explaining most everything, Theo paused, and Sophia's first thoughts were that Theo was stalking her—a fair assessment of the reality of things. Once that idea was quashed, things fell to the bottom of the barrel when Sophia asked if Theo was the father of her child.

Only through the pure volume of information that Theo knew about Sophia's life did he finally see her countenance change, and she started believing him. None of Theo's answers were sufficient enough, and he felt ridiculous throughout the process.

The last thing that Theo told her about was the money. Sophia did a double-take and exploded with several questions about where it came from and her old job at the bank. She insisted on going to the bank tomorrow, and for the first time, she appeared motivated.

When he and Jane stepped out of the room after over an hour of discussion, he felt exhausted, and Jane looked it.

"Follow me," Jane said, and she motioned for them to walk to the nursing station. "I can't believe her memory is gone like before. All this seems implausible, but she seems unharmed."

When they were halfway down the hall, the door opened, and Sophia peeked out. "I don't want to be alone. My life is a mess."

"We were going to get something to drink at the nurses' station. After that, I wanted to do an ultrasound and get some blood work, then we can get you a shower. Come on."

"Perfect." Sophia, still tired, slowly walked toward them.

After getting some cups of soda, they all hovered around, and Theo felt awkward. He knew he wanted to help Sophia again, but what if she didn't want his help?

Sophia voiced this thought. "What am I supposed to do now?"

Jane answered. "You and Theo made a great team before. I like what you said in the exam room. I think an important key is to locate where the money originated from."

Theo added, "If I remember correctly, your boss said that the money was sent to your account from another account, which was closed six months ago. Maybe he can see where that account was opened."

"It's worth a look," Jane said eagerly. She asked Theo, "What are *your* plans now?"

"That depends on Sophia."

Sophia glanced around nervously. "Why me?"

"The last time we looked into this, it got you back to where you started. You were taken again. This time we'll need to be extra careful. Your apartment is off-limits. Maybe Jane or I can go there, but you can't."

Sophia asked, "What if we go to the police?"

"My friend is with the police, and I have talked to him about you. He knows about you but is unwilling to get involved. Even after you went missing a second time, he wouldn't open a file. He called you an unreliable witness."

"What's that supposed to mean?"

"We don't really know what Dr. Haderly will say if cornered. My bet is that he will insist that there is patient/doctor confidentiality. He will say that he is worried about your well-being. He might have pictures and videos and lie about the entire thing. He will insist that you aren't reliable."

"That jackass." Sophia stood quickly. "I need to think about this for a few minutes. I think I'm ready for that check-up and that shower."

Jane added, "We can find you some clean underwear, a shaver, and a new bra. I'll help."

Sophia followed, but quickly stopped and faced Theo. "No one would've gone looking for me almost every day. Whatever happens, thank you for helping me."

Theo smiled, "I'm just glad you're safe."

Alone next to the nurse's station, Theo's stomach growled. He headed off to the employee lounge and found a few snacks, sat down, and ate. He was so relieved that Sophia was safe, and he needed to keep it that way. His hand shook for the first few minutes until he calmed down. He still had no idea what was happening. The thought of not helping her move forward was equally impossible to grasp. He became lost in his thoughts. For the first time, he wondered if they should cut their losses and relocate her away from San Diego. The hidden facts felt like a mounting tsunami.

When he was finished, Theo headed back to the nurses' station. The area was empty, and he found Jane leaning against the wall outside the girl's bathroom.

"How's it coming?"

Jane said, "The baby appears to be healthy and growing. Blood work was easy. She has some cuts on her back. If I were guessing, she was punished a month or so ago. Some are more recent. Most have scabbed over, but they looked to have been painful. There was a weird rash on the back of her head, the size of a dime. It was almost perfectly circular."

"I don't remember seeing that the first time, but when she comes out, I'll take a look." A moment later, Theo added, "When we drove here, she was hitting me. She was so confused. The only way I got her to listen was by telling her that Dr. Haderly was going to punish her. That stopped her immediately."

"I bet she was tortured."

"About what?"

"Maybe about what she found out while she was with you."

"We found next to nothing," Theo explained.

"Maybe you did…maybe you didn't."

"How is she?"

"She sobbed for the first ten minutes in the shower. I helped as much as I could. We found a chair for her. It went well after that."

"What should I do now?" he asked.

"You can't abandon her."

"Not planning on it." Theo leaned up against the wall. "Maybe I should have her leave town."

"To where? Your parents?"

"That wouldn't help."

Jane stared at him, unrelenting. "You need to solve this. Figure out what is going on."

"I don't know if I can. I don't want to put Sophia at risk."

"She'll remain at risk, always glancing over her shoulder."

Ten minutes later, Sophia emerged from the locker room wearing scrubs. She looked better and worse. She was clean, but emotionally she was vulnerable and a mess. She eyed them back and forth. "What the hell am I supposed to do now?"

Theo answered, "That's up to you."

A little testily, Sophia responded, "What in the world does that mean?"

Jane stepped forward and wrapped an arm around her. Sophia choked down a sob.

Theo added, "I set out to find you. I've accomplished that. I didn't have a great plan for what to do after I found you. You can have your purse back, and your money, and we can decide what to do next. You can leave the city, or we can try to find answers."

Sophia answered quickly, "I want to find out what happened to me."

"Jane and I will—"

"Mary's death is hard to swallow. I sort of remember some of the details. I was kidnapped twice. My memory is not worth five dollars, and I'm pregnant with no boyfriend. I can remember bits and pieces of what you told me. I'm frustrated...but I must find answers."

"We can help," Jane said.

Turning to Jane, Theo asked, "When's your next day off?

"Friday."

"For right now, you stay working here. If someone comes looking for Sophia or me, then call me."

"That's not fair," Jane said crossly. "I want to do something. I can help."

"We will need your help. But let me figure some things out. I need to find a way to keep Sophia safe."

Jane relented. "If I don't hear from you in two days, I'm coming after you with a freaking machete."

"I'll call." Theo added, "We should go." He led Sophia to his car. As they approached the window, Jane said, "What happened?"

"Oh, that," Theo said. "They really didn't want me helping Sophia to escape."

Sophia asked, "They attacked us?"

"They smashed my window and tried hauling me out."

Jane glared at him. "Why did you leave that part out?"

"A lot was going on. It slipped my mind." He opened the passenger for Sophia.

"Right." Jane slammed closed the door. "You'll need to get a rental. They might have written down the license plate."

"Okay. We'll ditch it."

Jane's next words were sobering. "Torch your car and call the police. Tell them that it was stolen."

"What?"

"Rent a car, pay cash, and find a hotel. Always pay with cash."

"What are you talking about?" Theo asked, puzzled.

Jane pulled Sophia to a group of trees east of the building. "Find a store and buy new cell phones. Never use your credit cards."

"Hold on here," Theo protested, trying to keep pace.

Jane shoved Theo back a few steps. "I've never told you this before, and I'll deny it. But I'm part of a group of women who help battered women escape toxic relationships. These are the same things that I tell them. The girls who escape are the ones who follow directions. Am I clear?"

"Perfectly clear," Theo said, shocked.

"Theo," she said, "give me the keys to your car and call the police. Get everything out of it that's important and valuable. After that, go back inside and do some charting."

"What are you going to do?" asked Theo, handing over his keys.

She handed Sophia her keys. "Sophia, will follow me in my car?

"I'm not sure she is well enough to drive."

Jane's tone was sobering. "Trust me. We don't have a choice." Wait thirty minutes after we leave to call the police. When they arrive, tell them that you were working late, paperwork and all. I would actually go log in and do some. Walk out the front entrance, on camera, and then run back inside and call the police. Tell them your car was stolen. They'll ask a bunch of questions. Say you don't know to most of them. We're so lucky that you parked in an area the camera doesn't pick up."

"Why does Sophia need to go with you?"

"How would I come back and get you? She can't be here when the police arrive. We'll be back in an hour, and I'll take you guys to your condo. I'll park in the alley two blocks away, the one by Jerry's Diner."

Theo shook his head. "This is insane. How do you know how to do all of this?"

"I've told you already. That alley is where I do a lot of pickups and drop-offs. It has been observed carefully. It should be safe."

Theo hesitated. "Should be?"

"Things rarely go as smoothly as we'd want them to."

The girls left, and he went back inside and worked. He followed her directions perfectly, and thirty minutes later, the police were called, arriving eight minutes later. Theo showed them his driver's license and work badge and answered a dozen questions. They followed him inside to his workstation. Two police cars had arrived initially, but one left after securing the scene. Theo talked with Officer Peterson, and the paperwork was started. Officer Reed went inside, where she reviewed the security camera. She returned ten minutes later and said that area of the parking lot didn't have a camera. Theo glanced up as if he never realized a camera was there. The officers finished their investigation, and Theo signed the report. The officers gave him the bad news that this was all too common, and the chances of a recovery were slim.

Officer Reed asked, "Can we give you a ride home?"

"No," Theo said dejectedly. "I'll call my roommate and he can come get me."

"Are you sure?" Officer Peterson replied.

"Yes. I've still got another thirty minutes of work. These dictations need to get done."

"Have a good night," Officer Reed said.

Theo stepped back inside and into an adjacent room. He watched as the officers glanced around one last time and got into their car. The police vehicle drove off, and Theo waited another ten minutes before he snuck out a side door and down to Jerry's Diner. Jane and Sophia were waiting for him.

He slipped into the back seat of the car. He asked, "Do I even want to know what you did with my car?"

"We have a place," Jane said.

Sophia added, "That was one of the coolest things I've ever seen."

Sophia and Jane shared a glance.

The car ride to his apartment was uneventful. Theo unlocked the door and slipped into his condo as Sophia remained in the car with Jane. The television was on, and his roommate was still awake and enjoying the show. Trying to act casual, Theo said, "Hey, Barrett, how was your night?"

Barrett paused his show and smiled brightly. "Terrific. This has been one of the best weeks of my life."

"What happened?"

"I found out I got a new job today. A girl emailed me back and agreed to go on a virtual date with me this weekend."

"That sounds fantastic," Theo said enthusiastically. "Where are you going to be working?"

"Delivering pizzas for Domino's. I'll get a discount."

"Even better."

"I know," Barrett said. He wore only boxer briefs, and Theo wasn't sure they were actually clean. Barrett asked, "Are you up for another late night of games?"

"Nah, I got to get some sleep. Only one of us had a good day."

"What happened?"

"First," Theo said, with all the anger he could manage, "my attending made me stay late to do all the paperwork. I was the last one there, and my car was gone when I came out of the building."

"Like, missing?"

"I had to call the cops and take an Uber home. What am I supposed to do without a car?"

"Finally," Barrett said, his happiness evident. "Your life sucks worse than mine."

Theo chuckled. "Thanks for pointing that out."

"Just joking. You can borrow mine."

"What about your new job?"

"Oh, yeah. You're totally screwed." Barrett stood, walked to the kitchen area, and pulled some beer from the fridge. "Want one?"

"Yeah, maybe."

Barrett reached for the beer just as Theo's cell phone rang. Perfect timing.

Theo answered, "Hello…yes, sir. I see." Theo sat on the couch. "Yes, that will work. I know, terrible situation. A hotel close to work. I guess that will work." Glancing up at Barrett, he finished by saying, "Thank you very much." Theo hung up the phone.

Barrett asked, "Who was that?"

"My attending. He has already heard about my stolen car. They want me closer to work for the next few days. I guess they're putting me up in a hotel."

"Wow," Barrett said. "That's super lucky."

"Only half lucky. I don't have a date with a girl like you do." Theo stood quickly.

Barrett suggested, "Maybe they'll buy you a new car."

"I doubt it." Theo chuckled. "I guess I better pack a bag for a few days. I've got to be back to work early tomorrow."

"I could give you a ride to your hotel."

Theo stopped quickly and turned around. "Dude, you're the best. But don't worry about it. They're sending over a car."

"Let me know if you change your mind." Barrett smiled tentatively. "I guess I'll have the condo for myself for a few days. I'm going to throw a party to celebrate my new job."

"Not a big party, right?"

"No way. Just a few hundred of my closest friends."

Theo covered his mouth so he didn't snort. He managed to say, "You deserve it," and he disappeared into his room. He collected Sophia's purse, the money, several days' worth of clothing, and his bathroom items. It wasn't long before he pretended to get another telephone call, and he rushed into the hall.

Barrett was standing there with a sack of food and three beers. "I doubt you even ate, and you need to relax tonight."

"Thanks, Barrett." Theo reached up and took the food. Barrett slipped the three beers into his bag and opened the door. Theo said, "If they have a hot tub, I'll call you, and you can stop by."

"Cool." Barrett smiled and closed the door as he walked away. Theo was relieved it went as well as it did. Jane's plan worked to perfection.

When he reached Jane's car, she asked, "How did that go?"

"Perfectly."

"I didn't know you lived here." Jane pointed to the front doors. "How old is this place?"

"I've been here just over a year."

"Perfect location. Is that a retirement community to the south? I bet you have no issues with noise complaints."

"No, we do not. This property used to be an old church. It caught fire, and they built condos instead. I was one of the first ones to buy. I had my pick of locations."

"Does that mean your roommate pays rent?"

"Yes. It works for both of us. He covers half the cost."

"You have a great view," Jane said. "There's a ravine, some trees, and a perfect view of that mountain."

"Yeah. I really enjoy it here."

Sophia interrupted and said, "Not to be a bother, but where are we going from here?"

Theo slid into the back seat as Jane drove away. "A hotel farther north. We'll get two rooms," he added quickly as he noticed Sophia's face.

As they drove in silence, Theo began planning. They had only a few answers and many more questions. He thought about going back to Cindy's train condo or maybe Club Jazzed. That club was sketchy, and he still had the black card. He wondered if Cindy might recognize Sophia, or if Sophia might remember something about Club Jazzed or one of the other locations. Theo had trouble keeping his eyes open, and he rested them for a moment.

Sophia asked, her voice soft and emotional, "Did Mary's funeral already happen?"

Theo exhaled. "I read in the paper that she had a nice service near her parents in Bakersfield. That was a couple of weeks ago. I thought about going but felt ridiculous being there without you."

"Did we ever figure out how I got pregnant?"

"No," Theo said. "Only theories."

"And you said someone broke into my apartment and trashed my room?"

"Looks that way." Keeping his eyes closed, he asked, "How well do you trust Derek and Clayton?"

"Why do you ask?"

"You and I met them. Clayton was very possessive of you. They also broke into your apartment, but it seemed they were worried about you. Clayton doesn't seem to like me."

"Clayton borders on a stalker. He's kindhearted deep down but goes about it the wrong way. Derek is a good guy. But neither of them could be the father. I can guarantee you that."

CHAPTER 15

The following morning, a rapid pounding on the hotel door pulled Theo from a deep sleep. At first, he thought it might be Jane coming back to check on them. He was exhausted, and it took a few minutes to react. Rolling over, he glanced at the alarm clock: 10:00 a.m. It had taken them until 3:00 a.m. to get situated in their rooms and another hour for him to fall asleep. Jane had promised a rental car would be delivered to their hotel by noon.

Theo tossed off his blanket and stepped to the door before the next round of violent knocking began. As he cracked it open, Sophia shoved the door and barreled into his room. Theo was knocked back a few steps. She wore the same scrubs from the previous day, and she was already showered. She wore no makeup, and her hair was tangled. Theo closed the door.

Sophia blurted, "I need some money to get a brush, some makeup, and other items. There's a Walgreens across the street, and before you tell me that I can't go on my own, just remember, I don't really know who you are. So relax."

Theo shrugged. "You do know me. I'm still here helping you. I'm not the enemy."

Her shoulders sagged, and she calmed considerably.

Theo said, "Here's the plan." He pulled out some money. "I'll shower, and after you are ready, we can get some breakfast. Once the rental car arrives, we'll go to the mall for some new clothes and get your hair cut and colored. We can't give anyone the idea that they can take you again. Sparkling necklace, earrings, and maternal clothing."

"Do you think that will matter?"

"We need to try. We will avoid St. Jude's at all costs. They're going to come looking for you."

"So you're okay with me going to Walgreens?"

"Just be careful."

She smiled.

"Let's plan on leaving in sixty minutes."

Theo showered and changed into slacks and a polo shirt. After Sophia returned, they found that they had missed the breakfast in the hotel. Sophia put on some makeup to cover her bruises. They waited in their rooms until a phone call came from the front desk saying that the rental car had arrived. Theo went alone, picked up the keys, and found Sophia at a side door.

"Nice car," she said as he drove up in a black Mini Cooper. "I hope it can fit all our shopping for today." Despite her annoyance with him from earlier, she winked at him.

They drove to the Fashion Valley Mall, and Theo did most of the talking. He told Sophia about himself, and she asked a few questions. They found some lunch and coffee before starting to shop. Theo had learned to loathe shopping, and the next two hours turned out to be as painful as a lumbar puncture using a crowbar instead of a needle. When they finished, Sophia had ten new outfits and half as many pairs of shoes. She had two outfits that cost more than his rent for three months. Theo was forced to try on several outfits and ended up purchasing five.

Sophia wore maternity jeans and a long-sleeved pink shirt with a diamond emblem near the chest. Her clothes transformed her into a fashionable and happy pregnant woman. Theo pointed to a salon near the food court, and Sophia grinned, handing him the bags of purchases. It had been more than five weeks since she had disappeared, and her hair was a mess. The stylist glanced at each of them as Sophia took a seat. As she explained the hair-color change and the cut she wanted, Theo walked the bags to the rental car. When he returned, he found a seat and began his endless wait.

An hour or five later, Sophia emerged as a new person once again. Her hair was dark brown, with a few blond highlights, and five inches shorter. She waited expectantly for the verdict.

"Perfect."

Sophia's dazzling smile revealed that this was the right answer. Her shoulders relaxed, and she wrapped her arm around his and pulled him off in the direction of a jewelry store. She purchased dangling earrings, necklaces, a watch, and some bracelets. The next stop was another makeup store, and this went quicker than he hoped. She knew exactly what she wanted. Lastly, they found a purse and several other items.

Once they had finished for the day, they headed out to the car. As they drove away from the mall, Sophia whispered softly, "Thank you, Theo." He noticed she had tears in her eyes.

"For what?"

"Making me feel special. I think it's been a long time since I felt like this."

"You deserve it."

They spotted a California Pizza Kitchen and enjoyed a simple meal together.

"Back to the hotel?" asked Sophia, when she was finished.

"We need to find a place to get disposable cell phones."

"Walmart," Sophia said without hesitation. "Jane told me while I was showering," she added after a side glance from Theo.

Sophia remained in the car as Theo purchased six disposable cell phones.

"Now what?"

"Back to the hotel," Theo said.

Nearing their hotel, Sophia said, "I think that our only choice going forward is to pretend to be a couple and stay in the same room."

Theo practically swerved off the road. "Are you serious?"

"I didn't sleep at all last night. I was so worried that someone was going to break in. We can put most of the clothes and other items in the second room. But I need to feel safe. Being with you makes me feel safe. Is that okay?"

"No problem."

Theo carried all the clothing and other items to the second room. He made several trips as Sophia moved her items into his room. They were situated on the first floor, near the middle of the hall. The pool and spa center were on the opposite side of the hotel. When Theo stepped back into his room, Sophia was in her pajamas, watching TV. She was slightly pale and uncomfortable but insisted that she was doing fine.

Theo showered, shaved, and slid into a T-shirt and shorts. They watched a movie for an hour, just enjoying the show and the silence. As the movie transitioned into the final scene, there were three loud knocks at the door. Theo, startled, leaped to his feet and rushed to the door, opening it only a few inches.

A disheveled man stood in the hallway. Theo asked, "Can I help you?"

The man blanched and glanced at the room number. "Sorry, wrong door," and he stumbled down the hall and out of view.

Theo didn't entirely close his door. A moment later, he slipped his head out and peered down the hall. The man was knocking at another door. When it opened, the man's head dropped as if in shame, and he stumbled inside.

After the movie finished, Sophia wanted to learn more about him. Theo retold some of his life stories, and he was surprised to discover a few new things about her as well. She was a great storyteller. She spoke about a time when she was at a slumber party with her best friend and they snuck out, stealing something and getting caught. The police were called, and so were both of their parents. Sophia added, "I can't even remember when the last time I talked to her was."

"Do you trust her enough to call her now?" Theo asked.

Sophia thought about this for a moment, then answered, "Besides Mary, she would be the first person I would normally call. She's married now and has two kids of her own. But with this mess, I can't involve her. There's no way she would believe me."

"Are you sure about the sleeping arrangements?" Theo glanced at the only bed.

"I doubt you're going to put the moves on me. I'm too tired to even worry about it. It's totally fine." Sophia disappeared into the bathroom. When she was back in bed, Theo used the bathroom, and by the time he returned, she was fast asleep.

Theo slipped into bed next to Sophia and stared up at the ceiling, trying to wrangle his own feelings. Surprisingly, so much had changed over the last several weeks. He loved being a doctor, and that meant something to him. But he also was surprised by how much he enjoyed helping Sophia. He felt she needed him.

Sometime during the night, he was awoken by Sophia talking in her sleep. She was mumbling. He caught only a few words, and fewer still that made sense. "All part of the job…Governor." The next few words were unintelligible. Then Sophia screamed, "No…Doctor…I won't." Sophia fell silent, and soon she was snoring. Theo rolled over and fell back asleep.

At breakfast, Sophia seemed rejuvenated, like she had gotten a full night's sleep. Theo woke early and showered. After they sat down to eat, Theo asked, "How did you sleep? Any bad dreams?"

"I slept great."

"You look like you're feeling better."

"I don't know. I've made it past the worst day of my life. It feels like my mind is so clear right now. I feel good."

"Do you remember who Dr. Haderly is?"

She concentrated on the name but finally said, "I think you asked me about him back at your work. But besides that, nothing. Why do you ask?"

"While you were sleeping, you spoke his name, and I wondered if you knew who he was."

"Honestly. Nothing. I can't match the name to anyone."

Theo told her about what he remembered about Dr. Haderly and St. Jude's. He also told her about seeing Dr. Haderly exchange something like a leather bag for a briefcase. Theo added, "We followed the black sedan, and it went to a pharmaceutical company called BioPharm. Have you ever heard of it?"

"Never."

"Not surprising. We should look into them as well."

"So, what's the agenda for today?" Sophia asked, stuffing a third pancake into her mouth.

"Following the money," Theo said. "You insisted on visiting your work again, and we need some cash."

Somehow, through her bites, she managed to say, "Sounds good."

After finishing, they drove to Lemon Grove and went directly to Bank of America. On the drive over, they came up with a plan. Theo would remain outside and monitor the building. Sophia wanted to talk with her boss alone and see what information she could get. Theo parked the Mini Cooper in the back of the building.

Sophia hesitated before exiting the car.

"What are you thinking?"

"I don't know if I can go in there on my own."

"You did fine before."

Sophia peered at him. "I can't remember doing that. You said that I talked to him a month ago. He'll probably pick up pretty quickly that I can't remember our last conversation." She glanced out of the window. "He'll know that my memories are gone again. He'll think that I'm an airhead."

"No," Theo said. "Ask him to look more closely into the money that was sent to your account. That's all. Either he can or can't. You just talked to him on the phone. This is the first time we've stopped by the bank. This is the only information we need, and you'll do fine."

"I don't know if I can."

"What if I came in with you? I could pretend to open an account."

She nodded, and together they stepped from the car.

Theo entered first, and Sophia came in two minutes later. Theo waited in line for almost ten minutes before he was ushered forward to talk to a representative. Sophia walked to a side desk and started speaking with someone she clearly knew. After a few minutes, an older man with red hair and rosy cheeks came and greeted Sophia. They hugged. A few more girls came over and appeared to be saying hi to Sophia, who unconsciously wrapped her arms protectively around her belly.

"Can I help you?" Theo turned to find a spunky appearing girl with brown eyes, who was eagerly waiting for the next customer. Theo sat down at her desk. This girl was calm yet confident and probably a few years older than he was. He said, "I need an account."

"That's easy money...pun intended." She laughed enthusiastically at her own joke, and Theo couldn't help smiling. She said, "Call me Anna."

"No problem. I'm Theo."

It took ten minutes to set up an account. Theo watched Sophia's slow progress to the bank manager.

Turning back to the girl, he asked, "Can I ask you a banking question?"

With a stern voice, she asked, "Is it... a 'can you stick up your hands so I can rob the bank' type of question?" Theo choked but couldn't say anything. The girl continued with a straight face, "Because I've gotten a lot of those lately, and they cause me so much extra paperwork."

"Wow," Theo said. "That wasn't the question at all."

"Thank goodness," A bright smile crossed her face.

"You must really love your job."

"I do."

Theo asked, "How can a second party, not my work, put money into my account? Do I have to give them my account?"

"Oh…" She winked knowingly and whispered, "A way to get your drug-dealer friends to put money into your account."

Theo gasped a second time. "No…no…not drug dealers."

"Sure," she said knowingly.

Theo waited for a smile; instead, she said in a professional voice, "Typically you give the company"—wink, wink—"or whomever a routing number and a copy of a deposit slip. It really isn't that hard. Even your druggie friends can do it. Since they're idiots and all."

"Um, Anna…"

She must've noticed the look on Theo's face because she quickly followed up by saying, "Look, this desk is like Doctor Phil…everything you say here is confidential. Everything except the bank-robbery question. If you do mention robbery, at that point, I'll be obligated to report you."

"Oh." Theo wasn't sure where this conversation had gone. He started to feel slightly confused.

"No, really." She smiled again at him. "I'm just joking. Try me. I'll tell you anything I can."

Theo rolled up his imaginary sleeves and glanced around. He noticed Sophia stepping into the bank manager's office. He said, "If my drug-dealer friends put money into my account, can they take it out at a later time?"

"No. Once the fruit of your work is inside the account, they cannot take it back out."

"What if it's another bank?"

"Well, that depends. If a check didn't clear, it leaves the account. But usually the owner of the account is the only one with access."

"What if a silent drug dealer put money into my account. Can I see what account it came from?"

"Most certainly. We can track the business name from where the silent partner placed your cash."

"That's all the questions I have."

"Those were pathetic. Come on, give me a hard question. I'm the best there is. I can do the impossible."

Theo ran through everything he could think of. "Sorry. You're a genius and answered a whole lot."

Before he stood, she said, "I noticed that you were looking at that girl talking with my manager. Do you know her?"

Theo hesitated. A moment later, he leaned in and whispered, "I'm a medical student. She was walking ahead of me when I came into the bank. She looked uncomfortable and very pregnant. I can't help but be worried about her. She looks like she might go into contractions at any moment."

Anna stared at the closed door Sophia had entered. "That was former employee of the year Sophia LaCross. I didn't even recognize her."

"Wait. You know who she is?"

"Yeah. She used to work here."

Anna added quickly, "Did you want a debit card for your account?"

Theo replied, "I haven't any money in it yet. I mostly wanted a savings account, so I can have a place to stock a few dollars and not spend it."

"Oh…" she said. She handed him his folder. "The routing number is on a separate sheet. Turn that in to your employer, and thanks for stopping by Bank of America."

"Thanks, Anna."

She glanced down, and for the first time Theo noticed her name tag—Julie Duprey. Before he could remark on her name, she said, "Next."

Theo was pushed out of the way as a father and his two sons came forward, taking his spot. Theo knew he couldn't just wait in the bank for Sophia, and he began making his way toward the front door.

When he was halfway to the door, the manager's door crashed open, and a man's voice echoed around the room. "Soph…I don't know what to say. I'll get this resolved by tomorrow."

Sophia asked, "Does that mean that the rest of my money is frozen?"

"I'm sure it's a misunderstanding."

"Unbelievable." Sophia took a deep breath to calm herself and nodded. "Call me when it's fixed."

"I will."

Theo reached the door, and without a second glance he stepped outside. When he was clear of the building, he scanned the area, unsure of what else to do as he tried wrapping his mind around what had just happened.

The door opened and Sophia stepped outside. She appeared as angry as Theo had ever seen her; however, her expression softened considerably when she saw him.

"What was that?"

"I'll tell you in the car."

As they hurried around to the back of the building, he asked, "Is everything okay?"

"Not sure. Something weird is going on."

Theo unlocked the doors, and they hurried inside. He started the car and drove out of the parking lot, turned left twice in quick succession.

Sophia said, "My account is truly frozen."

"What?"

"Someone tried pretending to be me and clearing out my money yesterday."

"At this location?"

"No. A bank downtown."

The car began to slow as Theo tried to process the information.

Sophia yelled, "Watch out!"

Theo jerked up and noticed Anna standing in the middle of the road as if looking around. They were almost directly in front of the bank. Theo swerved to missed her and Anna reacted by twisting to staring into the car.

"What the hell is she doing?"

"That's Anna."

"You know her?"

"She was the teller that opened my account. She was super friendly but I have no idea what she is doing."

"What is her name?"

"Anna," Theo replied. "But her name badge read Julie Duprey."

Sophia paused for a moment. "That wasn't the Anna that I know. Mack, my boss, told me that Julie quit five months ago."

Theo replied, "She told me that you were the employee of the year."

"I don't know that girl."

Glancing in the rearview mirror, Theo watched as two guys sprinted up to Anna. She spoke to them briefly and pointed in his direction. Theo said nothing but hit the gas pedal and turned the next corner. He did not like what he had just seen.

A few minutes later, Theo said, "That was quite the argument with your boss."

"Mack did that to throw off whatever is going on. He was helping me."

Theo asked, "How?"

"They tried closing my account. When I first called my boss, I guess I asked questions about the money in the account. At the time, he was confused about why I was asking about money in my own account. Mack admitted that he started watching the account closely. He also looked into who sent the money. It took some time to find out."

"He just had this information waiting for you?"

"Sort of." She turned slightly in her seat. "While he trying to identify who sent the money, he came across information showing that someone from a different branch was also looking into my account. He believes that they were trying to cover the tracks of the original sender. Mack got spooked and tried placing a hold on my account. It was denied. A close colleague at corporate finally traced the money to a separate account. It came from a company called Hartman Security LLC, but Mack couldn't access any additional information about them. Also hidden was who was looking into your account."

"Wow," Theo said. "I can't believe all this is happening at your bank."

"There's more."

"Like what?"

"Yesterday a girl showed up with a driver's license with my name on it. She intended to empty the account and close it. Fortunately, Mack was notified the moment someone started the process. He called over and was allowed to get it frozen. The girl ran off when she was approached."

Theo checked the rearview mirror as he entered the freeway heading north. No one was following them. "Now that you've escaped St. Jude's, maybe they're shutting things down."

"Exactly." Sophia leaned back. "But who was that girl?"

"Anna?"

"I've never seen her before."

"It seems unlikely that Dr. Haderly put a girl in the bank to watch for you."

"I can't explain it either," Sophia said, appearing puzzled.

Theo asked, "At what location did someone pretend to be you and try to withdraw the money?"

"Downtown. A bank on Island Avenue."

"Maybe we should go there and see if they will show us the security videos?"

"You think they will just let anyone inside?"

"It's worth a shot. Maybe Mack can pull some strings."

"I'll call him when we get to the bank. I also want to ask him, 'Who the hell is Anna?'"

CHAPTER 16

The Bank of America, on Island Avenue was an ideal location. It had easy access to downtown, with lots of foot traffic, and it was close to several outdoor stores, and close to several bus stops. They sat in the rental car as Sophia finished talking on the phone with Mack. Apparently, a few minutes after Theo and Sophia left the bank, a girl name Gwen, matching Anna's description, had told the bank manager that she was going to lunch. She had yet to return. Gwen had worked at the bank for the last two months and wouldn't have met Sophia. Sophia explained their plan to see the video and Mack said he would call the downtown location.

Theo stared out the window and watched a dozen shoppers pass by. It dawned on him that they were only two blocks from Club Jazzed. He doubted that this was a coincidence, but he also couldn't see a connection in his mind.

Theo stepped from the car and called his friend Zorn Davies. Like Patrick, Zorn had been uninterested in hearing about Sophia, her problems, and her disappearance. The first few times he approached the subject, Zorn remained impartial and didn't encourage Theo to provide more details. This time, he was slightly more interested in hearing about their findings at the bank and the two companies, BioPharm and Hartman Security LLC.

Zorn said, in his unemotional voice, "I'll do you a favor and look into both companies. Glad your friend is safe, but don't lose your job because you're pretending to be someone you aren't."

"Thanks for the vote of confidence."

"I just don't want you losing focus on what is really important."

"I won't."

Zorn added, "You and Patrick should come over for to watch a Padres game. We could do a barbecue."

"If I ever get all this figured out, I would love to."

Zorn added, "Patrick has been pretty busy himself. He's hoping to test for a promotion."

"I'm not surprised. Sounds like Patrick. What are you working on?"

"Just some things along the border. It's busy for a few days than nothing. It'll give me a chance to look into these two companies."

"I'd appreciate it."

Ever since he first met Zorn, he kept everyone at a distance, even at the bureau. He didn't like working with others but was tenacious at research. Theo didn't think he was well-liked by his superiors, but he was one of their top agents. He was loyal to a fault and had helped Theo get through losing Hannah. Zorn had helped solve her murder, and this opened the doors to the FBI. Her killer was now sitting on death row at Pleasant Valley Correctional Facility, the same location where Hannah had worked largely because of Zorn's relentlessness.

Theo asked, "Zorn, can you do me a favor?"

"Um…"

"Keep this information under wraps. This has to be off-the-books and low-key."

"I know how to do my job," Zorn answered, but not harshly.

They made plans to get together in a few weeks. Theo would call Patrick and share the details. Zorn would call back if he had more information. He hung up the phone and got back into the car.

Sophia, having already finished her call, asked, "Are we good?"

"Zorn is detailed and tremendous at uncovering any issues. He'll look into BioPharm and Hartman Security and let us know if he finds anything."

"Good." Sophia added, "Mack called the bank and I think we're good to go inside."

Theo asked, "Have you ever been to this location?"

"No. I knew they had a branch here, but that's it. I've never had a reason to come down here." There was a chime on her cellphone. She read it and said, "Mack says that we've been given ten minutes to look at the image on the screen."

"Here we go."

They stepped out of the car and approached the bank. It sat on the corner and took up three stories. Theo imagined that the upper two floors were strictly offices and the bottom floor was the bank itself. The automated teller machine was inside the first set of doors and could be accessed after hours, while the main doors were locked. Theo held the door as they entered the bank.

They found chairs against the sidewall, sat and waited. Fifteen minutes later, a portly man stepped from an office door that read, "Bank Manager." He waved for them to come over, but when Theo stood, the bank manager shook his head, and only Sophia was allowed in. The door to the office shut, and Sophia disappeared. A few minutes later,

Theo became fidgety. He couldn't sit any longer and started pacing. He felt anxious when Sophia wasn't next to him.

Finally, the door opened, and Sophia stepped out. Her face was expressionless. She approached and, without a word, walked past him and out the door. Instead of heading directly to the rental car, she marched toward the shopping area. Theo caught up and Sophia's arm intertwined with his.

They entered a Skechers store. Sophia found two pairs of shoes within minutes and moved to and area to try them on.

Theo whispered, "What are we doing here?"

"Looking at shoes."

"But why?"

"Maybe you should consider a few pairs yourself."

Theo added, "I've had enough shopping to last for the rest of the year."

As she tried on the second pair, she said, "The picture on the screen wasn't a great shot. She left a phone number, and they're considering calling her back in to close the account. If they do, they'll call me. They don't have any intention of closing the account. Mack must've really worked his magic."

"Really?"

"That's what he said. The bank manager recommended a pizza restaurant that would provide a great view of the front of the bank."

"They're going to call her now?"

"I hope so."

Theo sat next to her and asked, "So what's wrong?"

Her head turned, and she gazed up at him. "They have pictures of me before I was pregnant and during my pregnancy, coming to this bank and taking out money.

I was never alone, but whoever was with me couldn't be seen on camera. It was mostly from the ATM after hours. Each time, someone waited for me outside the bank or stood next to me out of the view of the camera. They found evidence that whoever was looking into my account, was erasing these withdraws."

"That's crazy."

Sophia said, "I'm going to buy these two pairs."

As they walked to the register, he asked, "Was it weird seeing yourself?"

"Totally. Especially since I can't remember what happened." In a different tone, she mumbled, "I hope these two pairs are on sale."

"Are we getting pizza after this?"

"You're damn right we are."

Sophia paid, and they hurried toward the pizzeria. As if reading his mind, Sophia said, "If I really wanted to torture you, I'd drag you into the Lingerie Lounge." She pointed to the store sign ahead.

"And I'd say—heck no."

"Maybe it would help me remember something."

"A pregnant woman looking for some lingerie opening a lost memory."

She shrugged playfully. "It happens."

Once inside the pizzeria, Theo ordered food while Sophia found them a seat. He grabbed some soda and sat across from her. They were near the front of the restaurant, with a perfect view of the front doors of the bank. They sat in silence until their food arrived.

Theo asked, "I think this might have something to do with Club Jazzed. We are just two blocks away."

"The club you went to while I was missing and hit on the waitress."

Theo snorted. "I wouldn't exactly describe it like that."

"But you were drinking, got buzzed, and ended up at her place."

"In a roundabout way."

"If I can't remember coming to the bank to withdraw money, I wouldn't be surprised if I was a dancer at Club Jazzed. Who knows…maybe that's where I got pregnant?"

"That place is weird and exciting at the same time. I never saw anything risky going on."

"Maybe you weren't looking hard enough."

"I could try to call Cindy and have her meet you."

Sophia's head lifted from her food. "I don't know if I can handle meeting anyone new."

Sophia's phone rang, and she answered it. She listened and finished by saying, "Thanks." To Theo she said, "The girl answered but changed her mind about closing the account. She won't be coming after all."

Theo sank into his seat and restarted eating. Sophia picked at her food and appeared to be dwelling on the bad news. Theo finished his pizza and drink and debated their next move. He was leaning toward going back to the hotel and relaxing for the afternoon.

Sophia's shoulders suddenly tensed.

"What is it?"

"I've seen that guy before."

Theo turned to see the well-dressed Mr. Jack strolling near the bank. Next to him were three women, all of whom were dressed as if they worked at Club Jazzed. Theo asked, "How do you know him?"

"I can't be sure," Sophia mumbled. "But I'm almost positive that I've talked to him before."

"He's an important person at Club Jazzed. He's the one that gave me a black card that will get me anything

I want. The other girls were frightened of him, like he would fire them on the spot."

Theo felt his heart racing as he watched Tina step away from Mr. Jack and march into the bank. Mr. Jack remained outside.

"What is it?" Sophia asked.

"My waitress from Club Jazzed just went into the bank. She introduced me to Cindy. What's she doing here?"

"Do you think it was her trying to pull out the money from the account?"

"I would've never guessed it, but maybe."

"What do we do now?"

"Wait and watch."

Ten minutes later, Tina stepped out of the bank, shaking her head. Even from here, Theo could tell that Mr. Jack was not happy. The bouncer glanced around as if searching for someone and Theo was relieved that they were nearly impossible to see. Mr. Jack grabbed Tina's arm and jerked her toward a Cadillac that pulled up. Tina was thrown into the back seat. The two other girls scurried inside, followed by Mr. Jack. The Cadillac rolled forward, flipped a U-turn, and raced back down the road, disappearing a moment later.

Theo and Sophia exited the pizzeria as quickly as they could. They hurried across the street. Theo rushed to get the car while Sophia ran into the bank. He parked the car directly across from the bank, and when she came out, she slid into the passenger seat.

"Yep. Same girl. The manager was surprised to see her. She came in to explain her actions. She admitted that she wasn't Sophia LaCross, but rather Amy LaCross, my sister, and she told a story of coming to California from Kansas to look for me. She had tracked me down to San

Diego. She had a matching driver's license and asked that he call her if he saw me again."

Theo stared back at Sophia, shell shocked.

A horn blared behind him, and Theo slowly drove forward. Two minutes later, they navigated past Club Jazzed and parked down the street. He couldn't see the Cadillac anywhere.

Sophia said, "I've been clubbing here before, one time. With Mary and some friends when it first opened."

"Did you ever work here?" he asked.

"Not that I can remember, but that doesn't mean a thing."

"Did you recognize Tina?"

She shook her head. She wondered aloud, "Should we go inside?"

"Not yet. I'm not sure how all this plays into it yet. We need to find a way to talk to Tina without Mr. Jack around. Maybe, we'll come back later tonight."

"Let's go back to St. Jude's," Sophia said.

Theo cried, "What? That's a horrible idea."

"We need to know more about Dr. Haderly. How can he be connected with Club Jazzed? Does he know Mr. Jack?"

"That's stupid. They're looking for you, and probably me."

"It's a chance we're going to have to take."

Theo ran his fingers through his hair and noticed the sweat running down Sophia's face. He kicked himself for dragging around a pregnant girl. He was about to voice his opinion when she grumbled, "Take me there or I'll go by myself."

Theo groaned and glanced at her again. The look on her face was fierce. He muttered, "Yes, ma'am. As you wish."

As he drove, Theo asked, "What are you going to do after the baby is born?"

Sophia visibly relaxed. "I've asked myself the same question a dozen times. I never knew where my mom went after she left my dad and me. Now that he's gone, my options are very limited. Logic says to give the baby up for adoption and start over. I'm just not sure that I can do that."

"Where will you work?"

"With the money I have in the bank, I'm thinking of going back to school."

"That's a good idea."

She punched his arm. "You sound surprised."

"Maybe a little."

She added, "I've always wanted to do something with numbers, maybe grad school in accounting."

Theo grinned. "Never saw that one coming. I didn't know that you were into constant boredom."

"Don't rain on my parade. Accounting is better than being a doctor."

"No way."

"Totally."

Theo took an indirect route to St. Jude's. He drove on streets he'd never been on before. He found an open space in a San Diego Transit lot. There were rows and rows of cars, each facing the shelter's front door. This was farther back than when he'd been with Jane.

"Are we too far away?" Sophia asked.

"This is as close as I am comfortable with."

Sophia pointed out, "I really doubt they would expect us to come back here."

"I'm not taking any chances."

"We don't even know if he's here today."

"Oh yeah, we do."

"How?"

"I sort of spent a fair amount of time here, looking for you." He pointed down the street to a car parked only half in view. "His car is the blue BMW 3 Series."

"Well, that doesn't stick out."

"He probably runs these streets, and no one would do anything to his car."

"What do you mean, runs these streets?"

"If he's meeting up with a pharm company or Club Jazzed, maybe his involvement is pain pills. Everyone uses those these days. It is a perfect party drug. If you recognized Mr. Jack, there must be a connection. Selling drugs on the streets is huge business. The few blocks around this shelter are some of the heaviest selling-grounds for drugs in Southern California. I think that Dr. Haderly has his hands involved somehow. Expanding to the club scene isn't too surprising."

"You think medications are a possibility of what caused me to have some memory issues?"

"High doses of pain meds can cause recall issues, as well as some antipsychotics, and others. But it's hard to understand how you would've forgotten months' worth of memories. There are possible side effects of personality changes, dissociations, and much more."

"But with no withdrawal issues?"

"Exactly." Theo asked, "Do you remember Dr. Haderly working with anyone else?"

"I can barely remember him. I'm going off the things that you said about him. It would be good to get a look at his face." She added, "A camera would help us identify anyone he talks with."

"Are you serious?"

"How do you expect to get any dirt on this prick if we don't have a camera? You going to use your prepaid cell phone?"

"Maybe," replied Theo.

Taking her new cell phone, she did a Google search and found a Ritz Camera store within a block of the BioPharm parking structure. It was still early afternoon, so they took a chance and dove directly to the camera store. Inside the store, they spent over $2,000 on a camera and more money on an extra telephoto zoom, an eight gigabyte memory card, a rechargeable battery, and a case. The store owner tossed in an extra battery for free, already half charged and ready for immediate use.

Forty minutes later, after stopping for some takeout food, they parked back in the same spot as before, sat back, and scrutinized the front door. The blue BMW hadn't moved an inch. The first hour was as uneventful. Theo found it extremely easy to talk with Sophia. They jumped from one topic to another. At one point, Sophia thought she noticed groupings of pregnant women like he and Jane had seen. She used the camera and zoomed in. Over the next twenty minutes, at least eight pregnant women walked through the front doors. Most appeared homeless and came from the same direction Sophia had been traveling, when he found her the second time, but the gated apartment building was out of view.

She whispered, "They look demoralized."

Theo was about to respond when he spotted a group of four or five girls huddled around a guy in his thirties or forties. He wasn't homeless, and he was dressed better than anyone within a ten-block radius. Suddenly, he motioned a few girls forward.

"Do you see that guy?" He pointed to the left. "Can you take his picture?"

There was no response.

"What is he doing with those girls?" Theo asked. "We need to get closer."

Theo glanced over at Sophia and was floored to find that she was crouching down in her seat shaking. "What's wrong?"

"Don't know," she mumbled. Her whole body shook. "My...my instincts took over when I saw that creep."

"You know him?"

Sophia shuddered. "Same feeling as when I saw Mr. Jack. I'm certain I've seen him before, just don't know how."

Theo reached for the camera and focused on the man. He seemed to be removing something from the wrists of two of the girls, possibly bracelets. Using the camera, he zoomed in, and the bracelets looked familiar. These girls weren't pregnant, but they weren't dressed up. It wasn't hard to imagine that they could be spruced up enough with clothes and makeup to work at Club Jazzed. Focusing back on the man, Theo noticed that he was tall, well-dressed, and skinny. He was strong and in control.

Twenty minutes later, long after the creep went inside and the girls left, Sophia still sat with her hands clenched, breathing rapidly. It took some convincing for her to return to her seat. It took another twenty minutes for her to calm down enough to speak. She took Theo's hand and whispered softly, "Sorry about that. I totally freaked."

"It's clear that guy is a problem. We need to find out who he is." He continued holding her hand. She squeezed it but didn't let go. "It's about time that you acted a little out of control. A little emotional. I was starting to get a complex that I was the only irrational one here."

She chuckled, but the sound died in her throat, and her grip on his hand tightened. Theo followed her gaze and saw Dr. Haderly and the well-dressed creep walking together. Theo managed to lift the camera and take a few pictures of the two men as they crossed the street. Dr. Haderly was angry, and the creep responded by stopping mid-step, pointing directly at Dr. Haderly, and saying something. The two argued for another few minutes. The creep's hand went to grab ahold of Dr. Haderly's shoulder, but the doctor knocked away the attempt. The creep raised both hands and quickly apologized. It was clear that Dr. Haderly was in control here.

The next few sentences appeared to be commands and the creep moved his head slightly to indicate he understood. When the conversation was over, the creep turned and walked back in the direction of St. Jude's. Instead of going inside, the man turned right and disappeared down an alley.

"My bet is that he works for the club," Theo said softly.

"Maybe," Sophia said in a breathy voice.

Dr. Haderly pulled out a cell phone as he unlocked his car and slipped inside. Theo backed out of the spot, drove to the corner, and waited. A few seconds later, the doctor pulled out, and Theo and Sophia began following the BMW.

CHAPTER 17

They remained several car lengths behind Dr. Haderly as he traveled across town. Theo drove and every few seconds, he peeked over at Sophia. She had calmed down but was still on edge. He handed back the camera, but there was no point in using it at this time.

"Where are we going?" Sophia asked. "Is the pharmaceutical company this far away?"

Theo responded, "No. BioPharm is back closer to the shelter, near where we bought the camera."

"He's not going to Club Jazzed."

"Nope."

Theo worried that they had chosen the wrong person to follow. He was eager to discover who the well-dressed creep was. What if Dr. Haderly was heading out of town, on vacation, and they were wasting their time. He was so focused on avoiding getting too close, that he almost missed the familiar road that Dr. Haderly turned on, Overland Avenue. An icy chill ran down Theo's spine.

"Theo. Are you okay?"

Shaking his head, Theo responded in a surprised tone, "You probably don't remember where we are, but up ahead is the medical examiner's office. This is where they did the autopsy on Mary and the last place I'd imagine we would end up."

"Why would he come here?"

"It better not be to see Dr. Celeste Lazar."

"Did I meet her?"

"No. But I told her a few things about you. She has helped more than once. I just hope that by working with her, I didn't make things worse."

Theo parked near the coffee shop, giving them a perfect view of Dr. Haderly's car. For an instant, he considered calling Celeste to see if she had any pending appointments. As the BMW came to a stop in front of the building, Theo's mind pictured the beautiful ME stepping from the front door and walking to the awaiting car. Instead he saw a man dressed entirely in black approaching the car.

"Who's that?" Sophia asked desperately.

"That's a colleague of Dr. Lazar. I can't remember his name."

Sophia asked, "And he works for the medical examiner's office? Why would Dr. Haderly be meeting up with him?"

"I have no idea."

The man slid into the car and the blue BMW pulled away from the ME's office and disappeared.

Sophia turned to him and asked, "Aren't we going to follow them?"

Theo debated what he should do. He was worried that following Dr. Haderly would lead Sophia directly back to him. "No," he replied slowly. "I think it might be better if we get some answers." He parked the car behind the coffee shop, in a hidden area. "I'll be back in fifteen minutes. Don't get out and call me if you see anyone."

"Are you sure?"

"No. I feel like I'm blind." He touched her shoulder. "I'll be back. It won't be long."

She did not appear convinced that he was making the right decision, or maybe she was afraid.

Theo pushed through the front door of the ME's office. It was early evening, and the receptionist was already gone. He continued to the back door and knocked loudly. Two minutes later, the door clicked open, and he found himself staring at Dr. Bowthorpe. Theo had forgotten his name, but fortunately, he wore a name tag.

"I'm Dr. Raden, looking for Dr. Lazar." Theo stepped forward without receiving a response. He walked down the corridor and into the unique office area.

"You can't just barge in here," whined Dr. Bowthorpe, trailing behind Theo.

Turning left, Theo went directly to the autopsy rooms but found no one and all the lights were out. He tried going down a hall where he thought she might be working, but the door was locked.

Dr. Bowthorpe said, "I recognize you. You were here a few months ago."

Theo said, "I'm still a medical student and I needed to do some research."

"This isn't a good time," said Dr. Bowthorpe. "You need to leave."

As Theo retraced his steps, a door without a nameplate opened, and Dr. Lazar stepped into view. She wore a long black elegant dress that matched her hair. Her makeup complemented her evening wear. Her eyes found him, and she smiled, warmly but with confusion.

"What are you…?"

Her eyes found Dr. Bowthorpe, and she stopped immediately.

Dr. Bowthorpe announced, "Dr. Raden is looking for you." His smile was full of contempt, and he didn't bother to hide it.

"And why is that?" Dr. Lazar said quickly. "I'm headed to a charity event at the Museum of Contemporary Art. I was supposed to leave five minutes ago."

"Isn't that two blocks from your house?" Dr. Bowthorpe said scathingly. "Couldn't you have the decency to get dressed there?"

"And miss your enchanting declaration of my looks? How could I miss that?" Her attention turned to Theo. "And Dr. Raden, to what do I owe this pleasure?"

"A quick question about…"

Dr. Lazar interrupted him. "Will you excuse us, Dr. Bowthorpe? This is about a patient we are working on, and I need to get some papers from my office."

Dr. Bowthorpe grunted and retreated down the hall to the offices. Instead of sitting down, he removed an old-fashioned coat from the rack and headed out of the building. He mumbled, "I was leaving anyway. This place has gone to the dogs. Who does she think she is?"

Dr. Lazar smiled the entire time; only a slight chink in her armor, a facial twitch, was effected by his rant.

"Well, Theo, please hurry. I do need to leave soon."

"Dr. Lazar. I need information on one of your workers."

"Call me Celeste, remember?" She glanced at him suspiciously. "Who and why?"

"A tall man. I've seen him before. He wears all black."

Celeste laughed emphatically. "You mean Dr. Daniels, who's about as flashy as it gets. What, did he beat you at poker, steal your clothes or your girlfriend?" As she tilted her head, he realized that she was sizing him up. "You're not his type. But he's worked here for about three years and has said less than five sentences to anyone, including me, his boss. But he does great work."

"So he's a loner?"

Her look changed so fast that Theo was unprepared for it. She marched forward, and a second later her finger thumped his chest twice. "Don't go knocking my employees, even if they do seem a little different." He didn't understand the severity of her mood change. Through a clenched jaw, she said, "I think I'm done here?"

Theo blocked her. "I'm not sure what's going on here. But I'm not leaving until I get some answers."

"Like what?" Her voice was icy cold.

"Did Dr. Daniels help you with any part of Mary's autopsy?"

The fierceness in her eyes blazed, but she remained calm. "He did. He helped with item identification, postmortem cleaning, and, in fact, he assisted me on the autopsy itself."

"Where was he before coming here?"

"ME's office up in San Francisco, I think."

Theo glanced around and found Dr. Daniels's desk. "Please don't take this as an attack, but for someone so colorful, he doesn't really decorate like he's staying for a long time."

"What makes you think he is colorful?"

"You're the one who said it."

Celeste stood there staring at him for several seconds, brooding. After a moment, he realized that she wasn't going to answer. Theo said, "I'll see myself out." He made his way in the direction of the outer door.

A few seconds later, he heard, "Theo, stop," but he kept walking.

Soft steps echoed behind him and soon Dr. Lazar had caught up. "What are you really doing here? I doubt this noble story about Mary is why you're here. Why can't you be honest with me?"

"I told you, I want information about Dr. Daniels."

"Come in here," she said, opening a door part way down the hallway. They entered a laboratory room with a dozen shelves, some equipment, and six large tables that would allow items to be placed in an organized fashion. "Look, someone is poking their heads into my department. That may not mean much to you, but I'm here to make sure nothing—"

"Is found out," he interrupted.

"No," she insisted. "What I was going to say is misinterpreted. Medicine has a big problem, especially when you're talking about autopsies of potential victims. One small step could lead to a dozen cases overturned. One misinterpretation could lead to a killer going free. My team needs to know that they aren't viewed as the enemy by the mayor, the governor, or any of their friends. If I find that you're a part of this witch hunt, I'll find a way to go after your license."

"Thanks for clearing that up for me." Theo pushed past her. "And threats on top of it all."

She grabbed his arm. "I just want you to understand. This is serious."

"Oh, I understand, but I'm not sure what it really means. Are you involved in a cover-up or is that just Dr. Daniels?"

"What are you so pissed about?" she asked.

"Just wondering why Dr. Daniels keeps popping up around Miss Sneider."

"He doesn't," Dr. Lazar said, exhausted. "Why are you worried about one case? Is this still about Sophia? What I'm referring to is much bigger than one case."

"I'm not part of whatever you're worried about. I don't even know who works here. The only person that I care about is Dr. Daniels."

"All right. Dr. Daniels has done a great job. He's the only one that doesn't knock me about my appointment here. Dr. Bowthorpe is the absolute worst. Dr. Marshall, whose desk has the palm tree and sand, thinks women are only good for bringing him a drink on the beach. He's asked me to join him several times, by the way. He'd have sex on the autopsy table if he thought it could be seen by the rest of the staff."

"For someone who is tight about her staff, you don't seem to like very many of them."

"Dr. Daniels is different. He hasn't said a single derogatory thing to me."

"I'm glad he is nice, but I'm trying to understand how Mary's death is connected with Sophia's disappearance."

"How could I forget? I was the one who gave you the list of clubs."

"Do you remember when I told you about that doctor at the homeless shelter?"

"I remember. Isn't he the one that prevented Sophia from leaving?"

"Well, I tracked her down. She was worse off than before. The doctor at the homeless shelter did something to her."

"I don't see what that has to do with me or with Dr. Daniels."

"Well, not fifteen minutes ago that doctor arrived at your ME's office, and Dr. Daniels got into his car, and they drove away.

"Are you sure?"

"In a city with thousands of doctors, it happens that one of your staff is friends with the one person who is somehow directly involved in all of this."

"There must be an explanation."

"I agree. Just not one that you're going to like."

"You don't know that."

"Mary went to one of the clubs on the list a few nights before she died. She was searching for Sophia, who had disappeared. You found a hidden list of clubs that were marked off in her clothing. It was placed in a plastic bag."

"Probably just a coincidence. It doesn't mean she didn't drown."

"Could it be possible that she didn't die in the pool but somewhere else?"

"Well, she definitely died by drowning. I can't guess other than what I know."

"I know that," Theo said.

"Then what are you saying?"

"I don't know yet. The clearer portion of the picture shows that Dr. Daniels, the homeless shelter, Sophia, and the death of Mary Sneider may all be connected. I need to find out how Dr. Haderly and Dr. Daniels know each other."

Celeste did a double take. "Did you say Dr. Haderly...Dr. Thomas Haderly?"

"That's the doctor from the homeless shelter."

She laughed derisively. "Dr. Haderly is incompetent, and he's been trying to get inside this building for the last ten years. Even my predecessor hated him." Shaking her head, she added, "Why would Dr. Daniels be meeting with him? He knows the problems we've had with him."

"What else do you know about Dr. Daniels?"

"He came to us from a small medical examiner's office in San Francisco. He'd only been working there a year. I knew that he had left some problems, but he assured me it was because of a personality issue with some of the other staff. He told me that San Diego is a better fit for him."

"Has he ever talked about Dr. Haderly?"

"Nothing more than adding his complaints to mine. Dr. Thomas Haderly has tried to form a friendship with the mayor. I have heard the rumors that he wants to be inside this building."

"Why would Dr. Daniels be meeting with him?"

"I'm going to find out," she said, pulling out her phone.

"No!" Theo shouted. "We can't let either of them know that we're following them."

"We?" asked Dr. Lazar.

"Some of my coworkers have been helping. And you need to get going to the charity event."

"That's the last place I want to be tonight." Leaning against the wall, she stared at him. Her eyes sparkled, and a small smile played on her lips. "Will you get some dinner with me tonight?"

"I can't." It took every ounce of self-control for him to decline.

Her smile widened slightly, and Theo wondered if she might have guessed at his inner conflict. Instead of pushing the subject, she asked, "Is Sophia out in the car?"

"Yes."

"Okay." Her tone returned to normal. "I'll call you tomorrow with what I find out about Dr. Daniels." Prodding her own dress, she added, "I better hurry to make the gala. There will be a lot of eyes on me tonight. Sorry if I came down too hard on you. I'm very protective, and you seemed to have an ulterior motive."

"Just trying to find the truth."

"Good luck with that. Want to walk out together?"

"Sure."

They left the laboratory room and walked down the hall. After exiting the front door, Celeste said goodbye, hugged him, and hurried to her BMW. Theo crossed the street to the coffee shop's parking lot, where Sophia stood waiting for him.

After he opened the door and sat down, Sophia asked, "Did you have to go inside and see her?"

Her tone surprised him. He turned to find her glaring at him. "That was Dr. Celeste Lazar, the medical examiner and Dr. Daniels's boss. I was trying to figure out if there could be a cover-up with Mary's case."

"And?"

Theo started the car. "We can't trust Dr. Daniels or Dr. Haderly. They're working together on something, and Celeste didn't know what it was."

"Celeste?"

"That's her name."

She grumbled, "I think we should have followed them."

"We need to be careful." He drove toward the freeway.

"Why?"

"Dr. Haderly and Dr. Daniels have a lot more power than I do. They could've said that I kidnapped you from a facility where they were trying to help you because of your mental health. I'm still a student and have no standing. Those two know each other, and going forward, we need to be extremely careful."

"I guess." Sophia stared out the window quietly for a few minutes. She turned back to Theo and asked, "What's next?"

"Let's call it a night, get some dinner, and make a plan for the next few days."

"Fine. I'm exhausted."

"Are you mad at me?"

She remained silent as he continued driving. "Not mad but frustrated. I felt we were on the cusp of getting answers and you went a different direction…to see your girlfriend."

"She's not my—" He didn't finish the sentence. When he spoke next, he said, "I'm the reason you got lost last time. I don't want it to happen again."

As they drove north to Mt. Soledad Freeway, they headed toward the hotel. Theo was exhausted, and Sophia kept him awake by reviewing everything they knew. She started speculating about Dr. Haderly. After this she tried to remember if she had seen Mary while she was pregnant. They went over Mary's autopsy report again—nothing surprising. Today's revelations with seeing Dr. Daniels meet with Dr. Haderly and seeing Tina at the bank provided more questions than answers.

They went through a drive-through, and Sophia ordered a variety of things. They barely had enough room in the back seat for the soda, burger, shake, and fries. Theo drove to a trash can and said, "Let's get rid of our cellphones. We can open new ones tonight."

"How will my boss get ahold of me?"

"We can call him again in a few days, but we gave our numbers to too many people today."

Sophia shrugged and they tossed their phones in a trash bin behind the fast-food restaurant. Theo drove away. He parked near the back of the hotel, and Sophia said, "We should scope out Club Jazzed tomorrow night. You can go in with Jane or something."

"Do you think that is a good idea?"

"She wants to help, and I clearly can't go inside." She shuffled to the door, with her hands full of food.

"Maybe," Theo said as he reached for the outer door. "I'll think about it."

CHAPTER 18

Theo woke up at 2:00 a.m. with the television as the only source of light in the room. The volume was barely audible, and glancing around, he saw that the room was empty. Throwing off his covers, Theo stood quickly. The bathroom door was closed. Theo knocked, but there was no answer. He pushed open the door, but it was also empty. He immediately began searching the room for the car and hotel keys but couldn't find them. Sprinting out to the parking lot, he found that a white minivan had taken the place of their rental car. Sophia was gone.

Theo circled the hotel twice but came up empty. Returning to his room, he couldn't find her purse or any of the money. Inside the second hotel room, all her new clothes and other items were neatly folded or stacked on the bed. Back in his own room, the toiletries, makeup, and cellphones were exactly where they should be.

He paced as wild thoughts drilled into his head. He imagined getting a phone call and learning that she had died. It was as if all the worst-case scenarios made complete sense. He had no idea why she hadn't woken him, or why she had left in the first place.

Twenty minutes later the door jingled open, and Sophia stepped in with her pregnant belly and arms full of bags of chocolate, Pepto-Bismol, soda, bottled water, iced coffee, and bags of potato chips.

Upon seeing that he was awake, Sophia asked, "Can a lady get some help here?"

Rushing to her side, Theo tried hiding his concerns, and took the bags from her. She was talking excitedly about getting out and how bad the traffic was. Theo listened as his heart rate slowly calmed.

Trying to sound as relaxed as possible, he said, "Next time you take off, could you possibly leave a note?"

She eyed him knowingly. "Did you miss me?"

"I was slightly caught off guard when you weren't here. I naturally thought something bad had happened."

"That's a natural thought for you?"

He chuckled. "Lately it is." He pulled out some glasses and a few plates. "I guess your cravings really did you over."

"Who doesn't want potato chips and milk chocolate at the same time?" She stuffed a fistful of food into her mouth.

"Good choices," he agreed.

Sophia asked, "When are you going to start dating Celeste?"

"What?"

"It was pretty obvious how she feels about you."

"We just met. She's a few years older than I am."

"I was missing for a few weeks. It seems like you've known her for a while."

"Right now is not a good time. My relationships are complicated." Theo couldn't deny his attraction to Celeste, and he thought she felt it too. He also hoped he was developing a friendship with Sophia. Then there was the mess with Danielle. He was in a horrible predicament, and with his history with Hannah, it wasn't a good idea.

"What is it?" Sophia asked.

"I don't think that anything is going to happen," he said honestly.

Sophia, as if perceiving his thoughts, added, "Not everything is supposed to make sense or be by the book. Just see what materializes."

"I guess."

Sophia stood and said, "I'm going to call it a night. I need to get some beauty sleep."

"Great idea." He turned off the lights after she had slipped under the covers. When he got in bed, he found a pillow between them.

"Is everything okay?"

Her voice was full of emotion when she said, "I'm fine. I can't afford to get too comfortable with you. I can't roll over and snuggle you; it wouldn't be fair for either of us."

"I can sleep in the other room if you want."

"I don't want that either. I want to be close with you, just not too close."

"I completely understand. Good night."

After five minutes of silence, Theo thought she'd fallen asleep. Her voice was low when she said, "In a few days, when we solve this, I probably won't ever see you again. That's fine but…"

"You probably can't get rid of me that easily."

"Good night," she whispered.

"I promise Sophia. Whatever happens, you and I are going to be good friends for a long time."

* * * *

Theo's phone began buzzing, and he rolled over, but it was on the table near the television. He assumed that

Dr. Jeffery was calling to demand that he come to the hospital for some sort of emergency. Theo eased out of bed, picked up his phone and the hotel key cards, and let himself out into the hall. Opening the second room, he stepped inside and said, "Dr. Theo Raden."

"Theo. Where the fuck are you, and what have you done?

Theo halted, and his head shot up. He focused on his phone. "Patrick. Is that you?"

"Don't play games with me, Theo." Patrick slowly hissed. "Where are you?"

"At a hotel. Where are you?"

"At my desk, at San Diego PD." Patrick's words held scorn and anger.

Theo recoiled at his tone. This was one of his best friends and it sounded like Patrick was speaking to him as a criminal.

"What's wrong Patrick? Not enough sleep last night?"

Patrick released a cynical laugh. "I'm playing tough-cop."

"Over the phone?" Theo questioned. "With me?"

Patrick's voice eased slightly, but Theo understood that something terrible had happened. "Can we meet for breakfast?"

"Why don't you tell me what's going on first?"

"Things are bad, Theo. You're wanted for questioning on a case by another detective."

Theo's mind turned to when he had broken into Sophia's apartment. She could square things away easily enough, no matter what Derek and Clayton would say. "Not sure what you're talking about. I'm with Sophia, and we're laying low."

"I need to see you today."

"Tell me why."

"Barrett Sanders was brutally killed last night."

Whatever Theo had previously understood about the bottom dropping out of a situation could not prepare him for the utter shock and devastation he experienced upon hearing this. "You've got to be kidding" was all he could manage to say.

"Not at all, my friend. You're chest high in this shit. We need to meet."

It took Theo several moments to recover. With a dry mouth and a thick tongue, he asked, "What the hell happened?"

Patrick whispered back into his own phone, "Theo, are you with me?"

He repeated, "What. The. Hell. Happened?"

"Detective Abbott has been out at your place since very early this morning. I shouldn't be telling you this, but a pool of blood was discovered leaking out from under your door. A neighbor saw it and called the cops. It isn't my case, but they want to talk to you."

"Oh heavenly misery, of all the ass-wipe things that could've gone wrong. This can't be happening!"

Patrick's voice was deep and commanding. "Where are you?"

"At a hotel with Sophia. I see you got my text last night about my new number."

"Yeah. Why *you* would need a new number is beyond my understanding. But I told you to stop playing hero. No one ever filed a missing report for Sophia. This is out of control."

"I haven't been to my apartment in a few days." Tears streamed down his face.

"They also found your car all burned to hell. You're the number one suspect."

"My car? I reported that stolen."

Patrick's voice was stern. "You idiot. You reported a car stolen just about the same time the medical examiner thinks your roommate was killed."

"There were cops at my work as witnesses."

"It doesn't matter. The ME found your blood at the scene, and a lot of it."

"What? How?" Theo couldn't believe what was happening. "Who signed off on the autopsy?"

"Why the hell does that matter?"

"Just tell me."

"I don't have it in front of me. Give me a second." A minute later, Patrick's voice came on the line. "Doctor Lucas Daniels."

"Incredible."

"Why? Do you know him?"

Instead of answering this, he asked, "Is Barrett really dead?"

"Yes, Theo. And you need to meet with me. I can facilitate your surrender."

"I've been with Sophia the entire time."

"I don't know Detective Abbott, but you're in a precarious situation by getting into the middle of this, and she's a pit bull, literally and figuratively. The first time you talk to her will be your only chance."

"I'm not coming in."

"They called your work this morning. Nurse Jane gave you an alibi, but it won't stick unless you have receipts for being out of town. You need to get somewhere far from here, and fast."

"Sophia can be my alibi."

"You know very little about her. My bet is, she has some instability."

"What are you saying?"

"She's unreliable. Either get out of town or turn yourself in."

Theo insisted, "We've been staying in a hotel for the last two nights. I haven't been anywhere near my apartment."

"How have you been getting around?"

"A rental car."

"Is it in your name?"

"No."

"You're screwed!" Patrick said.

"What are you talking about?"

"You've probably spent hundreds of dollars, and it will be tracked to your credit cards."

Theo laughed without humor. "Everything we've spent has been in cash. Don't you remember me telling you about Sophia's account?"

"You were serious."

"Something crazy is going on. I talked with Zorn yesterday, and he's looking into a few things for me."

"You've involved an FBI agent?"

"You weren't helping. We need some answers."

"Did Barrett get killed because of what you're looking into?"

"I don't know," Theo replied honestly.

"Look...stay low and keep out of sight until I can get a hold of the investigation report. I'll call you later today. I may be asking for you to come in and answer some questions. Maybe there is a way to keep your ass out of the flames."

"I appreciate that," he said honestly. "How did Barrett die?"

"His throat was slit, but it looked like he had been tortured. I heard that he was missing four fingers."

The phone disconnected, and Theo sat on the side of the bed. He was lost in his thoughts for a long time until he felt hands on his shoulders. His eyes focused to see Sophia standing next to him. She wiped at his eyes and waited patiently until he spoke. It took him well over half an hour to explain what Patrick had said on the phone.

When he finished, she said, "We need to get out of town."

"That's one idea," he said flatly.

"We're screwed." Sophia sat next to him on the bed. "What else are we supposed to do? We could go to the cops and explain things."

"I'm not sure we have any evidence that something has happened."

"But your roommate was killed."

"If we go to the cops, Dr. Haderly will swoop in and have some legalized paper saying that you're not competent to give any answers. He might show a video of you acting weird and out of control. They might have me on camera, dressed up and kidnapping you. You're my alibi for the killing of my roommate. If you're taken to the mental hospital or something, I'm going to prison for a long time. Dr. Daniels has linked my blood to the killing. Someone is trying to frame me." Theo's hand went to his head, where he had the laceration.

"We could leave, start somewhere new."

Her words were appealing. Reality would be far more difficult. They would always be looking over their shoulders, waiting to be caught. If they ran, he would be guilty. "If we leave, my career as a doctor is over before it really gets started. They'll put out a warrant for my arrest. No. We need to solve this thing. We need to connect Dr. Haderly to whatever is going on, and we need to find evidence of whoever is involved."

"And how do you think that will happen?"

"I'm going to take a shower and try to figure some of this out."

Thirty minutes later, Theo stepped out of the shower as Sophia began knocking on the door. "What's going on?"

Sophia said, "The manager and a police officer are at the door."

"What?" he asked as he opened the door with a towel around his waist, still dripping wet.

Loud knocking from the front door startled him. Theo yelled, "Coming!" Turning to Sophia, he said, "Get mostly undressed. Cover your stomach, so they don't know you're pregnant. Kick your leg onto the bed."

"What? Why?"

"Take off your underwear and your bra and toss them around the room."

"Are you serious?"

"Completely." Theo dried off as much as he could. He rubbed at his hair, causing it to become disheveled. He slid on some underwear.

The knocking at the door restarted for a third time, louder now. Theo hurried to the door and opened it slightly. "Hello."

"Good morning, Mr. Hunter. Is everything all right?"

"Without a doubt," Theo said in a slightly higher-pitched voice than usual. "But why in the world do you have the police with you?"

"Honey," Sophia called from the bed. "I'm waiting."

"Be right there, darling," Theo said, and the door inched opened slightly. He watched as the twenty-something hotel clerk and the fortyish male officer both did a double take. Theo's jaw almost dropped open. Sophia had her hands over her bare chest, and her leg was outside of the covers.

Somehow she had arranged herself to hide her belly, and she looked gorgeous. Theo had to pull his eyes away from her. Facing the two men, he said, "Hey guys, we're kind of busy. What's going on?"

The hotel clerk mumbled, "Someone reported some crying and yelling."

Theo quickly shrugged at the two men, his head tilting slightly. A newfound admiration was plastered on their faces. Theo smiled sheepishly "I don't think that was us."

The officer risked a glance at Sophia before saying, "Have you heard any strange noises?"

"Guilty," she said. "But there wasn't any crying or yelling."

"Oh…" grunted the hotel clerk.

"And"—Theo read the hotel clerk's name tag—"Ernie. Did you call the police?"

"No. No. He was already here on official business and decided to join me."

Sophia beckoned, "*Honeeeey, Pleeeease.*"

"Coming," Theo said quickly. "If we've been too loud, we're sincerely sorry. Officer McFarland, what is the official business of the police at a hotel?"

Officer McFarland stared at Sophia and mumbled, "We got a call last night about a possible kidnapping of a pregnant homeless women within this area. We're checking all the hotels in the area. Just part of the job."

Ernie said, "You have two rooms. Can we look at the second room?"

Theo knew that if they opened the door, they would find women's maternity clothes and makeup, and everything would fall apart.

He took a few steps out of the door, still in his underwear, and mostly closed the door. "Look, my colleague and I"—Theo used his head nod back into the room— "are in town on business. Our company pushed for two rooms. I can show you the other room, but we've decided that we only need one. We had to pay for both rooms to get reimbursed and to make it look...well...you know..."

"Politically correct," Ernie finished the statement.

Theo winked and the officer and the hotel clerk shared a knowing glance. They both turned back to him and smiled.

Theo said, "I really don't want to keep her waiting any longer."

"Understood," said Ernie.

The officer also gave a quick nod, and Theo slipped back inside the door. He said a little louder than normal, "I'm back."

Sophia giggled and Theo closed the door. As he approached the bed, Sophia whispered. "What's happening?"

Theo's eyes darted to the door, trying to clue her in. She finally realized what he was doing. In a pouty voice, she added, "Did you forget to grab my fruity drink?"

"Right." Theo leaped from the bed and made his way to the fridge. He opened it and returned with an empty bottle of water.

"That's better," Sophia sang. She began giggling so flirtatiously that Theo was almost convinced. He had to breathe deeply and picture in his mind the first cadaver he had ever touched for his heartbeat to slow down.

He heard the voices of Ernie and the officer talking as they walked away from the doorway. He heard Ernie say, "Lucky bastard."

Theo whispered, "These walls are paper thin."

As if just on cue, yelling and screaming echoed from a room above them, and soon they heard steps running toward the stairs.

When they were gone, Sophia asked, "What did they say?"

Theo stood and started searching for her clothing. "The officer received information that a pregnant girl who had been kidnapped was in the neighborhood, and he was checking all of the hotels."

"There's no way that this is a coincidence."

"Exactly what I was thinking."

"What now?"

"We probably need to stay another night, but you can't be seen. I have to tell you, you did an amazing job."

"Are you surprised?"

"Sort of."

She sat up. "Many women are great at flirting with guys. This was no different."

"I guess," Theo said. "You definitely had the officer and hotel clerk wishing they were me."

"All part of the plan." She glanced at him curiously.

He asked, "What?"

"Are you ever going to get me my bra and underwear?"

Theo felt his cheeks redden. "Right away."

He picked up the clothing and tossed them onto the bed, before retreating into the bathroom. Sophia said, "I don't think we should stay another night. We need to leave today."

"Why?"

"Too close for comfort. We need to keep moving."

"I told them we were here for a conference. We shouldn't check out, but we can find a different place."

"Fine," she said.

An hour later, Theo opened the back door, and he and Sophia made their way out to their rental car. They had gathered up everything from both rooms but left the do-not-disturb signs on both handles. Sophia got into the driver's seat, and Theo loaded all the luggage. As they drove out of the parking lot, they kept a lookout for any police cars but saw no one.

Theo leaned back in his seat. "I'm not sure how we pulled that off."

"Me neither." Sophia asked, "What's next?"

"Let's drive north and get another hotel."

"Okay," Sophia said. "But you'll need to call your nurse."

"What do you mean?"

"If they tortured your roommate, he probably gave out where you work. He never saw me, but that doesn't mean anything. Jane needs to be warned that someone might come to pay them a visit."

"I didn't even think of that. I'll call on our way."

"Make sure that you don't invite her to the club tonight. We can't get her involved."

"I won't."

The conversation with Jane was stunning. Instead of being afraid, she was delighted at the possible interrogation by whoever else came searching for Theo. She had already told the police that he was out of town. He tried warning her, but she was enjoying this far too much to be worried. Theo hung up the phone, shaking his head.

"She's crazy."

"No. She's from the South, and she kicks ass. We're good."

Sophia drove around for the next hour before they found a place to eat. They were north of San Diego, and their next stop would be to find a hotel. The food was greasy and tasty, and they both felt better afterward. They sprang for an expensive hotel near Pacific Beach and ended up on the third floor, with a perfect view of the incredible swimming pool and the oceanfront at the same time. They were only a few steps from the sand.

They quickly unpacked their clothing and belongings. It was easy to get help from the staff to get their items up to their room. When checking in, they said they were from Texas and paid cash. They didn't even have to show their licenses.

Once they finished, they settled on the balcony and drank some coffee from the hotel lobby. The view was spectacular.

Sophia asked, "Why did they come after your roommate?"

"I'm not sure. Jane was right to get rid of my car, but now it looks like I'm on the run."

"Or that your car was actually stolen. You talked to those police officers."

"I know. Patrick didn't think that would end up sticking. He thinks it will make things look worse."

"I bet if we pay the front desk, they'll say that we were here for several days. They required no address or proof. Once we paid up front, they didn't care about anything else."

"That's a great thought," Theo said.

After a few minutes of silence, Sophia said, "You said that your roommate was tortured, but it's likely that they already knew about you. That's probably how they found your condo. What were they searching for? The money?"

The realization hit Theo hard, and he gaped at Sophia. "They weren't looking for the money. They wanted to find you."

CHAPTER 19

"What are we doing here?" Sophia asked as Theo pulled up to the medical examiner's office. He hadn't really known what they should do this afternoon until he started driving. Going to BioPharm or coming here were his only options. He wanted to stay as far from Dr. Haderly as possible, until they had some evidence.

"We need to see if we can find something helpful on Dr. Daniels."

"Why him?"

"We can't go after Dr. Haderly without more information. He has seen both of us. Dr. Daniels feels like a safer option."

"So you agree that we should've followed him last night?"

"I'm not saying that."

"Well…I'm not staying in the car this time," Sophia said forcefully. "We either both go inside or we go somewhere else."

"Heavens. You are so stubborn."

"What's your choice?"

"We're not going through the front door."

"You think we can sneak inside?"

"That's the plan."

Sophia's eyebrows rose, and a dimple appeared on her forehead. "Well, if you ask me…your plan sucks."

"Good to know." Theo smiled for the first time in hours. They parked nearly on the opposite side of the building, far from the coffee shop. It wasn't a perfect view, but it gave them some cover. They backed into a parking spot next to a park with an overpass directly behind them. There were several large garbage containers on the edge of the asphalt. Beyond was a somewhat large field surrounding the backside of the ME's building.

After twenty minutes without a clear plan, Sophia asked, "Can we just wait until Dr. Daniels leaves and follow him?"

"We don't even know if he's here and we would have to go to the other side of the building and wait for him."

"If we don't find a way inside, I think that should be our play."

An opportunity presented itself a dozen minutes later. A tech wearing a white coat, someone Theo had never seen before, stepped out of a side door for a smoke. The tech began walking up and down the back wall, as if talking on his cell phone, with the back door propped open. At times, he would walk along the far side of the building and out of view. Without a word, they each bolted from the car. Despite Sophia's extended belly, she moved swiftly. They hurried to the end of the asphalt and waited between two large dumpsters. When the tech moved away from them, they sprinted across the field and ran directly into the building.

They stepped into a corridor that was dark and poorly lit. There were no paintings on the walls, and the floor was off-white linoleum. The corridor went on for ten feet and intersected with another corridor that traveled the distance of the building. Theo quickly realized that they must be on the first floor, a level below the lab and the other offices.

"Follow me," he whispered.

Sophia was breathing hard but signaled that she understood.

Creeping forward, they reached the junction. As he glanced left, Theo noticed several closed doors. A sign on the closest door read, "Gun range." Peering farther down the hall, he found several others, with signs such as X-ray, DNA Lab, and Forensic Anthropology. To the right were rooms entitled: Evidence Collecting, Bodily Fluids, Toxicology Lab, Histology Lab, more.

Sophia whispered, "I see an elevator. Should we use it?"

The loud slam of a door from behind them made them jump. The tech must've reentered the building. Theo clasped Sophia's arm, and they darted into the closest room. The temperature was frigid and was likely an easy thirty degrees colder than in the hallway.

Sophia hissed, "Don't tell me that there are dead people in here."

"What if I said it was for animals?"

"Even worse." Sophia started dry heaving.

"Put this on," he said, handing her a lab coat that was hanging on a hook off to one side. It didn't fit her perfectly, but she suddenly appeared as if she belonged there.

A few minutes later, Theo poked his head out of the room to find the corridor empty. Twenty feet down and across the hall was a stairwell leading up. Sophia shivered as they strolled down the hallway and opened up the door to the stairs. She breathed loudly as they ascended.

"Damn," Theo hissed.

"What is it?"

"No window to make sure the coast is clear."

"I could go first," she said. "They won't recognize me."

"Really?" he replied quickly. "Your stomach might not tell them who you are, but they will immediately know that you don't belong."

"What other options do we have?"

"Slow and steady." Theo reluctantly pushed open the door and tensed.

"What is it?" asked Sophia.

Theo eased the door close. "Dr. Daniels is less than ten feet away, talking with Dr. Lazar. She might have seen me."

"What do we do now?"

"Wait a few minutes and we'll open the door again."

In the next instant, the door was forced open, and Theo blocked Sophia. Doctor Celeste Lazar stood there with a pissed look on her face. The door didn't fully close.

"Seriously. Did you think you could sneak in here and no one would see you?"

"Not exactly," Theo lied.

"What are you wearing?"

"We found these downstairs."

"And…" She glared more fully at them. "What did you think you would accomplish by coming here?"

"We need information on Dr. Daniels."

"This is not a good time."

A voice called from down the hall. "Celeste. Do you have a moment?"

Dr. Lazar leaned out of the door and said, "Of course. But I need to talk to one of my techs. I'll meet you in the conference room in two minutes."

"Fine."

Before Dr. Lazar could say anything more, a man stepped into view behind her. Theo thought he saw two security guards flanking the man. He wore slacks and a polo shirt.

"Is that Dr. Daniels?"

"Quiet," she said. "The conference room is down the hall. I'll be there in a sec." After another few seconds, the man walked away and Celeste eased closed the doors and faced them. She looked Sophia up and down but said nothing more.

Theo asked, "Who was that?"

"Two people with Hartman Security, the company that provides our security."

"Are they looking for us?"

"I don't usually see them inside the building, so I'm not sure."

Sophia asked, "Is Dr. Daniels here today?"

"I don't have time to answer this right now." Shaking her head, she added, "Get to my office and close the door. I'll be there when I can."

"Which direction?"

Using her hands, she gestured a path going to the right, passing through the office section, turning left and then right. Theo signaled as if he understood. She rolled her eyes and stepped from the landing and disappeared. They waited until they heard no one and stepped out and strolled calmly down the hallway. Theo glanced over at Dr. Daniels desk, wishing he could take a look.

From down a separate corridor, Theo heard someone say, "We need to search the entire floor."

"You can't do that." replied Dr. Lazar. "There are some autopsies that we need to finish."

"We can and we will Ms. Lazar."

"It's Dr. Lazar."

"Well, Dr. Lazar…Dr. Daniels informed us that someone we're searching for may have been here recently. He's wanted for killing his roommate."

"I doubt that whoever it is is here now."

"We'll be the judge of that."

Theo's heart sank, and he felt trapped. What had the gotten them involved in?

Sophia asked, "What should we do?"

"Our only play is to go to her office."

"We better not get trapped." She looked terrified.

Theo heard Dr. Lazar explain, "Most areas in our building require a badge to get from one area to the next. No one is running loose around here. Do you have people at all the exits?"

"We do, ma'am. Our guys saw someone smoking on the side of the building and went to investigate. There could have been a breach. The door was closed, and the employee said he didn't see anything. We will begin our search now."

"Fine," she sighed. "Lucas must be with you at all times. He can show you around, but remember, much of what is in here is evidence. It cannot be contaminated."

"Understood," replied the man.

"I will be in my office."

Theo and Sophia turned left, and the voices faded away. They hurried forward and located the door with "Celeste Lazar" on the outside. They hurried in and shut the door. Five minutes later, Celeste stepped in, but she was irate.

"Am I harboring a killer?" she hissed. "Your roommate is dead?"

Theo took a deep breath, trying to calm the room. "We just found out this morning that my roommate was killed. I have no idea what happened."

Dr. Lazar glared at both of them. Finally she said, "What are you doing here?"

"We need Dr. Daniels's address," replied Theo.

She pointed to two chairs facing a large desk. Once they were seated, she turned and locked her door. Dr. Lazar moved slowly behind a large desk and sat in a chair. She scowled at them the entire time.

"We didn't do anything wrong."

Dr. Lazar silenced him with a look. "So this is Sophia LaCross. Mary Sneider was your roommate, and she is dead and now Theo's roommate is dead, and the police are looking for Theo."

Sophia hesitantly answered, "It was a mistake for us to come here. My life, and now Theo's life have been upturned. We're just trying to find some answers."

"How is Dr. Haderly involved?"

Sophia visibly jerked in her chair. "I don't remember much about him, but I saw him yesterday and I started shaking uncontrollably. He's involved."

Dr. Lazar leaned back in her chair. Her office was decorated tastefully. There were some expensive pictures of Napa Valley. She also had her degrees on the wall to his left. Black wooden pillars extended from the floor to the ceiling in all four corners, and the ceiling was made of the same wood. To his right was a wooden bookcase, and dozens of medical books were on the shelves.

Theo stared behind Dr. Lazar's desk, to a window, but immediately realized that this was not an avenue to escape.

"What am I supposed to do" Celeste asked herself. "If anyone ever finds out that I helped you, I'll lose my job."

Sophia answered, "Someone is killing our friends and we might be next. If you can help…"

Dr. Lazar lifted her hand and opened her desk drawer, pulling out some papers, and scribbled down an address. "Sooner or later, they're going to come check out this room. Did Dr. Daniels see you?"

"Was that him with the two security guards?"

"Yes."

"I don't think he saw us."

Her arm settled on the desk, and she rested her forehead as if thinking. When she spoke again, her voice was firm. "That means that Dr. Daniels is coming for me. He called the police to make it look bad for me. This is all for show."

Sophia asked, "How are we supposed to get out of here?"

Dr. Lazar thought for a moment. "I'll bring my car into the loading bay, and you guys will have to get into the trunk. All of the exits are covered."

"Both of us?" asked Theo.

"There is a detective out there that is convinced that something unusual is going on here. I'm being treated like a criminal in my own building."

There was a buzz on the phone, and all three of them froze. Dr. Lazar picked up the phone and answered, "Hello."

A woman's voice spoke through the phone, "Dr. Lazar...Franklin, the mayor's assistant, is still waiting for you in the conference room."

"Thanks, Debbie. I'm on my way." Hanging up the phone, she pointed to her left. "There's a bathroom back there. Stay hidden until I come back." She left the room without another word.

After the door closed, Sophia asked, "Can we trust her? I don't think getting into a trunk is the best idea."

"They're watching the building. I can't think of a better plan."

"She might inadvertently get us caught."

"Our backs are against the wall right now. We need a friend."

Sophia's arms crossed protectively over her belly. "If you say so."

Several minutes later, Theo started feeling antsy. Picking up a letter opener, he said, "Stay here. I'll be back in five minutes."

"What are you going to do?"

"Try to find a way out of here."

"Are you going to leave me here alone?" she demanded.

"I can do this," he said. "I'll be careful." Theo pulled out a medical face mask and a head covering that he had found downstairs. These, with his lab coat, made it nearly impossible to tell who he was. "How do I look?"

"If you're gone more than five minutes, I'm going to kill you."

Theo quietly opened the door and stepped outside. He hurried forward after seeing the area empty and stepped into the office area. He went straight to Dr. Daniels's desk and tried appearing natural. Opening the top drawer, he found nothing but pens, scissors, papers, and other office supplies. The second drawer was full of papers. Moving to the bottom drawer, he expected to see files or similar things. Instead, he found a locked metal box about the size of a book. Lifting it out of the drawer, he placed it on the desk. He couldn't find a way to open it. As he turned to put the box back into the drawer, something beneath the box caught his attention.

"Is someone at my desk?" a voice demanded.

Theo quickly picked up the clear evidence bag as he placed the locked metal box back where it was. Written on the outside of the evidence bag were the initials "M.S." and underneath them it read, "Fingernail clippings after drowning." In an instant he realized the infinite possibilities of this finding. There could be evidence, DNA, or something else inside this bag. He remembered Mary's autopsy and her recently cut fingernails.

Dr. Daniels's screamed, "Who are you? What are you doing at my desk?"

Theo's feet felt numb as he took two steps back, knocking over a chair. He twisted to run and sprinted down the hallway leading to the front of the building. Down at the far end of the corridor, two workers stepped into the entry. Theo curved right and crashed through a door into the conference room. Six people sat around the table. Dr. Lazar stood and screamed. Two security guards and a man in a suit appeared startled. Theo did not step and crashed into Dr. Lazar, pulling her close. He whispered, "Get Sophia out of here." He suddenly pushed her hard into a chair and, she fell back onto the floor.

Dr. Daniels crashed into the door behind him screaming, "That guy was going through my desk!"

"Stop!" yelled one of the security guards as Theo pushed open the door on the opposite side of the room. This hallway was clear. An adjacent door opened just in time as a girl carrying supplies stepped through. She didn't even see him slip past her and he tore down the stairs and into the hallway near the autopsy rooms. Screams echoed from behind him, but he didn't slow down. At the end there was a door, but it wasn't the same one they had entered through. Theo smashed through it and found himself outside of the building.

Instead of going around the back of the building to the rental car, he crossed the road directly ahead of him and turned right. He ran for several minutes before realizing that no one was chasing him. He pulled off the lab coat, mask, and head covering. He found a trash bin but decided against throwing these items away.

A minute later, he reached Famham Street, more than a block away from the medical examiner's building. The area directly around these buildings was open, but another half block ahead there was some shelter with a grouping of trees and fences. He jogged past the open area and ducked into some trees. Bending down, he tried catching his breath.

He spotted a van driving slowly around a building close by and he ducked down. This was farther west of where he had come from. A car drove into view from an alleyway between different buildings. The two vehicles approached each other. Theo watched as Dr. Daniels stepped out of the car and walked to the van's window. Theo thought he heard some yelling, but he couldn't hear what was being said. He assumed that whoever was inside was furious at Dr. Daniels. The doctor nodded and returned to his car.

Theo's cell phone rang and he answered it. "It's Celeste. Sophia is fine; she gave me your number. She's with me. Everyone left after you, and it was easy to get her out of the office."

"I want to talk with her."

He soon heard Sophia's voice, "You're an idiot. You left me back there."

"I found something in Dr. Daniels's desk. I don't know what it is exactly, but they are freaked out." Theo remained in his hiding spot and watched as the white van circled the area again, but there was no sign of Dr. Daniels's car.

Sophia added, "Celeste says that going to her house is probably not the best idea. There's a café—Dark Horse on Adams. Meet there in thirty minutes."

"I'll try. It's going to take a moment to get to the rental."

Theo hung up the phone and retreated deeper into the trees until he found a metal fence. He followed this back toward the ME's building for the next ten minutes. He was still far enough away that he could monitor the building. A single police car sat in front of the building, but five minutes later, it drove off. He needed to get to the opposite side of the building, and he thought he could follow the road they had driven back to the rental car. He left his position and began weaving between some buildings. He was making good progress when he heard a scrapping sound. Theo stopped and listened.

"Look who I found," a voice mumbled from a doorway. A man with broad shoulders stepped into view. "If I'm not mistaken, this is Dr. Theo Raden, friend to Sophia LaCross. Exactly the person that I'm looking for."

"Sorry. You've got the wrong guy."

Ignoring this, the man said, "Fritz is going to be tickled pink that I found you." The man was a security guard and the logo on his shirt was the name "Hartman Security" and the moment of clarity was enlightening. The man's hand held a knife pointed at Theo's stomach.

Theo asked, "What kind of name is Fritz?"

"Someone you don't want to be messing with. You're going to learn that in the worst way."

"I'm not who you think I am. Why would a doctor be out here?"

"Funny," the man said. "For a doctor, you're pretty stupid."

"Do I even look like a doctor?"

"My car is behind the building over there. You'll get into the trunk if you don't mind. I will ask you politely where to find Sophia and I won't lay a finger on you. Fritz will not be as kind when he asks, and he'll hurt you far worse than he hurt your roommate if you don't tell him what he wants to know."

Theo stared at the man. He knew that if he tried fighting him, he had no chance.

"Don't even think about running," the guy added. "I was a football player in college. I can run faster than you could ever dream." The man pointed at the building behind him. "Walk!"

Theo slowly turned and began walking down a slight slope between the next two buildings. In a dozen feet he would step onto the road he was aiming for. He furtively touched his front right pocket and felt the letter opener. He fished it out just as he took off running, throwing his gown behind him as a distraction. At first, he pretended to sprint away from the road; then he turned quickly and the instant he touched the pavement, he turned again, this time sprinting as hard as he could toward the parking where his rental car was. He had feared he would be caught within the first few seconds, but when that didn't happen, he thought he just might make it.

The enormous hand that clamped down on his left shoulder and squeezed surprised Theo so much that he almost dropped the object in his hand. He next felt a staggering blow to his right kidney that buckled him, and his knee smacked against the ground. A vast forearm went to clamp Theo's neck, and he was seconds from being asphyxiated unconscious.

The man hissed into his ear, "I knew you were going to run. You made it ten feet farther than I thought you would. So predictable."

The man grunted as he lifted Theo off the ground. Theo's vision flickered as he was being tightly squeezed. Somehow he managed to turn the letter opener backward.

He jammed it back once, twice, and a third time. Stars exploded on the outer edges of his vision and for an instant he thought he failed.

He thrust it back one last time, and this time, the man groaned, and the pressure lessened, and oxygen flowed blissfully into Theo's lungs, but he still wasn't free. The letter opener fell from his hand. He began kicking and using his elbows. He hit and hit and finally he was released. When Theo turned to face the security guard, the man was still standing, but his other arm was wrapped around his chest.

The unfocused eyes of the guard glanced up at Theo and back down at his wounds, as if his mind couldn't fathom what Theo had done. Blood soaked into the man's shirt. There was no way to know if any of the wounds were life-threatening. The arm protecting the body extended toward Theo as if trying to grasp him. The man stepped forward once, fell to his knees, and then toppled over.

Theo reached down and picked up the letter opener. Without another glance, he raced down the road, ran directly into the parking lot, and found his rental. He unlocked the car and satin the driver's seat. He reached for some napkins from earlier and quickly cleaned off the weapon and the blood on his hands. Using the cap from inside the ME's office, he wrapped up the letter opener and placed it on the front seat.

He shook as he turned on the car and pulled out of the lot. Thirty-five minutes later, he parked at the café and entered. Celeste and Sophia sat at a back table with an order of food. Theo limped toward the booth and gingerly sat next to Sophia.

"What happened?" Celeste asked.

"You've got blood on your shirt," whimpered Sophia.

"It's not mine. A security guard caught me." He explained what had taken place outside the ME building. Theo finished by saying, "He said he was going to bring me to someone named Fritz."

"I don't know who that is," Sophia replied.

Celeste leaned in and asked, "How bad is he?"

"He couldn't follow me or walk."

"Oh, shit!" exclaimed Celeste.

Theo reached for the water and, using some napkins from the table, started cleaning the remaining blood from his hand. His kidney throbbed and he felt blood running down his leg.

"That was the stupidest thing we could've done, going back to the ME's office," Sophia announced. "What did we really think that we were going to find?"

Celeste nodded her head, "You could have just texted me for Dr. Daniels's address."

"Thank you," said Sophia emphatically.

Theo pulled out the evidence bag and placed it on the table.

Celeste asked, "Where did you get this?" as she leaned closer to the table.

"From the bottom drawer of Dr. Daniels's desk."

"What is it?" asked Sophia.

"An evidence bag," Celeste answered as she gazed up at Theo. "Do you think the initials are from Mary Sneider? There were no nail clippings that I was aware of. Our only piece of examination were her nails…"

"…and they were cut short," Theo finished.

Celeste stared at him dumbfounded. "Dr. Daniels's performed this part of the autopsy on his own."

"I remember you saying that."

"Why didn't he just get rid of the evidence?" asked Sophia. "And what does it mean?"

Celeste answered, "It might mean nothing. We'll have to perform some testing."

Theo said slowly, "What if he kept it as insurance, like if anything went wrong. Maybe he didn't trust Dr. Haderly or whoever else is he is working with."

"In the drawer of his desk," responded Sophia.

"It's the safest place," said Celeste. "No one would suspect somewhere so open. No one would go looking there."

"Except for Theo," Sophia added.

"What do we do with the clippings now?" Theo asked.

Celeste said, "We need to get them tested."

Sophia leaned back, exhausted. "How?"

Celeste replied, "There's no way we can do it officially back at my lab. I think it's safe to say that we've been infiltrated. But I might know someone who can help."

"How long would it take?"

"Twenty-four hours at the earliest."

Sophia asked, "What are we hoping to find?"

Theo said, "Who killed Mary, and how. We need a shitload of evidence at this point and maybe then I can go talk to my friends."

"What friends?" asked Celeste.

"People that can get Sophia and me out of this mess we're in."

CHAPTER 20

"How long are we going to stay here?" asked Sophia as they sat in darkness inside their rental car, in one of the more prestigious housing communities near San Diego. It had only taken an hour to return to their hotel, shower, and change. Theo decided to bandage his knee, but there was a gash that could've used a few stitches.

"Maybe twenty minutes if no one else shows."

They had pulled into the neighborhood around 8:30 p.m. and found their spot. The only streetlight working was behind them a hundred feet away, and it wasn't very effective. A thick fog had rolled in from the ocean and completely changed the landscape. It had been the most exciting thing to happen in the last three hours. A slight drizzle began to fall.

Sophia complained, "I'm exhausted and hungry. In a few minutes I'm going to need to pee and I'm not using a cup."

Instead of answering, he asked, "How can Dr. Daniels afford this house? It has to cost more than ten million dollars."

"If it does, there might be a dozen security cameras watching the streets. I hope this goes better than what happened earlier."

"You're never going to let that go, are you?"

"Nope."

"At least we aren't being chased."

"It's still early." She pointed at the dash. "When the clock hits midnight, we're leaving."

Ten minutes later, Theo asked, "Is it legal to have cameras pointed outside of your property?"

"How the hell should I know?" roared Sophia.

A car turned onto a road, ahead of them, bisecting the one they were on. At first, they could see only the headlights approaching. Theo flipped the knob and the windshield wipers cleared away the droplets. In this lavish area, the houses were large and spread out, each with its own fence. The distance between houses and the location made this area feel secluded.

"This better be him," said Sophia.

The car drove up to the stop sign, and Theo's heart raced as he waited to see which direction it turned. If it veered away, then it wasn't Dr. Daniels, and they were leaving. The headlights turned toward them, and Sophia let out a sigh.

"We have a chance," said Theo.

"There are only three houses in this direction. It's more than a chance."

The garage door at Dr. Daniels's house started to rise.

"Go time," Sophia said.

They exited the car, and together they crossed the street. They each wore dark clothes and hoodies. The sidewalks alone were massive. They passed the only house south of Dr. Daniels's and found a path between the two houses. Theo searched but couldn't see any security cameras on this side.

"Do we still want to cut through here?"

"We won't be able to see anything from the front."

The path led them to one of the most exclusive golf courses in California. They skirted the edge of a long fairway that ran the length of several houses, including Dr. Daniels. From here they had a decent view into the backyards of three of the houses on this street. Farther down, the golf course turned away from the houses and was swallowed by the fog. Not far away, the beach gave way to a small rock cliff and the ocean.

The fog threw the lighting of the backyards of the closest two houses into a sort of enclosed feeling, like they were in a gigantic, mystical warehouse that no one had ever seen before. Music suddenly blasted into the night from a house next to Dr. Daniels's. Theo pulled Sophia into the tall grass, and they bent low. The neighbor's backyard door opened, and eight or ten guests came out with food, drinks, and intentions to use the swimming pool and hot tub.

Pointing to the house, Sophia said, "I guess clothing is optional."

Theo watched as most of the swimming suits, shirts, and shorts were removed. He added, "I have no idea how one person can do both of those things at the same time."

"One guy and two girls. It's not hard to imagine."

Theo glanced at Sophia. "Let's try to keep our concentration on the task at hand."

"At least I don't have to pee anymore."

"That's one benefit." Theo and Sophia slowly moved forward. He could see a large backyard, a hot tub, and several trees. All the windows were completely dark. "I don't see any motion sensors. Should we get closer?"

Sophia said hesitantly, "Why not."

They crossed the remaining tall grass. They found a golf cart path and crossed it. The ten or twenty feet that remained to the back fence were uneven with rocks, plants, and several smaller trees. The moaning coming from the neighbors made Theo blush.

"Where was our invitation?" Sophia whispered.

"I was wondering the same thing," said Theo. They reached the eight-foot mental fence and knew instantly that it was going to be impossible for both of them to get into the backyard. That had been the plan, but there was no way that Sophia would be able to climb this fence.

Theo glanced at her and said, "I'm going to need you to stay here. Keep hidden."

Before she answered, a single light in the kitchen turned on, and Theo and Sophia immediately ducked down. Theo felt anxious and didn't want to get spotted or caught. A movement from inside the kitchen alerted them to Dr. Daniels as he filled a wine glass from a box stored in the fridge.

"Does he look all right?" asked Sophia.

"Hard to tell from here."

"You're not leaving me."

"I can jump the fence and get closer."

"No," Sophia stated. "We're sticking together.

Dr. Daniels began gulping down wine from a glass, and soon he began refilling it. Even from here, Theo could tell that he looked more pale than usual. His black hair appeared to have lost its calmness and could best be compared to a bird's nest. He wore gray slacks and a gray vest. His white shirt was untucked, but his vest was still buttoned. His face jerked, and Theo thought there had been a noise or a slight movement from the front of the house.

Dr. Daniels lifted his glass as if toasting someone unseen.

"What a prick," Sophia whispered.

The doctor walked out of view.

"Where's he going?" Sophia asked.

"This is the perfect time for me to jump the fence."

"If you go in there, I'm leaving."

Theo rolled his eyes but he had turned his head so Sophia couldn't see. He added, "I think that someone else just arrived. We seem to be exposed right here. We also need a better angle."

Taking Sophia by the hand, they walked left along the fence line, and searched for a better window to look into. The party next door had momentarily slipped from his mind when he had seen Dr. Daniels, but now the festivities were fully on display. Even from here, he could hear the upbeat tempo, and the party was in full swing.

"Look at the windows of the third house," said Sophia. She pointed to an upstairs window, and Theo had to squint to see what she was drawing attention to. He was horrified to see that two young faces were plastered against the window, watching everything that was happening.

"That's disgusting," he hissed.

"We've got to do something," she pleaded.

"Right now we need to keep our focus."

"How's that going to be possible?"

Theo touched her arm, and she looked at him. "We can't solve all the problems in the world at once. We'll come up with a plan when we're done here."

"By then it could be too late."

"I doubt this is the first time they've seen this."

"How horrible."

Theo pulled Sophia into a crouch. From here, they had a view of three tall windows with their blinds open.

"I can't do this for very long," hissed Sophia.

Theo helped her stand, and they shifted to a grouping of larger trees. They still had a decent view inside. The room was a large living room with a gigantic flat-screen television.

"Someone is coming," Sophia whispered.

Dr. Daniels stepped into the large room flanked by two girls, one on each side. One girl slipped away and clicked on some music. Theo could hear the beats pulsating, and they watched as Dr. Daniels began dancing with the first girl. The second girl twirled around the room on her own. A third girl strode in from the kitchen carrying bottles of wine.

"I think I know one of the girls," Theo said.

"Which one? And how?"

The bottles of wine were placed next to the window. The girl peeked outside, and her face became discernible. "That one. That's Cindy."

"What's she doing here?"

"I don't know."

"Could the other girls be from the same club?"

"Stands to reason that they would be."

Cindy joined the other two girls, and they surrounded Dr. Daniels, danced seductively, and drank some more. Ten minutes later, the music was turned down, and all four disappeared upstairs.

"Not good," Sophia said. "Should we go around to the front?"

"Let's give it a few more minutes."

"Is that all the time it's going to take?"

"Let's wait and see. If nothing else helps us tonight, we'll find a way to talk with Cindy tomorrow." Theo's eyes searched the upstairs windows, but no lights were turned on. He was getting nervous, feeling exposed, when suddenly the back door opened, and music echoed out.

Cindy strolled out first, in a tight navy-blue bikini swimsuit. There was only a little light, but the fog brightened the area. She strolled knowingly to the side of the hot tub and flipped up the lid. Leaning over, she touched some buttons, and the water began turning gently.

"We're good," Cindy announced.

Dr. Daniels ambled out in a black robe. When he reached the stairs to the hot tub, he stopped. One of the other girls approached and removed the clothing from his shoulders. Theo was surprised at what was underneath. Dr. Daniels had no chest hair, and his skin was ghostly white. There were a dozen tattoos of different images covering his lean and muscular torso. The largest, on his back, was similar to a caduceus, but it was shaped in a unique and perverse manner. Typically, this was a well-known medical image—a staff entwined with two snakes with wings at the top. This tattoo was of a naked woman, both arms extended, her head drooping down and her hair wildly placed. The two snakes were there, but they almost cut in and out of her skin, and they ended by biting the girl's neck.

Cindy lifted a hand and Dr. Daniels took it, and he marched into the water without a second glance. The other two girls followed, and Cindy was the last one to settle in.

The girl's swimsuits left little to the imagination, with big curves and the least amount of material possible, but the other item caught Theo's attention. Cindy and another girl wore braided bracelets of yellow on their wrists, and the third girl wore a red one. He remembered finding a similar bracelet in Sophia's desk, except it was brown with a yellow bead. This had to mean something, but what?

"I didn't have much of a choice," Dr. Daniels explained, and Theo was surprised at how clearly his voice carried.

The girl wearing the red bracelet purred into Dr. Daniels's ear, and it seemed he was, in turn, speaking to her.

The girl answered in a musical voice. "What, poo-bear? You don't like coming around us anymore?" Her accent was unusual and reminded him of Nurse Jane's, a slightly Southern accent.

"Fritz didn't give me much choice."

Sophia squeezed his hand at the mention of Fritz. They were protected by the trees, and even if anyone in the hot tub looked directly at them, he doubted they would be seen.

The girl bent over, and Dr. Daniels gawked into her cleavage. She said, "Fritzy is just business, business, business. He needs to stop freaking out." Her voice changed to more of a pleading whine. "What's going on anyway? Why all these changes?"

"Do you really care? Or is it affecting how much money you make?"

Instead of answering, she said, almost pouting, "I just want things to go back to normal. Tell me."

"I can't talk about it." He shook his head as if coming out of a trance.

The other girl, next to Cindy, a slender brunette, said, "Lukey, tell us all your problems."

The curvy girl shot the brunette a look, but Dr. Daniels missed the exchange because he was reaching for a drink.

"They ain't problems," he declared, after taking a long drink. "I'm about to make it to the big time."

"Really," purred the curvy girl. "You going to Hollywood? You got a great face; you could make it up there."

"No, girl, I'm talking about here."

"Sounds like good business." The girl reached over and began rubbing Dr. Daniels's leg. "Is this a celebration?"

"Partly. It's an incredible business transaction. I'm going places."

"What kind of transaction?" the girl asked as she moved her hand to rub between his legs. The other two girls acted as if this happened frequently.

"The changing of the guard," he emphatically replied as he leaned back to enjoy the moment. "That hag had her balls handed to her today when that doctor came running through her own conference room. She looked like she was going to die. She is a step away from being fired."

Theo felt the prickles on his arms rise. All three girls stared at Dr. Daniels, perplexed. The curvy girl asked, "What are you talking about, silly?"

Dr. Daniels didn't seem to hear the question. He muttered with pleasure, "If only that pregnant girl had been with him. It would be all over."

The girl immediately stopped rubbing. Her face took on a dour expression. "Who is pregnant, Lukey, and who is this doctor?"

Dr. Daniels sat up, taking another long sip of his wine. "Why did you stop?" he demanded.

"We have questions we need answered."

"Are you here for me or for Fritz?" he asked, anger rising in his voice.

"For you," said Cindy quickly. "We're here for you."

"Better be," he announced. "Keep it that way. I've told Fritz that I'll handle my part. Don't go back to him saying otherwise." The curvy girl began rubbing him again. After a moment he answered, "The doctor is a no one, the pregnant girl is Sophia. You remember her?"

Hearing her name, Sophia dug her nails into Theo's arm so forcefully that he was convinced blood was about to drip onto the ground.

Once again, the rubbing stopped, and all three girls turned to face Dr. Daniels. He wasn't prepared for the resentment on their faces. He asked, "You were sent here by Fritz, weren't you? I don't know where she is, but I've got this covered. I'll call him when I find her. Hartman's Security will send over some more guys. We don't need help from Fritz right now."

Cindy said, "We just want to know that Sophia is safe. You promised that you would keep her safe."

"Safe?" demanded Dr. Daniels. "Everything was going perfectly. We set her up and had an ideal place for her. She was doing fine, and she was happy, but then she disappeared. That doctor took her from us."

Cindy answered, "Who's the doctor? What happened?"

"Everything is under control. The doctor was treating her for her pregnancy."

"Where is she now?" insisted the brunette.

"She's our friend," added the curvy girl.

Theo felt ridiculous. Cindy had known who Sophia was the entire time. She had lied to him. Who knows what else she had lied about?

Dr. Daniels slapped the girl with the Southern accent so fast that no one had time to react. Theo almost stood, but Sophia held him in place.

"Vickie. I swear to god that if I hear about your worries about Sophia one more time, I'll tell Fritz myself."

Cindy asked, "Why didn't you tell us she left because she was pregnant?"

"You know the rules," Dr. Daniels replied.

"You were supposed to protect her," said the brunette.

"Why did the other doctor take her?" asked Cindy.

Dr. Daniels shook his head. "Um. She almost lost the baby. We needed to get her to a specialist. She was starting to have bouts of paranoia." The words came from Dr. Daniels so easily.

The brunette added, "We've heard bad things from the other girls."

A flash of anger entered Dr. Daniels's voice, "Girls! What have you heard?"

Vickie folded her arms and said in a soft voice, "Nothing specific. A few girls on the street have said that they see things that aren't there. That's all."

The brunette asked, "What will happen if Fritz finds Sophia?"

"He'll teach her a lesson. But she's special."

"Aren't we special?" asked Vickie.

"Yes. You all are." After another sip of his drink, Dr. Daniels asked, "Have you heard anything else?"

Vickie answered, "Her friend came by the club and wanted to see her. Someone saw her talking with Fritz."

"Was it you?" Dr. Daniels asked calmly. "Did you ever talk to this girl?"

"No," Vickie answered. "None of us would. I was just worried about Sophia."

"I completely understand." He finished his drink. "I'm two steps away from becoming the co-medical examiner for the city of San Diego. Things are falling apart for my boss, and she doesn't even know it. Never asked for me to be her partner. Partner. Never wanted me to touch her partner. See will see the irony soon enough."

It was as if Dr. Daniels were no longer speaking to the girls but rather to himself. In a shrill voice, he added, "I know some very important people. In fact, *my partner* killed that girl who came looking for Sophia."

"What?" Vickie asked. "What have you done?"

Dr. Daniels's hand moved so quickly that nothing could be done. It held a knife, and it sliced through Vickie's neck as easily as going through water. Blood flowed freely before the brunette and Cindy began screaming. Vickie slumped into the hot tub. Dr. Daniels pointed the knife at each girl, and they stopped shrieking instantly.

Sophia had let loose her own scream that was swallowed up by the music from the orgy next door. Theo clamped his hand over her mouth, pulling her close to his chest.

Dr. Daniels spoke. "I own you two now. No one will ever believe two whores over a doctor."

Vickie's body was slipping under the water.

"As I was saying," he continued, "that girl that came looking for Sophia was killed by my partner. You just didn't know that I was working so closely with Fritz. I hid some of the evidence at my office, and I will suddenly find it. I'll blame Dr. Lazar's ineptitude at her job. When Dr. Theo Raden ran through the morgue yesterday, it underlined her lack of control. Things could not be more perfect for me."

"What's evidence?" the brunette asked with a tremor in her voice.

"Clues to how someone died."

The back door opened, and four guys stepped into view. "Hey Fritz," Dr. Daniels said.

Theo stared at the four men to see if any of them looked familiar. He thought there might still be someone inside, and then a muffled voice spoke, but Theo couldn't make out the words.

"Yes. You were right. Cindy here was speaking the truth. Vickie did know about that girl. I've taken care of the problem as you asked."

The brunette whispered, "I'm yours. I won't say anything. I'll do anything you want..."

Dr. Daniels screamed. "Then help me out of this damn water!"

A broad-shouldered, tall man, probably in his forties, with brown curly hair stepped outside. Theo didn't think he had ever seen this man before. Even from here, he spotted a large scar the went from the side of his forehead to his jawline.

The brunette leapt to her feet and tumbled down the stairs. Her knee hit the ground hard, but she didn't react. She stood and scurried over to Dr. Daniels and guided him out of the water. Cindy followed close behind, her chin pointed a little higher. She had just provided insight and had made a name for herself. Once the area was clear, the four men took out ropes, closed the lid, and secured it. The brunette situated the robe back on Dr. Daniels.

Dr. Daniels turned to face the tall man. "Your plan worked, Fritz,"

The man replied, his voice deep, "It always does."

A phone rang, and one of the other men answered. Once he hung up, he told the others, "The truck is here." Dr. Daniels followed Fritz inside, followed by the two girls. The man who answered the phone walked to his right, near the wall where Theo and Sophia had snuck to the golf course. He unlatched the gate. A large flatbed truck backed in, and the second half lowered to the ground. Within five minutes, the hot tub was loaded, and the truck and the house's occupants had vanished.

CHAPTER 21

Theo wasn't sure how long they remained hunkered down behind the trees. The orgy party had finished and was a distant memory. Sophia sobbed into his chest, and he held her tight. She had relieved herself on the ground at some point, but they were both too shocked to really notice.

"No. No. No," Sophia cried, and Theo imagined it had as much to do with her friend Mary as with the death they had just witnessed. Neither of them would ever be the same.

"We have to go," Theo said gently, and he pulled Sophia to her feet.

"I can't. I got Mary killed. Did you see Vickie's face when she realized she was dead?"

"Don't think about it," said Theo flatly, but he couldn't get her face out of his mind either.

He led Sophia out onto the golf course, and they headed south along the beach. He would find another place to cross back to the street. He needed to find a place to stash Sophia, and he would run to get the car. He didn't want her anywhere close to Dr. Daniels's house. That place was haunted.

It took an hour, but it worked. Sophia was quivering when he picked her up, and still crying. He drove south to their hotel. He parked as close as he could to the side entrance. Once it was clear, Sophia was ushered inside, a coat covering her head. The moment they stepped inside, Sophia hurried off to the bathroom and closed the door. Ten minutes later, he heard the water to the bathtub start and she remained inside for a long time. They slept together on the bed, fully dressed, as Sophia sobbed herself to sleep.

The next morning, Theo was up early after his mind had raced the entire night. While he slept, he had subconsciously imagined calling both Patrick and Zorn and telling them about the death of Vickie. He had no evidence, other than their word against his, and Dr. Daniels would parade in twenty people giving him an alibi. He knew that his only option was to find the evidence to show that Mary had died under suspicious circumstances.

"They killed Mary because of me," said Sophia from the bed as he sat on chair near the desk.

"They killed Mary because they are killers and have something to hide," replied Theo.

"Like what exactly? What could be this important, that they would need to hide me away and kill my friend?"

"That is impossible to know right now."

"What can we do? Now they've killed your roommate and that girl from last night, and they are undoubtedly searching for us."

"We need to find an ace of spades."

"A what?"

"Some evidence that will give us some leverage."

"Where are we going to find this?"

"Dr. Daniels mentioned some evidence in Mary's case. We locate that evidence, and we'll have a fighting chance."

"How?"

Theo pulled out his phone and dialed. The person on the opposite end answered, and he was surprised to hear the excitement and alertness in her voice.

"Hello."

"Dr. Lazar, it's Theo. We need to meet this morning."

"Call me Celeste."

"All right."

She whispered, "The morgue is being monitored closely right now. I've heard that something is happening today that could be very good for me. I don't think I have time."

Taking a deep breath, Theo put as much significance into his voice as he could. "I promise you, this will be the most important meeting you've ever attended. And if you don't, you will regret it for the rest of your life."

After a short pause, Celeste said, "I'm already at my office. There are a lot of people here. I will find a way to sneak away in twenty minutes. There's a mom-and-pop restaurant about a mile down Clairmont Avenue, on the right side. Meet me there in forty-five minutes."

"We'll be there."

He clicked off the phone. He showered quickly, and then it was Sophia's turn. They packed everything and drove off thirty minutes later. It still took twenty minutes to get there, but Celeste hadn't yet arrived. They entered and found a table in the back with a perfect view outside. If someone else turned up, they would have a few seconds' warning.

Ten minutes later, Celeste's BMW entered the parking lot, and she stepped out alone. Glancing around, she hurriedly moved toward the front door. Theo waved her over, and she sat quickly.

"I must say that I was surprised to hear from you," said Celeste. "I smoothed out everything that happened yesterday, but don't even think about going back inside the ME building."

"Good to see you too," said Theo.

"I don't have a lot of time. I snuck away, but I've been called down to a staff meeting. It is with Los Angeles County, several smaller counties, and their medical examiner staff. It is at 2:00 p.m. downtown. Dr. Bowthorpe and Dr. Daniels were asked to share some improvements we've made to techniques for getting fluids from clothes, difficult surfaces, and especially oral, rectal, and vaginal orifices. It is supposed to be cutting-edge. Rumor has it that I could be getting an award. If it is done in front of those two chauvinistic pigs, that could go a long way for me."

Theo said, "We were at Dr. Daniels's house last night. He didn't know that we were there."

Celeste glanced around, horrified. "Did you break into his house?"

"No. We remained outside of his fence, but we heard him talking to several people."

"And?" Celeste asked.

"Dr. Daniels said he was working with a partner, and that he hid certain evidence at the morgue that has to do with Mary Sneider's death."

"This can't be true."

"We both heard it," said Sophia.

"If we can find it..." said Theo.

"Absolutely not," countered Celeste. "If you're seen again, I'll be written up, or worse."

"We don't have a choice," said Sophia.

"Why's that?"

Theo explained, "We watched Dr. Daniels kill a girl from Club Jazzed. He is coming today to discover some new evidence and blame you for your incompetence. You aren't going to get an award today. Dr. Daniels's has plotted to get you fired.

"He wouldn't do that."

Sophia said, "Last night, he gloated about becoming the co-medical examiner for the city of San Diego, and I think he will be working with Dr. Haderly."

"What?" Celeste said as the color drained from her face.

"It sounded like they've been planning this for a long time. Sophia and I have thrown a wrench into their planning. They are coming after you."

"But why?"

"Can you imagine what would happen if the morgue was under the control of a criminal? Solving crimes for certain cases would become nearly impossible or flat out done wrong."

Celeste answered, "There's too much oversight."

"You can't manage a problem when it has already disappeared."

The waitress arrived, and they ordered breakfast. Celeste ordered some toast and jam, and Theo and Sophia ordered the daily special.

Celeste stared at him intently. "Tell me everything."

He reluctantly told her about running from the morgue and stabbing the officer, all while running for his life. He explained about who had come to Dr. Daniels's house and what had happened. She covered her eyes as he explained about the body being sealed up in the hot tub and it being hauled away.

He paused as the waitress brought them their food. Sophia began eating almost instantly.

Celeste asked, "What could Lucas have hidden?"

"That's what we need to find out," Theo stated. "But we need to find something, so they stop blaming me for everything?"

Celeste and Sophia nodded. Theo at last began eating. Once they had finished, Celeste returned to her BMW, and they drove behind her, keeping a good distance. They arrived at the medical examiner's office, and after ten minutes, she brought them through a side door unseen.

"Security is still here. I told them that one of the doors on the opposite of the building wouldn't lock. I had to smash it with a hammer."

"Where did you find that?" asked Sophia.

Celeste smiled mischievously. She said, "Let's get you guys some clothing that doesn't make you stand out."

Sophia replied, "How are you going to hide me?"

"In plain sight."

Sophia was rolled in on a gurney, under a sheet by a technician in training named Rory Finkelson. Theo wore scrubs, a white coat, and a badge pointing out that he was "in training." Dr. Lazar wore her lab coat, and to anyone it would appear like a normal day in the office. She had a secretary and another tech come and give her updates.

"Dr. Daniels is eating lunch with Dr. Bowthorpe downtown before the meeting this afternoon. If you want to go, just text him and he will send you the address. If you can't get away, Dr. Daniels wants to make sure that you aren't late."

"Thank you so much, Rebecca. I just have a few things more to do here, and I will head out."

Rebecca nodded and walked away.

"Where should we start?" asked Celeste. "There are a lot of places to hide things."

"What does he have access to the most?"

"The lab, the morgue, his desk, his locker."

"How about you start in the morgue, and I'll start in his locker."

Sophia hissed, "I'm not staying under here forever, so hurry up."

Theo retraced his steps and found the locker room. There were several metal lockers and benches. He found the one with Dr. Lucas Daniels on it and found that there was a lock. Next to it was Dr. Bowthorpe's. He went to find Celeste and returned with some bolt cutters. After two quick squeezes of the handles, he had broken each lock. He rifled through the contents of each locker carefully. He found clothing, money, cologne, showering supplies, boxes of supplies, and other random items. He found nothing suspicious.

Returning to one of the autopsy rooms, Theo found Celeste working on an old man on a steel slab. He was half draped with a white sheet; the body bag was off in the far corner. Theo savored the prospect of being here during this procedure. Looking around, he noticed that the back wall was concrete with a table, cabinets, and several highly valuable instruments. The two side walls were glass, but the clarity between the different rooms wasn't perfect. A slight glaze made the items in the other room look blurry. The outer glass was perfectly clear and pristine. The atmosphere in the room, caused by the glass, intrigued Theo.

Between her next cuts, Celeste said, "Franklin from the mayor's office just arrived. It must look like we're working."

"Who?" he hissed.

"The mayor's assistant. He has been here a lot recently. Put a mask on."

Theo nodded. Celeste began talking into an automated voice recorder. "Beginning autopsy on

Jonathan Stark, an eighty-four-year-old white male with a significant medical history. He was taking medications for hypertension, angina, hyperlipidemia, diabetes, and others. He was found dead in his bed approximately twelve hours ago."

She clicked off the recorder and asked, "Are you ready for this?"

Before he answered, he heard someone clearing his voice at the partially opened autopsy door.

Celeste barely turned, and said, "Hello Franklin. I am surprised to see you here today."

"Before the award ceremony at two, Mayor Reed has a meeting with the medical examiners from Los Angeles, Ventura, Orange County, and San Bernardino. Since our building is the newest, he wants to take some pictures and glance at the floor plan. You've done a terrific job of updating the building."

"Thank you very much, Franklin. Does the mayor want me at this meeting?"

"No need. Dr. Daniels was already available. He said you were swamped with a few autopsies today. I hope that is all right."

"Of course."

"I'll let you get back to work."

"Thank you, Franklin. I will see you this afternoon."

"Looking forward to it."

But Franklin did not leave. He stared, transfixed, at the body.

Celeste said, "Mr. Finkelson, what do you see?"

Theo almost didn't react to the different name. After a second, he said, "Well. This man looks young for being eighty-four. He appears to be in his sixties at the most. He seems healthy and fit." Theo walked around the body.

"There is some bruising along his flank. His face is devoid of any other trauma."

Celeste said, "The bruising is the key. What could cause this?"

"Injury during a fight, car accident, fall, or something else?" His eyes searched her face.

She asked, "Could anything else cause this bruising?"

He considered the question. He muttered, "Bruising is blood that becomes trapped in the interstitial tissue."

Celeste fired the next question. "Is this bruising post-mortem or ante-mortem?"

Leaning closer, he examined the back closely. "When he died, his heart stopped pumping, therefore there wasn't any way that this could be postmortem bruising—it cannot really exist."

"In this case, you are correct. The bruising occurred while he was alive. But post-mortem bruising can occur. But it is a rarity."

She asked, "Do you see any other injuries?"

"I don't."

"So, as far as you know, what was the method of death?"

"That's why we need to do an autopsy."

"Have you a guess?"

"Blunt force trauma from a fall. Internal organ injury, and he bled to death."

"It's possible, but this man was found in his bed."

"Heart attack?"

"Good guess. Let's open him up and see."

Franklin started coughing, and both Theo and Celeste glanced over at him. The man's face was white, and Theo thought he was going to collapse.

"Are you okay, Franklin?"

"Fine. Perfect, in fact. I just need to get some air. We will see you later." The man practically ran from the building.

264

Celeste immediately asked, "Any luck in the locker room?"

"Nothing."

"I didn't find anything out of place in the lab or any of the autopsy rooms."

"What other areas could he hide something in that only he has access to?"

"Besides his desk, nowhere really."

"I'll take a look while you start in here."

Celeste said, "They have added a few security personnel for today because of what happened. Make sure you don't get caught."

"Won't be a problem." Theo hurried to where Sophia was resting. She was sitting up, leaning against the wall.

When she noticed him approaching, she rolled her eyes. "This is taking forever."

"If anyone sees you sitting up, they're going to have a heart attack."

"If they're over here looking at me, they deserve it." She asked quickly, "Have we found anything?"

"Not yet."

"We've been here an hour. What have you been doing?"

"I checked some bathrooms, and I went into the locker room and broke into the lockers of Dr. Daniels and Dr. Bowthorpe. Nothing. Celeste has been in autopsy, and someone from the major's office stopped by. It had to look like she was working."

"Did she cut open someone?"

"Yep. She's probably working on that as we speak. I'm headed to their workstations. I'll be back in a bit."

Theo moved cautiously down the hall, passing the next two turns and taking the third. This went to the central area and the desks. Theo quickly went to Dr. Daniels's.

He stepped on the lush, black carpet and pulled back the chair. Bending down, he tried all the drawers, and they were each unlocked, like before. The bottom drawer still had the small metal lockbox. Pulling out some equipment, he went to work on the tiny lock. In thirty seconds, it lay open with cash, coins, and a bottle of blue elongated pills inside. After last night, Theo had a guess at what these were, and it wasn't Viagra.

The metal box was empty otherwise. He closed and locked it, placing it back where it had been. In the second drawer were personal items such as cups, plates, and some plastic silverware. There was some trash, and there were takeout menus and leftover sauces. Otherwise, there was nothing of value. The top drawer held pens, loose change, and other office supplies. Theo quickly searched the checkerboard and the lamp, and he even looked at the masks on the wall. Nothing.

Theo made a quick search of Dr. Bowthorpe's desk, but it was like looking through the drawers of a hoarder. There were dried food, trash, and other things he didn't want to know about.

Sitting in Dr. Bowthorpe's chair, he glanced around the area. Mary Sneider's picture was gone from the picture board. He stood and wandered around the edge of the room. There were no additional cabinets, water coolers, or anything. Glancing up, he noticed a small alcove with a fridge built into the wall and a small place for a coffeepot. Coffee was being brewed currently. When he arrived at the alcove, he found two different coffee machines. One had Dr. Lazar's name imprinted on the top. The other was a traditional machine, and this was the one brewing coffee.

Theo reached up and opened the cupboard above the machines. He found several bags of coffee. Two stood out to him. They had the name Partners Brazilian Coffee Roasters. Something felt unsettling. He plucked the closest bag, a blue bag, and found that it was completely closed. Standing on his toes, he reached for a second bag farther in the back. Theo brought down this bright red bag and pried at the seal. When he opened it, he knew something was different. There was an object that shifted inside the coffee beans. Using some medical gloves, he reached within and pulled out a circular metal case.

It wasn't hard to pry open the case. There was an evidence bag inside with a red seal and some writing on the outside. Through the plastic he could make out a black piece of fabric and there was possibly some dried blood on it. When he rotated it over, he saw a small portion of the fabric that had some bright orange decal. The color was familiar. Slowly the realization hit him, and he felt the oncoming panic attack.

CHAPTER 22

Theo staggered back to the autopsy room with what he had found. Dr. Lazar was working on the man from earlier; this time, his chest cavity was open. Theo stepped inside and said, "Celeste...we have a serious problem."

She glanced at him, exasperated. "Stop dictation."

"Sorry," he said. "I'm fucking screwed."

"What are you talking about?"

Theo lifted the evidence bag and the circular metal box. "I found this wonderful piece of evidence inside your Partner coffee."

"My coffee?" she hissed. "Everyone knows that my coffee is off-limits."

"I bet."

"What's that supposed to mean?"

"You have a coffee machine with your name engraved into it."

"So? It was a gift. A special gift." Her eyes narrowed. "How did you know to look inside my coffee bag?"

"Dr. Daniels loathes you, and he's completely jealous that you're the boss."

"This I know."

"He's also probably a narcissist and loves the idea of messing with you."

"How?"

"When Sophia and I were at his house, things were

strange. Dr. Daniels kept rambling, and I had no clue what he was saying. He killed that girl and all, but he was talking about how he was going to run the medical examiner's office. One thing that he said was thoroughly weird. He kept going on and on about…a partner. It was partner this and partner that. When I opened the cupboard and saw the name on the coffee bag, I got this feeling."

Celeste added, "Dr. Daniels hates that I don't allow anyone to touch my coffee. I've told him a dozen times where I get my Brazilian coffee from, but it's like he must drink my coffee."

"He's a lunatic." Theo held up the bag again. "The real problem is what is inside this bag."

"Looks like a piece of fabric."

"The writing outside the bag says: Fabric found inside Mary Sneider's hand. Collected by Dr. Lazar during autopsy."

"What?" Celeste stepped forward. "I've never seen that before."

"That's not the worst part." Theo shook his head as he realized the brilliance of their plan. "This is a piece of my shirt. And they're planning to disgrace you by showing that you hid evidence to protect me."

"Oh my hell," stammered Celeste. "What are we going to do now?"

Before Theo answered, there came a loud knock outside the autopsy room. Someone in work clothes stood next to Rebecca and he was pounding on the glass. Celeste walked closer to hear what the man was saying.

"What?" she said. "Can you open the door?"

Rebecca pushed open the door to allow the man to speak. "I'm here to drop off a shipment of Brazilian coffee."

Celeste glanced back at Theo and whispered, "What are the chances?" She turned back to Rebecca and said, "This isn't the best time."

Rebecca glanced over at the body on the slab. She stepped out to talk with the man and the door closed.

Theo's eyes focused on the face of the man outside the glass window, and he eyes fixated on the scar on his face. In a low voice, Theo said, "Tell that guy that we can't come out because we're in the middle of an autopsy. Tell him where to go to drop off the coffee, but make sure he goes the long way around."

Celeste replied, "We've never had someone drop off a shipment of coffee."

"Just do it."

Celeste walked to the door, opened it, and explained that he needed to keep this area secure, but she pointed to where he should go.

He nodded, smiled, and pushed a dolly bearing three boxes with the logo of Partners Brazilian Coffee on them. Rebecca set off in a different direction.

Once the man was out of view, Celeste asked, "Do you know who that is?"

"His name is Fritz. I've heard a lot about him. He knows Dr. Daniels. I just don't know why he's here."

Celeste returned to the body and placed the organs back inside the chest cavity. She hit a few buttons, and the body lowered into a space below the table. At the look on Theo's face, she said, "It will help store him until I can finish the autopsy."

"What are we going to do?"

"Find out what that guy is doing here."

Celeste and Theo pulled off their coats and placed them on hooks against the wall. She handed him foot booties, head coverings, and glasses. They also each put on a white gown that continued to their knees. He didn't recognize himself in the mirror.

"Hurry," Celeste implored. "Get Sophia and the gurney. We're going to use her to walk around. If we're caught, we'll say that we're bringing the body to the downstairs freezer."

Theo nodded. He sprinted to find Sophia, who appeared to be bored. "What's happening?"

"Found some planted evidence of my torn shirt. Fritz is here, and we're going to use you as a prop. I need you to lay down and keep still."

Sophia protested. "Fritz scares the hell out of me."

"I know. You'll be hidden the entire time," he insisted. "He's here for a reason."

"Fine." Sophia laid down. "You owe me big time."

Pushing the gurney forward, Theo and Sophia found Celeste lurking down a hall that bisected where the desks were. If they went forward and turned right, they would reach the coffee alcove. As it was, Fritz was speaking on the phone in a far corner.

"I thought you said the box would be in the fridge." The man paused. "No. I'm on the main floor. How would I know that the fridge you're talking about is on the third floor? What's that? Don't go in the room with six fridges, but the one across the hall. Fine. Your directions are pathetic."

The man did not glance back but moved forward. Celeste pointed to an elevator behind them, and Theo maneuvered the gurney down an adjacent hall as Celeste hurried to catch up. Fritz's voice carried. "Yes, Lucas. Dr. Lazar is busy. She's in the middle of an autopsy. She has no idea who I am."

Celeste used her badge to open the elevator. She said, "Upstairs is where we keep the bodies before we perform an autopsy. The room across the hallway is seldom used but has a backup generator and two extra freezers in case things get hectic in here. There are some additional workstations and other equipment. It's a logical place to store something."

"How is he going to get up there?"

"I'm sure Dr. Daniels gave him a key badge."

Theo said frantically, "He's going to get up there before we do."

"Maybe," said Celeste as the doors closed.

On the upper level, they crept down a hallway, intently listening. Celeste silently opened a door and whispered, "In here."

"What is this?"

"A storage room."

The moment the door close, Sophia sat up and asked, "Why is Fritz here?"

Celeste said, "Searching for something."

"I'm going to go find out. The two of you stay here." Theo ducked out of the room and ran down the hallway. A doorway of the staircase rattled, and the handle began to turn. Theo ducked into the nearest room and hoped it was the right one.

On the left were four workstations with microscopes, tables, chairs, and computer screens. Theo hurried to the third station and dove behind it, hiding behind a few boxes. He came to a stop suddenly as he hit something that dug into his ribs. He let out a gasp then covered his mouth. Gazing through the tears in his eyes; he was relieved to see that he had a direct view of the fridge.

Fritz strolled into the room as if he owned the building. He kept the lights off and stepped forward. He opened a brown carrying case and pulled out a set of gloves. They appeared to be green medical gloves but were nicer—surgeon-quality. He ambled to the first fridge and pulled open the door. It didn't budge. The second fridge opened, and the vapor of aerosols shot into the air. Theo silently hoped that it was a poison attacking Fritz's airway and lungs, until he realized that the same poison would reach him within seconds. He settled for it knocking Fritz unconscious, but nothing happened.

When the air cleared, a smile spread across Fritz's face. He plucked out a black plastic box and placed it on a nearby counter. Theo crawled forward to get a better look. On the outside of the box were the two letters— "M.S."

Fritz carefully opened the lid. The first item he removed was one of the most interesting devices Theo had ever seen. It was a grand total of eight inches in length. For all intents and purposes, it resembled a metal, gun-like device, with a syringe on one end. There were two handles, though the one further back was thicker and fit into Fritz's palm. The second handle was almost equally long. Theo puzzled over its possible uses. Then he noticed the trigger on the second handle. The barrel of this item, if that was what it could be called, had a syringe at the end, where something could be injected into something or someone. It was devilish in its design.

Fritz carefully placed it on the counter and pulled out a black case that was only a few inches thick. A plastic lid kept the items from moving around. When Fritz turned it over, there were two rows of blue bullets. Theo silently groaned. These same items were in Dr. Daniels's desk. What he was looking at made no sense. The next item out of the box was a group of white, small pieces of paper—

receipts, or something similar. Fritz threw these onto the table, unconcerned. A stack of photos was removed, and Fritz looked through them quickly. A piece of tape, some hair samples, and two smaller circular bottles were held in separate plastic bags. The next item was a piece of cloth or paper, and Fritz opened this carefully. It was a folded-up drink napkin with the words—"Club Jazzed."

The last item removed was a large bag with a purse, keys, a wallet, a small case that was black in color, and a few cosmetic items. Fritz took this and tossed it back into the box. He pocketed the napkin, the receipts, the metal gun, and the capsules. The trace items were tossed back into the box, and it was returned to the fridge. The small black case he'd seen inside the purse slid across the counter, and Fritz tried gathering everything. He grunted and shoved it into his pocket.

Fritz exited the room, and Theo struggled to get to the door before Fritz started downstairs. He poked his head out and watched the door close. Following Fritz to regain those items was fruitless, so he retreated down the hall and found Celeste and Sophia where he'd left them.

"What happened?" asked Celeste.

Theo explained what he'd seen.

Celeste said, "Okay. He has a gun of some sort, these weird vials or pods, and a napkin. But he left some trace elements, some evidence, and a purse."

Theo said, "Still trying to make you look incompetent and frame me."

Sophia said, "But that will open the case into Mary's death."

"Not for long," replied Theo.

"Because of the evidence you found downstairs."

"Yes." Theo nodded.

Celeste said, "I've already started having the fingernail clippings analyzed. Let's grab the other evidence, and they'll have nothing to point to."

"Let's go," said Sophia.

Theo pushed her to lie down, and Celeste opened the door. Theo maneuvered the gurney out the door and around the corner.

"Oh, shit," hissed Celeste.

A voice boomed from the far end of the hall. "Is that you, Doctor?"

She answered, "Just placing this body into the freezer. I'll be with you in a minute."

Theo guided the gurney forward, and Celeste opened the door. Fritz followed them into the room. He felt horrible as he opened a latch on the wall, and he and Celeste moved the slab from the gurney onto a rolling shelf. Without a second thought, Theo pushed closed the door and it latched tightly.

She asked, "How did you get up here?"

"The door was unlocked, ma'am. I just need a signature."

Celeste took the paper and signed it. "Is all the coffee delivered?"

"Yes. The finest coffee in the world."

"My favorite," she added with a broad smile.

The man said, "Could you walk me out? There were several people outside, and I don't want them thinking I'm not where I shouldn't be."

"Certainly," she said.

Theo tried giving her a look, but she just said, "Doctor Finkelson, please prepare our next autopsy. I believe it is Barrett Sanders. We need to hurry as I need to be leaving in an hour. This is an active case, so be careful. Get things set up and I'll be back in five minutes."

"Right," Theo said, stunned. His roommate, who had been killed, and whom he was suspected of murdering, was about to be autopsied in the same location as Mary Sneider. It was as if everything had come full circle.

Theo pushed the empty gurney back down the hall.

Fritz asked, "Where is he going?"

"To the elevator. It is the only way up to this floor for us. But you and I can take the stairs."

Once Theo reached the elevator, he hit the button and waited for the elevator to arrive. As the door opened, he knew Celeste and Fritz had already headed down. He still pushed in the gurney and hit the button for the bottom floor. He stepped out as the doors closed. He sprinted back down to where Sophia was, opened the latched door, and helped her out. She was nearly hysterical, cold, and pale. They didn't have a ton of time, so he helped her back into the corridor and across to the other room. He retrieved the items left behind by Fritz and headed back to the elevator.

Nearing the elevator, Sophia asked, "Where is Celeste?"

"With Fritz. We need to get you back on the gurney and out of sight." He hit the elevator button, and it rose up from the bottom floor.

"I can't get back onto that gurney."

"Just for a little longer."

"I hate all of this," she whispered.

The door opened, and the gurney was still there. Sophia lay down, and they descended to the main floor. As the autopsy rooms came into view, Celeste appeared to her left, walking up the corridor. She came and sat on a chair just outside of the autopsy room. She tore at her lab coat, face covering, and booties. She shook.

Theo asked, "Did anything happen?"

"He told me to enjoy my coffee for as long as I could. The threat was there, but if I didn't know who he was, I would have never seen it."

"What now?"

"Show me what Fritz left behind."

Theo pushed Sophia into the autopsy room and helped her from the table. He pulled in a chair, and she sat, trying to regain her composure. As Theo worked, he asked, "Did you happen to find the cause of death for that older gentleman?"

"You mean Jonathan Stark. Yes, I did. It was from an aortic aneurysm. It ruptured, and his death was immediate. It was also what caused the large amount of pooling blood. He must have been lying on his back, so the blood naturally settled."

"Interesting." Theo pulled out all the items and handed them to Celeste. The first item was the fabric from the coffee bag. "You're sure that this will have your blood on it?"

"That is a piece from my Texas Longhorns shirt. It will match."

He next handed an evidence bag with several strands of hair. "What could this be?"

"I keep my hair samples in a protective barrier, not a bag like this. Did you see if this bag was added to the pile?"

"I didn't. Why would they do that?"

She held up both evidence bags, and Theo noticed the difference between the two. "If I had to guess, I would say that this is also yours."

Sophia said, "It does look like the same color."

Theo reflexively ruffled the back of his head.

They looked at the receipt and the bag. There was the name of Mary Sneider on the receipt, and the purse was clearly hers as well. Celeste said, "This links everything."

Sophia asked, "I think we need to leave."

"Soon," said Celeste. "I need to work on a few things. I'll show you to my office, and you can rest there for a bit. I need to document what we've found and check in on the nail clippings."

Sophia said, "I need some food."

"I have a few protein bars in the fridge in my office and we have a break room."

"How long is this going to take?"

"A few hours."

"That will be dangerously close to the time of your meeting."

"It can't be helped. I'm not showing up to that award ceremony without something to defend myself."

Theo and Sophia sat on a luxurious couch in Celeste's office and ate some of the food they found.

Sophia said, "I can't believe we were just here, running around like our heads were cut off."

"A lot has happened over the last few days," said Theo. "I think we are getting close."

"Do you think they'll find something that will point to Mary's killer?"

"I hope so. But I think we know it was Fritz."

"Really," Sophia said. "How?"

"Dr. Daniels said his partner killed Mary."

"I can't handle all of this." She lay back on the couch and rested her eyes. Ten minutes later, Sophia fell asleep on the couch, and Theo leaned his head back, deep in thought.

Sometime later, he heard footsteps and voices approaching the office. Theo placed a hand over Sophia's mouth, waking her and dragging her to the bathroom. The door mostly closed as Theo heard the office door click open.

"Mayor Reed," said Dr. Lazar, wearing her white coat and appearing to be in control. "I can assure you that there is no impropriety going on here at this office."

Theo had only the slightest view of Dr. Lazar's profile and the side of the face of the mayor. He felt that others were in the room as well.

"I'm sorry for the commotion, Celeste," said a male voice, practiced and sophisticated. "There has been an open investigation on your office for several weeks. We've interviewed several staff members. Most everything seems up to par, but we have concerns about a few cases that you are working on."

"Which ones?"

"Mary Sneider and Barrett Sanders. Dr. Daniels has indicated that you did the autopsy on Miss Sneider and are scheduled to perform Mr. Sanders's autopsy today or tomorrow. He feels that both cases are connected, and he is worried that your judgment might be skewed slightly."

"And why is that?"

Dr. Daniels's voice cut through the air. "You allowed Dr. Theo Raden to come look at the body of Mary, and now he is the person of interest in the death of Barrett Sanders. I sent an email to you about my concerns just yesterday. The same doctor broke into the office here, likely to steal evidence that he had left behind. There were reports of a security guard being stabbed. Last week I informed you that there was evidence missing in both of their cases. Apparently you don't have the time or inclination to respond to my questions or emails." His voice was filled with contempt.

The mayor added, more diplomatically, "There have been reports of gross misconduct and tampering with evidence."

Celeste pointed to her computer. "Dr. Daniels. You and I both know that you didn't send me an email. I answer every email that I get. I can also bring up the camera in this facility when I questioned you about the evidence in Miss Sneider's case. You did the preliminary on Mary Sneider but failed to finish your report, likely on purpose, so that I would have to turn in the final product. I have been reviewing it and have it readily available."

A voice added, "It has been confirmed through an email sent to Dr. Bowthorpe detailing Dr. Daniels's concerns. It does not appear that you were sent the email."

Theo recognized the voice from earlier today. Franklin, the mayor's assistant. Had he been here checking up on Celeste, Theo wondered.

Sophia squeezed his arm, and Theo turned to stare at his friend. All the color had drained from her face. She mouthed, "I recognize a voice."

"Which one?" Theo mouthed back.

Sophia shrugged her shoulders.

Another voice added, "We were initially told by your office that the death of Mary Sneider was a simple drowning."

Doctor Lazar quickly answered, "That's not exactly true, Detective Yang. I called your office and spoke directly to Detective Fisher. I told her that we had found new evidence and that the case was ongoing and suspicious."

A high-pitched squeal erupted from Dr. Daniels. "What new evidence?"

"We have some hair samples and a piece of tape, and a second look at the body produced some fingernail scrapings. It was supposed to have been done by one of my staff during the initial autopsy, but I looked at it again and reevaluated things."

Dr. Daniels countered, "Dr. Lazar, how come this new evidence wasn't brought to my attention?" Theo smiled at the voice change of Dr. Daniels; it was as if helium had attacked his vocal cords.

"I did." Doctor Lazar moved, and Theo thought he heard her rotating her monitor. "I sent you this three days ago. It is unopened and unread. It wasn't specific about the evidence, but I've been running it. Again, as you did the preliminary but didn't finish, I thought it was my obligation to inform the police of these changes."

"Dr. Daniels," the mayor spoke with perplexity in his tone. "You called my office and reported that you felt that some evidence was in a fridge upstairs being intentionally hidden from your investigation. You also said there might be some missing evidence in other locations."

"Yes," he gloated. "It is upstairs."

"I'd like to see that evidence right now. Detectives Yang and Franklin, please accompany Dr. Daniels upstairs. I want this to be well-documented." The force in his voice was clear. Theo heard people leaving the room. Mayor Reed's voice softened when he next addressed Dr. Lazar. "Celeste. Tell me what is going on here?"

A clinical voice responded, "Mary Sneider was a twenty-two-year-old female who was found at the bottom of a pool. Initially it looked to be an accident. But samples taken from under her fingernails hinted at a possible attacker. We're looking into a piece of tape that may have been used to keep her nostrils open and some hair samples."

"Why would Doctor Daniels believe that evidence was being misplaced?"

"Sir, if I could speak freely."

"Please."

"You know me. I understand that our relationship could not continue. When I was brought here, I hope that you did so because of my experience."

"It was."

"Doctor Daniels sees me as someone who was given this post and didn't earn it."

"Jealousy?" Mayor Reed questioned.

"And maybe something a little more sinister."

"Why would the possible killer use a piece of tape?"

"If I am right, she might have been drowned somewhere else and brought to a pool at her apartment building. Once she was submerged, water would naturally seep into the mouth and lungs and potentially contaminate the scene."

"What do you mean, contaminate?"

"Drownings are difficult because the water ingested into the lungs while the victim is alive will at least partially be absorbed into the body. This occurs through the stomach and lungs. If, say, someone died in a muddy pool versus a bathtub, the expected findings of the lung fluid would be different. By placing the body in the pool, it could potentially contaminate the findings."

"Why not communicate your concerns with Dr. Daniels or Dr. Bowthorpe?"

"I wanted to do a thorough investigation of everything we had, to either rule it as a simple drowning, or something more."

"What about Dr. Raden? How is he involved?"

"I really don't know. He arrived and was convinced that Mary's death was no accident. He pushed me into taking a second look at the body."

"Where is the evidence that you are working on?"

"Some of the hair and fingernails are being worked on in the basement. I have my best technician, Mark, working on it."

"Can we go down there after we're done here?"

"Certainly, sir."

"I should have given you fair warning that you were being investigated," replied the mayor.

"Why, sir. You wouldn't have done that with anyone else. This is the proper way."

"You are full of surprises," whispered Mayor Reed. "Always trying to do things on your own."

The rest of their conversation was cut short by the sounds of the office door opening and people entering.

"Welcome back, Dr. Daniels," said the mayor. "Where is this evidence that you were referencing in regard to the gross misconduct in this office?"

Detective Yang replied, "Dr. Daniels became distraught upstairs. He swore repeatedly that some box was inside a fridge."

"And it was empty?" the mayor asked.

"It was."

Detective Yang continued, "He next took us to a cabinet with coffee supplies and other items, but again, nothing."

"Coffee?" questioned the mayor.

Franklin added, "We didn't find a single thing that could be considered as evidence."

The mayor turned to face Dr. Daniels. "Tell me what you think?"

"I don't really have an answer for you right now."

"Then tell me why you called me."

After a long pause, it was Celeste who answered, "Our team is working hard to identify the real cause of Miss Sneider's death, and we will work tirelessly until the case is solved. Our entire team will work closely with Detective Yang. I think that over the next few days, we will learn more about the evidence we have. This is one of our top priorities, and I will keep you in the loop daily, sir."

"That is the answer I wanted to hear. Thank you, Dr. Lazar."

"Will we still be having our meeting this afternoon?"

"No, I don't think so. Our focus should be on our current cases." In a more firm and angry tone he continued, "Dr. Daniels, you called my office on this matter and informed my staff that there was some evidence missing. I hope that this was a mistake rather than an attempt to discredit Dr. Lazar. I hope in the future, this sort of behavior will not happen. Do you understand my meaning?"

"Certainly, sir."

"We'll be going now."

"Thank you, Mayor," replied Dr. Daniels calmly.

Theo was tempted to step out and reveal all of Dr. Daniels's dirty secrets. He had killed a girl and tried to take over the MEs office. For all he knew, Dr. Daniels had killed Barrett. But if he did, he would be arrested on the spot, making things far worse for himself, Sophia, and Celeste.

Dr. Lazar added, "Detective Yang, Mayor Reed, would you come with me to the basement for an update on the evidence we've collected?"

"Gladly," replied Detective Yang.

CHAPTER 23

A few minutes had passed since the door closed and everyone left. Theo was listening intently to ensure no one had stayed behind. Turning to Sophia, he asked, "Which voice did you recognize?"

She tapped the wall repeatedly. "I can't be certain."

"Was it the mayor?"

"Possibly." Sophia's arms were crossed over her chest, and she was rubbing her arms as if cold. "Maybe it was Dr. Daniels. I can't be sure right now. He's such an evil person.

Theo nodded.

Sophia asked, "What do we do now? Should we stay here or go?"

Theo wanted nothing more than to escape the building, but he worried that if they walked out, they would see the mayor and Detective Yang standing outside. "I think we wait until Dr. Lazar comes back."

"You like her, don't you?"

Theo wasn't sure how to answer. "I'm not sure. Maybe...but we need her help to get out of here and to solve this case."

"Could you see yourself with her long-term?"

Theo was surprised by this question. "Why do you ask?"

Sophia looked at the ground. "I just don't know if, after all this is done, you would want to spend some time with me?"

"I totally would," Theo answered quickly.

A huge smile spread across Sophia's face.

"But as friends," Theo continued. "I see you like my sister if I'd ever had one."

Theo remembered the look that had started all of this, one that had matched Hannah's. In this moment, he realized that he needed to move on from her death. He had never allowed himself to think like this before.

Sophia's words cut through his thoughts. "This is a bathroom, and I really have to go. Could you stand out there until I'm finished?"

With a smirk, he said, "You better hope that I don't get caught."

"Well. I must go more than pee, and I can't do that with you in here. Hide under the desk."

"Fine," Theo said. He slipped out of the bathroom, ducked down behind the desk, and waited. There weren't a ton of windows, but he couldn't be certain that Celeste would be the only one who came back. Sophia let him back into the bathroom ten minutes later.

Dr. Lazar arrived and closed the door. She was alone and most of the tension in her shoulders disappeared as she leaned against the door. Theo asked, "Can we come out?"

"Yes. They're gone."

Sophia said, "I need to sit down."

"Are you feeling all right?" Celeste asked.

"I started having small contractions this morning. They aren't regular, but they're painful at times."

"Having you been drinking enough water?" asked Dr. Lazar.

Sophia glanced up with a sarcastic look on her face. "Trying my best. It's been a rough few days."

"Of course," Celeste replied.

"Did you check on the nail clippings? I thought you said that you didn't trust anyone here?"

"I don't trust that inside this building that the process won't be contaminated. I mentioned Mark working on the clipping, but that isn't really true. I have a professional in the city doing the testing, and he can perform everything safely if this goes to trial. We've used him before."

"And…what?" asked Theo. "He'll call when he gets something."

"Yes." Celeste moved to her desk, but something changed in her countenance. "But if we get something, we'll need to match it against someone else. That might be easily done, or not."

"That's good news."

"Yes and no," said Dr. Lazar.

Theo was taken aback by her crestfallen gaze. He asked, "What's wrong?"

"Fritz coming here means that they are confident and unafraid to pressure me. He saw me and you here. He left thinking that the evidence was still here. That's why he notified Dr. Daniels that he could come here with the mayor. But now both Dr. Daniels and Fritz know that we have the purse, the piece of your shirt, and the rest of evidence is gone. We're all going to be in more danger."

"Did Fritz kill my friend?" asked Sophia.

"I believe so," replied Celeste. "Now we'll need to prove it. Her drowning is no longer accidental."

"Tell me more about that gun you saw," Sophia said.

Theo explained the two levers, or a handle and a squeeze mechanism. He wasn't completely certain what he had seen or how it could be used.

"How would Mary have found that?" asked Sophia.

Theo said, "I have no idea." Turning his attention to Celeste he asked, "Who would have performed the evidence list when her stuff arrived?"

Celeste clicked a few keys and said, "Dr. Daniels did."

"But now that the evidence is gone, it means nothing," replied Sophia.

Theo said, "A part of me thinks that's how Sophia became pregnant."

"How, though?" asked Celeste. "I don't know anything that fits your description."

"Maybe a special procedure or something. That's still being developed."

"But why?"

"A test subject?"

Celeste said absentmindedly, "A test subject for medication that can increase the possibility of getting pregnant. It's already been done, but in a clinical setting. If they figured out how to do it on the black market, that would be worth a ton of money. Do you know how much is spent each year to get pregnant? We're talking hundreds of millions of dollars. If a company found a better way, I can only imagine. And, if they are using test subjects among the homeless or college students, what a perfect set-up."

"It still doesn't account for how she lost her memory."

Celeste said, "A side effect of the medication."

"Oh. I like it," Theo replied. "That would explain a thing or two. But we still have several unanswered questions and no evidence. If I explained this to Patrick or Zorn, they would just laugh at me."

Sophia said, "How could we get our hands on that metal gun and those capsules?"

"We could follow Fritz around," Theo suggested.

"He'll probably be at the club tonight."

"I could go with you," suggested Celeste.

Sophia insisted, "I feel well enough to go."

"None of us can go," Theo pointed out. "Fritz knows what Sophia looks like. He was here today, and if he saw you or me at the club, he would realize that we have caught on to something. Fritz is going to know that the evidence was misplaced in a matter of minutes. Hopefully, he blames Dr. Daniels."

What are we going to do?" asked Sophia.

"Celeste should stay here and continue trying to identify the evidence we found today. Maybe you'll have better luck identifying that metal gun-looking device."

"What about us?" demanded Sophia.

"We're headed back to Mary's apartment and to see if we can find anything else that she may have hidden."

"We've already been there," Sophia hissed. "We found nothing."

"But we didn't know what we were looking for."

Sophia added, "There might be someone watching the apartment. We could call Clayton or Derek to sneak in and see what they find."

Theo considered the option. Finally he said, "I'm not sure it's a good idea to involve anyone else."

"Fine," Sophia thundered. "But I need some real food…and it better be good."

Celeste led them out of the MEs office without any further incidents. An hour and a half later, Theo and Sophia pulled into a small auto-repair shop just off of Broadway in Lemon Grove. They parked about two blocks from Sophia's apartment complex. There was a metal fence encircling a portion of the parking lot. Directly behind the repair shop was a field that approached the apartment complex. If the complex was being watched, this would be a perfect spot to see them before they were seen.

There was an abandoned white house next to the auto repair building, on the far side of a dirt road. The road went up a slight rise and disappeared into the field. Theo explained his idea as they finished eating their tamales, rice, and beans.

"Ready?" asked Theo.

"Not really. We better not have to sprint back here all of a sudden."

"I could go on my own."

Sophia glared at him. "Stupid option."

After throwing away their trash, they found a small area near the back of the fence that was separated enough to squeeze through. The walk to the back portion of the apartment was longer and harder than they had planned. Fatigue, uterine cramps, and being eight months pregnant depleted Sophia of her energy and stamina.

They stopped a few times to rest. If a woman with a distended abdomen, dirty clothes, and sweat trickling down her back were the fashion, she'd be setting trends. After climbing the back wall, they moved from tree to tree until they reached the first building. From there, they circled the building and found the walkway. It was mostly deserted. They held hands as they strolled ahead, trying to appear as if they belonged.

They changed directions, turned right, and went directly to the dumpsters. Lifting the lid, Theo pretended to toss something inside.

"I can't see anyone watching the apartment," whispered Sophia.

"Me neither."

From there they went directly to her front door, she placed her key into the lock, and it opened easily. The front room looked exactly how he remembered. Closing the door, he moved the closest couch to block the doorway. They continued to Mary's room, not wanting to waste any time.

The next thirty minutes were fruitless, and they found nothing. Theo, feeling helpless, sat on the edge of the Mary's bed. Sophia was already lying on her back exhausted.

Theo grumbled, "Well, this was a total waste."

"The black underwear you discovered is quite revealing," smirked Sophia.

"I saw that last time."

"You did?" Sophia tried sitting up.

"I'll search the kitchen. Try to get some rest."

Theo was about to turn around when a deep voice spoke from the kitchen. "Hey, you asshole. Take another step and I'll shoot you in the head."

Theo twisted slowly and found Clayton pointing a gun at his head from ten feet away.

"Sophia! You okay?" Clayton called. "Can you come out and step toward me?"

"Dude," Theo said. "You are so annoying."

"Shut it."

Sophia stepped out of Mary's room with a bat in her hands. "Leave us alone, Clayton."

"Whoa. When the hell did you get pregnant?"

"You need to leave."

"I can't do that," Clayton insisted.

"Why are you pointing a gun at us?"

"Not you." He steadied the gun. "At him!" Glaring at Theo, he asked, "Are you the father?"

"You're brainless," Theo responded.

Clayton's eyes fluttered to Sophia, and Theo felt that something was off. He stepped in front of Sophia.

"What are you doing?" screamed Clayton. "I'll kill you here and now!"

"Clayton. What the hell are you doing?" demanded Sophia.

Using the gun he motioned for Sophia to come closer. Theo shook his head and extended his hand to make sure Sophia didn't step away.

Sophia asked, "Why are you doing this?"

Clayton answered softly, "I'm saving you."

Sophia spit at Clayton. "Saving me from what? Did you kill Mary?" Theo registered her anger and this new line of thinking.

"I'm saving you from him." He pointed the gun at Theo.

Theo asked, "Do you know a guy named Fritz?"

"Who?"

Sophia said hotly, "I'm going to ask you one more time. Did you kill Mary??"

"No freaking way."

Sophia shook her head. "Then why are you pointing that gun at me?"

"I'm pointing it at him."

Theo asked, his voice calm, "Can we tell you a story?"

"Who said you could talk?"

While he raised one of his hands, he used the other to grip Sophia and move her directly behind him. He nodded to the living room and the couch. "Sophia is going to sit down, and you're going to lower your gun. She'll explain everything as I sit next to her."

Before Theo took a second step, the gun discharged, and a bullet crashed into the ceiling above them. Theo stopped instantly.

The loud sound appeared to startle Clayton as much as them. Sophia began screaming, and Clayton flinched. Theo lunged, and despite Clayton having twenty pounds on him, Theo hit him directly in the shoulder of the arm holding the gun. He angled his elbow at close range, and it connected with Clayton's jaw. The boy staggered back, the gun dropping to the floor. Theo crouched as a fist flew above his head. Theo's next punch was an uppercut that was perfectly timed. It connected under the jaw, and Clayton stumbled to one knee. Theo knew that a kick to the side of the head would knock Clayton out completely. But instead, he stepped away and picked up the gun.

Sophia rushed forward and lifted her arm as if she were going to clobber Clayton. She screamed, "Clayton Shephard, I'm going to kick the shit out of you until you tell me what the hell is going on!"

"I thought you were in danger…" His voice trailed off. To his credit, Clayton didn't block the punch that connected with his nose.

She screamed, "For hell's sake. You shot at Theo and me."

"To protect you."

"You are brain-dead."

Clayton stood. "Give me a chance. Let me call Derek and Rachael. They can explain everything."

Sophia retorted, "Right now I don't trust you at all."

The glass door behind Clayton slid open an inch. A voice entered the apartment. "How are things going in there? What was that noise we heard?"

"Derek. Get the hell in here before I slap Clayton to death. He tried shooting us."

The door slid open farther, and Derek and Rachael, dressed in black jeans and hoodies, strode into the apartment.

"It's not a real gun," replied Derek, but he glared at Clayton. "I told him not to do it, but he wouldn't listen."

"What?" Theo replied. "Was he shooting blanks?"

"Clayton, you idiot!" Rachael screamed. "You were supposed to call us before you did anything stupid." She looked from Theo to Sophia. "Oh my god. Are you pregnant?"

Sophia said curtly, "Yes. I. Am!"

Derek frowned at Theo. "Care to explain?"

Theo replied, "We will when Clayton backs the hell off."

"But I saw them sneaking inside and wanted to make sure they didn't get away," Clayton stated.

Sophia's high-pitched scream drowned out everything. "By pointing a gun at us!"

"I pointed the gun at him—not you."

"Enough!" Derek roared. "We need to get out of here. Come on Sophia, you're safe now. You're coming with us."

"I'm not going anywhere."

Derek pointed at Theo. "Is he working for whoever was following Mary? Is he the father? We glimpsed him sneaking into your apartment and looking around."

"He's been helping me the entire time."

Rachael put in, "I told you. He didn't even know about Mary's death until I told him. But he lied about her being sick."

Clayton hissed, "Shut up, Rachael."

Sophia stepped forward and slapped Clayton. "Stop acting like a dick and pushing people around. I'm totally sick of how you're behaving. Someone better tell me what's going on or I'll never talk any of you again."

"Whoa," Derek muttered. "Everyone needs to relax."

Theo replied, "We're here to try to get some idea of why Mary was killed."

"We can't stay here," Rachael insisted. "Someone has been watching the apartment."

Derek offered, "We can head to our apartment."

"You haven't given us a single reason to follow you," Sophia hissed.

Derek glanced back and forth between Theo and Sophia. "When you went missing, we helped Mary look for you. We've kept pretty good details on who has come searching for you. Your friend seems awfully suspicious. He has snuck inside this apartment a few times and won't let you out of his sight."

"He has rescued me a few different times. He has sacrificed everything. Why didn't you tell me that you helped Mary look for me?"

"When?" Clayton demanded. "We've been to your work and your favorite places, and we even tried hacking into your phone. You keep vanishing."

"That's the point!" Sophia shouted.

"We need to go," Derek said.

Sophia hissed, "We'll follow you."

Rachael said, "Make sure all the lights are out. That's how it has been."

They left through the kitchen door and ducked through some of the shrubs. Again Sophia held Theo's hand while Derek held Rachael's. Clayton was the fifth wheel, and he gave the impression that he wasn't happy about this. They stayed close to the back of the buildings and crossed to the opposite side of the complex.

Derek and Clayton had a corner apartment with a partial view of Sophia's front door. They snuck around to the back of the building and in through the sliding glass door.

Once inside, Derek said, "Lock all the doors and check the windows."

Rachael and Clayton hurried off and returned two minutes later.

Clayton said, "Clear."

"Let's pull up some chairs and talk."

Theo nodded.

"Are you guys dating?" asked Clayton.

No one answered. Instead, Rachael said, "We've been looking for you for months. Then you showed up with this guy who was slightly suspicious. We didn't see or hear from you again for weeks. Why wouldn't you at least tell us that you were okay?"

Clayton answered, "Because she was mind-controlled."

"You mean brainwashed?" Theo retorted.

"Look at the prick."

"Stop being childish, Clayton," Derek said. His focus landed on Theo. "What about you?"

"I'm her doctor."

Rachael coughed into her fist.

Clayton replied, "Shut the hell up and call me stupid."

Sophia shook her head. "You called it, Clayton. It's true enough. He's my pregnancy doctor. I met him when I was really out of it. But we're not saying another word until you tell us what you know about Mary's death."

"She drowned," Clayton mumbled, but his voice was no longer angry. He stared at the floor as if reliving something.

"You've been missing for months," Derek started. "Why do we need to tell you anything. Can't you remember?"

Theo answered, "Sophia has some memory loss that dates back to before she got pregnant. Explain to her like she knows nothing."

Derek nodded but still appeared confused. "It first was an issue a couple of weeks after we last saw you.

There was a huge fight between you and Clayton in this apartment. He wanted to go on a date with you. You didn't. Do you remember that you threatened to move out of the apartment?"

Clayton interrupted, "Do we have to rehash this?"

"Not at all," Sophia whispered.

Derek continued, "We didn't see you again. We thought you had moved out. There were some new friends at the bank, and you had been going to these late-night parties. You went off the deep end and wouldn't talk to any of us. Even Mary said you were acting weird."

Theo asked, "Why didn't you mention this when we saw you the first time and Sophia asked you about Mary?"

Clayton answered, "Because we trusted you so much. How did we not recognize that Sophia was pregnant?"

"Keep going," Sophia urged.

"You would come home late, then not come home for weeks. One night, you came back, and it was the first time we'd seen you in a month. We were partying here, and you knocked on the door and pulled Mary out to talk with her. You were all dressed up but refused to go into your apartment. You and Mary walked to the back, near the dumpsters. She later told us that you asked her to help you, but before you explained what you needed, a black sedan pulled up and demanded that you get inside. That was the last time any of us saw you until we bumped into you weeks ago. Mary was so worried about you and then she died…"

"Did Mary start looking for me?"

"At first she thought it was a new boyfriend." Derek glanced at her belly. "You had told her that there was someone rich in your life. She hoped it was no big deal; we all did. But after two months of not seeing you, and after she learned that your rent was being paid by direct deposit, she got worried. At first, she tried to find out who was sending the money. She went to your work, but everyone thought you had up and quit. Nothing made sense. It was about two months later that she started searching through some of your things. She found receipts from a half dozen bars, clubs, and restaurants. She began hunting for you at these places. She came to Clayton and me for help. We recruited Rachael while we were trying to get information on how the rent was being paid."

Theo asked, "Did you find anything?"

"Sort of," replied Derek. "I have a friend of a friend who's pretty good with computers."

"Do I know this person?" asked Sophia.

"Probably not."

"That's convenient."

Ignoring this, Derek said, "The money came from a company called Hartman Security LLC."

Sophia nodded. "We learned the same thing but couldn't get any further."

Derek said, "We did."

Sophia's eyebrows rose slightly. "I'm impressed."

"Hartman Security LLC is a shell company for another company and another company. It all leads back to this pharmaceutical company called BioPharm. It was them who sent the money."

"You're kidding," Theo gasped.

"It didn't make any sense to us," added Rachael.

"It that all you found?" asked Sophia, slightly disappointed.

"No way," Clayton said.

Derek continued, "Mary hit the jackpot when she saw you coming out of one of the clubs. She left out the part about you being pregnant."

"Get to the point."

"Mary told us that she talked to you and you were someone totally different. You didn't remember her or any of your friends."

Theo asked, "How long was this after Sophia came knocking at your door during that party?"

Clayton answered, "Four or five months."

Derek continued, "Mary was so worried that she took you to a doctor. The entire time, you kept talking about something called Alethomne. Mary thought you meant a homeopathic pregnancy, but weeks later our hacker friend connected BioPharm and a drug trial in Europe that was shut down two years ago because of some crazy side effects. Buried deep in the paperwork was a medication for anxiety called Alethomne. Does that mean anything to you?"

"Nope." Sophia smiled humorlessly. "But Theo has tracked a crooked doctor to BioPharm and a club called Club Jazzed."

"That was the club that Mary found you at," Clayton barked.

Theo asked, "Why didn't you stop Sophia from getting away from Mary?"

Clayton replied defensively, "We weren't there, bro. Sophia escaped Mary, and a few weeks later, she was dead."

Derek stood and began pacing. "Mary searched and searched, but she couldn't find you again. That was when she came to us with a plan."

Sophia asked, "Do I even want to ask?"

Derek added, "It was a brilliant plan, all of us thought so, but it may have been what killed her."

"What?" Theo hissed.

"Mary was convinced that something had happened to you rather than you choosing to stay away." Derek's eyes were dark and serious. "She had been to Club Jazzed a few times, and things were fishy. Something was happening behind the scenes."

"Fishy." A laugh escaped from Sophia.

Clayton continued, "The same girls worked the bar or were waitressing. But these other girls were coming in and out like a merry-go-round. These girls attracted a certain type of guy. The rich and powerful. This is a high-end club."

"Have you been there?" Theo asked.

Clayton pounded the countertop with his fist. "We were supposed to be with Mary the night she died."

"What do you mean?" Sophia leaned back, her hand falling across her belly.

Derek answered. "Mary asked us to follow her, as she was planning to go inside alone. We helped her get ready for her mission. We thought she would be fine, but we ran into a problem when we tried to get inside the club. We didn't have enough money to buy our way in. We tried finding another way into the club, but they had security around all the other sides. The next day, Felix and Jeremiah had a huge party. We were there, hoping to see Mary, but she never showed up. A fire alarm went off in the main building. Someone had put dry ice in one of the toilets, and some of the water flowed across the floors. Rachael was called to clean up, and Clayton and I helped. Someone noticed that something was in the pool and I dove it and found Mary."

Sophia leaned forward as if she was going to vomit. "This is unreal."

Theo asked emphatically, "Why didn't you tell the police?"

Clayton growled, "Tell them what?"

"That you knew exactly where she was the night before."

Derek shook his head and said calmly, "You've got to understand. Mary had a special camera that we gave her for her visit to Club Jazzed. It's a simple idea, yet the reality is that this camera is very complex. It's about the size of a pack of gum and holds the information on a micro-SD card. It can record for up to two hours, and it can be in color and with audio. It isn't illegal per se, but it isn't something you want to point back at you."

"It's a what?" Sophia demanded.

"A micro DVR camera."

Theo said hotly, "You didn't tell anyone because of your stupid little camera. You thought you were going to get into trouble."

Derek answered, "Hell no. But the camera probably caught exactly what happened. We wanted to find it before we said anything, because then we would know exactly what happened."

"What did it look like?"

"It's entirely black, fits in a small gum wrapper, like the kind that holds five or seven pieces. There's a small hole at the top that the screen or recorder works through. It would be darn hard to spot this. It is much more than those stupid things you can buy on Amazon for home security."

Theo tried thinking through the fog. "I might have seen it."

Clayton asked, "Where?"

"In the morgue. It's a long story, but a guy from Club Jazzed has it now. It'll be damn hard to get back."

"Crap," Clayton said, and he kicked the wall softly.

Sophia asked, "What did Mary think was happening?"

"Drugs," Derek and Clayton responded simultaneously.

"That's one of our theories as well," Sophia added. "But what about Alethomne?"

"I don't get it," said Clayton. "You're here acting like you don't know what happened to you."

"I can't remember most of what has happened to me since I got pregnant. Sometime after Mary took me to a doctor, I made my way to Scripps Mercy. Theo here is Dr. Raden, and he helped me get out of whatever psychosis I was in. I was good for a few days when I saw you guys last, but then I got lost again. Theo found me again, and we've learned quite a bit. Mary's death was ruled an accident, but recently it has been changed to suspicious."

They took the next hour to explain what had happened to each of them. As the discussion went on, both Clayton and Derek warmed up to Theo and what he had been through. It was sobering, talking about the death of his roommate and watching Dr. Daniels killing the girl in the hot tub. When they finished, they all sat back, and it took ten minutes before anyone spoke.

It was Derek who said something first, "What's our plan now?"

Sophia smiled, "Are you sure you want in?"

CHAPTER 24

Approaching the door, Theo walked unsteadily, and he was unsure if he could actually pull this off. For his part, he had consumed a few drinks already, but he was sure that he was going to be forced to drink his weight in alcohol tonight. He fumbled the black business card from his back pocket. When he finally collected the card from the ground and glanced up, a huge mammoth of a man stood over him. Theo had shaved his head and used some tanning cream. He wore a white, collared shirt, a black sport coat, and brown pants. This outfit had cost nearly $8,000 and was made of Italian wool.

"What do you want?" the bouncer purred.

Theo shrugged, unalarmed, and showed the man the card. The bouncer would not touch it but smiled knowingly.

The lights outside the club were vibrant, and the line to get inside was two and a half blocks long. This was a special celebration, even for a Friday night. Word had spread quickly that a rookie all-star from the Padres and a Hall of Fame player were meeting with a few other players and celebrating an important series win, among other things.

"You here for a special reason tonight?"

Theo pulled up his pant leg, and a red bracelet came into view. Nothing else was said, and Theo was granted access to the front door as the man pulled back the rope blocking the entrance. A light flashed on the ceiling of the doorway as a second bouncer touched something on the wall.

Theo, Sophia, Derek, Clayton, and Rachael had staked out the doorway for the last three nights. They had set up cameras and rented an empty apartment room a block away from the club. The six cameras gave them a perfect view of the front doors and both alleys on each side. The only part they couldn't capture was the back of the building. Derek and Clayton were outside on the street, while Sophia and Rachael sat in the apartment.

Theo pulled out two hundred-dollar bills and passed one to each of the bouncers as he disappeared inside. They plucked them from his hand as expertly as the master bartenders inside created their own concoctions.

A bombshell of a girl materialized inside the door of the club. Theo had never seen her before. They were in a space between the outside and the club itself. The girl was curvy and perky, and her smile was dazzling. She wore a baseball jersey pulled back tightly to reveal her incredible figure, with a cap, short shorts, and no bra.

Theo's mouth opened on its own. He managed to mumble, "Mr. Jack gave me this card and said that I would be welcome."

As the black card came into view, the girl smiled even more genuinely, if possible. "Welcome, sir…we expect you to have the most pleasurable night."

They stepped into the club itself, and the atmosphere was purely volcanic. The ground shifted as loud music rumbled. There were spotlights, laughter, dancing on bars by girls in expensive outfits, and free-flowing alcohol everywhere. Theo was drenched in vodka by a short Asian girl with spiky hair. He was hugged and kissed, and phone numbers were thrust into his hand by three or four girls. This had all happened before he had taken a dozen steps into Club Jazzed.

He was led to a small table near the back wall of the main room. It was a typical bar table but had two leather chairs, and as he sat in his chair, he found that it was incredibly comfortable.

In a sweet voice, the girl said, "I promise I'll be back. Relax and enjoy the moment. This might turn out to be the best night you've ever had."

"Promises, promises," he said, toying with her.

She winked and disappeared into the crowd. The second and third floors were buzzing, but much of the excitement was on this main floor. There were twenty similar tables, an expansive bar, and a small dance floor. There must be nearly four hundred people on this level currently. No one sat at the bar, as everyone stood and danced, drank, and kissed. Just to the left of the bar was a large table with a dozen beautiful girls leaning against the wall, massaging backs, and talking with the customers. Theo recognized a few of the baseball players as they were hollering, singing, and enjoying themselves.

Five minutes later, two large glasses, one the color of apple-green, the other a toxic blue, were set on the table. He sipped each to appreciate the taste and siphoned some into small bottles inside his jacket. He needed to appear that he was enjoying himself. Derek had shown him this trick. Businessmen and women of every color, age, and size filled the room. Girls and boys danced, passed drinks, and went to join the hundreds of partygoers upstairs.

Theo switched seats and glanced up to where he had talked with Cindy and Tina. A tall black man dressed entirely in black was celebrating something fierce. He was surrounded by an entourage of three men with several girls giving them all their attention. They were having the night of their lives.

Moving back to his seat, Theo took a long drink from the blue cup. It was a frozen cocktail with a pineapple. He could taste the vodka, coconut, and blue curaçao. A flash of light caught his eye; someone was taking pictures of the crowd on the dance floor. Theo had just seen the flash from the camera at the right moment. However, someone else had seen the flash too; a door opened from inside the wall, and a large man stepped out. This area was near where the baseball players were, but none of them noticed a thing. The large man effortlessly cut through the customers next to the bar, and within seconds he had grasped the woman on the wrist, and a camera the size of her hand was ripped from her grasp. She tried to pretend she was with a group of women at a table near the front glass, but they all shook their heads. The camera was confiscated, and she was thrown out of the front door.

The vibration of his cell phone brought Theo back to reality. He stared down at the name on the ID of his phone—Dr. Celeste Lazar. He knew he needed to answer it, but he wasn't sure this was the right time.

"Hello, sweetie?" he shouted into the phone.

"Are you talking to me?" Celeste bemused. "Where are you?"

"That's 'cause I haven't said anything."

"Are you drunk?"

"Not yet."

"I thought you didn't drink."

Theo hissed, "Only when I go to the best club in town."

"You went without me after everything you said earlier."

"It was time to make a move."

Glancing up, Theo saw Fritz standing on a balcony on the upper floor, on the opposite side of the room. The man might be looking at him, but he couldn't be certain. Fritz wasn't the plan, but at least he knew that he was here tonight.

A tall, curvy girl wearing a tight purple dress with skinny straps arrived at his table and delivered a tall glass of red wine and a plate of food. Theo saw some crusted bread slices with chicken salad toppings, a bowl of potato soup, and some corn fritters. The smell was incredible.

Theo said, "I think me gots to go."

"I'm coming to get you."

"It's fine, I'm fine."

Theo smiled, and the girl nodded and walked away.

"You don't sound okay."

"Ewery twing is A-okay."

"I'm coming now."

Theo replied, his voice as clear as ever, "No, Celeste, stay away."

"I've got something important to tell you."

"What's that, babe…you finally going to cook me some dinner when I get back from this trip?"

"I see." A small pause followed, then Celeste added, "There wasn't any DNA evidence under the nails."

"Oh, shit," hissed Theo.

"What?"

"Sorry," he mumbled. "I was hoping for a smoking gun."

"Whatever that means." Celeste continued, "I found material under her nails that is a combination of algae, sediment, and coral."

"Are you saying she dug at the bottom of the ocean?"

"I don't think so."

"Then what?"

"I think that she was drowned in a fish tank—a saltwater fish tank."

Theo instinctively searched the entire room, expecting to see a fish tank in one of the walls. He came up empty. "That's totally cool, babe."

"There was a sticky substance on her nose, and I believe that it was taped open, postmortem, to get the chlorine water into her lungs and stomach."

"I've got to go now. See you soon."

"I'm coming to get you."

"I'm fine, Celeste." He felt more than saw someone approaching him, and he finished by saying, "I've got to do this. I'll call you when I get back to my hotel."

Theo took a long sip of his drink, emptying half of it, and when he came up to breathe, a man sat in the chair opposite him. Theo peered at Mr. Jack, who had two stunning brunettes on each side of him. He didn't think they were from the United States, and they were twins.

"Hello Mr. Reynolds from San Francisco," Mr. Jack said pleasantly.

"Mr. Jack," Theo said loudly. "You have a fantastic memory."

"It's my job. Love the new haircut. Are you ready for a good night?"

"Completely."

"You showed my card to Belinda, and now you have this first-rate table. Can I have the card back?"

Theo produced the black business card and handed it to Mr. Jack.

"These girls are spoken for. Let me pass them off, and I'll be right back."

"That was mischievous of you." Pointing to the empty seat, he said, "I'll be waiting for you."

Mr. Jack answered, "You won't be disappointed." Both girls winked and smiled at Theo before they strolled away.

The temptation to follow them was shockingly strong. He wasn't sure if it was the drinks or his adrenaline, but he wasn't thinking straight.

His phone started ringing again, and he silently swore. It was Celeste again. This time he declined the call. He took another deep sip of his wine, and it smoothed and calmed his nerves. He silently promised that he would never drink again after tonight. Finishing the wine, he moved on to the green-colored drink. It was both sweet and sour, delicious, and it caused his eyes to water. He noticed at least three staff members watching him closely. He suddenly felt the room closing in on him and desired nothing more than to run away.

"Sir, we have quite a night planned for you." The voice reached him from behind him and toward the front door. Theo rotated and found Mr. Jack strolling toward him. This time, he recognized the girl with him. It was the brunette who had been with Dr. Daniels inside the hot tub.

Mr. Jack sat back down, and the brunette rushed to Theo's side. She began rubbing his back and kissing his neck. "This is Darla, and she'll be with you for the first stage. Each phase gets better and better."

Theo took a long sip and hissed, his throat burning, "This is my kind of place."

"How was your week of business?" asked Mr. Jack.

"To say that I hit it out of the park is putting it mildly. This could become a monthly affair."

"We would be the recipient of great fortune."

"I'll drink to that." He gulped some of the remaining frozen blue drink and ate the pineapple.

"Do you prefer ice or coal?" asked Mr. Jack with a hint of a smile on his face.

Theo was taken aback by the question. He considered that this might mean something. He replied, "Both."

"I've got the perfect choice for you. Fracking is the first level. It'll be twenty-five hundred, and the drinks will be on me."

Theo didn't argue and pulled out a roll of bills. "Fifteen hundred now and the rest later."

"Certainly."

Fritz stood and said, "Follow me."

As he stood, the brunette rubbed up against him so forcefully that he felt the small bottles inside his jacket dig into his ribs. She didn't mind and wrapped her arm around him.

"Thank you, Darla," Theo said.

In a seductive voice, she said, "If you thank me for all the tiny things I do for you, you're not going to have a voice after tonight."

"Fine by me," he said as she led him next to the dance floor and toward the back wall. Two of the baseball players started hollering at him and Darla as they passed. One guy pounded his back as if congratulating him.

"He seems happy for you," she said.

"And why shouldn't he?"

Theo felt the phone in his pocket vibrate and knew that it was a text message.

"Do you need to answer that?"

"Maybe," he said, but made no attempt at his phone.

"I might punish you if you do."

"How about a peek?" Theo stopped next to Mr. Jack near the side wall.

"I'll let you peek at something," she whispered, and licked his ear.

Mr. Jack nodded, and the access entry opened, and then he was ushered inside. A man, thinly built and dressed in a tux, welcomed Theo and Darla. They stepped onto a red carpet. The walls were dark, but there was a glow in the ceiling. The corridor was a good twenty feet or more. The door closed behind him, and Theo tensed as he wondered if he was about to get attacked.

"Nervous?" Darla asked.

"Excited," he answered.

Mr. Jack said, "This is the true VIP of our club. You've made it to the big time. We only allow a handful of guests to see this inner sanctum."

"What should I expect?"

"Rousing and thought-provoking excitement that you'll beg to come back to over and over again."

"Wow," Theo said honestly as they marched into a chamber that reminded him of an enormous health spa. His eyes focused on the water in the center of the room. There were columns, and the air was humid, and a dozen men and women were in the water, with other nearly naked men and women outside performing for those in the audience in the water.

"This is the Garden of Eden," said Mr. Jack. "It is the next stage after Fracking, if you make it to that point." The man pointed to a small corridor to the right.

Pretending to be gazing around the sauna room, Theo noticed two more halls going off from the main room, farther to his left. Looking right, he noticed some offices and large televisions in the opposite corner.

"Is that salt water?" Theo asked, pointing to the large pool.

"No," said Mr. Jack. "But there are some propriety ingredients that make it the most pleasurable in California."

Theo nodded his approval, and he was led down a corridor to the right and entered a space with the glow of soft, yellow lights. Theo was led to a closed door on the left, the third along this section. Mr. Jack stopped on the far side of the door. He whispered, "The room behind this door is a once-in-a-lifetime opportunity. We've never allowed someone to enter this room twice. They've tried paying us obscene amounts of money to get in here a second time. Trust me, no one ever does. Don't let this moment go to waste."

"That's a helluva description. I hope it lives up to your hype."

"It will."

Mr. Jack knocked twice, and the door was unlocked. A man dressed as a servant opened the door. He doesn't smile or acknowledge Theo or Mr. Jack, and he stepped out of the room into the corridor. Theo's mouth nearly fell open. He recognized this man as someone who had been outside of St. Jude's when he and Sophia were watching Dr. Haderly. Theo turned away to avoid drawing attention to himself. For the first time, Theo saw the opulence of the lavish room. "I just might never leave," he sighed.

Mr. Jack said, "This is Samuel. He is here for you. He'll stand outside and make sure that you aren't disturbed. He'll knock twice when it's time to sample your choices."

Theo stepped in, and Darla followed him. Before the door closed, Theo said, "Please don't keep me waiting."

"Well. You will need a little time to spend with Darla. But it will be well worth it. Your entire night is just beginning. You'll never be the same after we pamper you like you deserve."

The door closed, and when Theo turned, he found Darla completely naked, standing on the bed, her finger demanding him to come closer.

CHAPTER 25

Theo was far from prepared for the direction things had turned. He knew that sex and drugs were likely central to Club Jazzed. But this was rapidly turning into an implausible fantasy. He gazed around the space, awestruck. The room was luxurious and could rival any suite in any local hotel. Extravagant red, gold, and yellow wallpaper wrapped the room like a present. There was a couch, black in color, large enough for two people to lie down on, against one wall. A champagne bucket and a bottle sat on an expensive table in the middle of the room. He could see an open closet with every imaginable toy within reach. There was a four-poster canopy bed with curtains, and Darla was dancing erotically.

Soft music played in the background. There were rings in the wall for handcuffs, and the walls appeared fortified. Theo heard nothing from outside this room.

Darla again motioned for him to come closer, and he followed her command. When he was a few feet away, she spoke. "Rule number one, you can't video anything that happens inside this room. I need you to put your cell phone on the table."

"Okay," Theo replied, trying to look at her without seeing her. She was attractive, and despite knowing that she had been in a hot tub with a killer, his heart was racing, and he was breathing fast.

"Rule number two. For now, I'm here to look at only. No touching or otherwise until I get the approval. Do you understand?"

"What?" Theo blurted before he could help himself.

"Part of the rules."

"Fine," Theo said. "I don't understand what is going on."

"I think you do. It's all part of the game." She smiled sweetly at him. He shook his head. The smile was eerily similar to Belinda's, who had walked him into Club Jazzed. "Phone."

Theo pulled out his phone, and as he rotated it over, he saw that he had a text from Celeste. He read part of it, and a wave of terror ran through him. He walked to the center, intending to put down his phone. He said, "What should I expect?"

"We are here to make sure you have the time of your life. You can choose a lot of different things. Some come here to watch and others to play, but most enjoy a combination of the two. We have medications that can help you last and relax. So many different options. But what happens inside this room only happens once." She pointed to a lever on the right side of the room, near a full-length mirror. "When you pull that lever, your time in this room is over forever. If I pull it, it is because you didn't follow directions, and the night ends. Don't leave with any regrets."

As she spoke, he poured himself a glass of champagne.

"Do I pour you one?"

"Maybe later. We don't want to rush things." She began twirling around the bed, using the silky drapes along the top and the poles to put her body into positions that were impossible.

Theo drank his glass and clicked on his phone. Celeste's text came into view. "Received call from Detective Yang. They found Dr. Daniels's body inside a hot tub. Water and acid were used, and he was only partly submerged. Neighbors found him before finished. Those responsible got away. Be careful."

He watched Darla for several minutes. His thoughts were jumbled as the reality of what he was risking set in. Dara's movements were hypnotic, and he suddenly became anxious that he had been led here on purpose. He took another sip of the champagne, and after another few minutes, he relaxed slightly.

Darla suddenly stopped and waited for his response.

Theo wiped his mouth and said, "Holy shit. That was the best dance I've ever seen. Incredible."

"Pour me one of those glasses."

"No problem."

Theo filled two glasses and nearly sprang from the table and away from his phone. He asked, "Where do you want me?"

"Let's have you take off your jacket and sit on the bed. Don't lie down, at least not yet. We will start with a massage." She accepted her glass, drank its entire contents, and encouraged him to do the same. She took the empty glasses from him, her hand running across his chest, and she walked to the table. Theo began to remove his jacket.

The only thing on Darla was a red bracelet that he had now seen several times. She took his jacket and tossed it onto a chair. She stepped in front of him and unbuttoned the top three buttons. She took his hand and guided him to the bed. She pushed him against it, came close, and kissed him passionately. His hands never touched her. He remained standing, unsure if he was supposed to sit down.

"I see that you understand the rules. You could have gotten away with a little there, but you did well."

Theo was out of breath, and he forced himself to picture the body of Dr. Daniels.

She climbed onto the bed, touched his shoulders, and pulled him back into a seated position. For the next fifteen minutes, she rubbed his back, kissed his neck, and snuck her hand down his shirt. Somehow he managed to scrutinize the room. There were no windows, but red curtains hang in a pattern to mimic a window. Against the left wall was a large, decorated marble fireplace.

There was a knock at the door, and Darla strode off and opened the door. Mr. Fritz stood there as if alone. He nodded almost imperceptibly at Darla, and she must've winked or something. Mr. Jack reached out of view. When he moved into the room, he was dragging two girls behind him. The girls were cuffed to each other near their ankles. They had gags placed over their mouths. They hobbled into the room, but to Theo's horror, they were happy, and their eyes glinted with excitement. They were beautiful and unafraid. He struggled to understand the distinction between the situation and the joy on their faces. He wanted to leap from the bed and unhook the girls, but that would be pointless. Each girl wore long silk pajamas, half hanging off their shoulders and flowing all the way to the floor. The first girl was dressed in white, the next girl in black. Their pajamas were sheer, and neither girl wore any underwear.

Mr. Jack's voice was professional. "Hope these choices please you."

The man must've misunderstood the expression on Theo's face, and he began nodding rapidly.

"Before we continue, Mr. Reynolds, I'll need the last thousand dollars."

Theo stood and walked to his coat. From the inside pocket, he pulled out $10,000. He counted out ten bills and stepped back to Mr. Jack. "This is going to be the best money I've ever spent."

"I completely agree with you."

Cindy stepped in wearing only lingerie and a fake smile. She had bruising on her face, a cut across her chest that likely spread onto her left breast, and several other abrasions. As the girl placed four fruity drinks onto the table, Mr. Jack hissed, "You could have this girl instead."

Theo shook his head, turning his back on Cindy. He felt that this was a test somehow. "Not interested. Not my type."

Mr. Jack said, "Just making sure you have all the options."

Theo shrugged and walked to the other girls. He bent down, gripped the chain, and pulled it toward the bed. The girls practically tumbled forward, laughing through their gags. "I have all that I need. I'm ready to be punished."

Before he had taken two steps, the skinny man that Theo had seen earlier reentered the room and grabbed Cindy by the neck, nearly lifting her off the ground. At the doorway, he pitched her onto the ground. Mr. Jack, acting if nothing was happening, said, "A few more rules."

Theo glanced over at Mr. Jack. "Like what?"

"You've got an hour. You cannot harm our girls. They are essential to what we do. We do not watch what happens here, but we'll examine our merchandise afterward. If there's a problem, that's when you'll pay. Samuel will make sure all is well, and he will remain outside the door. If you need more time, all you have to do is slide some cash under the door. Darla will remain here to help in any way she can."

Mr. Jack paused as if waiting for a response. Theo could not think of anything to say. Mr. Jack's left foot began taping the ground. Theo said, "The only thing I care about is if the girls are clean."

"What sort of clean?"

Theo laughed. "I don't care if they do drugs or whatever. I hope they want to party a little. There's only one true type of clean."

Mr. Jack said, "We pride ourselves in customer satisfaction. If we didn't have clean girls, who would ever want to come here in the first place? They're checked a few times a week."

"That's all the assurance I need."

"The last rule is that our club manager, Mr. Fritz, meets with everyone afterward to make sure that nothing went wrong."

"No problem," Theo said, and shouldn't have been surprised.

Mr. Jack retreated from the room with a smile on his face. "I envy you. The first time is always the best."

The door closed and locked. Theo dropped the chain immediately and strode to the table. He started picking up fruity drinks and passing them out. Darla accepted hers without a second thought.

"Any plans?" she asked. "Do you need a pill?"

"I have a few ideas, and yes, I would love one."

She drank her drink as she walked to a drawer next to the bed. She pulled out a key and unlocked the door.

Theo turned to the two girls. One was blond, and she wore white pajamas. The other girl was black, with black hair, and she wore black pajamas. They couldn't be more than seventeen or eighteen.

The girls accepted their drinks with practiced hands as Theo lowered their gags slightly. Both girls smiled. Theo lifted his drink, and they did as well. The glasses came together, and Theo put his to his lips. The girls drank greedily. Darla returned. He clinked glasses with her, and he pretended to drink. He accepted a pill from her, allowing her to put it in his mouth. He drank but put the pill under his tongue before swallowing.

Darla smiled. "Where were we when we were interrupted?"

"On the bed. But I still had my clothes on."

"We can remedy that, but it's more fun if we do it slowly."

"Whatever you think."

"Bring the dessert with you." And Theo knew she was talking about the two girls.

He pulled the gags back over their mouths, and towed them to the bed, and sat where he had been. He removed the pill from his mouth and into his hand. He shoved it between the mattresses. The two girls bent down and started massaging his feet and legs with their bodies. Darla worked on his back and arms, rubbing up against him at every opportunity.

Theo hoped that things would start progressing more quickly. Five minutes later, he thought he noticed a change in Darla. She began swaying, and her hands moved less confidently.

"Did you do something?" she hissed.

"Not yet. But I want to."

DOUGLAS VAUGHN

"No. I can't lose control," she muttered.

Theo glanced into her eyes and saw that she was starting to get drowsy. That part had been the hardest to get right. Before coming here tonight, he had practiced opening the small container that held the Rohypnol. He had poured a little into the other three glasses.

"I think you're going to be fine," he said.

"No," she hissed. "They will hurt me if you get away."

Theo wondered at her words. The other two girls were already passed out on the floor. However, when Theo stood, he did so with unsteady steps himself. It was clear he had drunk more than he intended. He found a bathroom just off the main room, to the left. There was a standing shower and a double sink. Turning on the water, he switched it to icy cold and splashed his face. He repeated the process, even pouring some water down his back. He hurried back to the main room, feeling slightly more confident about what he needed to do next.

321

CHAPTER 26

When Theo returned to the room, he returned to his clothes and got dressed. He grabbed his phone and began filming the area of the room. He walked to the bed and filmed the unconscious girls. Once finished, he began searching the room quickly, trying to find another way to get out of the room. He combed through Darla's clothes and found a set of keys. One of them open a locked drawer in the nightstand, which Darla had opened to get some pills. Taking the keys, he continued exploring the room. All along the right side of the room were large red curtains. When Darla had been kissing his back and giving him a massage, he had been searching for a way to escape. Theo pushed and pulled and finally separated the curtain enough to locate the door he was looking for. He was relieved that he wouldn't have to go through the main door, with Samuel keeping guard outside.

He tried three keys before he found the correct one. After he turned the lock, the door swung inward. The area was dark, and it took a moment before Theo realized that there was a small corridor adjacent to each room, like a hidden passage. Only faint light shone in this space. Glancing left and right, he was relieved that this was one empty. Silently stepping in, he closed the door behind him. He turned left and walked to the far end of the corridor, toward the back of the room. The hidden space connected with another corridor beyond the boundary of the room. At the intersection, he took a deep breath and quickly peeked his head around the corner. It was again empty.

Looking right, he found that the corridor continued for another two rooms. Each of these rooms had a camera set up that was pointed into the area. The lights were off, and he didn't think these rooms were occupied at the moment. He pulled out his phone and recorded what he saw. As he, Sophia, Derek, Clayton, and Jane had met together over the last three days, they came up with the plan to get into Club Jazzed. Early this morning, Jane mentioned that there was a likelihood of blackmail cameras being used. She had been convinced that sex had to be involved. She had not been wrong. Theo was relieved to see that nothing was pointing into his room.

Turning left, he walked along the back corridor. After a dozen steps, he was unsurprised to find a corridor going along the opposite side of the room he had been in. Ahead, there were two more rooms without cameras. As he passed the next two rooms, he heard a commotion in the farther one away. He plugged his ears and kept walking. The area directly in front of him became less visible with light. However, Theo could see the outline of a door.

Once he reached the end, he stretched out his hand to push open the door, but it was locked. Using the light from his phone, he began using each key. He went through about a dozen before the right key worked. The door opened, and light splashed down the corridor. Theo rushed forward and slammed the door behind him. He cringed as he found himself alone in a sex-toy supply closet. He snapped a dozen pictures. There was a significant amount of different clothing, cosplay items, make-up, toys, and much more. There were shelves, hooks, and closets full of items. The only doorway was at the far end of the room. He was about to step out of the room, when he saw a walking stick leaning up against the wall. He grabbed it.

Poking his head out of the closet, he oriented himself and recognized that he was inside the large sauna room but at the back. The pool and water were diagonal to his position. He was hidden by a wall and some fake trees that added to the ambiance of the area. On the far side, there was a gazebo and three people, naked, were getting massages. There were another four guests in the water. The ceiling was fifteen feet high or more. He didn't think the water was deep, but the people inside were laughing and playing some sort of a game. Steam rolled off the surface and collected throughout the room and near the ceiling. The lights were dim, adding to the ambiance, along with music and a fresh scent that covered the chlorine smell.

Theo had used his camera phone to collect enough data on what was really going on inside Club Jazzed. Kneeling down, he filmed the massage session happening, which was quickly turning into something more erotic. If Patrick or Zorn saw these recordings, they would have this club raided in an hour. He stopped recording and almost vomited onto the floor. Keeping to the far wall, he forced himself to crawl forward.

A minute later, he had made it to the edge. Peeking around the corner and down the hallway, he saw Samuel standing outside the door he should have been in, talking on his phone.

Samuel suddenly swore loudly. "Are you fucking sure? Doctor Theo Raden … the one we've been looking for … is the guy we let into our luxury sweet?"

"My pleasure. I'll bring him to you."

Samuel spun around, pulled out a stick with a Taser on the end, and placed a key into the door.

The instant the door opened, Samuel stepped in, and Theo sprinted across the hall to where he had seen some glass windows. The hallway leading to the main space of the club was blocked by two large men. Neither of them saw Theo as he ducked into the first room that he came to. This was a copy room with a computer and printer and plenty of brochures getting boxed up. Theo tiptoed down the hall as running footsteps echoed around him.

The next two doors that he came to were locked, and he clambered forward.

Someone yelled, "Check the back door and the alley."

He bent low at the next door and reached up to the doorknob. It turned slowly, and it opened. He snuck into the room, closing the door. When he stood, he was shocked at what he found. There was an exam room table bolted to the floor with straps to hold down someone's arms and legs. There was a metal gun, like the one he had seen before, sitting on the counter. Theo moved forward and grabbed the gun. There were a dozen of the blue capsules in a small box.

He stopped momentarily and typed a message on his phone, "Emergency."

An instant before he was going to retreat out of the room, he spotted a fire alarm. Reaching over, he pulled the lever. The lights erupted, and he exited the room.

He made his way back to the corridor, but there were too many guards still at the door. There were several people running in every direction, and Theo decided to head back in the direction of the sauna room. Guests were being escorted from other areas of the back building, and towels were being placed on those pulled from the sauna. Theo inched around the corner, intending to sprint down a hallway, but before he went two feet, a man stepped out from the shadows. Theo halted as Fritz glared at him with a spine-chilling stare that caused Theo's legs to wobble.

"You asshole," Fritz shouted as he swung a small, black club. It collided with Theo's hand, and the metal gun fell to the floor.

"I'm Mr. Reynolds," Theo said weekly as he clutched his hand. "I found that on the floor as I was leaving my room. Samuel was supposed to be standing guard."

"You didn't think we were ready for you, Dr. Raden," Fritz hissed. "It was just a matter of time before we caught you. Mary might have snuck in here once for some evidence. She got what she deserved. We certainly weren't going to let it happen twice."

"Not sure who you're talking about," said Theo as he looked at his hand. It was pulsating and he thought it might be broken. "I paid a lot of money to be here with Darla and Ice and Coal. I was thoroughly enjoying Fracking."

Other guests were now screaming, and Theo hoped he could use one of them as a distraction. He still had the bottles in his coat.

"I bet you were."

"I'll be going now."

"I don't think so," Fritz said as he stepped closer, raising his weapon.

Theo swung the walking stick at Fritz's left leg. It collided perfectly with his knee, and the man stumbled into the wall. Theo thought he could slip past him, but before he took even a single step, someone collided with his back, and he was knocked forward. Time slowed, and

Theo found himself soaring through the air, only to land hard with someone on his back. He tried rolling to the side but couldn't.

A voice hissed into his ear. "I found you, my pretty. Did you think you could trick us?"

"Samuel," Fritz screamed, "get this douche to his feet and into the boss's office!"

Both of Theo's arms were pinned behind his back, and he was lifted to his feet. Samuel squeezed Theo's hand, and his knees buckled. He fell to the floor and Samuel rewarded this behavior with two quick kicks to his ribs. He was yanked back to his feet and found Fritz standing before him. Fritz unleashed a punch to Theo's stomach that sent a large volume of his stomach contents pouring out of his mouth onto the floor. Theo tried to crumple to the floor, but Samuel held him tight. The second punch hurt far more than the first and Theo heard a rib or two crack.

Fritz hissed, "We have someone that wants to see you."

"Terrific," Theo mumbled.

The ringing of the fire alarm was turned off, and the cheers from the front of the club were deafening. The music restarted, and within seconds, new guests were being escorted back near the water. The lights and smells changed almost instantly. New performers emerged from a doorway in the back.

Theo was shoved forward, and he hobbled. Samuel hissed into his ear, "You drugged my girls. That was very stupid of you. If they're hurt in any way, I'll find a way for you to work off their debts to me." Samuel was wiry and strong, and Theo was starting to believe that he might be the boss.

Theo gritted his teeth and, through the pain, asked, "Do Fritz here and Mr. Jack both report to you?"

"Everyone does."

Theo nodded. "Like puppets."

Samuel said, "Why don't we have a chat in my office."

Two large bodyguards stepped forward, and Theo was shoved into their hands. There was tremendous pressure placed on his shoulders and his injured hand. He was forced back near the corridor leading out of the back room. Instead of going to the passageway where he had found the exam room, he was brought to a metal door with a number pad next to it. Samuel punched in a few numbers and the door unlocked. Theo needed to find enough time to stay alive in order for the cavalry to arrive, whoever that would be.

"Help," Theo screamed, and some of the people about to go into the pool turned and stared at him.

Instead of helping, or caring, they started pointing fingers and laughing. In the next instant, they were ushered into the water laughing as pills were placed inside their mouths, and Theo knew any thought of him had vanished in their minds.

"They don't care about you," Samuel whispered into his ear, "…except that you interrupted their pleasure. I might have to comp their stay; they're important people."

"I could care less. You should tell them to leave. The police know that I'm here and they're on their way."

Theo was propelled into a lush hallway hidden by the metal door. There were three doors open, and Theo was led to the middle door. It was pushed open, and he was shoved inside.

Samuel's tone mocked. "You didn't breathe a word to Detective Yang or anyone else. He would have told me. I'll have the mayor entangled in this in less than a month. You tried to protect Dr. Celeste Lazar but her keeping her job is only temporary. She'll be gone by the end of the summer."

"Like you did with Dr. Daniels?"

"You heard about that?"

Samuel pulled out a knife and stabbed it into Theo's right thigh. He buckled toward the floor but was pulled to his feet before he landed. In the next instant his head was shoved into some water in a tank in the center of the room, dousing him awake. Theo hadn't been expecting this and swallowed more than he should have. When he was pulled out, he came face to face with Samuel. "You think this is all a game, Dr. Raden? You really have no idea who I am."

Theo's vision blackened, and he saw stars. He was dunked two more times into the water, and his energy vanished. Unable to stand or walk, Theo was carried back out of the torture room and into an adjacent room. He vomited two more times, but the floor was marble or concrete, and he watched one of the goons spraying it down as he left.

Theo was unceremoniously slammed into a chair, and his head rolled back and forth as if he had a concussion, and somewhere in the back of his mind, he wondered if the camera in his pocket or his cellphone had been damaged.

Samuel demanded, "Make sure he doesn't bleed out onto the floor."

A roll of duct tape was tossed to the two bodyguards. One of them held Theo tightly as the other man wrapped enough tape around the wound to sink a ship. There was a noticeable increase of pain in his leg with the pressure. Samuel strolled confidently to stand behind an enormous wooden desk. Behind him was a bookshelf with a television in the center.

Between Theo's wounds and his waterboarding, he barely had enough strength to keep his head from bobbing up and down. The two goons kept a hand on each of his shoulders. A sound caught his attention. He heard sobbing; true fright and despair seized his heart, and it nearly stopped. With guilt and apprehension, he turned his head, expecting to see Sophia. Instead, he found Cindy sitting next to him, with Mr. Jack holding a gun to her head.

Fritz stepped into view, swinging the club in his hand.

"If I remember correctly," Samuel said and motioned for Fritz to step back, "you've already met Special Agent Cindy Cummings from the Portland office. She told us that you spent the night at her house."

Theo tried denying it, but Samuel continued, "She did say that you were rather drunk that night. What do you remember her saying? Who have you told about our little enterprise here?"

"Nothing," Theo replied. "But the cops are on their way."

"We already know what she told you, and I've already explained that Detective Yang is keeping me in the loop." Rage spread across Samuel's face, and he demanded, "Now I want some fucking answers."

Theo was jerked back in his chair so that his eyes stared at Samuel.

"Who did you tell about what Cindy told you?"

Theo tried to recall what she had told him. Did he know that she was an FBI agent?"

Samuel continued, "She's not here in any official capacity. She came looking for her sister, who went missing a year ago."

These words triggered memory fragments. Theo mumbled, "Faith."

"So, you do remember," Samuel grumbled. "Well, she was one of our dancers, but she had some suicidal thoughts and wanted to find a way to fix them. At the time, we were just getting started. We tried the drug on her, and she had an adverse reaction."

"You killed her," screamed Cindy.

Lightening fast, Mr. Jack used the stock of the weapon and smacked Cindy's head. She immediately stopped speaking.

"Drug?" Theo asked.

Ignoring this question, Samuel said, "Cindy screwed up a few different times. She tried contacting her office when a friend of hers was killed."

"Inside the hot tub. Yeah," Theo said. "We got that on camera. Saw it from the backyard. The police have copies as well."

Theo thought he saw a glimmer of a smile cross Cindy's swollen and beaten face.

Fritz stepped forward again, facing Samuel. "I was there. If that's true, I'm on camera."

Samuel lifted his hand and silenced the man. He continued, "Fritz started having concerns about Cindy the day Mr. Reynold came into the club. We started watching her very closely. If we hadn't, we would not have overheard her report to the Portland FBI office. We didn't think anything of Mr. Reynold at the time. You slipped past our defenses the first time, but not the second."

"The FBI also knows about what is going on here."

Samuel nodded, and Fritz whirled around and clubbed Theo in the side of the head so hard that Theo thought he lost consciousness for several seconds. When he finally opened his eyes, the room was spinning, and there was a flash of light in his right eye that only partially resolved.

"After you dismissed her in our pleasure room, we brought her here for some questioning. That's when we realized Mr. Reynolds and Dr. Theo Raden were the same person. You were so close, yet miles away from doing any real damage."

"A room full of idiots," Theo said with as much confidence as he could find. "You've been too focused on Cindy and Sophia to see that the real threat had already walked into your club. Did you know that I have close friends in the police department and in the FBI here in San Diego? They've been working on a case for months. Kidnapping Cindy and I will be your downfall."

"You're a funny man." Samuel sat partially on the desk. "Being a doctor has caused you to think that you're smarter than the rest of us."

"Well, I am," said Theo. He tried sitting up a little straighter despite his head, arm, and all the pain he was feeling. Theo noticed the gigantic saltwater fish tank built into the wall behind where Mr. Jack stood, not far from Cindy. Theo added, "I would've been smart enough to know that you shouldn't kill someone in your own office, especially by drowning her and then throwing her into a pool at her apartment."

Fritz stepped forward, lifting his club once again.

Samuel raised a hand to stop him.

"I'll give you a little credit. Even after you met with Dr. Haderly, we didn't think you were anyone. You found Sophia again and have made quite a little stir within our group. Coming here was reckless, especially after being at the morgue and trying to follow Fritz. We have all the evidence, and you have nothing."

"Keep dreaming," said Theo, though he felt things might be unraveling. Too much time had passed since he entered the building.

Samuel said, "The thing is …you're going to kill Special Agent Cindy Cummings here. Detective Yang will be called, and he will kill you as you try to kill him. You're already a suspect in another murder. That will wrap up things nicely. The moment Cindy called the FBI about her sister, we sent her body to Alaska. It will be found in the wilderness partially eaten by savages."

"You assholes!" Cindy screamed.

"Great plan," joked Theo as his heart thumped in his chest. "I'll counter that with a video of Fritz in the morgue retrieving evidence from that fridge on the second floor in the case of Mary Sneider. And we'll double that by showing the video of Dr. Daniels killing Vickie with Darla and Cindy in the hot tub and Fritz and four goons coming and stuffing her in a van. Now, Dr. Daniels is dead, in another hot tub, and we have a clear connection to this club. As I've already told you, we've sent the evidence to the FBI in San Diego. The club will get raided in the next five minutes."

"You'll be dead, and we can move on."

"How do you figure?"

"Because," a voice said from the doorway to his right, "eager young people, drugs, sex, and advancing pharmaceutical research is available in every major city in the country. With what we have developed, we're unstoppable."

Theo turned to see Dr. Thomas Haderly standing in the doorway, holding tightly to Sophia.

Sophia wept. "I'm so sorry, Theo. I thought that you were in danger."

CHAPTER 27

"Congratulations, Dr. Raden, I'm completely shocked that you had the guts to come here. No clue why you didn't at least try to send Sophia out of the country. Either way, it was pointless. We would have never stopped looking for her." Dr. Haderly stepped farther into the room. "When I was told that you were here, I knew that Sophia had to be close by. I sent some of my crew and found her trying to sneak in through the alley. That was not a very smart move."

"I'm sorry," Sophia muttered.

"Leave her alone." Theo tried standing, but this time, Samuel allowed Fritz to swing his club into Theo's stomach. Pain shot through his body and the room began to swim. Theo lost it again, collapsing to the ground, he started dry heaving.

Dr. Haderly shoved Sophia to Mr. Jack, who pulled out a third chair and forced Sophia to sit. He approached Theo and took something from his pocket, shook it, and stuck it under Theo's nose. The involuntary shudder and energy that was transferred to Theo caused him to recover quickly. He was lifted by the goons into his chair.

"Do you know why Sophia is so important?"

"She's proof of what you're doing here."

Dr. Haderly said, "I guess that's true. But really, she's the blackmail piece that we need. See, the mayor's assistant,

Frederick Jones, is the father. He came here early on and thought he was in love with Sophia. He paid a lot to make sure that Sophia was only for him. It worked for a few months, but then she got pregnant. We tried blackmailing him, but he was smart enough to wear a disguise when he came here. Our cameras couldn't pin anything on him. But, inside of her, is his DNA. With that evidence, he will do anything for us."

"I don't know Frederick," cried Sophia. "He isn't the father."

"Such naivete and stupidity." Turning back to Theo, Dr. Haderly said, "There's no evidence that Mary was murdered. I will take the stand against Dr. Lazar any day of the week. Anything that she finds will be dismissed from court due to a lack of chain of command. There will be no match to Fritz, who killed her, of course, because he's not in the system."

Theo said, "You killed Mary because she found out that Sophia got pregnant by Frederick Jones."

"Mary had no clue what she had found. It wasn't about Fredrick."

Sophia asked, "Then why did you kill my roommate?"

"She did find out about our drug testing. That is the key to everything that we're doing."

"With BioPharm?" asked Theo. "I was just telling Samuel about the videos that we have. We also watched you meet with BioPharm. We have plenty of pictures. These things have also been sent to the local FBI."

"I heard your threats earlier," said Dr. Haderly. "I just don't believe them. If you sent them to the FBI, it would be them, not you, who walked through our doors."

Theo understood that Dr. Haderly had seen through their plan. He refused to give up. He added, "Dr. Lazar saw Fritz, and he talked to her. We know that he is involved. She knows the entire story."

"That's what I wanted to hear," said Dr. Haderly, and he nodded at Samuel. The man pulled a gun and shot a round directly into Fritz's chest. As the body fell to the floor, Dr. Haderly leaned in and added, "So careless. One of our fringe employees trying to make some money for himself. He killed Dr. Daniels and got caught on camera at the morgue." Dr. Haderly moved to stand over the dying corpse. He pointed a finger down at Fritz. "You were supposed to be our head of security, and you let this imbecile into my house."

Sophia screamed, but Cindy appeared to smile as Fritz died.

"What are you smiling at?" asked Dr. Haderly. "You'll be next."

"He killed my sister. Karma is a bitch."

Dr. Haderly's face contorted, and he nodded at Samuel. He moved the gun and pointed it directly at Cindy.

"Wait," Theo shouted. "The metal gun that Fritz found was a fake. I switched out the real one a day before he arrived. If we don't all get out of this alive, Sophia's friends will send it and the videos to the FBI. BioPharm will be raided."

"So you're not working alone," replied Dr. Haderly, and Samuel lowered the gun.

"What does it do?" Theo asked.

Dr. Haderly said to Mr. Jack, "You've been promoted to head of security. You and Damian here need to get rid of Fritz's body. If the police do come here, there can be no evidence. Can you do that?"

"Yes, sir."

"Have Gregory stand guard outside.

"Copy," said Mr. Jack.

From the cabinet in the back, a black plastic morgue bag was removed, and Fritz's body was stuffed inside. Mr. Jack and Damian, one of the bouncers, worked as if they were experts. The body was removed from the room, and Theo watched as the second man guarded the outside door.

"What do you think you know?" asked Dr. Haderly.

Theo began calmly. "There's a connection between drugs, Club Jazzed, and BioPharm industries. Sophia worked here and became pregnant. You say it is because of Frederick Jones, but Mary found out about that metal gun and those blue bullets and snuck them into her purse. No one thought she had." Theo nodded at the saltwater tank. "You must have caught her, but not before she hid the gun. Did she come here a second time looking for Sophia? Fritz drowned her in the saltwater tank in this room. There has been a lot of death in here."

Dr. Haderly answered, "Mary got in and out cleaner than you did. It took us a few hours to realize she had the injector. She didn't get in a second time. We caught her and brought her here for an unhealthy conversation. It wasn't hard to catch her and kill her."

Theo continued, "You taped open her eyes and dropped her in the pool at her apartment and hoped that no one would know. Like I said before, we have the gun and two bullets. We have Fritz in the morgue and Dr. Daniels slashing throats. But it's all over now."

"You're dead wrong, Dr. Raden. You see, Fritz will be blamed for all of that, along with Dr. Daniels. Those two will be discovered selling drugs. Club Jazzed will burn down tonight, and we've already started a new project near Petco Park. It will be finished in two months. We'll have so much more security and much more fun will be had by our guests. Fredrick Jones will ensure it all happens. Soon enough, we'll have the mayor himself entangled. The other stuff, you have mostly correct."

"You're a psychopath Dr. Haderly," said Sophia.

"No," Dr. Haderly screamed. "I'm not insane or unstable. Me and the CEO of BioPharm are trailblazers. This club stuff is all a front. We have a breakthrough discovery of a mediation that will revolutionize the military, police, and thousands of other people. We have found a medication that can wash away unwanted memories."

"Ridiculous," replied Theo. "That's not possible."

"You saw the results first hand. Sophia had no idea that she was pregnant. Even more importantly, we can control which memories are created in the future. In science, we've termed the theory an 'Echo'. Sophia had no idea of what she was doing. She was dancing and having sex with multiple people. She can't remember a single thing that happened. That's because her memories were washed away, and we control the echo."

"What's an echo?" asked Theo.

"The echo is the connection between a thought, a smell, or even something you see, and it being stored in the mind. Our new drug regulates it all."

"How?" asked Cindy. "Why? Was that what you were trying to do with my sister?"

"Dr. Sommers and I have worked hard for two years to get to this moment. He worked for a pharmaceutical company in the UK called Teva UK. Unfortunately, he was placed on administration misconduct for testing on subjects unbeknownst to themselves. He left before anything was formally done, and he moved to the U.S. That's when I met him, and we established common ground. He already had the framework for what he wanted to do, much of the science, and I had plenty of unimportant test subjects and grants to further his research. We worked and worked and came to understand where memories are stored and how. The echo is a beautiful thing. You need neurotransmitters, hormones, and the capacity to remember."

"Sounds nearly impossible," said Theo.

"What do you know about your memory and the connection with your brain?"

"If I remember neuroscience correctly, memories are from the pre-frontal cortex which allows for sensory input."

"That's just the beginning," Dr. Haderly retorted.

Theo continued, "There is a difference between short and long-term memory. The pre-frontal and parietal lobes are involved. It's all in the study of cognitive neuroscience, a lot of large words."

"After our hard work, we can overcome memories. We can prevent them from getting inputted into the brain permanently. Soldiers get PTSD from something they saw, smelled, or felt, and their lives are ruined. First responders see a dead baby after a car crash and are scarred for life."

"These are things you can't change," said Theo.

"But we have."

"How?"

Dr. Haderly pulled out a box and removed a metallic gun with two handles and a case of blue bullets. "This injector is cutting-edge science. See, you place this end at the base of the neck and squeeze the trigger. A drug that we made enters the body and changes the brain. It attaches like a coating around a portion of your tissue. New memories are formed, and you can interact with your old memories. These new memories do not become permanent because the echo isn't allowed. They don't connect with the receptors and can be washed away later.

"That sounds awful," said Sophia. "You forget love, life, and experiences."

"Who cares, girl? They become the perfect soldiers. The perfect responders. The perfect people."

"No," Theo replied. "They become brainwashed."

"Is that so bad?" Dr. Haderly pointed to Sophia. "She was picked out by someone in her class. She came here never having had sex before. She was pretty and pure. I could show you what Frederick did to her. But she will never remember what happened."

"That's sick," Sophia whispered, tears rolling down her face. "You treated me like an animal."

"No," Dr. Haderly said. "Like an angel. You are blessed beyond belief."

Cindy interjected, "Why did you kill my sister?"

After a pause, Dr. Haderly said, "She was a casualty of science. We did not know at the time that if you had diabetes, this medication causes you to go into diabetic ketoacidosis. Your sister was not killed, she suffered a medical complication."

"She didn't get to choose this."

"She took our money," replied Dr. Haderly. "And she wanted to be here. She was in a different arm of our research. You see, we are learning to change the thoughts and processes of some humans. Faith was constantly suicidal, and she wanted to never have those feelings again. She willingly asked to be a subject. We just didn't know about the medical complications. It happens."

"You killed her."

"No. We tried saving her."

Theo pointed out, "Sophia's mind cleared up. She started to remember things. How do you account for that?"

Dr. Haderly said, "You must have used Ativan to calm her down. That medication counteracts our medication."

"Unbelievable. We tried Valium the second time, but it didn't work."

"Ativan is the only medication that works."

Sophia cried, "You'll never succeed in controlling people's minds."

"We already have. In fact, I'll show you. You see, memories are often our sense of moral judgment. You see your dad hitting someone, and you either think that it's okay or you don't. A moral imprint has been placed in your mind. Imagine soldiers with no moral compass. They do exactly what you say and then don't worry about it afterward. You will come with us, Sophia. You have forced us to change our plans. Club Jazzed will burn down, and Dr. Raden will become a serial killer. He will admit to setting this place on fire and killing Cindy, Fritz, your roommate, and Dr. Daniels. In the morning, he will confess."

"I won't," Theo replied.

"The evidence will be confusing. But your testimony will be sufficient to convict you."

Dr. Haderly removed one of the blue bullets and placed it into the top of the canister area of the metal gun. The first thirty minutes after you receive this injection, your mind is willing to accept whatever it is told, also part of the echo. This is the most crucial moment. It is when you tell a soldier whom they are supposed to kill, a whore that they will fuck someone, and a serial killer the exact details of what they have done. FBI agent Cindy will suffer greatly at your hands."

Theo felt the horror of that possibility. "I won't let you."

"You can't stop me," said Dr. Haderly.

Sophia asked, "What did you tell me in the first thirty minutes?"

Dr. Haderly smiled. "We've given you the shot three times. The first time, you were told how to please our customers. The second time was when Mary stole information from us. You called her and told her where to meet. That is why she was so easy to catch. The third time was that Theo Raden was the enemy. I'm surprised she didn't try to kill you."

"Wait!" Sophia shouted. "Did I lure Mary so that you could capture her?"

"You did. Cindy helped too. She calmed you down during the ride from and to St. Jude's."

Cindy spoke, "I didn't know that you were going to kill that girl. After I heard what happened, I took Sophia to a different shelter so that she could escape."

Dr. Haderly smiled. "That's how Sophia got away from us. Now it all makes sense." Dr. Haderly turned and nodded at Samuel, who raised his gun, pointing it at Cindy.

Dr. Haderly spoke. "If you move a muscle, he will shoot her in the stomach and in the chest. She will suffer as you've never imagined."

Theo asked, "What are you going to do?"

There was no answer. Dr. Haderly stepped behind him, and Theo felt the cold chill of something at the base of his neck. The whooshing sound and slight burning sensation at the back of his neck spoke volumes. Immediately, Theo heard ringing in his ears and mounting pressure on his temples.

"Done," Dr. Haderly said.

From the corner of his eye, Theo watched as the door opened two inches, and something was thrown inside. With everything that he had, Theo lunged at Sophia and Cindy, pulling both off their chairs and onto the floor.

"What the?" cried Samuel.

Theo covered his ears and protected the girls.

In the next instant, the flash-bang grenade detonated inside the room. The shrieks and shrills exploded, and ten masked men entered the room. Theo felt the room spinning and was convinced that the entire building was going to fall on them. Shots rang out in the room, but Theo could not tell from what direction. Finally a hand rested on his shoulder, and Theo knew that one way or another, everything was over.

CHAPTER 28

"We need a medic and some Ativan," cried Sophia, and Theo tried watching her crawl over to him through the haze in the room. How did she have this much energy? His ears were ringing, and he couldn't stand on his own. "It must be Ativan!" she screamed into the room.

Theo felt a hand grip his arm, and he was relieved to see that it was Cindy on his left side. She was dazed but in one piece. There was a commotion in every corner of the room. Dr. Haderly had been knocked to the floor, and Samuel was lying behind the desk with a red stain spreading across his chest. Dr. Haderly was forcefully rolled over, and handcuffs were placed on his wrists. His head turned, and his eyes connected with Theo; a faint smile played on his lips. The man was jerked into the air and hauled from the room. Someone was checking Samuel's pulse, but Theo knew that he was gone.

Sitting up slowly, Theo shook his head. A medic arrived a few seconds later, and Theo was given a shot in his arm, just like Jane had done to Sophia those weeks ago. His leg burned where he had been stabbed, and he was confident that his hand and ribs were broken.

Despite the haze and the oncoming headache, Theo focused on his two best friends as they stepped into the room. When it had mattered the most, they came without a single complaint. Patrick Mulder and Zorn Davies, both wore black vests, goggles, and helmets, and they were smiling at him with approval and hesitation.

"What the hell?" screamed Theo. "Don't tell me that it was your choice to send Sophia in here. You should've had enough footage to sink this place."

"It wasn't our call," Zorn said.

"Then who?" demanded Theo as he was helped to his feet. The medic was dragging Sophia to a gurney situated in the hallway. Sophia was refusing. "Help," she cried.

"You're all headed to the hospital to be checked out," Zorn replied.

Patrick said, "From my boss."

"Unbelievable."

"No," Zorn retorted. "Unbelievable is you thinking that you could come in here and have your friends call us with what was actually happening."

"You would have never allowed me to come in here and bring down Fritz and Dr. Haderly."

"We could have come to some sort of agreement," Patrick retorted.

"I tried."

Zorn added, "When you went into the water, you lost all your video imaging. Sophia volunteered to go in after you. She said that you had saved her, and it was time she saved you."

"And you didn't stop a pregnant woman?"

Patrick answered, "We tried. She was having none of it."

Cindy said, "I thought we were all screwed. I'm grateful to still be alive."

"We had a plan," Theo said.

"It was a terrible one." Zorn finally smiled, and he half-hugged Theo. "I'm glad it worked out in the end."

They were led out of the office, past dozens of agents who were searching every inch of the club. Sophia insisted on walking. Zorn guided them to the front part of Club Jazzed. Cindy limped for a few steps, and a wheelchair was brought to help her the rest of the way.

The lights were on in the club, and it was empty of partygoers. Clayton, Derek, Rachael, and Jane were standing on the far side talking with an agent. They broke away to approach Theo, Sophia, and Cindy.

Clayton asked, "Is Sophia okay?"

Sophia screamed, "I'm fine!"

"She's better than fine," Derek said.

Jane punched his arm. "I'm glad you called and got me involved, but you two are the stupidest people I know, and I deal with crappy people all the time. That could have gone sideways a dozen different ways."

"But it didn't," Sophia said.

Theo countered, "I totally had the situation handled."

"No, you didn't, bro," replied Derek.

Theo smiled. "Regardless, you don't send a girl who is eight months pregnant into a club with these psychotics."

"It worked," insisted Sophia. She glanced at Theo and asked, "You're not sexist, are you?"

"No. Just practical. You need to be a little more careful."

"I can be now that we've solved Mary's murder."

Cindy spoke. "You guys also helped solve my sister's disappearance. I'm not sure we'll ever find her body, but at least I know what happened to her."

Theo said, "Everyone, this is Cindy Cummings. I met her here at the club when I first visited. She was working here undercover, looking for her sister, and happens to be an FBI agent."

Patrick said, "Truth be told, I bet there are a lot of girls missing. This is going to take weeks to put together. And Special Agent Cummings, I'd bet that we can find one person willing to tell us where she might be."

"It won't be Dr. Haderly," said Theo. "I hope that guy never gets out of prison."

"Uh, Theo," said Zorn. "I think there's someone at the door looking for you."

Theo turned and found Celeste Lazar pounding on the glass and pointing directly at him, waving for him to come outside. Theo glanced back and found Sophia staring at him with genuine happiness. She nodded, not giving permission but urging him to move forward. In an instant, he was brought back to the hospital room, and the tragic look of profound sorrow on the face of a lost girl. That look was gone, and so was the girl.

Without saying another word, he ambled past several agents, broken tables, and dozens of shattered lives to the front door. Stepping into the night, he appreciated that everything in his world had changed, some for the better and some for the worse. She reached out and pulled him into a hug.

She whispered, "Did you find what you were looking for?"

"Almost."

EPILOGUE

Theo felt more exhausted than he ever thought possible. Medical school had been nothing compared to the first few days of babysitting at the hospital and trying to recover. His eyes felt heavy, and there was a pressure on his chest that had nothing to do with an actual force. However, the emotions of fear and joy mixed together were equally powerful. Marianne Theo LaCross had been born on Wednesday the third at 2:47 a.m. She was healthy and strong, and she cried and was fed within minutes of being delivered.

"Did you have the baby or did I?" Theo asked as the nurse stepped out of the room.

"I'm pretty sure that was me." Sophia glowed and appeared more relaxed than Theo had ever seen her. Her water had broken two days after the raid on Club Jazzed.

"Then why am I hurting so much?" asked Theo.

The scowl he received from Sophia said everything. "All you did was sleep on the couch and check on Marianne now and then. I did all the real work."

"I know. There's no way that my body could handle giving birth. Halfway through the night, I couldn't feel either of my legs. I've been cramping all morning. I feel miserable."

"From sleeping on a small couch in a hospital?"

"It was painful."

"Well, my breasts are on fire from nursing. They are red and chapped. No one tells you how uncomfortable yet soothing this process is. I won't even tell you about my tearing."

"That part, I understand, but I'll take your word for it." Sophia's musical laugh echoed in the hospital room and Theo smiled.

"You look great," he said. "And happy."

"I am." She took the plastic container from her bedside and gulped down half the water. "Derek, Clayton, and Rachael will be here in a few minutes. Will you stay with me?"

"Sure."

"They turned out to be good friends."

"That they did," Theo agreed. "It was rough for a bit, but it worked out in the end."

There was a knock at the door, and Patrick and Zorn entered, each carrying flowers and a stuffed animal. They placed them near the window and smiled.

Patrick said, "Theo told us that the delivery went well. We are both happy for you."

"I couldn't have done it without my personal doctor," she said.

Zorn added, "Your daughter will be ridiculed forever with a middle name like Theo. It should have been Zorn."

"That was the second choice," she said. "Are you here on official business or something else?"

"Both," Patrick said. "We wanted you to be the first to know that Theo has officially been removed as a person of interest in the death of Barrett Sanders. Dr. Lazar just matched the DNA to Fritz. I just heard it from Detective Abbott, and since Fritz is in the morgue, case closed."

Sophia asked, "What about the CEO from BioPharm?"

"They executed a warrant on him yesterday. A lot of information, technology, and computers were seized. Dr. Sommers was arrested and asked for a lawyer immediately. There is already a lot of evidence against him. He and Dr. Haderly will turn on each other soon enough."

"That's good news," said Sophia.

Zorn added, "We also found five of those metal guns at BioPharm and another two at Club Jazzed. A third, the one we think Fritz took from the medical examiner's Office, was also found with Mary's purse and a stick of gum, among other items."

"What did the gum show you?"

"The camera ran out of batteries weeks ago, but once it was recharged, it allowed us to solve Mary's death—again, Fritz, with Dr. Haderly and Samuel present in the room when it happened."

"Who was Samuel?"

"He was the owner of Club Jazzed when it first started. He was approached by Dr. Haderly and Dr. Sommers. Fritz was brought in as a bodyguard. Mr. Jack was previously the club manager. Both sides came to an agreement on how to bring in new clients and have girls and boys willing to provide the services available. Lots of people come to California looking for a new opportunity, and there were people waiting to exploit them."

"What will happen to those caught up in this?"

Patrick said, "Great question. We know that Ativan can counteract the effects of the trial medication, but how do we know which ones were given the medication in the first place? There are dozens of people insisting they were brainwashed. We have nearly sixty people that have been tracked down and some arrested."

"St. Jude's Village was closed down," said Zorn. "We know that Dr. Haderly was using this for those girls who got pregnant or didn't react well to the trial medication. Most everyone there seems to be good-natured, but Dr. Haderly had his fingers in everything. This is going to be a long process to sort things out."

"What about the medication itself?" asked Theo.

"It is called Alethomne. And it is really close to being reviewed by the Drug Administration."

"What do you mean?"

"It's big business, and we found hundreds of thousands of doses of the medication at BioPharm. There were two arms of the research. The first is what the government knew and what reports they were being given. Dr. Sommers was working with Dr. Haderly on the side and getting a profit from the club. They still had a dozen people working on getting approval for Alethomne. From what I've heard, they expect the approval in the next six months, and this entire misunderstanding will turn out to be a minor setback."

"How's that possible?" asked Sophia.

"Money. Drug companies and the medical community see significant potential for Alethomne in treatment of mental health, PTSD, fear, and much more. The government gave a significant grant for the work in the field of soldiers."

"There's no way."

Patrick said, "What Dr. Sommers had found was that Alethomne in its purest form, which is what was used by Dr. Haderly, can coat the memory pathway as he explained. But Dr. Sommers also found a way to add particles so that the medication wasn't in its purest form when injected. This doesn't take control of the mind or require

Ativan. It shows significant improvement in patients with schizophrenia, bipolar disorder, PTSD, mood disorders, and more. This drug will revolutionize mental health. At least, that's what we were told during our debriefing this morning. They have scientists who will strongly back the data."

"Who will have access to Alethomne in its purest form?" asked Sophia. "Could this happen again?"

"That information has become classified," answered Patrick. "There's nothing we can do about it, and the government has taken control of BioPharm. It is no longer in the private sector."

"Perfect," said Theo.

Zorn and Patrick said their goodbyes and promised to see them again soon. After Theo and Sophia had eaten another round of hospital food, and Marianne had been fed, Derek, Clayton, and Rachael arrived.

They also came prepared with gifts for Sophia and Marianne. They each declined to hold Marianne and preferred to stare at the new addition.

Rachael asked, "Can I ask you a question?"

"Sure."

"A few nights ago, you learned that the father was Frederick Jones. Is that going to complicate the parenting process?"

Sophia sat up a little. "Honestly, I'm not sure. I did not put down a father's name on the birth certificate. I don't think Frederick has been arrested, but he has been put on leave by the mayor's office. He has not contacted me, and I don't need him involved. I can do this on my own."

Theo added, "You have plenty of friends."

Sophia smiled, but her voice was cautious when she said, "That I do."

"What are your plans?" asked Clayton. "You coming back to Lemon Grove?"

"No," said Sophia quickly. "My contract goes for another few months, but Theo sent some movers, and they cleaned out my apartment. I can never go back. I have some money and need to get a bigger place, with some security. There will be a settlement with Club Jazzed, with what happened and all. I'm not sure if I will stay in San Diego, head back to San Francisco, or try somewhere new. My parents are dead, so I'm not sure of my next step."

"You could stay around here," said Theo. "All of us can help in one way or another."

Sophia glanced up at him. "I didn't want to assume that you guys would stick around after things ended."

Derek said, "We're not going anywhere. It might be a good thing for all of us to leave Lemon Grove in the past. Clayton and I were just thinking that we needed a new start. What do you think, Rachael?"

"I'm totally in. I bet we can find better."

"What about you Theo?" asked Derek. "What are your plans?"

"I'm happy to report that I wasn't kicked out of medical school. So, I still have that going for me. Patrick, Zorn, and Dr. Steven Jeffery have cleared everything with my dean and any charges against me. I get to continue working here at Scripps. In fact, I talked with Dr. Jeffery this morning, and I start back up next week with my rotations. The same company that helped Sophia move also cleaned out my condo and I moved into a new one. I'm near Sunset Cliffs, and I get to be right on the ocean."

"What should I do?" asked Sophia, but the question was directed at Theo.

"I found you an apartment at Sunset Cliffs as well. It is on the opposite side of the complex, but it has security and a great view. There's another complex a mile or two away that would be perfect for Derek and the others. We could all be close enough to help, but far enough away if you need some privacy."

"You mean when Dr. Celeste Lazar comes to stay at your place," she said, with a half-smile on her face. "And you want *your* privacy."

"Well," said Theo. "She is extremely attractive, and she has shown a lot of interest. We have a ton of fun together, but we're going very slowly. Who knows what will happen."

"Are you saying that you don't already have a girlfriend?" said Clayton. "I always got the vibe that you had someone else."

"There has been this girl coming in and out of my life. It was convenient for both of us. But Danielle and I ended things recently. She has some issues, and so do I. She's a good friend, but not someone I should be dating."

All eyes turned to Sophia, and she sat there thinking. "Is this condo place far from Lemon Grove?"

"Far enough. But there is a branch of Bank of America nearby and your boss has already put in a good word."

"You guys want to continue helping me?"

Derek said, "We are friends. We've bonded as we've gone through hard times. We will always be here; however you need us."

Sophia stated, "It's a relief to know where Marianne and I will be going when we leave here."

Sophia was discharged the next day and agreed to move to Sunset Cliffs for a trial period of six months. A part of her seemed hopeful at the possibilities for the future, but despite everything, she was still brokenhearted that Mary was gone. Sophia insisted on being positive for Marianne and Mary would never be forgotten.

As Theo turned the key, Sophia said, "There better not be any surprises."

Theo shrugged and said, "Sorry. I don't do surprises."

The door swung open, and the celebration began. The entire apartment was full of people. Patrick and Zorn and their families were there, as were Dr. Lazar, nurse Jane, Dr. Jeffery, her old bank manager, several other work friends, and some others from Lemon Grove. Derek, Clayton, and Rachael sat on the couches with broad smiles. Sophia began crying as the door closed. Theo held Marianne as Sophia went around the room, hugging everyone. There were hours of stories, smiles, and more hugs.

It had just taken a day to fully furnish the apartment, and even Marianne's room was decorated. The kitchen had brand-new items, and the couches were leather and comfortable. The television was perfect. Sophia had a third room that would become an office one day.

After everyone but Theo had left, Sophia admitted, "This feels like it could be home, but I'm not sure I can do this all alone."

"I'll stay in Marianne's room until things get more comfortable."

She nodded. "I always thought that becoming pregnant was the worst thing that could happen to me. With my mom and dad, I wasn't sure I wanted kids. Certainly, how it happened wasn't ideal, but we've been through some terrible things, and we survived. Hopefully, raising Marianne will be a breeze."

"I doubt it."

"I couldn't be here without you."

"Like you said…you have your own personal doctor."

"A great doctor, and a passable friend."

Theo smiled. "You're a comedian."

ABOUT AUTHOR

Douglas Vaughn is semi-retired and transitioning into what he has always wanted to do...write a thriller. He has intimate knowledge of medicine, hospitals, medical advancements, the pharmaceutical world, and much more. There is something exciting and empowering about science and the infinite possibilities. That excitement transitions well to the fictional world. There are dozens of stories to be written.

Douglas lives with his wife, and two dogs, and is always searching to find time to escape into the wilderness around their home. He often contemplates human interactions, the search for happiness, mental health, and our place in the world. Join him as he brings forth a new medical thriller series.

One of the best ways to support an author is to leave an honest review. If you enjoyed reading this book, please leave a review on Amazon and Goodreads.

Additionally, you can sign up for my Newsletter at my Author Website https://authordouglasvaughn.com/

I send a Newsletter monthly with up-to-date information, recommendations, progress updates about the next book, and much more.

Thank you so much.

Made in the USA
Middletown, DE
12 March 2023

26619264R00215